WHITE LIGHTNING AND WHITE HEAT

"Open your mouth, Hannah," Henry Lee whispered. "I want to kiss you."

She tasted good. She tasted so good. Nothing that he had ever tasted was better than her. She was like his whiskey, warm and smooth.

Whiskey! his mind screamed at him. The whiskey must be burning up, either that or spoiling. *It's the wedding whiskey.* If he let the wedding whiskey ruin, it might ruin the marriage.

With a groan of pure agony, Henry Lee pulled away from her. He stared down at her; she was flushed from her cheeks to her waist, her eyes were hooded and sleepy with desire. Her breathing was quick and short. No man could leave a woman like this.

"Easy, darlin'," he consoled in a whisper. "I'm going to make it fine, real fine." He accented his words with tender kisses along her neck and strong, skillful strokes of his hand.

"It's like a prairie fire," he whispered against her flesh. "You get ahead of it and start your own flame. When the two fires meet up, they consume each other."

Bantam Books by Pamela Morsi

HEAVEN SENT

COURTING MISS HATTIE

Pamela Morsi

BANTAM BOOKS

NEW YORK · TORONTO · LONDON · SYDNEY · AUCKLAND

HEAVEN SENT

A Bantam Book

PUBLISHING HISTORY
Bantam edition published March 1991
Bantam reissue / July 1995

ISBN 0-553-76192-7

Published simultaneously in the United States and Canada

Bantam Books are published by Bantam Books, a division of Bantam Doubleday Dell
Publishing Group, Inc. Its trademark, consisting of the words "Bantam Books" and
the portrayal of a rooster, is Registered in U.S. Patent and Trademark Office and in
other countries. Marca Registrada. Bantam Books, 1540 Broadway, New York, New
York 10036.

PRINTED IN THE UNITED STATES OF AMERICA

For my husband who cooked all the meals, my son who washed all the dishes, and my daughter who reminded all her dolls to "be quiet, Mama's writing her book."

PROLOGUE

The first gray light of dawn illuminated the white clapboard house that sat like an island in a sea of corn near the border of the Indian Territory. The Reverend Farnam Bunch, pastor of Plainview Church, stepped out his back door, bucket in hand, and headed down to the wellhouse.

He was a simple man who loved the country. He drank in the smell of the early morning air, anticipating the prospect of a fresh day. He had come to the Oklahoma Territory from Kansas five years earlier, seeking a new challenge and a new church. He wanted his family to be a part of the territory, where they could grow and the future was bright.

Today the future seemed to be just dazzling out on the horizon as he whistled the catchy melody to "There shall be showers of blessings."

As he opened the door to the wellhouse, his whistling stopped. He stood frozen, contemplating the shocking sight.

On the floor of the wellhouse, a young couple lay wrapped in each other's arms. He knew them both, and yet surely he was mistaken. He threw open the door wide, hoping that the meager morning sunlight would show his error. It could not be true. Even as his mind denied it, rage boiled up in him like a volcano and came spewing out in a torrent of angry words.

"You trifling, no-account scoundrel! By God, I'm going to send you to hell!" he thundered. The preacher

1

had never been a man to curse. He struggled, his hands shaking at his side, with the vile language that rushed to his lips. The situation didn't call for civilized discussion. In red-eyed fury he yelled back to the house, "Violet! Bring me my gun!"

Inside the wellhouse, Hannah Bunch woke from her warm, pleasant dream, startled to hear the sound of her father's angry voice. Disoriented at first, she quickly realized that everything was going as expected. This was a crucial part of her plan, a difficult part, but one that was essential. Her father would be understandably angry, she had known that from the beginning. But it was her father who had taught her that nothing worth having was achieved without sacrifice. A few embarrassing moments could hardly be counted against a lifetime of contentment.

People came running from every direction. The whole community had camped at the Bunch farm the previous night for the church raising and all of them had heard their preacher's angry cry.

Hannah had never seen her father in such a rage. His face was a vivid red and his teeth were bared like an animal's as he spat thunderous blasphemies into the doorway of the wellhouse.

She knew that more than one couple from the community had anticipated their wedding night, and rather than condemning them her father had always been understanding and forgiving. She had counted on that spirit of forgiveness, but there was no mercy in him right now. He was furious and he seemed to Hannah to be talking crazily, directing his anger to the man who stood silently behind her.

"People told me not to trust you, that you're a heathen with no morals, a son of a drunken squawman. But I said a man must be judged on his own merits! The more fool me! I invite you into my home, feed you at my table, and this is how you repay me, by ruining my daughter!"

The preacher's deep booming voice was raised to a pitch that surely made it audible halfway to Guthrie. "Violet! Where is my gun?"

Hannah was frightened. Her brothers drew close at

the door behind her father, their angry words more hateful and vile than her father's. They would not hesitate to come to blows on Hannah's behalf. She had to calm the situation, and quickly.

She'd expected it to be difficult, but she hadn't thought her father and brothers would be beyond reason. And she was shocked at the things they had to say about Will. They had always seemed to like him. She couldn't bear such hard feelings among the family. She could feel his presence behind her and she wished he would say something. Clearly, she must make an explanation and she must make everyone watching believe it.

"Papa, please don't be angry," she pleaded, leaving the door of the wellhouse and walking toward her father with her arms outstretched, entreating him. "I love him, Papa, and I think that he loves me," she lied.

Her father's look, if possible, became even more murderous. Her brother Leroy snorted an obscenity in protest. She grabbed her father's clenched fists and brought them up to her face in supplication. "He's a good man, Papa. You know that as well as I."

The crowd of people stood watching in shock as Violet, who had heard the commotion and her husband's call for a weapon, came running with his old squirrel gun, as though she'd thought some rabid animal had got shut up in the wellhouse. Seeing her stepdaughter, clad only in her thin cotton nightgown, she stood stunned in disbelief, but retained the good sense not to give her husband the weapon.

"Papa, we want to be married," Hannah pleaded, praying silently that Will would not dispute her statement. "Please, we want your blessing."

Her brothers exchanged looks of furious disbelief and righteous indignation.

"You're a dead man!" Rafe, the youngest, threatened.

Hannah was tempted to go over and box his ears.

"Give me that gun!" Ned ordered Violet, but she gripped it tighter.

Hannah's patience with the whole group was wearing thin. It wasn't as if she were a green girl, she was a grown woman of twenty-six and was thoroughly entitled to make her own mistakes.

"I love him, don't you understand?" she lied. "I want to be with him."

"That low-down snake doesn't deserve the likes of you, Miss Hannah!" a voice just to the right of her father shouted in anger. "What's got into you messing with a decent farmer's daughter?" he yelled at the man behind her.

The voice captured Hannah's immediate attention. She turned toward it, shocked. Will Sample, the man she planned to marry, was standing in a group of men staring angrily at the wellhouse.

With a feeling of unreality, Hannah turned toward the object of their anger. In the doorway of the small building, with his hands upraised like a captured bank robber was Henry Lee Watson, a man Hannah barely knew.

ONE

Practical problems have practical solutions. Hannah May Bunch had always believed that. Perhaps that was why, with only the merest twinge of guilt, she had set herself upon the plan. As a solution, it would have been good for all parties concerned. It had seemed perfectly reasonable, and except for some of its slightly underhanded aspects, it was essentially biblical.

Or it had seemed so yesterday.

She had begun the previous morning at first light, leaving her bed and her still-sleeping younger sister to start the morning fire. It was no longer her job, but years of habit forced her to be the first to rise. In the kitchen she opened the grate on the stove and stirred the ashes.

This is the day, she thought. *The day that will change my life.*

She'd finally decided that her situation was not going to get any better. She needed to take action. Action to get what she wanted, or more specifically *who* she wanted.

Moving to the water pitcher, she lifted it and poured half into the bowl and began washing. Hearing movement behind her, she glanced back, offering her father a pleasant "good morning," which he answered with a yawning "hello" as he headed for the wellhouse. Water drawn the night before was fine for washing, but Papa insisted that his morning coffee be made with freshly drawn water.

A well close to the house was the nearest thing to a luxury that one could find on the prairie. Most farmers either lived next to the small creeks and streams of the territory, or built the difficult and undependable cisterns to collect rainwater. Finding water right next to the homestead was such a stroke of good luck that it could only be considered a gift from heaven. Hannah's father was very proud of his well. So proud in fact, that he built a house for cooling and washing right around it. Wellhouses were common in Kansas, but here in the territory they were rare.

Checking first to see that the fire was going to catch, Hannah returned to her bedroom to dress and awaken her younger sister.

"Myrtie, you better get up," she ordered the rounded pile of bed linens. "The sun will be up any minute and there is a world of things to do this morning."

Myrtie snuggled deeper into the covers and made an unintelligible answer.

Hannah pulled her blue gingham from the hook in the wardrobe. It was her most attractive work dress. She reasoned that looking her best today could be important. For her plan to work, the entire community might need to believe that she was capable of attracting the opposite sex.

"Come on, Myrtie, everybody in the country will be here in an hour. You don't want them to catch you with your hair a mess."

Myrtie sighed loudly and moved to rise. Hannah knew that prodding her sister's vanity was the one sure motivator. Myrtie was the prettiest girl in Plainview, everybody said so. Even if she was just sixteen, there was not a doubt in anybody's mind that she was something to see. Unlike many sisters who, being older and less attractive, might have struggled with sibling jealousies, Hannah was proud. Maybe it was because she felt more like a parent than a sister.

At fifteen, Hannah had taken over the job of raising two-year-old Myrtie and her three brothers, even before her mother had died. The vicious, painful cancer that had slowly choked the life out of her mother had caused young Hannah to put away her childish things forever.

Hannah had no regrets. Her brothers were all married now. They had their own places and a start in the world. She was an aunt twice over already. And seeing young Myrtie—pretty, sweet, all primed to run a house, the most sought-after girl in the territory—was evidence of a job well done. But the job was over now, and it was time she made a life of her own.

She examined her reflection in the small glass that had belonged to her mother. The gingham dress did nothing to disguise the broad shoulders and sturdy appearance that Hannah had inherited from her father. It was a simple and rather severe style and was not exactly blue anymore. Lack of bluing on the prairie generally, and in the territory particularly, meant that most everything faded to a dull gray that seemed to be almost a part of the landscape. Hannah had often prided herself on being a practical, hardworking woman. This day, however, with the task she had set for herself, she wished she had just a fraction of the dainty, dimpled appearance of young Myrtie.

In fact, Hannah was pleasant enough to look at. She was tall and strong, the way a farm girl should be. Her features were comely, and her figure was definitely female. Her hair, which she considered her best feature, was an in-between color, not quite brown, but not quite blonde. It was a riot of thick natural curls that she kept tightly braided and wrapped at the nape of her neck. Her eyes were the color of storm clouds over a lake, but with none of the foreboding.

Now they settled on her sister, who had yet to move from her comfortable cocoon. "Come on, Myrtie, all those sweet-looking boys are going to be disappointed if you're not down there to greet them."

Throwing back the covers, Myrtie sat on the edge of the bed with her eyes still closed, trying for that last minute of a long night's rest. As her sister finally began her morning ritual, Hannah hurried out of the bedroom and into the kitchen.

Her stepmother, Violet, was seated at the table rolling out biscuits, the water already steaming on the stove.

The two women greeted each other cordially. Hannah

went to the coffee tin and measured a pot's worth into the grinder.

"Have you taken care of everything for the meal?" Hannah asked. "These men are going to be very hungry and you can't count on the other women to bring enough."

"Oh, there'll be plenty," Violet answered, with a smiling confidence that Hannah didn't possess. "I've never yet been to a community dinner where there wasn't twice as much food as needed."

Hannah started to suggest that was true because the women always planned ahead, but she managed to hold her tongue. "I suppose," Hannah suggested instead, "if things start to run out I could come in and fry up some of that ham. It won't be as good as the other, but if you're hungry you can eat anything."

Violet smiled at her stepdaughter. "I'm so excited about the new church, I could hardly sleep all night," she told her. "I just kept imagining all the angels in heaven cheering and singing for joy that a new house for the Lord would be going up in the territory."

Hannah could not imagine lying awake in the bed thinking about the doings of angels. It was one of the things that was so difficult for her to understand about her stepmother—her flights of fancy.

"We'd best get those biscuits in the oven," Hannah muttered dryly, "or do you think the angels might send us breakfast from heaven?"

Violet's laugh was tinkling, like a little bell. "They just might!" she replied, her eyes bright with mischief. "Do you think your father would prefer grits this morning or manna?"

The air was still cool as Hannah hurried out to do her chores, but there was no doubt that it was going to be a hot day. That would fit in perfectly with Hannah's plan. By now, she had convinced herself that she was doing the right thing. After all, the idea had come to her from the good book.

One evening during her father's daily scripture reading, when her mind wandered from his droning voice, she'd gotten the idea. At first, it seemed quite daring and sinful, but after examining it more closely, she had decided that it was, in fact, very sensible. Men married women for many reasons and most of those turned out to be terribly shortsighted. This was a very practical solution, not done up with hearts and flowers perhaps, but one that would offer a measure of happiness and security for both of them . . .

As she gathered the eggs, her father hailed her on his way back from the barn.

"Looks like a perfect day for building a church," he said, glancing toward the road as if he couldn't wait to begin. "Figure those boys will be heading in anytime now, you better hurry up and help Violet, she's not used to feeding a crowd."

"I will, Papa," Hannah assured him. Her father's choice in a second wife continued to be a mystery to Hannah. Violet was sweet and loving and very unlike the type of woman her father needed. Her faith was childlike and her experience at making a home almost nonexistent. Hannah found it hard to understand how her straightforward sensible father could find happiness with a woman who seemed more Myrtie's contemporary than his own.

"I'll take care of things, Papa," she said. "But it's best if it looks like it's Violet's spread." Hannah was well aware that a woman's place in the community was judged by the way she set a table. It was true that most of the congregation seemed to accept Violet's peculiarities, but Hannah didn't think it would do any good for the women to think that it was Hannah who continued to keep her father's house.

Hannah glanced up at the rise on the east side of the house. A foundation of sandstone, quarried from the local hills, was surrounded by fresh timber, just waiting for the hands of carpenters.

"It's going to be a wonderful church, Papa."

"Yes, I think it is," he said, beaming at his oldest daughter.

Reverend Farnam Bunch had waited five long years to have a church of his own. He might have waited even longer if his new wife, Violet, hadn't encouraged him. The grassy prairie that had appealed to farmers because it lacked the stumps and roots that they had had to remove in former homesteads, meant that lumber was hard to come by. It also meant that homes and barns and other necessary buildings had to be raised before using precious lumber for a meetinghouse. Now, finally, he had convinced the congregation that they were ready to build a church. With everybody helping out, two days would be plenty of time to see his dream become a reality. His eyes rested warmly on Hannah.

"I like it that you are so pleased about the church. You didn't seem to much like the idea when Violet came up with it."

"I explained all that, Papa," she sighed. "I just thought that if we built a bigger barn, which we really need, we could make do with the old barn as a church."

His frown admonished her as he spoke deliberately. "The house of the Lord shouldn't be in a barn, Hannah. Violet's right about that."

"Yes, I'm sure she is," she admitted and then lifted her chin in mild defiance. "But, we do need a bigger barn."

He laughed. "Don't forget what the Bible had to say about building bigger barns, you can get yourself in a peck of trouble there, sister."

"You're right, of course, Papa." Hannah shook her head at her father's attempt at humor.

"Anyway," he said wrapping his arm around her, "aren't you about ready for a nice, clean, little, white church, like the ones we left behind in Kansas? I thought all ladies liked nice, clean, little, white churches."

Hannah smiled. What would her father say if she told him she planned to be married in that nice little church tomorrow. He would be shocked. Hannah had never had a regular beau. It wasn't that she lacked interest in men. But she'd had a house to keep, a farm to work, and the children to raise. Gentlemen callers were a luxury for which she had no time. When she was prime age for men to be giving her a long look, she knew that her father and her brothers and sister needed her too much to leave them.

Because Hannah had never allowed any man to sit with her in church or walk out with her in the evenings, her father believed her to be one of those women fulfilled by spinsterhood. It had never occurred to him that her lack of a husband was due to his overburdening her as a daughter.

Hannah might have been content if her father hadn't remarried. But now it was Violet's house and hearth. And Hannah felt in the way.

Of course, it wasn't only for her father and Violet that Hannah had come up with her plan. She wanted a family and a man of her own. At her age, it wasn't easy to go husband-hunting, although she knew that she would make an excellent wife. She was capable, diligent, used to hard work, and of an even temperament. She needed a man who would accept her for those practical qualities, but that kind of usefulness didn't generally catch the eye of young men.

As Hannah headed back into the house, her father continued to gaze at the top of the rise. He'd named it Plainview Church because you could see nothing from that rise but just plain view.

Hannah's eyes, however, did not linger on the church that was going to be, but on the house that was, and had been, her home for so long. If her plan worked, and she was sure it would, this would be one of the last mornings of her life here. Would her new home be as loving and peaceful as this one? Surely with a man like Will, it would be.

Will Sample had moved to the area over a year ago, setting up a dry goods store down near Pearson's Creek. For Hannah it had not been love at first sight, or even the nearest thing to it. Will was not the kind of man to set a woman's heart aflutter. Most women would have said he was big, and shy, and homely. But Hannah thought he was much like her. Hardworking and eminently practical, he was a man of few words, and though he had few friends not many would have stated that they disliked the man.

Almost from the day he moved to the area, he had latched on to Hannah's family. He was there most Saturday nights for supper. He never missed a Sunday service. If there was anything extra to be done, if a man's hand was needed, he was available, right along with her brothers.

For a while, Hannah was puzzled by this. People had reasons for the things they did, and at first, she couldn't fathom Will's. Then she realized that he must be coming around to see her, and she was flattered, and mildly amused. After her father married Violet, she became interested.

Hannah was certain that she could make him a good wife. She didn't love him, of course. But that would come in time, she knew. A good marriage should be based on comparable purpose and ambition. Hannah knew that she had good business sense and could be a help to him in making his store prosper. Both of them being matter-of-fact and sensible, they would work well together.

But that had been several months earlier. With each passing week it had become more difficult to wait for Will to work up the courage to begin a courtship. It had become increasingly obvious to Hannah that he was so shy he could only rarely manage even a few words for her. She tried to give him opportunities to see her at her best, to be alone with her for as long as was proper, and to try to make him as comfortable as possible in her presence.

Hannah had maintained her patience as long as possible, and finally she knew something had to be done. Then suddenly the perfect plan was right before her eyes. Now all that was needed was the doing of it . . .

The morning was a busy one for Hannah. She expected to feed close to a hundred people, counting the children. She knew that every woman would be bringing food, but it was still the responsibility of the preacher's family to see that everyone had plenty to eat.

As she sat on the wash bench under the blackjack

tree snapping beans, Myrtie and Violet came over to join her.

Her sister stood before her, smoothing her hair and preening as she admired her ruffled skirts.

"What do you think of this dress, Hannah? I do look all right, don't I?"

"You're a vain child, Myrtie," Hannah answered, but there was a smile on her face. "If you do as well as you look, then you'll be doing all right."

Violet laughed. "Oh Hannah, Myrtie always does what she is supposed to do, and when you are especially pretty you can't help but be a little vain about it."

Hannah didn't know that she truly agreed with that, but she held her tongue. Violet was such a cheerful person she was difficult to scold.

Hannah and Myrtie settled themselves under the tree and began the process of snapping the beans and transferring the snapped portions to another saucepan. Myrtie's help was halfhearted this morning and her talk inevitably turned to boys. Hannah listened as she always had. She wished she could share her own excitement and nervous anxiety about the events coming up in her life. But telling Myrtie would be like advertising in the Gazette. This was something that Hannah would have to keep to herself, at least until tomorrow, when everyone would know anyway.

"Look, Hannah, someone is coming down the road already." Myrtie quickly grabbed the edges of her apron, forming a safe pouch for the beans she held in her lap, and stood on her tiptoes to get a better view.

"Who is it?" Hannah asked.

"I can't tell," her sister answered, shading her eyes against the sun.

Hannah stood up and looked down the road at the wagon coming slowly toward them. Hannah noticed the driver's shiny black hair and her heart began beating quicker. Will Sample, the first to arrive. Hannah struggled to control her breathing and tried to remain unconcerned as her future rode toward her.

"Oh, it's Henry Lee Watson!" Myrtie exclaimed.

Hannah looked again and realized Myrtie was right. She guessed that she was so anxious to see Will that she saw him even when he wasn't there.

"I can't imagine what he's doing here," Myrtie said. "Why, he doesn't even attend church."

Hannah knew Watson lived out near Pearson's Creek just across the line in the Indian Territory. He'd been here long before the Washington policy that had offered any willing farmer one hundred and sixty acres just for tearing up the prairie grass and planting in the remaining dirt. The change had not been without incident, and cattlemen and farmers still weren't on the best of terms. But Henry Lee was neither farmer nor cattleman. He held a rather unique position in the community. Revered by some, despised by others, he refused to take the judgment of the community too seriously.

Hannah knew little of him except that it was said that if more than two people were meeting together, Henry Lee Watson would soon be showing up. To Hannah, this meant that his interest was in trifling pursuits and idleness. Not the type of steady, hardworking man that she could respect.

"He's here because I asked him," Papa said, as he came up behind them, "and don't you be making eyes at that one, little sugarplum. He's a grown man who's lived a full life, I've no doubt, and he's no match for the likes of you. But he is one good cabinetmaker. To my mind he ought to take up cabinetry full-time, but I guess it's his choice. Anyway, I want him for the finish work for the church."

Henry Lee rode up into the yard and waved. Six foot two inches of lean, muscled man, he rarely went unnoticed by females of any community.

"Reverend Farnam," he said, doffing his hat to the ladies with a handsome smile, "the devil must still be sleeping this morning, looks like a perfect day for building a church."

"That it does, Henry Lee, and I hope you're feeling like working."

"I will surely try, Reverend, but with pretty ladies

like these around, why it nearly puts me out of the working mood altogether." His words and charming smile were directed at the women sitting on the wash bench. Myrtie giggled and covered her face with her hands. Violet laughed lightheartedly, as if flirtation with the preacher's wife and daughters was perfectly normal. Hannah just stared at him wondering how a grown man came to be so frivolous. Oh, she could see why Myrtie found him interesting, he was a fine-looking specimen, broad enough in the shoulders to make his height seem everyday. And the black hair that betrayed his distant Indian heritage was thick and straight and offset by the most amazing blue eyes that seemed perpetually to be dancing with amusement.

Hannah found him fascinating, almost like a rattlesnake. He was just the type of man she'd warned Myrtie to avoid.

"What are you bringing us here, Henry Lee?" Hannah's father asked.

"Venison," he replied unloading the contents of the wagon and hoisting the haunch of meat on his shoulder.

"To tell you the God's truth, Reverend, I had this terrible nightmare last night." His eyes scanned Farnam and then the ladies, keeping everyone's attention.

"I kept hearing something calling 'Help us! Help us! She is going to kill us all!' and do you know who was calling me? Why those fine laying hens of yours. I could just see Mrs. Bunch saying she was going to have to do away with every last one of them to feed this crew." He flashed a dazzling smile at Violet, causing her to blush prettily.

"You could say," he teased her, "that I'm bringing this deer to insure the future of eggs in the territory."

Everyone laughed.

"I trust that this is *all* you brought, Henry Lee." The preacher's tone was serious.

"It is, Reverend," Henry Lee told him cheerfully. "Even I can forget about business for a couple of days to help build a church."

The preacher seemed to like his answer. "Have you

had your breakfast, Henry Lee?" he asked. "Seeing how you're here first, you'll have time to try some of those eggs you're so fond of and maybe some of my wife's biscuits. Light as air, they are. That's why I married her, for her biscuits."

Henry Lee said something quietly under his breath to the preacher, who laughed heartily and clapped him on the back as they headed into the house.

As the morning lengthened, others began arriving and the air of a festive occasion blossomed. The men all headed up to the rise with a wagon load of lumber brought by Mason Dillary. Will's arrival almost passed unnoticed by Hannah, who had finished up the beans and was shucking corn.

Will bypassed the house to go straight to the rise, and had someone not called out to him Hannah would not have known that he was there at all.

She wanted to speak to him and set her plan in motion, but apparently that would have to wait until later.

The sounds of shouts and hammers filled the morning as the men began laying out the foundations for the church. By late morning the frame was up and it was possible to see at last that all the noise was really producing a building.

Myrtie asked to carry water to the men, and Hannah was sorry that she hadn't thought of it. That would have been the perfect way to have a moment to speak with Will. Of course Myrtie would think of it. Hannah decided that she would just have to wait until she had dinner on the table and then confront him.

The women had arrived with baskets of breads and jars of pickles and dressed hens for dinner. Just as Violet predicted, there was going to be plenty to feed everybody, not only for dinner, but more than enough left for those staying for supper.

Many of the church members lived long distances away and would be staying the night, bunking down in the barn or out under the stars. It was perfect for Hannah's plan.

Sawhorses were set up about twelve feet apart and planks were laid to make a temporary table. It took three of Hannah's mother's tablecloths to cover it. The food was laid out and everyone filled their plates. It was called having dinner on the ground because there wasn't enough room for everyone to sit at the table.

Myrtie graciously volunteered to pour lemonade and Hannah was obliged to run back and forth to the kitchen to replenish her supply, along with a thousand other errands.

The mood was happy and cheerful, with everyone in high spirits and children running wild. Hannah, however, was becoming more nervous by the minute, afraid that she would miss her opportunity to speak with Will.

At the last possible moment, before the men went back to work, Hannah spotted Will taking his plate back to the table and intercepted him.

"I'll take that, Will," she offered with a smile. "Did you get enough to eat?"

"Yes, ma'am," he replied, immediately becoming red-faced. "Your stepmama sure sets a fine table, Miss Hannah."

Will was a goodly sized man, with large features and a round face. His complexion was naturally ruddy, but it had been Hannah's experience that anytime he spoke to her his face and neck were constantly flushed red.

"Would you like another piece of pie or maybe some of that berry cobbler?"

"No, ma'am, I'd better be helping the others," he said, turning to go.

"Will!" Suddenly Hannah had his attention but didn't quite know what to do with it. "It sure is powerful hot out here today."

"Yes, ma'am, a real scorcher." Will ran his hand through his thick black hair as if to relieve the weight of it.

"I certainly feel sorry for you men coming here to do this good work and then having to try to sleep out in this heat." Hannah could feel her face burning as hot as the summer sun she was talking about.

"Oh, it's no problem, ma'am."

"Yes, well." She hesitated as her mind screamed *have courage, Hannah*. She couldn't look him in the eye, but gazed off into the distance.

"I imagine the best place for sleeping tonight would be the wellhouse, it's always a mite cooler there." She watched his reaction closely to see if he read anything into her comment, but he didn't appear to.

"Yes, ma'am, I suspect so."

"If I were you, Will, I'd get that place for myself."

"Sounds good, ma'am, thanks for the advice."

Will stood there waiting to see if she wanted to say anything else. Hannah wanted to, but she seemed to have lost her ability to speak. With a nod of her head she dismissed him and he headed back up the rise to the church.

Hannah felt ill. She had never been so afraid in her life. She couldn't decide if she wanted to lie down or take off running. But the deed was done. Will would be in the wellhouse tonight.

Hour by hour, the church seemed to take shape. The laughter involved in putting on the roof was unseemly to Hannah, who was getting more nervous by the minute.

"They shouldn't be carrying on like that," she grumbled. "Laughing and joking while they work on the Lord's house."

"Good heavens, Hannah," Violet said, "You are always far too serious for your own good. Don't be so sour. The Lord expects us to be happy, he'd never be insulted by a little laughter in his house." Then her stepmother looked at her more closely. "Are you all right, Hannah?" she asked.

"Yes, Violet, I'm fine, just a little tired, I guess." Hannah rubbed the back of her neck to ease the tension that had settled there.

Violet's eyes softened. "I'm sorry I wasn't more help at dinner. You never seem to mind doing it all so I just let you. I promise I'll do better at supper."

"It's not you, Violet, truly," Hannah said. "I guess I just have a few things on my mind."

"Here," Violet said, handing her the water bucket,

"you take this up to the men and it will get your mind off your troubles."

The last thing Hannah wanted to do was to stand around under the scrutiny of the men, and she certainly wasn't going to say another thing to Will, but she took the water bucket and headed up the rise.

As she walked up to the first group of men she noticed that they were all gathered around Henry Lee Watson.

"There were these two sisters from Cincinnati," Henry Lee was saying. "The fat one was named Ima and the skinny one was name Ura. Well, when the brush salesman came to the door—"

One of the men signaled to Henry Lee and he immediately stopped his story and turned to face Hannah.

"Miss Hannah, you've brought us water!" he said loudly as if he were speaking for the benefit of everyone. "There's nothing more encouraging to a man hard at work than the sight of a pretty girl concerned with his comfort."

All the men seemed to be looking at Hannah and she felt distinctly out of place. That was another thing about Henry Lee Watson that she truly didn't like. He made her feel uncomfortable. It was as if, when he was around, the differences between men and women were somehow more marked.

He took the ladle from her and drank deeply, then he poured a second ladleful over his face.

"On a day as hot as today, ma'am, you could offer a man a drink like this and he would give you anything." He spoke the words in a stage whisper that seemed to insinuate some sort of intimacy between the two of them. It made her flustered and she searched for a scorching reply.

As he drank another ladleful, she said as haughtily as she could manage, "It's only water, it's not as if I made it myself!"

Henry Lee spewed the water out of his mouth nearly choking and laughter rang out all around them. Horrified, Hannah realized the implication of her words. The idea

that she "made water" was the most humiliating thing
she had ever said in mixed company. And he was laughing at her.

"Here, take it." She handed him the bucket and, with
blazing cheeks, headed back down the hill at a controlled
and moderate pace, her back stiff with anger.

He better not be interested in Myrtie, she thought to
herself furiously. He was terrible, but a young girl like
Myrtie wouldn't be able to see past that handsome face.
Surely Papa would never allow a crass man like him to
court little Myrtie.

Supper was served late. The men wanted to use
every last bit of daylight so they could finish early tomorrow. The high spirits of the afternoon had given way to
an overall tiredness. Hard labor for ten hours made the
supper table a quiet place.

Hannah was quiet also. Time seemed to drag, and
yet the hour for implementing her plan was almost upon
her. She kept reminding herself that this was all in the
good book, but she was beginning to have some doubts.
As the men got up to leave the table, she came out to
clear it.

She watched Will head toward the wellhouse and she
reminded herself of the prize she sought. A good, hardworking man to live her life with, to give her children,
and to grow old beside. Hannah finished her chores and
returned to her room.

Myrtie flounced into the bedroom and peered over
her sister's shoulder as Hannah sat on the bed, poring
over her Bible.

"Honestly, Hannah! Don't you get enough of that
with the family? Papa just finished reading us the
scriptures."

"It's just something I wanted to look over one more
time," Hannah answered distractedly, and returned to
her studying.

Myrtie was already fast asleep and the candle burning
low when Hannah finished. She closed her Bible, pressed
it to her breast, and whispered to herself, "and Ruth
sought Boaz on the threshing floor—"

She closed her eyes and placed her hands over her face as if to hide from herself. "Please give me strength to do this," she prayed. "If this is the only way it can be, then please give me the strength to do it."

When the house was completely still Hannah moved slowly out of her bed. She wished she could dress, but that would defeat her purpose. Donning her wrapper, she headed out the door, and nearly came up short as she heard snores coming from the backporch where some of the men had bunked down. She decided that if anyone should rouse, she would simply be headed for the privy. No one did, and with amazing ease she found herself at the wellhouse.

She looked around to see if she was being observed, but the whole world seemed to be asleep. She eased the door open and peered inside. The light from the moon did not allow her to see too far past the doorway, but she could make out the form of a man sleeping on the floor. She opened the door wider and the moonlight revealed a head of thick black hair. Hannah's breath caught in her throat for an instant, but before her courage could leave her she whispered to herself the verses she had memorized.

"And it shall be, when he lieth down, that thou shalt mark the place where he shall lie, and thou shalt go in, and uncover his feet, and lay thee down . . ."

Hannah took a deep breath and stepped gently inside, it certainly would not do to wake Will up. The embarrassment would be impossible to live with and he would surely send her back to the house and everything would be ruined. Ruth had wanted a man to marry her, and her mother-in-law had directed her to go out to the fields and lie beside him. If she were caught in a compromising position with Will, he would have to marry her. It had worked for Ruth.

She slipped off her wrapper and gently laid it out beside him. She gave quick thanks that his face was turned away from her or she might not have been able to go through with it. She eased herself down beside the man she intended to marry. Stiff, frightened, and wary, she lay beside him and waited for dawn.

For the thousandth time she felt a twinge of guilt. But she knew that she would make Will happy. No other woman would try as hard as she would to be a good wife to him. Still, it seemed unfair for him to have no choice in the matter at all.

But then, why had the scripture so captured her imagination if it had not been meant for her? Why even have such a story in the Bible if not to serve as a useful guide for someone in the future? She could not imagine God allowing a story in his book that served no useful purpose. It was undoubtedly there to give guidance to women like herself, who otherwise might have no opportunity of getting married.

The man beside her suddenly made a noise in his sleep and rolled over. His arm came in contact with her body and he immediately clutched her to himself.

Hannah nearly screamed in fright. In the Bible story Boaz had awakened at midnight to find Ruth. "Please don't let Will wake up!" she begged silently.

Her prayers seemed to be answered, he slept on with her tucked into his chest. How could he sleep like that without noticing her? Surely it was a sign that they were meant to be together. They already slept like old married people.

With that she began to relax. She was right to do this, she was sure now. After the worries of the past hours and with the most important day of her life coming tomorrow, Hannah slept.

TWO

Henry Lee Watson stood in the door of Reverend Bunch's wellhouse with his hands raised high over his head.

Damn! he swore to himself. He knew he had no business hanging out with these churchgoers. Now he'd really bought himself a peck of trouble.

He prided himself on being a man who could control his temper. His father would nearly tear the house down in fits of rage. Vowing never to be like him, except for an occasional unexpected expletive, Henry Lee had learned to maintain a calm control.

It enabled him to keep his peace as a semicircle of angry men surrounded him. Not one face was softened by sympathy. Out in the middle of the fray, the preacher, a man whose good opinion he valued highly, raged at him for his duplicity. He had done nothing wrong, and he wanted the reverend to know that. But perhaps it was the Indian in him that urged him to wait and see how the land lay.

He turned his eyes on the girl. Not a girl, he decided quickly. She was obviously a woman. Her hair hanging like a long braided rope down her back, slightly mussed from sleeping, gave her a certain wanton appeal. She had modestly crossed her arms over her chest, which was exposed in the thin summer nightgown. But from Henry Lee's perspective, the morning sun shone through her skimpy covering, distinctly displaying her feminine charms. She was a tall woman, but her limbs were neither lanky nor coltish. Through the shiny veil of cotton he could see the outline of strong, well-turned legs and shapely thighs. He wondered why her family didn't take care to cover her. Shouldn't one of the women have brought a blanket or a shawl?

He stared at her for long moments, his clear blue eyes trying to understand the look of bewilderment in hers. She had set him up. It was obvious. But he didn't know what he could do about it. None of these men would believe it, he was sure. It was difficult for him to believe himself. He could still feel the heat from her body on the front of his shirt. Hatred would be the appropriate reaction to this little tramp; he should be boiling with fury. But as he looked at her lost, incredulous expression, he felt only pity. She seemed to be worsening the situation, with her nonsense about his love for her. The crowd had enough of a spectacle at their expense, it was time for him to take charge.

Henry Lee dropped his hands to his side. With a close eye on his back, he reached into the wellhouse and retrieved Hannah's wrapper from the floor. He walked toward her slowly. He sensed her fear and was careful not to make any threatening moves. If she were to visibly flinch in front of this crowd, they might lynch him as a rapist. He draped the cover around her shoulders with the gentle courtesy of a man who knows to treat even the shadiest lady with special respect. Looking straight into Hannah's eyes, he saw vulnerability that rode ill on the starchy spinster's face. Her lower lip trembled slightly, causing a well of protectiveness to surge through Henry Lee. He turned to her stepmother and spoke with careful politeness.

"Mrs. Bunch, you had better take Miss Hannah up to the house. If the preacher intends to kill me it's not a thing that she should see." He watched as she was led away from the confrontation, too overwhelmed with the calamity that she had produced to protest.

Myrtie and Hannah's sisters-in-law, June, Velma, and Earline, were waiting a few feet away. All of their faces registered stunned disbelief.

"Oh, Hannah, are you all right?" Myrtie asked.

"Fine," she answered absently. "I'm fine," she said more strongly. Hannah turned to look back at the scene she had left, the men seemed to be closing in around Henry Lee, itching for trouble. She saw her youngest brother, Rafe, well-known for being a hothead, step right in front of Henry Lee, their faces not more than two inches apart. She felt a wave of guilt. This was all her doing and she'd left him to answer for her.

"Violet, you can't let them hurt Mr. Watson, it's not his fault," she pleaded with her stepmother.

"Not his fault!" Velma snorted. "Heavens above! Do you expect us to believe that an innocent, Christian woman forced herself upon a man with a questionable reputation?" The others nodded their heads in agreement.

Hannah couldn't expect them to believe it, even though it was absolutely true.

Violet hugged Hannah sympathetically, and placed a comforting arm around her shoulder. "Your father can't hurt him much," Violet promised her, patting the stock of the double shot firearm she held reassuringly. "I've still got the gun."

They stepped into the house, and as if on signal, the sound of a scuffle began near the wellhouse.

Hannah paced frantically and tried to see what was happening. Her kinswomen seemed to immediately form a conspiracy to keep her from the windows.

"Oh no, we've got to stop this," Hannah exclaimed. "As big as he is, he could hurt Papa!"

"A minute ago you were worried about him, now you're worried about Papa," Myrtie pointed out.

Hannah ignored this reference to her inconsistency and continued to listen to the yelling of the crowd with trepidation.

"He won't hurt your papa, not with all those men around, and not a one of them is on his side, you can be sure of that," Violet told her. "Besides, he knows he's done wrong."

Hannah tried to sort out what had happened. *What had Henry Lee been doing in the wellhouse? Will was supposed* to be there. *Why didn't she make sure who it was! How could she have made sure? Lighting a lamp would have wakened him, and that would have ruined the plan completely.* But the plan was shot to pieces anyway. *Better to have had to explain herself last night, than to explain herself this morning. What would she tell Henry Lee? Worse than that, what would she tell her father!*

If there was one thing her father always insisted upon, and one thing she had prided herself upon, it was honesty and integrity. How could she explain that she'd attempted to coerce a man into marrying her. And failed!

And poor Will, now he would never find the courage to walk out with her. If he were to court her now, it would make him a laughingstock.

Everybody in the territory would hear about this escapade. And what they would make of it, she knew, was even worse than it appeared: A lovestarved spinster seduces a handsome young man, right under her father's nose.

It was going to be a terrible embarrassment for her entire family. The only women likely to stand by her were her relatives, and even they were totally scandalized.

The shouting from outside and the sounds of the fighting ceased. When after a moment there was no cry for help, Hannah sighed heavily. No one was seriously injured, no permanent damage done. Only her shame would linger.

"Thank God, it's over," she said aloud.

"I doubt seriously, Hannah," Violet stated sternly, "if it is over."

"What do you mean?"

"What I mean is, that while I do blame that man out there for enticing you, he did not come and steal you out of this house. You went out to him, of your own free will. Even though you think that you love him, that's not cause to break the commandments."

Hannah's mind was in turmoil. Of course the whole territory would assume that she had carnally sinned. But she could outlive that. It would just take time. She'd heard stories about women who had fallen from grace.

Some even had illegitimate children as permanent reminders. But it was said that if a woman confessed and lived an exemplary life thereafter, eventually she would be tolerated by the community.

She blushed, thinking of how long it would take for the community to forget the scene they had witnessed this morning. She remembered pleading with her father and claiming she was out there for love. Oh, how embarrassing that was. People would think that she had been swept off her feet by that smooth talker and his well-known charm. She hated for anyone to believe that of her. She'd rather they thought she was wanton than gullible.

But how much worse was the real truth. She was out there to trick a man who couldn't bring himself to propose. She couldn't get a man any way but by her trickery, and even as she had been trying to lie herself into a marriage, she had managed to embroil an innocent party into a scandal.

With all the conviction that any jaded sinner ever had, she suddenly knew that she could not, would not, ever tell the truth about what she was doing in the wellhouse. Far better for everyone concerned to think that she was a foolish, credulous old maid with flexible morals, than the deceitful conniver she really was.

Straightening her back and raising her chin, Hannah said, "I have nothing to say about what happened last night. I'm a grown woman, responsible only to God for my sins, and I do not have to confess them to you."

Myrtie's eyes were as big as saucers.

"We'll see what your father has to say about that," her stepmother replied.

"He can say whatever he wants, Violet, but I don't intend to discuss it with him, or you, or anyone."

Reverend Bunch walked in through the door and sat down at the table. His step was weary and sweat was running in rivulets down the side of his face. He wiped at it half-heartedly as his wife came quickly to his side.

"Get me some salve, Myrtie," he said tiredly.

"Are you hurt?" Violet's face was lined with worry.

"Just my knuckles," he said. "He didn't even swing

at me." He glanced at Hannah. "But I like to broke my hand on his jaw."

"Is he all right?" Hannah asked.

"Well, I suspect he'll be all right. He's got a busy day ahead of him, he'll have to be building a church all day and he's got a wedding to attend this evening."

"Wedding?"

He rolled his eyes in disbelief. "You said you wanted my blessing. Well, you've got it and I think, honey, that you're going to need it." Her father reached up and took Hannah's hand. He gestured for her to take a seat beside him at the kitchen table. He continued to hold her hand as he gazed into her eyes with fatherly love and apprehension.

"Child, he's not the kind of man I would have chosen for you. But you made this choice yourself."

Shaking his head, he looked up to heaven as if for guidance.

"It has always been a mystery to me why good Christian women always seem to fall in love with the wildest living men around. I guess maybe it's the need to reform them. I'm not sure, though, how much reforming you can do on Henry Lee Watson. You two will have to get along the best that you can."

Hannah felt a sense of rising panic as disbelief turned into a waking nightmare.

"Papa, I can't marry this man! I hardly know him and we just are not suited."

Reverend Bunch looked genuinely confused.

"Hannah, what do you mean? Only a few minutes ago you were begging to marry him."

"I know, Papa, but now that I've had a moment to think about it, well, I've reconsidered." Hannah floundered, wondering how to explain without explaining. She was willing to pay for her mistake, but the price being asked was too high. "At the time, well . . . it might have seemed like a lasting sort of thing, but I'm sure, now, that it was just, well . . . it was a moment of, well . . . it was just the 'lust of the flesh.' "

Violet and Myrtie both gasped. A strange noise emanated from her father's throat that sounded somewhat like a moan of pain.

"Myrtie! You must have chores to do!" her father said sternly and the younger girl quickly left the kitchen.

Hannah's father was now red-faced and seemed to be taking several deep breaths, as if to calm himself. His speech was especially slow, as if he were making a desperate attempt to make himself understood.

"I understand, Hannah, how you could have second thoughts about your actions. I believe that I am certainly understanding of weakness of the flesh, but I'm afraid it's a little late for undoing the past. In my book, young lady, when you met him in that wellhouse, that was the same as agreeing to marry him. And he knew it too, didn't even try to argue about it. I suggest that you do the same!"

Henry Lee Watson shored up the trim in the new Plainview Church. Normally it was work he enjoyed but today he concentrated on it grimly, hoping to free his mind from the morning's disaster.

The men working around him followed his direction as they had the day before. But yesterday there had been a camaraderie, an easy friendliness. Today that was missing. He understood. They thought he had seduced the preacher's daughter. How funny that was. If they really knew him at all they would never have believed it of him. He had a reputation with the ladies, but pretty prostitutes or willing widows were his style. Respectable young women meant trouble.

His face was still tender and puffy from the blows he'd taken this morning. The pain only served as a reminder of how easily he'd been caught in such a simple little trap.

And he would never have done anything to anger Farnam Bunch. He considered the preacher a fair and honorable man. A man whom he could respect. There hadn't been many of those in his life. And that was why the circumstances of the morning had resolved themselves in the way they had.

Imagine that girl of the preacher's sneaking outside

to sleep with him in the wellhouse. She knew she'd be caught; he was sure of that.

She'd known, too, that her father would come out there, she'd known they'd be trapped and it was just what she wanted. He shook his head in disgust. He knew women were partial to him, he'd seen it all over the territory. He was good in the blankets and built to please, but it had never occurred to him that a woman like Miss Hannah would even be interested.

He'd been outrunning calf-eyed young girls and buxom widows for a lot of years now, and not one of them had even come close to catching him. Who could have imagined that some starchy spinster would compromise herself for him. And why? She had never seemed to show much interest in him, not like that saucy little sister of hers. In fact, he had the distinct impression that she didn't like him much.

He remembered hearing her pleading with her father, claiming to love him. Poor, foolish girl. What was he going to do with her?

He certainly didn't need a wife. Farmers needed wives. They lived little two-by-two existences. Every farmer had to have a woman to work and raise up more hands. That was their way, but Henry Lee didn't see how it could work in his life.

Had it been anyone else's daughter, he might have taken off and the devil take the hindmost. But for Reverend Farnam he had to do the right thing. Was marrying the foolish woman really the right thing to do?

Agreeing to marry her seemed like the only thing he could offer, and the only thing that these farmers would accept. If he expected to continue to do business among these men, he had to live by their code, accept their way of doing things. And that didn't allow for deflowering well-brought-up young women.

And she had looked so pitiful. It was as if she couldn't quite believe that she had done it. She must have been afraid that he would expose her. He could have told her daddy what she had done, but chances were, no one would have believed him anyway.

He smiled ruefully, it was kind of hard for him to believe himself. He hadn't been with a woman in a month of Sundays. He'd been making plans to go to Ingalls next week to see if that little redhead still worked at Edith's place.

If he had known that Hannah Bunch was lying there, he could have made her lie into truth! No, he shook his head, the last thing that would interest him was a straightlaced farm girl who'd want to keep her clothes on and her eyes shut. But, damn it, in a few hours he'd be married to one!

"No, absolutely not!" Hannah declared. "I will not wear mother's white wedding dress. I don't want you baking a wedding cake. I am not getting married to Henry Lee Watson and that is final!"

The words were spoken to the mirror, no one else seemed to be listening. She was still certain that her plan to brazen out the scandal was best, but no one, not her father, not Violet, not even Henry Lee Watson was cooperating.

Violet had pulled her mother's wedding dress from the trunk and it was airing outside at this very moment, waiting for Hannah to wear it. Her sisters-in-law were alternately laughing and arguing in the kitchen as they cooked dinner and decorated a cake for the wedding. Hannah was supposed to be packing up her things, but she saw no reason to do so. She wasn't leaving. She wasn't marrying anybody. All of this was just going to disappear.

She was sure Henry Lee Watson was playing some kind of joke. He was biding his time, maybe planning revenge. Any moment now he would either tell Papa the truth, or just grab his horse and ride away and never return. Hannah hoped he would do the latter. It would be easier to be left standing at the church than to try to explain to her father why she had sneaked out to the wellhouse last night.

She must have been out of her head to think that heaven would send her on such an errand. Folks in the

Bible did plenty of strange things, but that didn't mean that people were supposed to do them nowadays. She'd been foolish and selfish, trying to force poor Will Sample to take her for a wife. Will would have done it, of course, and would have tried, no doubt, to make the best of it. But Henry Lee Watson would never stay with her. He'd be gone in a minute. What Hannah couldn't understand was why he hadn't left already!

Peeking out of her room, she was dismayed at the flurry of activity taking place in the house. Cooking for the building crew took up a lot of time, but it was obvious that the women of her family were heavily involved in planning a celebration. It amazed her that Violet, who had always seemed so unorganized, had taken charge of the wedding. She seemed to be thriving on all the details that normally Hannah would have handled.

Violet glanced up and noticed Hannah at the door. She smiled warmly and wiped her hands on her apron and came to her. Her earlier disapproval and censure seemed to be completely wiped away.

"Don't worry about a thing, Hannah," she said cheerfully. "I know it seems like it is very hurried, but we are going to have a real wedding that you'll be able to remember with pride for the rest of your life."

"Violet," Hannah said nervously, drawing her into the bedroom for a private consultation. "You have got to help me. I just cannot go through with this."

Violet sat down on the bed and patted the place beside her. When Hannah joined her, she took her hand.

"I know exactly what you are going through. When I married the late Mr. Bradford, I was so nervous beforehand that I was sick to my stomach. And even as a widow, when your father and I tied the knot my knees shook like jelly for a week before the wedding."

"I wish this were only nerves!" Hannah said, honestly. "I know that Henry Lee does not want to marry me."

"Well, of course he does!" Violet insisted. "You just put that idea right out of your head. You're going to be a wonderful wife to him, I just know it."

"Violet, he would never have married me if Papa hadn't caught us out there."

Violet seemed to consider for a moment. "Well, maybe he wouldn't, Hannah, but you've got to remember that the Lord works in mysterious ways. There's more than one man that found himself on the way to the altar before he'd planned, but heaven has its own time and place for things and this is your time for marrying Henry Lee."

"You don't understand," Hannah pleaded. She wanted to confide in her, but knew it was pointless.

Violet merely gave her a hug of encouragement. "Now you just get busy and get your things packed. We'll be spending most of the afternoon getting you prettied up for the wedding. You're going to dazzle poor Henry Lee so much, he'll plumb forget that this whole thing wasn't his idea."

Although the men had planned to work until they finished, eat a late meal and head on home, the wedding plans had changed the order of the day. The whole community seemed to be involved in the planning of the festivities, and speculation about the wedding and the bride and groom was on everybody's lips.

Hannah knew they were talking about her, but her family stayed around her like a net, not allowing anyone close enough for embarrassing questions. However, plenty had their comments. When the noon meal was laid out and the men came down to eat, the net began to have gaping holes in it.

"You sly thing!" Mary Beth Thompson said to her. "How long has this been going on, and you not letting on by even the slightest sign!"

Hannah just stared at her, not having the vaguest idea of what to say. Mary Beth was still young and attractive enough to be eager to spread the worst kind of stories about courting couples. Whatever Hannah said, it would be twisted and retold to make Hannah seem more foolish than she already was.

She was rescued by an unexpected source.

"Now, Mary Beth, we had to keep it a secret." Hannah tried to keep her mouth from dropping in surprise as Henry Lee walked up behind her and placed his arm gently around her shoulders. "Miss Hannah wanted to be married in that church and wouldn't let me say a word to her daddy until it was nearly finished. She was afraid he'd take a shotgun to me." Leaning down conspiratorially to Mary Beth, he added, "and I guess she was right!"

Mary Beth giggled, totally bedazzled by his teasing words, and around them everyone within hearing distance joined into the laughter.

After that Henry Lee did not stray an inch from his betrothed and his unfailing politeness and obvious deference was slowly winning over the churchgoers. Everyone seemed gradually to become delighted with the wedding and the apparently happy couple.

Hannah couldn't understand it. Surely no one believed that they had actually been seeing each other. Why did a few silly words from this man make things all right again? And why was he saying them? If he didn't go ahead and leave soon, they would actually have to go through with it.

Henry Lee filled two plates and insisted that Hannah come and sit with him to eat.

"No, I really must help out," she pleaded, not wanting to be in close proximity to him any longer than absolutely necessary.

"Nonsense, you are the bride."

Had he given the word an unusual emphasis? She saw in his eyes a strange mixture of admiration and pity.

"Come and sit down, nobody expects the bride to wait on us, do you, boys?"

"Come and sit a spell, Miss Hannah," a grizzled farmer told her. "There're plenty of women here to help that ain't getting married this afternoon."

With Henry Lee at her elbow carrying the plates, Hannah made her way to the swing that her father had put up in the grape arbor. The grapes didn't thrive, but the arbor was the coolest, most pleasant place to sit in the yard. As the men came over and seated themselves around the couple, Hannah couldn't decide if she was glad of their presence or resentful of the lack of privacy.

She felt foolish and out of place. All around her were men she had known all her life, but she had hardly ever spoken to any of them. Now she was too ashamed to look at them.

Henry Lee kept up a running conversation about the church, and the other men, and the crops, as if to discourage talk of the wedding. Just talking and visiting seemed to come easy to him. He put the men at ease.

However, not everyone's curiosity could be redirected.

"Where're you two going on your honeymoon?" Clarence Hopkins asked, drawing out the word to nearly three times its normal length.

Henry Lee looked the man square in the eyes. "Well, Miss Hannah and I are somewhat partial to the wellhouse."

Hoots and howls followed this statement, Hannah noticed that even her father was genuinely laughing. Personally, she was mortified.

Henry Lee reached over and raised up her chin. "You see this, gentlemen? My daddy always told me when you're thinking to marry a woman, it should be one who still knows how to blush."

THREE

She would be the wallflower bride of the charmer of the territory, Hannah thought miserably as she stood in her room dressed in her mother's wedding gown. Once white, the dress was now faded into a color reminiscent of frosty cream. The high collar and tight sleeves identified it as a dress from another generation and the detail of fifty-two buttons down the back clearly showed that it was sewn for a wedding very different from this one.

Surely he'll make his getaway soon, she told herself hopefully. But she no longer quite believed it.

Myrtie had bounced back from her earlier shock and was lying on Hannah's bed practically giddy with excitement.

"To think of you and Henry Lee Watson," Myrtie sighed. "I just would never, oh, Hannah, he is so handsome!"

"Myrtie, really, you mustn't say that!"

"Oh, you know I wouldn't say it to anyone else. But he's going to be my brother-in-law after all." She sighed again. "All the girls talk about him. He's so handsome and such a cutup. They say that he goes to every party in the territory. Just think, you'll be going to parties all the time."

"I'm sure I won't be going to any parties. And he surely doesn't go all the time, Myrtie," Hannah replied, somewhat concerned. "I'm sure there is plenty of work to be done on his place."

"Yeah," Myrtie agreed, sounding somewhat disappointed. "And married men just don't go to parties all that much. They just want to eat and raise corn."

Myrtie's observation was so sorrowful that Hannah smiled for the first time in hours.

"You have to raise corn to live, Myrtie. And believe me, there will come a time when you'll want a man whose interest is more in working to provide for his family, than partying to enjoy himself."

Hannah thought of Will and his quiet hardworking life with a pang.

Myrtie worked on Hannah's hair, fixing it higher up on her head than she usually wore it, and leaving it looser and fluffier, a curl slipping free in several places. It gave Hannah a more vulnerable look, which went along perfectly with how she was feeling. The dress looked beautiful on her, although it was the type of gown that she would never have chosen. Too delicate, she thought, for a woman like her. The contrast from her usual attire made her seem too attractive, she thought as she looked at herself in the mirror. She didn't want him to think that she was trying to impress him. Or perhaps it was really true what people always said, that all brides are beautiful. Even those who became brides by devious and underhanded means.

Henry Lee stood inside the new church. He had been alone with his thoughts for a quarter of an hour and he wasn't sure that it was for the best. Reverend Farnam was to meet him here and he would undoubtedly have a few things to say to his future son-in-law. Henry Lee dreaded the confrontation.

The church smelled of fresh wood and new paint and sawdust. He examined the finishing work that he had done, discovering several places he wanted to touch up, but it would have to wait for another day. He'd sent Dillary's youngest son over to his place to get his best suit. Now that he was dressed he couldn't just start sanding.

He was determined that the wedding look as ordinary as the scene this morning had not. He had thought it all through carefully, and had decided that the marriage wasn't such a bad idea after all. Henry Lee was a man who tried to deal with his troubles as they came along and not to get too involved in plans for the future. He thought it was a pretty good way for a moonshiner to be. He rose every day to take care of what needed to be done. He didn't spend his time worrying if next year's corn was doomed to fail, or whether the still would get struck by lightning, or the Federal marshalls would come looking for him, or if the current batch would scorch and he wouldn't have anything fit to sell.

Worrying about the future was a useless pursuit, as far as he was concerned, and with the carelessness of youth he had avoided doing it.

Yet when something couldn't be avoided, Henry Lee turned it into an advantage. It wasn't that difficult to see advantages in a marriage to Hannah Bunch. She was reputed to be level-headed—although this morning's behavior put that somewhat in question—and she was undisputedly a hard worker. There was plenty of work to be done around his place. He liked cleanliness and order, having someone else to take care of that would free him up to spend more time at his business.

There would also be the advantage of a regular partner to warm his bed. She wasn't really his type, but on a snowy winter evening, a man couldn't be too choosy.

The main advantage, as far as Henry Lee could see, would be to permanently align himself with the good people of Plainview Church. He enjoyed a reputation for honesty and fairness throughout the Twin Territories. That was saying a lot for someone in his line of work. Like many men who live on the wrong side of the law, the desire for recognition and respect was always unfulfilled. He lived on the fringe of this community, but with a decent woman at his side, a woman from their own ranks, he could be a part of it.

"Henry Lee," Reverend Farnam hailed him as he approached his future son-in-law. "I wanted to have a few words with you before the service."

The preacher waited a minute, drawing together his thoughts. Henry Lee was discomfited by the silence, and tried to start the discussion on an agreeable track. "It's looking real pretty, don't you think? I've seen a few small things that I want to redo, and then of course, it needs pews. I won't have much time to do them before winter, but by next year at this time, it'll be as nice as any church in the territory."

The preacher nodded in agreement, looking around proudly. Then he focused his attention on Henry Lee. "I didn't come here to talk about the church, Henry Lee. I came to talk about Hannah."

"Yes, sir." He was ready to be taken to task. His swollen lip was still visible, but he knew that a couple of punches wouldn't dispel the trouble between them.

The reverend seemed to be waiting for him to speak, but for once Henry Lee didn't know what to say. A full minute of silence was louder than any sound Henry Lee had ever heard.

"If it helps to know this," he said finally, "nothing passed between Miss Hannah and me last night or any other night for that matter."

The older man looked at him speculatively. He remembered the sight of the two of them curled up together on the floor of the wellhouse, Henry Lee's arm around his daughter's waist and his hand splayed open on her abdomen. Yet he had some inner sense that his daughter had not been changed, that there was still an innocence in her eyes. He looked at Henry Lee and realized that he was not lying. "I think I already knew that," he said.

"I want you to understand something about Hannah," he told Henry Lee. "When my first wife took sick, little Hannah was not much more than a girl. Without anyone so much as saying a 'would you please,' Hannah just took over the keeping of the house and the raising of the little ones. She scrubbed and cooked and taught the children their lessons, all the while that she was watching her mama die. I wasn't any help to her at all. I was just bowed down in my own grief, couldn't even see at the time what was going on. She took on burdens that would have crushed many women."

The reverend looked directly at Henry Lee, as if trying to underscore his point.

"My Hannah is a fine, strong woman that any man would be lucky to have for a wife. I hope that you know that."

His voice became lower and almost threatening. "I don't claim to understand what is between you two, and truth to tell, I guess most would say it's no longer my business, but I value my girls very highly and I never intend to give them up completely. If I ever see a bruise on her or hear that she or her children are going hungry, you'll be having a reckoning with me."

Henry Lee was stung by the words. He felt anger roll through him like a wave. Hadn't he already saved this stupid female from public embarrassment and her family from shame? How could the preacher think that he would mistreat her? But then, the preacher didn't really know what he had done for him and probably never would. The reverend still thought that Henry Lee had lured her outside to take advantage of her.

As quickly as the anger had come, it left him. Henry Lee almost smiled. Doing a favor for someone, and having them not know it, or be able to thank you, made it seem more right somehow, more selfless. It was a novel experience for the moonshiner.

"Don't worry, Reverend," Henry Lee said, "Hannah and I may have some problems, but I've never hit a woman in my life and I couldn't starve a polecat."

Henry Lee extended his hand to his future father-in-law and, after an instant of hesitation, the older man took it.

"Now the real problem, Preacher Farnam, is how are we going to get all those people who've come to see the most talked-about wedding of the year into this church?"

The two men laughed together.

Less than an hour later the church was filled to capacity. The families of the church builders had stayed for the ceremony. Curious folks from all over had come to see what was going on, and as it turned out it was good that there were no pews. With all the guests standing there was still little room for an aisle.

Henry Lee stood at the door, talking and greeting everyone and acting the role of cheerful bridegroom.

Reverend Farnam looked a bit more nervous. "I forgot about the ring, Henry Lee. Will you need to make one from a horseshoe nail?"

Henry Lee pulled his watch out of his pocket. Attached to the fob was a small gold band. "I have my mother's." But, even as he said it, he wasn't sure that he wanted to give it. He hardly knew this woman and certainly didn't want to trust her with his mother's ring. It was a tiny gold circle decorated with a garnet. It wasn't a wedding ring at all. It was given to his mother by her lover, Henry Lee's father. And it had been the only thing that she'd managed to keep away from her husband. Now her son was expected to hand it over to some stranger. But Hannah was to be his wife and it would look curious now, if he didn't give her the ring.

"Then I guess we're ready," Reverend Farnam said.

Myrtie was watching from the porch. When she saw the two men enter the church she squealed with excitement.

"They've gone inside, oh come on, Violet, let's hurry, I can't wait another minute!" Myrtie was dressed in her "Sunday Best" dress, a pale pink confection, and was carrying a little bouquet of flowers she had picked herself. It was her contribution to the wedding, bouquets for the bride and the bridesmaid just like in town weddings.

Hannah was numb. She had waited all afternoon to hear that she had been "left at the church" but for some reason he hadn't left. She was like a sleepwalker now as they led her up to the church. Her stepmother was giving instructions, but Hannah wasn't listening at all. She stared at the new building as if mesmerized. She couldn't seem to get her mind functioning.

She was really going to marry a man she barely knew and didn't like.

The walk up the rise to the little church, now the

color of ripe wheat from the unpainted pine boards, seemed to last forever, and at the same time everything seemed to be moving too fast for Hannah.

Myrtie made a last minute check of Hannah's gown, seeming totally wrapped up in her own chatter. Her excitement was in sharp contrast to Hannah's faraway expression.

"All right now, are we all ready?" Violet asked.

Hannah nodded. Violet hugged her and squeezed her hand as if to give her strength, then entered the church.

Myrtie and Hannah stood together outside. Myrtie hugged her too.

"Oh, Hannah, I am so happy for you," she said before she too went inside. "It's like all my dreams for you coming true."

For a moment, she was alone. Then the door opened and there stood Will Sample. "Miss Hannah, your father says you can come in now."

Hannah stood and stared at him. This was the man she had wanted, the one with whom she could make a life. But, truly, she didn't deserve him. She deserved the punishment of being married to Henry Lee Watson. He was a frivolous, trifling man and she in her own deceitful way was just as bad. This was something that she had brought upon herself and wishing it away would not make it so. She had made her bed and now she would have to lie in it. She cringed slightly at the literal truth.

She was her father's daughter and would just have to make the best of the situation she had created for herself. She would marry Henry Lee Watson.

"Thank you, Will, I'm coming right now."

He held the door for her as she entered the church.

She stopped immediately. Inside, there seemed to be a solid mass of people all straining to see her. She raised her chin and reminded herself that she was Miss Hannah Bunch and began to march forward.

Henry Lee was clearly startled at the sight of her. She was pretty today. It was funny that she had never tried to make more of her looks before. He might well have noticed her if she had always taken such care with her appearance. In fact he was betting that a lot of men in this room were wondering why they hadn't noticed her before.

He glanced quickly around the room and grinned at the surprise on many faces. He knew lots of folks were wondering what this marriage was all about. Well, let them think that he saw beauty in her before they did, it would make for a lot less speculation.

Hannah kept her eyes on the front of the church until they were drawn to Henry Lee. He was dressed up as fancy as a riverboat gambler. His handsome face was marred by a bruise or two, and there was a small cut beside his lower lip. Looking at his lips, Hannah realized that he was grinning. Grinning in church and during such a terrible twisting of the sanctity of marriage. She was a sinner, there was no doubt, but this man was just plain wicked. Well, she could certainly teach him a few things about living a clean life. Her punishment might well prove to be the salvation of this unworthy sinner.

When she came up beside him, he took her hand. He meant only to clasp it loosely, but he grasped it and was surprised to find it cold as death, unthinkingly he enfolded it into both of his.

Hannah wanted to pull her hand from the enveloping warmth of his, but had the good sense not to. Steeling herself, she looked up at her father.

Farnam Bunch kept the service brief, not in consideration of his daughter, but because the packed church had become unreasonably hot.

"Do you, Henry Lee Watson, take this woman, Hannah May Bunch, as your lawful wedded wife?"

Henry Lee spoke his "I do," with conviction. The girl had turned out not to be such a bad looker, and if she was as good a worker as well, he'd have a cook, and laundress, besides an extra hand, and a bed partner. It seemed not a bad trade. He smiled at Hannah. It was not going to be a bad trade at all.

Having and holding, for better or worse, in sickness and health, until death do part; Hannah accepted her fate with all the courage that she could muster.

When Reverend Farnam asked for the ring, Henry Lee brought it out of his pocket where he had safeguarded it, and turned to Hannah. Moving it to the third finger of Hannah's left hand he tried to put it on her. It moved past the first knuckle and stopped abruptly. Henry Lee's mother had been a tiny woman who apparently had much smaller hands than Hannah. He slipped it on to her smallest finger and offered a smile of apology. To Hannah it was a symbol. They were mismatched, a marriage that didn't fit.

But when he spoke the words, "With this ring I thee wed," it didn't matter whether it was meant to be or not, it was, and forever, no going back.

Henry Lee leaned down and planted his warm lips gently against hers and the deed was done.

By lit torches and the sounds of fiddle playing, the community of Plainview Church celebrated the wedding. Reverend Farnam didn't wholeheartedly approve of dancing so the folks mostly just listened and talked and swayed in place to the music. Henry Lee was wishing that someone would turn up with some corn liquor; however, he wasn't too hopeful. Preacher Farnam had preached far too many lengthy sermons on the evils of strong drink and no one wanted to be the cause of another one.

The cake Violet and Myrtie had baked was three layers high and light as a feather. Hannah was obliged to cut it and feed the first piece to Henry Lee. She seemed so nervous that Henry Lee didn't try to joke with her and took his bite of cake without incident. By now the bawdy humor of the men was growing worse. Fortunately for Hannah, most of what they said she didn't understand. That was what was intended. The joking was not meant to upset the bride, but to disconcert the bridegroom.

Finally, after what seemed to Hannah to be an endless party people began to make ready to leave, but remained as if waiting for the final act. Reverend Farnam had the good sense to prompt Henry Lee, who seemed content to just talk and laugh with the men all night.

"Henry Lee, you'd best tell your wife to go on up for the night," the preacher told him. Henry Lee knew that he was right. These folks were tired, but were waiting to see the couple to bed before they left.

Henry Lee moved through the crowd laughing and fending off jokes as he went. He spotted Hannah in a group of women apparently all talking to Hannah. Hannah was saying nothing and looking like she was not sure what was happening. The women abruptly quieted as he walked up.

"Evening, ladies. It sure was a lovely wedding, wasn't it?" The women quickly agreed, but before they could get started explaining what they liked about it, he continued. "Miss Hannah, I mean Mrs. Watson, has had a very busy day and I suspect it's time she retired."

The women all giggled meaningfully and Henry Lee noticed Hannah turned a bit pale. Just what he would have expected from her type. Suddenly, her attention was drawn to something behind him. Before he had time to turn around he was grabbed from behind.

"Shivaree!" he heard someone cry out and then he saw Clarence Hopkins's laughing face just before the blindfold came down over his eyes.

Hannah had no time to react. When she realized what was happening someone had already grabbed her. She had heard stories about shivarees. Brides being tied to logs and sent afloat down the river. Grooms being smeared with honey and left in the hills for bears to find. Terrible deeds done in the name of a wedding custom to force the bridegroom to earn the right to his bride.

"Papa, Papa, help me," Hannah screamed. "Stop this," she told them struggling and kicking. She landed a good blow on the shin of one of her captors. He cried out and the other men laughed heartily.

"You got yourself a fighter here, Watson," a man said, "I wonder who'll pin who in tonight's wrestling match."

Laughter and jests continued as they forced Hannah into a wheelbarrow.

"All right, Henry Lee," a voice said, "we're letting

you off easy. You ride your new bride three times around
the church and back down to the house and we'll let you
take her in."

Shouts of laughter and agreement were heard as
Henry Lee protested. "I can't see a blame thing, I couldn't
even find the church!"

"Your bride's eyes are wide open, she'll tell you
which way to go."

"Yeah," another man added, "that's what you have
to learn, to be a married man. Let your wife tell you what
to do."

Henry Lee even laughed at that. Grasping the han-
dles of the wheelbarrow and raising it up he asked, "You
ready, Hannah?"

"This is ridiculous!" she said. "Let me out of here at
once!"

"Seems the bride is in a hurry to go to bed," a voice
called out. Hannah felt her face flame with embarrassment.

"Hannah, just tell me which way to go. They are not
going to be talked out of this."

Hannah resigned herself to being pushed around in
the awful wheelbarrow and began to direct Henry Lee
around the church. Unfortunately, from inside the wheelbarrow it was impossible to see the ruts in the yard and
twice he spilled her out. The men quickly grabbed her
and put her back into the barrow with jokes about the
bridegroom's clumsiness and the inability of women to
give directions.

Finally they made it back to the porch of the house
with much shouting and celebration. Henry Lee tore off
his blindfold and before Hannah could climb out of the
wheelbarrow he reached into his pocket and pulled out a
handful of coins that he scattered behind him then
pushed the wheelbarrow, with Hannah in it, onto the
porch, through the front door, and into her bedroom. He
slammed the door behind him and dumped Hannah on
the floor, wedging the barrow into the door frame so that
the door couldn't be opened. Then racing across the room
to the window, he quickly slammed the shutters closed

and secured the wooden bar to hold them. Almost immediately, the sounds of banging pans and shouting jests
commenced both at the door and the window.

Hannah, still sitting on the floor, put her hands on
her ears.

"Hopkins! You're no friend of mine!" Henry Lee
shouted through the door. This statement was met by
hoots of laughter. "Now get away from our door, you've
had your fun."

"Don't mind us, Henry Lee," Hopkins called back.
"Go on about your business, the racket is meant to keep
us all from hearing the bedsprings rattle!"

Henry Lee shot a look at Hannah, her eyes widened
in shock and her face blazed crimson. She averted her
eyes from Henry Lee and helped herself off the floor.

"Just ignore them," Henry Lee told her. "It's late and
everybody is tired. They'll stop in a little bit."

"I can't imagine why my father didn't put a stop to
this," Hannah said angrily.

"Because you are not his responsibility anymore,
you're mine."

Hannah looked at him, startled at the truth of that
statement. He was right. She was his wife now, for better
or worse, and her father no longer had any say over her.
It was a frightening thought. She hardly knew this man,
and suddenly he had complete control over her. Wasn't
she just planning yesterday to take control of her own
life?

Hannah turned away from him, but found that there
wasn't really any place much to turn. The small bedroom
that she shared with Myrtie seemed dwarfed by the huge
man now occupying it. The tight space and the closed
window served to make the room uncomfortably warm.
Hannah wanted to take off the beautiful silk dress that
now felt more like a sticky blanket.

She glanced up at Henry Lee, who leaned indolently
against the wall. The sounds had died down and now
they were singing "Oh Promise Me." Hannah was surprised at the blending of female voices with the male. She
wished that they would all just go home. At least with

the women with them, they were not likely to do any more nasty tricks.

"It's so hot," Hannah said, hoping that Henry Lee would take the hint.

"Yes, ma'am, it surely is," he answered, wondering if talk of the weather was typical of wedding night conversation. He wanted to take off his coat, but he was afraid it would frighten her. He certainly didn't want her screaming with people just outside the window. He decided that the best thing to do would be to try to relax her with a little conversation. He'd always been told that he had the gift of gab and could talk pretty near any woman right off her feet. But for some reason, he couldn't think of one light, amusing story to entertain a nervous bride.

"At my place we have a big red oak that shades the house, it helps to keep the heat off the house. And makes it a bit more tolerable in the summertime."

"Yes, well," Hannah murmured, "it's too bad we don't have some of that shade here." She looked around as if trying to find her courage in the walls or the furniture. "Do you think you could leave now?"

"What?"

"Do you think you could leave now? I know they are still singing, but perhaps they wouldn't bother you if you left," Hannah said.

Henry Lee's expression was condescending. "Where exactly am I supposed to go, ma'am?"

"Why, I don't know," Hannah answered uncertainly, "but surely you can find some place to spend some time so that I might have some privacy."

Henry Lee roused himself from the wall and running a hand impatiently through his hair he came over and sat down on the bed. Unconsciously Hannah moved away from him. He rubbed his temples as if to soothe a pain.

"I can't go anywhere tonight, I have to spend the night with you. It's expected. You do understand that married people sleep together?"

"Well, of course I understand that." Hannah's face flamed red. Did this man think that she was totally ignorant? "Could you just go somewhere for a while, this dress is so hot, I've just got to take it off."

"I can turn my back."

"No, I'll have to have help, my mother or my sister."

"Hannah, I can't leave and your mother or sister can't come in, that's why they are singing out there, this is our wedding night." Henry Lee cursed silently. How had he become stuck with such a naive girl? "We aren't supposed to have any privacy, this is how married people get to know each other."

Hannah, who prided herself on her usual maturity and bravery, found herself feeling very young and afraid.

"Couldn't we start getting to know each other tomorrow?"

Her request sounded like a plea. Henry Lee, looking around at the closeness of the room, could not help but commiserate with her. It was an impossible arrangement. Half the territory was standing just outside their window, and they just total strangers. Nothing good could ever come of such a wedding night.

"Turn around, I'll unbutton you."

"You can't!"

"Of course I can. Turn around or you'll have to wear this dress all night." Shaking his head in exasperation, he added, "You were wearing less out by the wellhouse this morning."

Blushing at the truth, Hannah bravely offered her back to him and Henry Lee, still sitting on the bed, pulled Hannah between his spread thighs facing her away from him and commenced undoing the buttons on the wedding dress. Hannah cringed at the close contact. She could smell the clean male scent of him and his big hands gently touching the silk of the dress. It gave her a curious light-headed sensation. It must be even hotter in this room than she thought.

"This thing sure has a lot of buttons," he said.

"Fifty-two," Hannah answered. "One for each week that my parents were engaged."

"That's a pretty long engagement."

"Long engagements allow people to really get to

know each other and to make sure that they can make the other person happy," Hannah unthinkingly repeated the position that she frequently had explained to Myrtie.

"You like long engagements?" he asked teasing her.

"I wouldn't have known. Ours wasn't even fifty-two hours!"

"But ours was a . . ." Hannah's voice trailed off.

"A what?" he asked, completely stopping his progress with the buttons and concentrating on what she was about to say. He wanted to know, what she had thought she was doing forcing him to marry her.

Hannah wanted to say that theirs was a mistake, but she knew that she couldn't say that. She didn't really know this man, and she wasn't sure what his reaction would be. Suppose he got violent?

"It was," she answered lamely, "an unusual engagement."

Henry Lee gave a kind of half laugh, half shrug and resumed his work on the buttons. "Yes, I guess you could say that. Unusual. A very good word for it."

His progress on the buttons had reached almost to her waist. The lower his fingers moved, the more uncomfortable and exposed she felt. Henry Lee was concentrating on the buttons, trying not to think how long it had been since he'd undone a woman's dress.

When he got past the waist he could see the laces on her corset and ties for her underskirt. His mind conjured up the image of firm young flesh underneath these layers and his body responded accordingly. He squirmed slightly adjusting his posture to accommodate the change in his anatomy. His thigh, now resting comfortably against Hannah's hip, had a disquieting effect on Hannah.

Hannah's mother had only briefly talked to her about the duties of the wedding night, and that had been years ago. Being a farm girl, she had a fairly basic idea about what was involved in mating. She had witnessed the birth of many animals and she had even gone along to help when Greta Snyder's last baby was born, although she was sent to the kitchen just before the miraculous event occurred. However, she had never chanced to witness the mating of any animals in the wild, and because Reverend Farnam believed that the propagation of God's creatures was not a fit sight for his innocent young daughters, her father had never allowed either of his daughters around the stock during breeding.

Hannah's main source of information on sexuality was Bessie Turnball. Although Bessie was more Myrtie's contemporary than she was Hannah's, she seemed to know a great deal about the subject of men and women and never hesitated to explain it to whoever would listen.

To Hannah, the whole thing sounded a bit untidy, embarrassing at best, but she was sure that she could survive. What she was not too sure of, however, was what these flustery, warm feelings were all about. She wanted to move away from him at the same time she felt the need to ease up more closely.

Henry Lee undid the last button and gently pushed her away.

"You'd best change into your night clothes and get into bed," he told her. "We'll have a very busy day tomorrow."

She looked at him with anxious confusion. Fortunately Henry Lee was sensitive enough that she needn't express her hesitation.

"Don't fret now, Miss Hannah, I'll turn my back." Which he proceeded to do, staring at the door, his hands jammed into his trouser pockets. Hannah was held frozen in place for a moment and then with incredible haste, but almost total silence, she went to the hook in the far corner that held her nightgown. She changed her clothes without taking her eyes off Henry Lee for one moment. She tried to be very quiet, thinking that not drawing attention to herself somehow made her safer. As if he were a wild animal that might not know that she was there if she didn't disturb the leaves or grass.

Even as quiet as she was, Henry Lee was very aware of what was happening behind his back and was busy trying to drown out the telling silence with his own silent admonitions. She was a virgin, and not a ripe one, but rather an overripe spinster who undoubtedly was horri-

fied at the idea of sex. And even if she weren't so terri-
fied, she did, after all, seek this marriage in a very
desperate manner. She was so anxious he would surely
hurt her, and he certainly didn't want her screaming or
crying with her parents and most of the community right
outside the door.

No, he told himself, he would wait a few days until
they got a little more used to each other and he would
start out slowly, a few kisses tomorrow, some serious
hugging the day after until she was more used to him. If
there was one thing he had learned about women it was
that patience has its rewards. Tonight he would be
patient.

Hannah, dressed in her flour-sack cotton nightdress,
stood uncertainly beside the bed. She couldn't decide
what her next move should be. If she just stood there, he
would turn around and see her, but if she were to hide
herself in the bed, it would seem as if she were anxious
to couple with him. Finally she gave up the effort of making a decision, and turned the problem over to Henry
Lee.

"Should I get in bed now?"

"Yes, go ahead," Henry Lee answered as he waited
for the sounds of her movement into the bed. After he
was sure she had settled herself, he turned without looking at her and lowered the wick in the lamp, and then
blew it out completely. Normally, on these hot summer
nights, he slept naked, but he wasn't ready to do that
with Miss Hannah. He stripped down to his small clothes
and decided it was enough.

He carefully moved over to the bed and eased himself
in beside her. Even without touching her he could sense
how stiff and frightened she was. He congratulated himself on his superior judgment and control in not breaking
her tonight in her parents' home. He made himself as
comfortable as possible and waited for sleep.

Hannah lay tense and wary. She wasn't sure what
was to happen next. She remembered overhearing Nettie
Haskell saying once that the carnal needs of men were

disgusting, but that a Christian woman had to tolerate them so that her man would not be tempted into sin.

Hannah felt that she would gladly allow Henry Lee to be tempted into sin, if he would just not do anything disgusting to her. It felt so strange to have him beside her in the bed. She had shared this bed with Myrtie, and for years it had always seemed a reasonable size. Now with Henry Lee lying in it, it seemed miniscule. It was hard to imagine how a man could be so broad and so long. Even though she knew herself to be a robust, country girl, he made her feel small and vulnerable. She was still fearfully waiting for something to happen when she fell asleep.

The sun was well up when Henry Lee drowsily awakened, realizing that a warm female body lay in his arms. Actions born of memory and instinct led him to pull the woman more closely to his body. Her hair brushed his face and the warm clean smell drew his lips to her neck and collar. He felt her breasts against his chest, so soft, but with hard points, and it encouraged him to run his hand along the length of her back. She was smooth and soft and warm. His hand found her firm buttocks and he could not suppress his need to press her against his erection. It felt so good that he gave a small moan of pleasure as he continued to move himself against her.

Hannah awakened to a strange sensation of heat rushing through her body. She felt the hand that caressed her behind and felt the hardness of him pushing up against her. It answered a need inside her and instinctively she pressed back. Her heart seemed to have dropped to that warm place between her legs and it was pulsing and throbbing as if she had just run half a mile. She opened her legs instinctively to bring relief and he pressed against her so strongly it caused her to gasp. The sound brought her fully awake and Hannah suddenly realized where she was, and what she was doing.

It was her sharp intake of breath that brought Henry Lee back into reality. Reality being a new wife who was not ready for him and a stiff member that was ready for anything. He released the pressure on her backside, but moved his hand only as far away as her hip. It felt too good to let her go completely.

"Good morning," he whispered, his voice gravelly from sleep. "Remember me? I'm your new husband."

Hannah gazed into his languid blue eyes, as his handsome face softened and smiled at her lazily. The enticing fire still sparked through her veins as she felt the firm, possessive hand on her hip. His long brown arms were corded with muscle, but held her with the strength of tenderness. Marriage to Henry Lee Watson abruptly, seemed not such a punishment, more a prize.

FOUR

Henry Lee was securing the harness on his team on the first day of his married life, feeling almost light-headed. He was encouraged by Hannah's behavior this morning. Maybe she wasn't as starchy as he'd thought. She was obviously quite taken with him, enough to risk her reputation, and that always made a woman more malleable. And it certainly wouldn't hurt his business, either. Becoming a member of Preacher Farnam's family could be a real boon.

With these pleasant thoughts, Henry Lee joked easily with the last of the campers heading out and laughed off the most raucous jokes about his wedding night. He seemed, to himself and to all those who spoke to him that morning, a man content with his life.

Henry Lee ate his breakfast with enthusiasm, complimenting Mrs. Bunch until he had her giggling. When Violet assured him that Hannah could make biscuits just as light, he gave his new bride a warm smile and an agreeable nod.

Hannah was also strangely cheerful and content. It was apparently true that things always seem better in the morning. Yesterday, the idea of marrying Henry Lee Watson had seemed the height of idiocy, but today it seemed no more strange than marrying Will Sample. After all, she could be a good wife and helpmate to either man. Making a quick perusal of her new husband through lowered lashes, she also admitted that, if the truth were told,

55

Henry Lee Watson was a good deal more handsome than Will Sample.

Yesterday that handsomeness had seemed almost threatening. But today she was no longer afraid. Certainly, he was a man who was going to need a good deal of churching and would have to be schooled in good manners, but with the confidence of the new day, Hannah felt up to the challenge.

After breakfast, Myrtie volunteered to help Hannah sort her things and finish packing up.

"Anxious to have the room all to yourself?" Hannah asked her curiously as they walked to the room.

Myrtie giggled nervously. "I'll really miss you a lot, Hannah, but I'm so excited for you."

Myrtie gave her sister a quick hug, dropping the sheet and towels that she had clutched.

"Now look what I've done!" she exclaimed in exasperation, dropping to her knees. "Violet wanted you to have this extra bedding and towels." She lifted an armful, shaking it clean as she deposited it in Hannah's outstretched hands, then rose to her feet with her own bundle clutched firmly.

As the two began folding Hannah's clothes into her trunk, they giggled like young girls. Now that they were starting separate lives, the differences between them seemed to have disappeared.

Flushed and giggling, Myrtie looked slyly at her sister. "You've got to tell me what it was like," she said, gesturing dramatically as she threw herself across the bed like a fainting heroine, scattering linen in her wake. "I want to know every romantic detail!"

Hannah shook her head comically at her sister's antics, but couldn't conceal her involuntary blush. "Myrtie, you know it's none of your business."

"Of course, it's my business!" she insisted indignantly. "I'm your baby sister and you've always been willing to give me the benefit of your knowledge."

Hannah scooped a pillowcase from underneath Myrtie's shoulder and folded it, thinking of all the things she had shared with her sister. She'd taught her to read, and quilt, and turn the seams on a dress, but, being her sister and not her mother, there were some facts in life for which she had not been able to offer instruction. Now she wasn't able to look Myrtie in the eye. "I don't really have that much to tell you yet, Myrtie. At least not much that I think you'd want to hear." It was the closest Hannah could come to admitting that her husband had not elected to assert his rights on their wedding night. Unfortunately, Myrtie took it all wrong.

"Oh, no!" she wailed miserably. "Was it awful then? Did he hurt you?" She clenched her fists in anger and looked mad enough to spit. "I don't care how cute he is, if he was mean to you, Hannah, I'm going to hate him!"

Hannah waved away her sister's anger, sorry that she'd got Myrtie on the wrong track. "No, no, he didn't hurt me." She thought about the tender caresses of the morning and found herself blushing. "He was very kind actually, but you'll just have to wait until your own wedding night for the details."

Myrtie rolled to her side, propping herself on her elbow with a look of disgust. "I just can't believe you're not going to tell me," she complained. "You've always said that these things were natural and that our bodies were nothing to be ashamed of, now finally you've done it yourself, and you get as closemouthed as all the other married women!"

Hannah smiled at Myrtie. She hated disappointing her, and having her sister's undivided attention was something that happened less and less as she got older. Hannah just wished that she had more information to share.

"Okay, I'll tell you this much," she said leaning down beside her sister and whispering conspiratorially. "He was very gentle and it wasn't unpleasant at all and it made me feel all kind of fluttery inside."

Hannah congratulated herself on not exactly lying. She had accurately described what she had felt in Henry Lee's arms this morning, and she had given her sister enough information to stir her imagination, but not anything that was totally untrue.

"Oh Hannah, I just can't believe that you are really married. Just think, by next spring you could be coming to church with a pretty little cotton-head baby of your very own."

Hannah smiled prettily, surprised at her own delight at such a prospect, but quickly corrected her sister.

"A baby of Henry Lee's would have coal black hair," she said, picturing in her mind the child she would give him. "I'd tie that gorgeous hair all up in pink ribbons and she'd be the prettiest baby the territory had ever seen."

"What if it's a boy?" Myrtie asked laughing.

"Well." Hannah flopped down next to her sister on the bed, allowing her imagination full sway. "Maybe not pink ribbons, but he would still be the prettiest baby in the territory."

"You'd want him to look like his papa then?" Myrtie teased. "Henry Lee is so good-looking! All the girls think so. And you always acting like you never noticed."

Hannah smiled with a bit of pride, pleased at the thought of finding herself the envy of young girls.

Her voice was stern, but teasing, threatening mayhem. "You just tell your friends to keep their eyes off my husband!"

The two sisters collapsed together on the bed, laughing and hugging.

Henry Lee heard their merriment as he came through the house. He'd parked the wagon at the front door and he wanted to load up Hannah's trunk. Truth to tell, he was ready to get out of here. Nearly everyone had stopped by the wagon to wish him and Hannah the best, and to let them know that the community had forgiven them for, as one farmer put it, plowing the corn before the fence was in. He didn't wish to discuss it any further with anyone. He and Hannah would make a good life together, and the sooner the gossip about them stopped altogether, the easier it would be to make that life.

He was just about to knock on the door when he heard the sweet music of female laughter. One voice high and tinkly, the other low and throaty, like a burgundy wine. Somehow he knew that laugh belonged to Hannah.

It spoke to him in a way that sent strange hot sparks through his veins, warming him inside as well as out. As he tried to reason out the peculiar feeling, he just caught the words in Myrtie's voice.

"Oh Hannah, I'm so happy at how well everything has turned out for you. I can hardly wait until you have that baby. You'll be such a wonderful mother, and I'll be the best aunt you ever saw."

"Now Myrtie, don't you be talking about that where anybody can hear you. We've had enough scandal involved in this marriage already. I don't want anybody talking any more about me if I can help it." Hannah laughed thinking what someone might think to hear a woman talking about having a baby the morning after her wedding.

"Oh Hannah, you know I won't tell a soul, I swear it!" Myrtie giggled tauntingly. "My sister, Hannah, a mother at last, I can hardly believe it."

Henry Lee stood stock-still, frozen in place. All color drained from his face and a hollow pit seemed to have opened inside him. He turned abruptly and returned to the wagon. Somebody spoke to him, but he ignored them. He could barely hear for the roaring rage inside his head.

It all made sense now, perfect sense. She needed a husband and he was simply the one best able to fill the bill. His reputation had done him in. No one would doubt that the genteel Miss Hannah had been seduced by the Whiskey Man.

And he had believed her. He thought her sweet and innocent and foolishly smitten by him. He remembered last night, how she had pretended to be so frightened and he had wanted to spare her. He had wanted to spare her, and she had been rolling in the hay with God-knows-who for no telling how long! He slammed a hay hook into the back of the wagon in anger. The movement startled the horse and he had to hurry to the front to quiet the young gelding.

He stood beside the animal, crooning softly, trying to calm himself as he calmed the horse. She had made a fool of him. She and her lover were probably laughing at him right now. He had thought he was doing her a favor, what a joke. It was a joke all right and it had been played on him. At least the rest of the community didn't know what a fool she had made of him. At least they didn't know it *yet*.

He wondered why her lover hadn't married her himself. Maybe he was already married, or maybe she'd had so many men that she didn't know who the father was. No, he ruled that out. Had she been round-heeled, he surely would have heard of it. Things like that couldn't be kept secret. But an affair with a married man could be. Obviously it had been.

Henry Lee stroked the soft nose of the horse and worried about what he should do next. He'd given her the benefit of the doubt when they'd been caught at the wellhouse. He didn't feel obliged to accommodate her anymore.

How in the world did she think she would get away with this? Did she intend to pretend innocence in his bed and then claim the baby had arrived early? He heard of women trying to play those types of tricks, but he never thought that it would really work. In his heart, a man would know the truth, or his suspicions would drive him crazy.

Henry Lee was tempted to just hop in the wagon and ride off into the sunset forever. He felt like such a dolt, falling right into her devious little scheme.

He knew he wasn't the first man to have been tricked into claiming another man's son, but he sure as hell was not going to let her think that her evil little plan had worked. She was his wife now, and she would learn to rue the day she tried to make a fool out of Henry Lee Watson.

By the time Hannah and Myrtie had everything gathered up, she was very excited. She was going to have her own home, her own husband. It was like a dream come true. She had discovered a new closeness with her sister, and a kinship with her stepmother, and other women of the community. She was a married lady. At last, all the rights and privileges of that blissful state had been visited on Hannah.

Talking with Violet as they sorted linens and packed baskets of fruits and vegetables, the conversation drifted to the concerns of governing a household.

"Now I doubt that Henry Lee has much of a garden," her stepmother told her. "You best start right away getting whatever you can out of the ground, it's really too late to plant much but maybe squash and turnips."

"Do you think he'll have much put up already?" Hannah asked her.

"I doubt it. I suspect that bachelors don't even know how to put things up. Making his place into a home should keep you busy for a while."

Hannah was suddenly very anxious to do just that. She knew she was an excellent housekeeper. She would make such a wonderful home for Henry Lee, he would never regret having to marry her.

Her father carried out her things to the wagon as quickly as Hannah, her stepmother, and sister could get them ready. She kept waiting for Henry Lee to come back inside the house, but for some reason, he continued to tarry by the wagon.

Finally when everything had been taken out and loaded up, Hannah said her good-byes and went out to join her new husband.

He was standing by the wagon, leaning against it and staring out at the distance. As she watched, his gaze turned to her. She smiled broadly at him, but he only continued to stare, his face completely expressionless. This abrupt change in his attitude disconcerted Hannah. However, since her family was beside her, all expecting hugs and kisses and saying good-bye and wishing her luck, she had no choice but to act as if everything were fine and that her future was secured.

Tying on her sunbonnet, Hannah stepped down from the porch, and with only a slight glance back, she went to join him.

Henry Lee helped Hannah into the wagon seat and

pulled himself up beside her. Thankfully, most of the
other folks had already gone, he thought. It was difficult
enough being in front of her parents, who surely didn't
know what she'd done to him. He didn't know if he
would have been able to tolerate a crowd where, possibly,
the father of Hannah's baby stood by watching their progress and laughing at Henry Lee.

Her smile when she had come out of the house had
made him flash hot then cold. He still remembered the
pleasure of this morning, but the betrayal was more vivid
and infinitely more important. He decided it was best not
to look at her at all. He released the brake on the wagon
and with a curt wave to her parents, snapped the reins,
urging the horse out into the lane and headed east toward
his own place.

The warm summer breeze felt cool against his angry
cheeks as Henry Lee kept his eyes unfalteringly on the
head of the horse and the line of harness running toward
the wagon. After a quick glance at her husband's dark
visage, Hannah concentrated on the beautiful morning
and the countryside. Unlike Henry Lee, Hannah had only
good feelings for the day. Even his less than enthusiastic
reception when she came out of the house did not upset
her greatly.

She assumed that he had been thinking about the
trick she had played on him. He would probably want
her to explain herself. She wasn't sure yet what she was
going to say, but she had confidence now that, as his
wife, and the future mother of his children, he would be
able to forgive her.

The day was hot, but the nice breeze blowing in from
the south made it all seem bearable. The activity of the
bees in the clover made a lazy sound that, for all their
activity, was strangely relaxing. The sky was an unusual
shade of steel blue, so different from the sky she remembered from her childhood in Kansas. She'd come to think
of it as Oklahoma Blue, always accented with wispy feath-
ers of clouds hung way high, as if to remind you continu-
ally that the weather was changeable.

"It's a beautiful day, don't you think?" she asked,

deciding that a good marriage would need to start with amiable conversation.

"Hot."

"But the breeze is nice."

"Yeah."

"Think we'll get some rain pretty soon for the crops?"

"Maybe."

Hannah was surprised at Henry Lee's reticence. He'd always appeared to be a man quite willing to talk, but this morning he didn't seem to have much to say. If he was angry, she wished that he would just say so. It was best to just tear into a sore spot and wrestle it through. She didn't believe in letting bad feelings fester.

The countryside was mostly still in prairie grass, although here and there she could see the beginnings of farming. The land here was hilly, but free of rocks and trees. What trees there were grew concentrated on the banks of creeks and ponds. Since Hannah had never been to Henry Lee's place before, she was curious about her new home. She knew it was located in the Indian Territory, an area much older and more settled than the new Oklahoma Territory just beside it. But up till now she had never had any cause to venture that far.

"You live on this side of Pearson's Creek, or do we have to cross?" she asked, trying to draw out her new husband.

"Cross."

"Does it look like this?"

"Like what?"

"Like this. Like you can see for miles, just grass and sky."

"Woods."

"What?"

"It's woods, it's in the hills, it's not like this." His voice was impatient and there was an undertone of unmistakable anger.

"Oh." Hannah was rebuffed. Obviously Henry Lee considered her attempt at conversation feeble. Well, she supposed that discussing the lay of the land was somewhat like discussing the weather.

"What about the house?"

"What about it?"

"Is it big or little, white or clapboard, tell me about it."

"It's a poled cabin."

"A poled cabin?"

"Straight logs, no split rails."

"It's a log cabin?" she asked excitedly. "I've never even seen a log cabin!"

"There's more timber around the creek and up on the hills."

"Oh, how romantic! Just like the real pioneers. I wonder if it looks like Abe Lincoln's did."

He turned finally to look at her, his face like a thundercloud. "Abe Lincoln was a Republican!" he said sharply.

"Well, yes, I suppose he was," Hannah replied lamely. Politics was obviously another poor choice of subject. She had always been a Jayhawker Republican, because her father was. She wondered if now being married to Henry Lee automatically made her a southern Democrat. She decided that it was best to stick to subjects more suited to a wife.

"I'm sure that I will love the house."

"It's plenty good enough for the likes of you!"

Hannah was taken aback by his rudeness. It was as if he had slapped her. She guessed it was time to try to explain what had happened in the wellhouse. *How would she explain it?* she wondered. Well, she wasn't going to lie anymore. She would tell him as little as possible, but it would be the absolute truth.

She took a deep breath and said a silent prayer for help from heaven.

"I know I owe you an explanation of what I was doing in the wellhouse," she started, staring straight ahead, not able to meet his eyes. "I realize how angry you are, so it seems to me that we ought to go ahead and discuss it, get it out of the way."

"I never get angry!" Henry Lee barked at her, realizing that he had been furious for the last two hours!

He was looking straight ahead again and clenching his jaw. He wondered if she had managed to think up some plausible lie to try to get him to swallow. Somehow he was sure that she had, and that when she told it, things would be worse than they already were. It was time that he took the situation in hand. She was no longer deciding how the game was to be played. Henry Lee Watson was the man she would answer to now!

"I already figured out about what you were doing in that wellhouse."

Hannah looked at him, startled. What could he possibly know?

"Do you think I'm a complete fool? Did you think that I wouldn't find out?"

Hannah was totally unprepared for this. She hadn't told a soul about her plan, how could he have guessed it? Had anyone else suspected?

"How did you find out?"

Henry Lee's look was rough and angry.

"I know, that's the important thing. So there is no need for you to continue to pretend that you have any feelings for me. I never could abide a liar."

Hannah was stung. She wished, unrealistically, that she could just jump off the wagon and walk back home, but she couldn't. She'd made this trouble for herself, and she knew she would have to accept the consequences it had generated.

"I planned to tell you eventually," she answered guiltily. "But I was hoping by then you'd be more used to me and that you wouldn't mind."

"You were hoping that I wouldn't mind!" He was snarling through clenched teeth. He took a deep breath to control his rising anger. "Maybe I'm not a churchgoer, Miss Hannah, and maybe my folks weren't the finest, but believe me, I mind! I mind just as much as any of those damn farmers."

"Well, of course I knew that you would mind," Hannah backtracked reasonably. "I know that you would not have intentionally chosen to marry me, but I was hoping that now that it is done, well, I . . . I think we could make a life together."

His angry silence seemed to last forever. Henry Lee could not make his thoughts coherent. He was a jumble of anger, and he deplored that emotion, considering it a weakness. He concentrated fruitlessly on the horse in front of him as he tried to corral his shaking fury. His stillness seemed to say to Hannah that he didn't want to make a life with her. She had no idea what to say to that. "I'm sorry," was her final choice.

"Yeah, well, I'm pretty goddamn sorry, too!" His voice was rough and his eyes were blazing.

Hannah was not shocked by his language, but the force of his disdain was frightening. For an instant she feared that he might strike her, but as she watched he seemed to gather his control.

Henry Lee was outraged. It added insult to injury for Hannah to think that he would be so glad to have a woman like her that he would quickly forget that she had been another man's first. It seemed to him the ultimate in conceit, that because she was a so-called decent woman, he should be glad to have her at any price.

She thought she was better than him because he wasn't the offspring of stalwart citizens like those in her daddy's church. He was Skut and Molly's brat and no matter what he tried to do with his life, no one ever let him forget that.

The man he called father, Skut Watson, had moved to Indian Territory after the Confederacy's defeat. Not that politics had meant anything to Skut. He was only thirteen and custom made for trouble when he'd joined up with the rebels. Burning, stealing, and killing became little more than recreation to the rough group he rode with, but it wasn't enough for him. Skut Watson had hoped to make some money out of the war.

He was one of those men who were always just a minute away from success. All his life he spent looking for the easy way, the fast way, the get-rich-quick scheme that never quite materialized. It had led him near and far after the war, searching for that big payoff. Finally it had led him to Fort Gibson on a snowy afternoon in February. The commander was in a mess of trouble. He was, unbeknownst to his faithful wife, keeping a half-breed Cherokee mistress. The pretty, light-skinned beauty was pregnant and demanding the commander marry her. She was threatening to make trouble and he needed to get rid of her in a hurry. The arrival of Skut Watson was timed perfectly; the commander paid real gold to have her taken away.

Skut had not intended to wed her, but when he found out that her half-breed status could get them a piece of land, he immediately tied the knot. Feeling safer once he'd taken her away from friends and family, he'd traded her allotment in the Cherokee hills for a useless piece of hilly, wooded ground in the Creek Nation. It was as far away as he could get from those things familiar to her.

The woman, Molly Fish, had not been particularly happy with her new marriage, but she was young and scared and pregnant and she really had no other choice. She knew that Skut had received gold and she wanted to stay around long enough to take it away from him.

First she needed someplace to winter and have her baby, so she stayed with Skut for a while. As it happened, she never left. She was sickly after Henry Lee's birth and kept waiting for her strength to return.

Lulled by the pleasure of watching her handsome son grow, the weeks stretched into years and she stayed with Skut. Their marriage could never have been called a happy one, but she had learned to just turn her thoughts inward when life around her became too hard. Seeking a quiet corner, the reality of her life faded away as pieces of tree branches came alive in her hands. Her talented fingers held the knife as she formed the small wooden creatures that pleased her bright, blue-eyed son as he played near her.

Over the years, Skut became involved in one get-rich scheme after another. He'd always managed to keep body and soul together, but he had never made the big success that he desired. His most successful venture had been whiskey.

Alcohol was in great demand among the Indians. Skut remembered stills back in his home in Tennessee, but he could never quite get his attempts at distillery to work. So instead, he carted in wagon load after wagon load of moonshine from the stills in the Ozarks and made a good living for several years.

Eventually, he took Henry Lee with him to help, and ultimately to do most of the work. Skut had developed a taste for liquor and felt it necessary to sample every shipment heavily.

Henry Lee, who was quick and sharp, learned faster than Watson. By observing and listening to the whiskey makers, Henry Lee soon understood the whiskey business in a way that his adopted father never had.

As Hannah and Henry Lee, on that first morning of their married life, rode silently down the road, Henry Lee ruminated on the irony that he had been claimed and raised by a man who was not his father, and now he was going to have to do the same for another man's child.

Henry Lee felt both glad that he had let her know that she wasn't fooling him, and angry at the situation and at her for choosing him as the scapegoat. He decided, philosophically, that since his mother was a whore, having a wife who was no better than she should be certainly made sense. At least, she could never throw up his background to him. The fancy preacher's daughter had proved to be no better than trash herself. It was hard to believe that Hannah Bunch was of such low morals, but she hadn't even tried to deny it.

Henry Lee despised himself for hanging onto his anger and purposely put it away. She was here; she was his wife and he needed to accept her duplicity. He had learned long ago that a man's blind rage only served to make him prone to mistakes and miserable in his mind. He'd schooled himself to vent his anger in quick little explosions and then get on with his life. Taking a deep, cleansing breath, he did just that.

His bride was a light skirt. She had been with another

man and carried his bastard. Those were facts, he would grow to accept them. The past was past, he would see that she never strayed again. The first one might not be his, but he'd be damn sure the rest would be. He wasn't the first man to make that vow, he knew. But he would keep it if he had to tie her to the kitchen door.

Hannah concentrated on watching the scenery and not making any moves that might catch Henry Lee's attention. Apparently Henry Lee knew that she had been out at the wellhouse to trap another man. She couldn't imagine how he'd discovered that, but she was glad that it was finally out in the open, and that the embarrassment of explanation was behind her. She wanted to stay out of his way until the anger cooled. She knew that she wouldn't get off scot-free, but she wouldn't volunteer for a dressing-down.

They passed a couple of miles in silence until they reached a place where a small trail wound away from the road and down to a creek bed. Henry Lee turned off and drove the wagon down the steep sides. The water was only about knee-high and the creek had a quiet peaceful feeling to it.

"Is this Pearson's Creek?" she asked him tentatively, her voice quiet with inquiry.

When he nodded, she could see that he was in control of his temper, and smiled animatedly. "I thought I recognized it. We held a baptism downstream last fall. It's so peaceful and serene; it's like I think the River Jordan must be."

"I don't know much about the River Jordan, but come spring, this little creek runs so fast, it's one quick way to die. You'll have to watch my pigs, make sure they stay clear of here during the rain."

"Is that what you do for a living? Raise pigs?"

Henry Lee turned abruptly to look at her. Was it possible that she really didn't know how he made his living? He always assumed that everyone in the community knew of his clandestine business interests, but he guessed that it was quite possible that the farmers would spare their womenfolk the horrifying experience of knowing they had a moonshiner living in their midst. He thought of how shocked and embarrassed she was going to be when she learned the truth, and it brought the first smile that Hannah had seen on his face since they started the trip.

"Yes, ma'am, I do indeed raise pigs," he told her. "Some of the most well fed duroc hogs in the territory live right on my premises."

Hannah was encouraged by his smile and decided that she had finally found a subject to discuss with him, his hog business. Not knowing much more about the creatures than how to feed them and make them into ham and sausage, she began eagerly questioning him on hog farming. Henry Lee seemed to find this very amusing and was delighted to fill her in on the secrets of swine husbandry.

As they came up on the other side of Pearson's Creek, the landscape made a clear change. The wide open prairie had given way to a rather loosely wooded area, and the trail headed generally upward.

When they reached the site of Henry Lee's home, Hannah looked about eagerly. It was a good-sized cabin looking to the west with a porch running the length of the front, facing the creek. On the north side was a well-kept cornfield, green and prosperous. To the south a huge red oak, at least four feet across at the base, sheltered the cabin, its outstretched branches enfolding the small house and yard like a canopy.

Henry Lee drove the wagon around back. From there Hannah could see the outbuildings. One was obviously a barn and another a pigsty. There was an outhouse, a workshed, chicken coop and a couple more whose purpose was not immediately discernible. The yard was well-kept and clean. An outdoor hearth, undoubtedly used for doing laundry, was in evidence and a cord clothesline ran along the back of the cabin, one end hooked to the henhouse and the other attached to a freestanding wooden crosspole.

A strange sort of snorty bark caught Hannah's attention and she turned to see a herd of pigs heading for the wagon. Probably a dozen or so rust-red swine of varying sizes rushed toward them in minor stampede.

"What's going on?" Hannah asked, gripping the side rail as the strange rumbling chorus drew closer.

"Don't worry, they're friendly little beasts," Henry Lee assured her. "Just looking for something to eat. They like acorns plenty fine, but after two days they're anxious for something a bit more filling."

He jumped down from the wagon, securing the horse to the hitching post. Then by yelling, stomping, and kicking, he discouraged the hungry pigs from invading the wagon area.

"Let me go slop them and get them back in the pen," he told Hannah, offering a congenial smile. "You can have a look at the cabin," he suggested as he headed toward the pigsty, the snorting hogs following him as if he were the pied piper.

Hannah helped herself down from the wagon. At the back of the cabin was a lean-to section, obviously built after the original structure, through which she made her entrance to her new home. The lean-to was a porch of sorts, a wash porch she would have thought, but there was no evidence of wash having ever been done there.

She walked into the main cabin through the back door. It was very neat and in good repair, although it looked like a good bit of dust was building up in the corners. The cook stove was practically brand new. As she admired it, she noticed that it was nicer than the one back home.

There were cabinets and counters built from local pine that shone with a glaze that seemed to add light to the room. The table and chairs were oak, strong and sturdy enough to last a hundred years, with a glaze that matched the cabinets. A huge gray stone fireplace dominated the room. In front of it sat a hand-hewn fruitwood rocker, beautifully carved and finished. Hannah remembered that her father had said that Henry Lee was an excellent cabinet maker. She knew now why he wanted Henry Lee to do the pews for the new church.

Off to the right of the main room were two doors.

Hannah opened the first one to find sawhorses, wood supplies, carpentry tools, and a lathe. She rightly decided that this must be Henry Lee's workshop and proceeded on to the next door.

The bedroom contained an extra-long four-poster bed with posts shaped like stalks of corn. Hannah had never seen such a thing in her life. The bed was at least four feet off the floor and a small step had been constructed on one side.

A matching table with the same unusual cornstalk design sported the water pitcher and basin. A wardrobe was built into the wall. It was made of a different type of wood, and was more crude in aspect. It obviously had already been in the room when the furniture was made.

Hannah slowly turned, looking about the room, reminding herself that she now lived here. She tried to imagine having her babies in the cornstalk bed, but just couldn't seem to see it. The intimacy of the bedroom disconcerted her.

Mentally shaking herself, she decided to stop daydreaming and get to work. There were all her things from the wagon to be brought into the house, and dinner was late already.

FIVE

When Henry Lee had finished feeding and penning the hogs, he headed down a well-worn trail toward the creek. Turning off the main track, he continued in a parallel direction on a path that was so well disguised only the very best trackers would have even noticed it. He automatically took the careful precautions necessary for traveling to the still, pondering the events of the last two days.

Seeking peace in those things familiar, he decided that today would be a good day for starting a new batch of corn liquor. He hadn't planned on doing this yet. He liked to time it so that the distilling took place during the waxing moon, which was a good ten days away. But with his temper so close to the edge and his confusion of feelings, he decided that making a good batch of corn liquor would be a good occupation.

The unexposed trail that he had been following abruptly ended at a sandstone bluff that rose high above Pearson's Creek. He moved along the side of it until he found the "bench," a small ledge about three feet across and a couple of feet deep. He hopped up on the bench, and finding small toeholds in the sandstone he continued upward. About ten feet higher was what appeared from the ground to be a small indentation in the rock. Actually the indentation was a well-disguised overhang that hid a cavern that went far enough back to be completely private. At that height the smoke from the fire could diffuse easily and was rarely seen or smelled. There was a spring at the very back of the cave that fed into Pearson's Creek. Having water up so high made the site perfect. When he'd first stumbled upon it, it had seemed too good to be true. But, after looking around and checking out the site from all angles, he decided that his luck had really made a turn for the better.

The two things most necessary for running a still were abundant water and ventilation of the smoke from the fire. Originally, Henry Lee had followed the advice of Ozark moonshiners, and for years had moved the still every two or three months. When he'd found this site the winter before last, however, it had just seemed foolish to move to some place less-suited.

He'd decided that practicing caution would make the still as safe as moving it around. He was not, after all, being pursued by revenuers. Revenuers, or tax men, were experts on discovering whiskey, but Federal taxes were not being collected on distilled spirits in the Indian Territory. His main concern was from his customers, many of whom would love to do a little private raid on his business, and from the federal marshalls, whose job it was to keep liquor out of the hands of the Indians.

Slipping into the overhang, Henry Lee had to stoop down through the entrance until the area was tall enough for him to stand. His new cookpot, which had come all the way from Kansas City, sat shiny and clean on the raised grate that he had constructed. He kept his equipment clean as a church. No one had taught him that, he'd decided on his own that clean whiskey just plain tasted better. He even boiled the copper coil, or worm as it was called, to make sure that nothing came out of it but moonshine.

Stacked on the far side of the overhang was at least a cord and a half of cut wood. Distilling took a hot and steady fire. A moonshiner couldn't just walk off and go foraging for timber, he had to have enough on hand to keep the fire going until the mash was cooked.

Opposite the woodpile was the area that passed as home during whiskey making. A cabinet with a few foodstuffs, a chair and table, a deck of cards and a bed were all that was necessary to live here for sometimes as long as three days. Near the front of the cave stood a couple of oak barrels. Both were empty now. Henry Lee knew that he'd have to get busy and make some corn grits this evening if he wanted to start making sweet mash in the barrel tomorrow. He was thinking about how hard it would be to get the corn grits done by tomorrow, when it suddenly occurred to him that he was no longer alone in this world. For better or worse he had a wife of his very own and tonight she could help him make whiskey.

Hannah had discovered that cooking as a married woman was proving to be a good deal different than it had been in her father's home. Her inspection of the pantry had yielded a surprising result. Rows and rows of store-bought tin cans full of vegetables and fruits crowded the shelves. The cans were expensive and highly prized, not for the food in them, which was considered poor quality at best, but for the tin. Once you cut the ends off the cans, the tin was flattened and used for roofing shingles. Hannah suspected there was enough right here in the pantry to finish a good-size shed.

She congratulated herself that she had already found one way she could show her worth to Henry Lee. From now on she'd put up her own fruits and vegetables and Henry Lee wouldn't have to pay a penny for them.

Hannah found a slab of bacon sitting in a salt tub and started frying it up. She also found a sack of greens that weren't too wilted and she put them on to cook, seasoning them with a bit of the salt pork and vinegar. Figuring that if she stirred up a batch of cornbread to cook on the top of the stove, that would serve as a meal. Not an auspicious beginning to her new life as wife and housekeeper, but it couldn't be helped.

She was beginning to wonder what had happened to Henry Lee, and how she would go about calling him for his evening meal, when he showed up at the back door carrying a washtub.

"Are you bringing in laundry?" she asked when she

saw what appeared to be wet towels on the top of the tub.

"No it's corn," he said shortly. "We need to dry it out. Go start a fire in the fireplace."

Hannah looked at him as if he were losing his mind. Wood was a precious commodity to her, being raised on the plains, and even though it seemed in abundance here on Henry Lee's place, she wouldn't dream of wasting it by starting a fire in the fireplace in the middle of summer. Hannah's first instinct was to question his judgment, but she thought the better of it. Keeping her opinion to herself, she found wood in the wood box and did as he asked.

She watched Henry Lee get out a contraption that looked very much like her mother's quilting frame. He set it up in the main room and stretched a bedsheet tightly across it. Digging soggy, sprouted corn kernels out of the washtub, he spread them along the sheet.

Hannah was so curious about what he was doing, that she kept looking back to see what was happening next. This did not help her attempts to start up a fire. He seemed so calm and determined, nothing like the rather ne'er-do-well farmer who was more interested in fun and games than in farming that she'd imagined. His face in profile revealed a stronger jaw than Hannah had previously noticed and his high cheekbones seemed to accentuate the straight, sparse brows above his eyes. With his sleeves rolled up to keep them out of the wet corn, his powerful brown arms and big hands were in sharp contrast to the whiteness of the bedsheet he was working with. Hannah remembered the strength of those arms as he had pulled her close that morning, and the remembrance of those hands moving slowly down her body, stroking and caressing, brought a flush to her cheeks and strange fluttering in her abdomen. Henry Lee finally looked up and caught her staring at him. She didn't have the fire going yet, so he thought to give her a hand.

"Here, you spread these out nice and even all along the sheet," he instructed, "and I'll get that fire started."

She leaned closer, watching him as she imitated his movements. "What is this for?"

"I'm drying them out so that I can make corn grits."

"My heavens," Hannah exclaimed. "What army are you planning to feed, there must be a bushel of corn here!"

"I feed it to the hogs," he told her, turning his face away from her so she didn't see his sly look. "They're low on feed, I need to get these dried and ground by tomorrow."

His look was a challenge. "I'm not sure that I can get it done by then, by myself. But then I remembered that I had you as my helpmate. Are you my helpmate, Miss Hannah?"

The look on his face, sort of teasing and flirty, was the same he had given her when she had brought him the water at the church. It had distinctly annoyed her at the time, now, strangely, it made her feel warm and friendly toward him.

Hannah vividly recalled the vows she had made yesterday evening. She was his wife and she wanted to show that even if he hadn't chosen her, she could still prove to be a bargain. Never in her life had she heard of pigs that had to have special food. Her father's pigs ate fodder and leftovers and whatever else they had put in front of them. But if, for some strange reason, Henry Lee's pigs ate corn grits, then she would help him make corn grits: bushels and bushels of corn grits.

"Of course, I'll help," she said enthusiastically.

Henry Lee smiled back at her, pleased with his own private joke: the preacher's daughter making corn liquor.

He seemed content with the supper put before him, even with Hannah trying to apologize for not cooking something up special. He considered himself a pretty fair cook and had always taken care of himself. But the greens were better than they ever tasted when he cooked them, and her cornbread was so smooth and slightly sweet that it was almost like cake instead of bread.

"It tastes fine," he told her. He was not yet willing to give more of a compliment than that.

"Well, of course, you didn't have anyone to cook for you, but now that I'm here, I can do for you."

"You just worry about getting that corn ground into grits tomorrow, that's what I really care about."

Hannah shook off his concern. "I'll have all that corn ground before noon tomorrow, don't give it another thought. You really are an unusual man, to care more about the food you feed your hogs than about the food you feed yourself."

Henry Lee choked slightly on a bite of Hannah's warm cornbread and swallowed his laughter. Could this ignorant female really believe that he would go to all this trouble to feed hogs? She was either crazy, or she thought that he was!

"Now, about the food for yourself," she began, talking to him as if she were an adult and he was a rather slow child. "It's a bit late in the year, but I thought I would try to start up a garden. We won't get too much from it this far into the summer, but everything we do will be just that much that you won't have to buy."

"Don't worry about it," he said, wondering how he would explain his trading without mentioning the whiskey, "there's no need for you to start up a garden."

"But I want to. It's part of my job to set your table."

He shook his head and waved off the idea. "Like you said, it's too late in the year. There's no need for you putting in all that work for what you'd get out of it. I don't even have any ground that's been turned, it would take a team and a prairie cutter just to dig you out a space."

"I should put up stores for the winter," she protested. "I'm your wife, it's just not fitting that you should have to get store-bought to provide for your table."

To Henry Lee it almost sounded as if she were jealous. He was a bit surprised at her anxiousness. Being a hard worker fit his former image of her as the preacher's spinster daughter. It didn't fit at all with what he knew now to be the truth about her.

She was right about a woman providing for the table

from her own garden as being more fitting, and if they only ate food that she'd put by, at least they'd be sure that it was plenty clean and good. He guessed that would be important to her, being in the family way.

Just reminding himself of that soured his disposition. His eyes automatically dropped to her stomach, the sight of which was hidden by the table. He wondered when she would be showing; hopefully, not until winter. People sort of lost track of time in the winter and maybe her early blossoming wouldn't start that much gossip. Though he hated the idea of being saddled with another man's child, he liked children well enough and he thought he could tolerate this one. He'd just have to think about it as an orphan.

"You're right about needing a garden and doing your own canning. I think that's a good idea, but it's too late for a garden this year. I'll trade with some of your farmer friends for fresh produce and you can do with it what you think best."

"Trade? What will you trade?"

"Pigs." That was the answer he gave and at her surprised expression he began carefully studying the food on his plate. He knew it made no sense to suggest that any local farmer would trade table crops for pigs. Everyone in the territory kept pigs. You could ship them out as a cash crop or take them into town and get something for them, but for the locals they were the main source of meat for territory cooking.

"Who around here would trade you for pigs?" she asked him.

"Pretty near anyone," he replied deciding that the bigger the lie the more likely it would be to be believed. "That's why I only feed my pigs corn grits, makes the best ham and sausage in these parts. Everybody wants one of my pigs, I'm surprised that you haven't heard of them before."

Hannah hadn't.

After the meal, Henry Lee went to work carefully stirring the corn on the quilting frame. It was very important that the kernels were completely dry or they would not grind properly. The fire going smartly in the fireplace now made the room about one hundred degrees. With sweat running down the side of his face, he wondered why he'd been so impatient, not allowing the corn to dry out in the sun for a couple of days. It was all the fault of that woman, he decided. She had the power to make him do things that he wouldn't normally do.

Thinking about her, his eyes were drawn to the sight of her standing at the sink washing dishes. From his perspective he could see only the back of her, the tall body flanked by unfemininely broad shoulders that served to emphasize the very feminine nipped-in waist. The contrast was accented by her apron strings that gently smoothed the outline of her rounded hips. Her behind was one of her best features, Henry Lee decided. He had always preferred tiny, petite women. They made him feel massive and strong, but he suddenly understood what the appeal was for women who were "big of breast and broad of thigh." To relax in the comfort of that big, lush body seemed a worthwhile goal. And that generous rump, it almost begged a man to run his hand across it. He remembered his sleepy, waking dream this morning, when he had done just that. And just the memory of it had him hard as a blackjack stump at Christmastime. How had he failed to notice that enticing backside before? And who was the man who had noticed it before he did?

He quickly rose and headed out through the back door, grabbing up a bucket. "Getting fresh water for morning," he said tersely.

"Could you get an extra bucket for me?" she asked him. He stopped to turn and look at her. She seemed more her usual self if he looked at her in the face, not nearly so enticing.

"Sure, what do you need more water for?"

She blushed prettily as she answered him. "I wanted to wash up a bit before bed."

Henry Lee jerked up a second bucket and headed out

the door, anger and desire struggling for dominance in his thought.

Unlike Hannah's father, Henry Lee had dug no well at his place. The creek was only a hundred yards or so down the hill and it had just not seemed worthwhile; however, he now thought that it might be hard for a woman to tote water that far up the hill several times a day. Especially a woman big with child.

He tried to imagine Hannah a few months from now, her belly stretched out before her like a ripe watermelon. He briefly thought of his poor mother. Childbearing was no sure thing. He remembered her lying so white and still in the bed, she had given up trying to expel the baby and only moaned in pain and waited to die.

His father, drunk in the corner, had done nothing but curse at her. And the Indian woman he'd brought to help her only shook her head and told him, "Baby dead. Both be dead soon."

Henry Lee reached the creek bank and knelt, ostensibly to fill the water buckets, but in fact the memory of his mother's death still had the power to frighten and grieve him. She was nothing but used goods, she'd drop her drawers for any man who had the price. His father had said that a million times. But she had been gentle too, and had cared for him. Somehow that seemed to make up for what she was. And watching her die in such pain, surely she hadn't deserved that, no matter what she had done.

She had been so young when Henry Lee was conceived. A pretty, light-skinned half-breed living near Fort Gibson, she had soon captured the eye of the fort's commander. She told Henry Lee about dances and parties, pretty dresses and a little house of her very own. Whether she had loved his father, Henry Lee never knew, but she had lived well as his mistress, and given him the son he'd never wanted.

Being little more than a child herself, the childhood that she offered Henry Lee was full of games and fun. She had no rules and made none for him. They ate when they were hungry and washed when they felt dirty. They worked too, when it was necessary. And Molly taught her son the only thing that she really knew, whittling.

Molly could pick up a fallen branch and make three toy soldiers, or a bird, or an axe handle. She knew the best wood for each task and she always sought out whatever was inside.

"You can't make a bowl from a stump, if there isn't a bowl in there already," she told him and showed him how to read the lines of the wood to see what was inside.

Henry Lee was never the carver that his mother had been, but he learned a lot about wood and used his knowledge for practical things. Where Molly had made figures and whirlygigs, Henry Lee made chairs and tables.

When Henry Lee was seven, his mother had become pregnant again. He remembered Skut being very pleased about it, his mother was not. She felt poorly almost from the first and her death climaxed weeks of increasing agony.

His thought shifted from his mother to Hannah. Would she die crying and moaning as his mother had? No, he quickly discarded the thought. His mother had been tiny and delicate, breeding too early, she was never in the best of health. Hannah was built for birthing. She'd be one of those farm women who drop their babes in the field, and then go on to finish the row. No need to worry for her on that account. She'd put this one out early next spring he supposed, and after that, by God, he'd keep them coming spring and fall until he had enough young 'uns to populate his own territory! And every damn one of them had better look just like him. Except, of course, the first.

He had decided to forgive her. He had decided to make a life with her. He would accept this other man's baby. It wasn't the young 'un's fault at all. A child was a child. And it wasn't that he was jealous, he told himself, he had no feelings for Hannah. He just hated the idea that he had to take another man's leavings. Skut had done the same and he was determined that he would be a better father than Skut had been to him.

He just wished the baby was here and over with, so that she would be his and they could get on with their lives. That was the rub. As long as she carried another man's child, another man's mark was on her. She could not be Henry Lee's.

He knew with certainty that he would not, could not, spend his seed where another man's had taken root. He would not share a bed with Hannah until she was delivered.

Having come to this decision, Henry Lee headed back up to the house, to explain to his bride just exactly how things were going to be.

Full darkness had fallen as Hannah lit the lamp in the main room and surveyed the drying corn kernels. It was so hot in the house now, that she doubted the possibility of sleep. If he really wanted these dried out by morning, someone would have to mind the fire.

She felt the sweat running down the back of her neck and decided she was wearing far too many clothes. In the bedroom she slipped out of her petticoats and removed the binder that she routinely wore on her bosom. The binder, which Hannah thought gave her a more youthful appearance by restricting her more womanly contour, was extremely bothersome in the heat and she gladly discarded it.

She stared at the cornstalk bed and imagined being in it with him tonight. The memory of the morning was still sweet to her, but because he had been grouchy on and off all day, it was tempered with a bit of embarrassment. She wondered if that tenderness in bed had not affected him as it did her. Perhaps he engaged in such things on a frequent basis and found them pretty usual. Since he regularly attended all the parties and shindigs for miles around, maybe he regularly took women to bed. Maybe those other women were more attractive and exciting than herself. The thought was not very comforting.

She decided she would just have to be the same type of wife that she had been as a daughter. It had always been Myrtie who was pretty and sweet and lovable. It was Hannah who had been responsible and hardworking. Freed from her hot, constricting underclothes and feeling a good deal cooler, Hannah returned to the quilting frame and carefully stirred the kernels as Henry Lee had. Maybe he would never see her in the same way as he might one of those other women, but she would prove her worth to him. Make him glad that he had taken her on. Prove that she could be a very good bargain.

When Henry Lee walked in the back door of the cabin, his mind was quite made up. He would move his workroom out to the shed and bed down next door to her until after the baby was born. Then they could use the workroom as a nursery and he'd move into his rightful place as husband, beside her in his own bed. He was ready to sit down and discuss it with her calmly and rationally. However, the sight that greeted him as he stepped into the cabin took away all rational thought.

Standing in profile next to the quilting frame with the fire to her back, Hannah was more exposed to Henry Lee's eyes than if she were stark naked. The light through her thin cotton dress revealed in detail the luscious curve of buttocks that he had already admired, as well as strong, well-muscled thighs that tapered into long well-turned calves. Her bosom, released from its confines, strained against the bodice of her gown like a ripe fruit begging for a hand to pluck it. She turned her face toward him and smiled eagerly, as if to say, "I want to please you."

His resolution disappeared like ice cream in hell as Henry Lee bridged the distance between them and grasped Hannah from behind. He captured those breasts in his hands and pressed his aching desire against her firm, yielding bottom.

She was wanton, desirable, and out to tempt him, he thought. But he would show her who was in charge. He was not a man to be led around by petticoats. His lips found her tender throat beneath her hair, and blazed a trail of sparks and flame up to her ear where he hoarsely whispered, "I want you."

Hannah was startled at his touch and frightened by the roughness of his embrace. Her breathing and her senses vividly alive, she could not seem to react to the onslaught of emotions and feelings that were bombarding her. The intense heat surrounding their mingled bodies blazed hotter than the fire behind them and Hannah had no coherent thought for responding to it. Her young, healthy body, however, knew exactly how to answer the flame he was stirring.

Henry Lee's need prodded him to harsh handling of her tender bosom. Through the thin summer blouse, he felt the hard nipples straining against his hand. His attention to them was both tender and crude as he alternately teased and treasured. His own desire was throbbing and plethoric as he brushed it hungrily against her backside.

Instinctively, her bottom squirmed and wiggled, pressing eagerly against him. Henry Lee's reaction came gasping from his throat, part moan, part cry, as he answered her squirming pressure with his own heated thrusting.

His right hand released the pouty nipple it had been worshiping and headed down the front of her dress, hoping to find her hot, feminine core wet and ready for him. As his hand splayed across the smooth curve of her abdomen, he suddenly thought of what lay beneath his touch. Another man's get. The result of her passion with some unknown male before him sparked his humiliation and anger.

Henry Lee released her abruptly and stepped away turning his back to her, so that she wouldn't see his body's obvious eagerness, so accurately displayed in the front of his trousers.

"Get some clothes on, Hannah!" He slammed his fist angrily against the wall. "Damn it, woman! Would you have me mount you on the table? Have you no shame at all?"

Hannah stood bereft, as if something vital was now lost. Her womanly parts were throbbing. The blood in her veins was pounding and every nerve in her body was awake and alert. His hurtful words sank through the red haze in her brain and suddenly she was ashamed. What had she done? What had happened to her? The image of her mindless lust was as clear to her as if she had watched herself. Her wanton loss of control and her animalistic display of carnal appetite was completely unforeseen in her life thus far. She had shocked herself and was sure that she had disgusted Henry Lee.

Her mind filled with confusion and her eyes filled with tears of humiliation she fled to the bedroom, slamming the door behind her and slithering to the floor as she leaned against it. She folded her arms across her knees and as tears of mortification coursed down her cheeks, she willed herself to cry silently.

Henry Lee was also ashamed. He knew that his words had hurt her and knew that he had lashed out at her in anger at himself. She was no better than she should be. A woman of doubtful morals would be expected to try to entice a man when no one else was around. And it wasn't as if she were being dishonest about it. She must have been wanting a man pretty bad, the way she flashed to fire so quick. It must have been a while since she'd been with her lover. Henry Lee wondered why. Had the man voluntarily given her up when he found out she was in the family way? It was possible, but it seemed more likely that he would have continued to take his pleasure while scheming to find a way out.

Maybe he wasn't from around here. Henry Lee remembered an old tinker once sitting up drunk all night telling him stories of all the skirts of farmers' daughters that he'd raised in his travels. He made it sound like a traveling man could have most any woman he set his sights on.

That would actually make more sense, Henry Lee decided. She wasn't really such a trollop. She was just a very foolish old maid that fell for a peddler's fast talk, and then had to find someone to make an honest woman of her.

He thought on it as he began stirring the corn kernels again. He could live with that a bit better, he decided. And he wondered if he was right to wait until she was delivered to share the bed with her. If the sparks between them could fly so easily, it would be a long winter.

Anyway he needn't worry about sharing it with her tonight, he thought bitterly as he heard the faint evidence of her weeping through the bedroom door. He had corn grits to make tonight.

SIX

The morning sun spread only a bit of warmth on the stone ledge at the entrance to the cave. Sitting on the cool stone Henry Lee could see a good distance both up and down the creek and all the way to the main road. But he was not looking in any of those directions this morning. His attention was focused on the opened doors of the shed near his cabin where Hannah was grinding the corn into grits.

The hominy mill was two round grinding stones that lay one on top of the other like stacked pancakes in a bowl. The lower stone sat on a metal fulcrum, its top was lined with furrows. Exactly on top of its mate, the upper stone had no furrows, but a hole about three inches in diameter was cut out in the center. Hannah would pour a bit of corn into the hole and as the stones turned, the corn would be crushed. As the particles became small enough they would fall into the furrows and be pushed out into the bed of the mill as meal and grits.

He watched Hannah as she whirled the stone round and round, her motion almost dancelike in its rhythm. She tried to continue without stopping as much as possible. Once the wheel started to turn, it was not so difficult to keep it going, but she had to stop every few minutes to fill the hole with more corn.

It was tough work, and Henry Lee wondered why she hadn't asked for help, but he knew the answer. She had barely spoken to him since last night. She didn't seem angry at him, but rather embarrassed and uncomfortable around him. He knew that it was his fault. She was trying to make it a normal marriage and she undoubtedly expected that lovemaking would be a part of that.

Well, he'd gone into the house last night to set her straight. And he'd sure done it, but not with the calm, rational explanation he had anticipated. He knew that he should go down there and apologize. Try to explain to her why he had spurned her. That was what he should do, he was very aware of it.

For most of the night he had sat up stirring the drying corn kernels. It had given him a good deal of time to think, but thinking really did no good. Where there were no answers, pondering for hours on end was merely a wasted effort. He sat now, watching her rhythm at the hominy mill. The strength of her arms did not match her determination, but still she kept on without missing a beat. He shook himself from his near trance and, heading into the cave, followed her example and went to work.

Hannah Bunch Watson stood at the mill, grinding corn as if her life depended on it. Her arms were so tired that each time she had to stop to replenish the stone they trembled. But she continued. There were dark circles under her eyes, betraying her lack of sleep the night before. For most of the problems of her young life she had looked to the Bible for solutions. For her current predicament, she had no idea where to turn. Twisting scripture to suit herself had got her into this marriage, but untwisting it could not make things right again.

Her behavior the night before had her completely puzzled. Such intensity of feeling was a new experience, and she'd had no inkling of her susceptibility to carnal desire. Searching her mind for an appropriate Bible passage, only the declaration in Paul's epistle that it "is better to marry than to burn" came to mind. Once she'd imagined that scripture to be a warning of hellfire, but after last night she thought perhaps he was speaking of a more earthly burning.

As the morning wore on, she began to worry about Henry Lee. She knew he had headed down toward the creek as soon as he had the corn set up in the mill, but that had been hours ago. For a moment she had a wicked thought that perhaps he had fallen into the creek and drowned and she could return to the bosom of her family as a respectable widow. But that thought was immediately followed by genuine worry. Although the past few days had been awash with unpleasant experiences, she had decided Henry Lee was a decent fellow and the unfortunate victim of her mislaid plans.

As noontime approached, the corn was nearly finished, and Hannah began to plan what she would make for Henry Lee's dinner. This morning when she was fixing his breakfast she had discovered the cellar. She would never have known that it was there; built so neatly into the back of the house and entered through a trap door on the wash porch it was almost invisible. She had not had time to explore it yet, but she was sure that Henry Lee must have some meat stored there, because she had glimpsed several oak barrels inside. After last night, she wanted more than ever to prove herself an excellent cook and worthy housewife.

Finishing the corn, she lined a bucket with clean cotton cloth and transferred the rough-ground meal into it. At one end of the mill bed was a chute that could be raised to easily transfer the grits to the bucket. The pouring created a small cloud of corn dust that tickled her nose. Willing herself not to sneeze, she covered the bucket with another cloth and carried it to the porch.

Leaving the corn grits in a safe corner, Hannah went immediately to the trap door to the cellar. She was surprised that the door had no pull. It had been carefully cut out of the natural grain of the wood on the floor and was so perfectly matched and fitted that it was a bit difficult to open. In fact, she thought, if she didn't know that the door was here, she would never have noticed it at all.

Hannah lit a candle on a small shelf just underneath the door. She headed down the sturdy wooden ladder to see what kind of stores were in the oak barrels.

The cellar was about ten feet square and not much higher than Hannah's head. The floor was lined with baskets and buckets and an unusually large number of earthenware jugs. She looked around, somewhat disappointed that there were no shelves on the walls for potatoes and onions. When potatoes were stored for winter in a sack, they went bad in no time. But set out on shelves, most would survive until April or May.

The barrels, however, were as fine as any Hannah had ever seen. Sturdy white oak gracefully bent for a perfect fit and held together by slim metal bands. She knew that Henry Lee could not have purchased them from a local cooper. These were made special by a skilled craftsman.

Eagerly Hannah opened the first of the handsome oak barrels, only to discover that it was empty. Her mild disappointment immediately turned to dismay as the trapped odor in the barrel assailed her nostrils. Something had been allowed to spoil in the barrel, the air was pungent with the smell of fermentation. She shook her head in disbelief.

What on earth had Henry Lee put in this barrel and then left to ruin? She quickly placed the cover back on it and checked the second barrel. It too was empty and smelled to high heaven. Hannah disapproved, but secretly she was a little bit glad. Henry Lee kept his house very neat, his little pig farm seemed to run well, and he had made arrangements in the community for foodstuffs. At first glance a wife seemed a bit superfluous. But here at last was evidence that Hannah was needed and that she could make a difference in Henry Lee's life. She vowed that this very afternoon she would start making things better for him by cleaning these barrels.

Her attention finally turned to another barrel on the other side of the cellar. It was not made of fancy white oak and looked a good bit the worse for wear. However, Hannah decided to check it out anyway. Holding her nose in preparation for the worst, she lifted the lid. No putrid stink awaited her, but a sea of white. Reaching down with one finger she touched the contents of the barrel and then lifted it to her lips. Sugar.

With a small cry of delight, Hannah began digging down into the barrel of sugar until she found what she was looking for: ham. Sugar-cured ham was her very favorite and she seldom ate it. Her father preferred his pork cured in salt so that was the way she had always prepared it. It was only visiting at other people's houses or eating at the community socials that Hannah had enjoyed sugar-cured ham. And it looked like Henry Lee was very good at curing. The ham looked and smelled perfect. She thought of the other ruined barrels. Maybe, she thought, after making such a mess, he learned to take his time and do it right.

Carefully securing the lid back on the pork barrel, Hannah headed up the ladder to the cabin carrying her prized ham with her. She was going to fix Henry Lee the most delicious meal he had ever eaten. Everyone knew that the way to a man's heart was through his stomach. Once Henry Lee fell in love with her cooking, he would begin to get used to the idea of Hannah as his wife.

With that thought in her mind, she began her dinner preparations and for the first time in many days began singing in her unfashionably husky soprano.

> *"There shall be showers of blessing,*
> *This is the promise of love;*
> *There shall be season's refreshing,*
> *Sent from the savior above.*
> *Showers of blessing, showers of blessing we need;*
> *Mercy drops round us are falling,*
> *But for the showers we plead."*

Henry Lee headed down the side of the bluff and made his way by circuitous route to the creek side trail and then back to the cabin.

He heard her singing as he came up into the yard. Not having spent much of his time in churches, or in the company of churchgoers, he was unfamiliar with the song, but he knew that it was a hymn. He was quite fond of music, and as far as he was concerned, the only difference between hymns and regular music was that you weren't supposed to dance to the hymns.

He stopped beside the shade tree and listened. He liked the sound of her voice. It wasn't high and breathy like he imagined churchgoing women to sing. It was deep and husky and reminded him of a girl he'd heard sing in the Pink Slipper up in Wichita when he'd gone to buy his whiskey barrels. He'd wanted to get a chance to lift the girl's skirts after the show, but he hadn't had enough cash. Hannah's voice was as sexy as hers had been.

Maybe he'd missed something by not going to church all this time. He smiled to himself. Who would have thought that Henry Lee Watson could get himself stirred up by hymn singing. Lately, it didn't seem to take much, but this was downright blasphemous. Laughing away his foolish reaction Henry Lee went into the cabin.

Hannah stopped in mid-verse at the sight of him. He was smiling at her. She knew he had always been a man with a ready smile; people had said that about him for years. But now, his dazzling smile was directed at her and it made her heart beat a little bit faster and a flush seep into her cheeks.

"Don't stop singing on my account, ma'am," he said.

Hannah lowered her eyes in embarrassment; he was not smiling at her, he was laughing at her singing.

"I know I haven't much of a voice," she said quietly, "but the Bible says to 'make a joyful noise,' so that's what I do."

"It is joyful and a pleasure, for sure," he told her. "I like the sound of your singing. It's unusual, but the tone is real nice."

Hannah looked at him gratefully, assuming that he was being polite. Her husband might be rough-hewn, she thought, but he was a gentleman.

Today's noon meal was a vast improvement over the previous day, Hannah thought, and Henry Lee apparently agreed. He complimented her outrageously, although he was a little surprised to find one of his Christmas hams on his summertime dinner table.

"I'm going to grind the rest of that corn right after lunch," Henry Lee told her conversationally.

"Oh, the corn is all done, I left it in those buckets out on the porch."

His jaw dropped in disbelief. "You finished all that corn this morning?"

Hannah nodded, glad that she had surprised him and shown herself to be a good worker.

Henry Lee was pleased at her obvious industry and decided that he'd put up his sweet mash first and then fix himself a bed for the workroom. He thought about explaining to her now that he didn't plan to sleep with her. But she seemed in such a good mood and the meal was going so smoothly, that he decided not to bring it up. He would just move into the workroom and if she wanted to know why, she could ask him.

After putting away an amazing amount of Hannah's good cooking for his noon meal, Henry Lee slipped down into the cellar and brought out one of his prized oak barrels. Hoisting it on his shoulder, he set out to find the perfect spot to make sweet mash. Normally he made it out on the south side of the front porch. It got good sun there, and it was easy to keep an eye on it. But Henry Lee imagined that a fine-looking barrel sitting on the front porch was bound to raise Hannah's curiosity. He thought it best to head for a less obvious location.

He stopped at the outdoor hearth and checked the small fire burning there. Hannah was certainly efficient; she hadn't let the little fire go out all morning. Filling the big, black, iron kettle in the creek, he hung it on the crossbar. As the water heated, Henry Lee inspected and rejected several potential spots to set up the barrel, finally deciding on a spot facing the creek behind the pigsty. It had all the sun that it would have had on the porch and the barrel was close enough to the sty that, if an animal came out of the woods to investigate, the pigs would let him know.

He placed it securely in the spot that he thought best, adjusting it slightly a couple of times to get it just right. He placed the corn grits that Hannah had so dutifully made for him in a layer at the bottom and poured a half barrel of hot water over them. He replaced the tight-fitting cover over the mix and hoped for the best. It would take three or four days for the grits to ferment. Until then, the corn was on its own.

Hannah made short work of the mealtime dishes and the small amount of housework that needed attention. She was anxious to get those oak barrels out of the cellar and get them cleaned up. If Henry Lee was impressed with how fast she could grind corn, well he would be amazed at how thoroughly she would clean up those fancy barrels.

She was surprised to find only one barrel in the cellar, and hoped that Henry Lee hadn't thrown away the other. She knew it would take a good deal of scrubbing, and some strong lye soap, but she was sure that she could get the barrels clean and fresh again.

It was late afternoon as Hannah headed into the house to start supper that she heard the sound of an approaching horse. Shading her eyes from the sun, she looked up to see her father riding into the yard.

Surprised to see him, she was glad too. She was happy he had shown up this afternoon instead of this morning. He would have known that there was trouble in her marriage. But now, after the congenial dinner with Henry Lee she was optimistic again that things would work out.

Her father stopped beside her smiling a little tentatively and seemed to be examining her closely. Hannah misread his look of concern and thought he must be able to tell how she behaved last night in front of the fire. Her face flamed fiery red and her father, seeing it, blushed himself.

He cleared his throat several times, and shifted on one foot and then another.

"How are you, Hannah?" he asked her. "I was heading out this way and I wanted to stop by and see that you two had got home all right."

With a shy smile she told him, "Everything is just fine, here. How are Myrtie and Violet?"

"Oh, they're fine, fine," he answered nodding. They stood in uncomfortable silence for a moment. "I'll be going into town this weekend," he said. "Violet was wondering if you're needing anything."

"No, I think I have everything I need. Tell Violet that the house was in very good shape. Henry Lee is very clean and neat," she boasted. "And it will take me no time at all to set the place up to suit me."

"That sounds good," the preacher said, obviously pleased that his son-in-law was neither slovenly nor unclean. "If you think of anything you might need, just send word. I thought I might take Myrtie and Violet to Ingalls with me if the weather holds out. I suspect they both will have some ideas of things for me to spend my money on," he joked feebly.

"I was just fixing to start supper," she said. "Can you stay for a bite? Henry Lee's out working, but he'll be showing up for supper pretty soon."

Reverend Bunch tied his horse to the front porch and followed his daughter into the cabin.

Henry Lee had left his barrel of corn grits and water working to become sweet mash and brought his cot down from the cave. It was nothing fancy, he'd used it for years to sleep in the cave when the mash was cooking. It wasn't as comfortable as a real bed, of course, but he figured that he'd only have to sleep on it a few months. And he figured there was no way to really be comfortable when sleeping next door to the woman he wanted to sleep beside.

He smelled his dinner cooking as he neared the house and hurried his step. Unfortunately, the horse tied to the front porch was out of his range of vision. When he walked in the back door, carrying what was obviously a bed, to find his father-in-law sitting at his table, he was speechless.

The two stared at each other for a minute and Henry

Lee saw the reverend eyeing the bed with curiosity. Henry Lee couldn't for the world think of one explanation that he wanted to give to Farnam Bunch. Fortunately, the man didn't ask any questions.

"Evening, Reverend," he finally offered and quickly moved to put the bed in the workroom and out of sight. Returning to the table, he tried to be congenial.

"Nice of you to drop in this evening. You staying for supper?"

"Hannah already asked me. Guess I will sample a bit of my daughter's cooking, if that's fine with you?"

"Of course," he answered tightly. "My father-in-law is always welcome at my table."

Feeling distinctly unwelcome the reverend went on quickly to explain, "I'm taking my wife to Ingalls on Saturday and was wondering if Hannah was in need of anything. I haven't bought you two a wedding gift yet."

Henry Lee didn't believe his excuse for a minute. He knew that he was being checked on, but he was determined to be gracious about it.

Hannah passed by him as she placed a bowl of redeye gravy on the table. Henry Lee reached out and wrapped his arm around her waist. Drawing her close, he smiled up at her.

"Just having Hannah for my bride is gift enough for any man," he said, trying to reassure the older man that his daughter was happy and safe.

He hoped that the reverend wouldn't make a habit of dropping in unexpectedly. That could embarrass his customers and hurt his business. Although he normally took his moonshine elsewhere to sell it, sometimes a customer came by looking.

Hannah served supper to her husband and father with a great sense of pride. She'd fried up some Indian bread to go with the ham and gravy and a huge mess of poke salad seasoned with just a dash of dill weed and a mountain of white potatoes whipped up to a frothy texture and sprinkled with big chunks of real black pepper.

To their credit, the men ate heartily and dispensed

compliments liberally, until they had Hannah thinking herself to be a housewife of exceptional quality.

Hannah's father leaned back in his chair and crossed his arms on his belly in a gesture of sated appetite and smiled at his daughter.

"You planning to drive Henry Lee's buggy in to church on Sunday?"

Rather than answering affirmatively as Henry Lee expected, she turned to him for permission.

"Would that be all right, Henry Lee?"

Surprise that she sought his approval, as well as having a full mouth, gave Henry Lee a moment to consider before he answered. Even so, he was stunned to hear the words come out of his own mouth.

"It's pretty far for you to be driving that buggy alone, Hannah. I suspect that I can drive you over once a week for Sunday service."

Reverend Bunch raised his eyebrows.

"Well, I'm pleased to hear that, Henry Lee. I know that you don't care much for the services, but it's real fine of you to come and bring my Hannah."

Henry Lee shrugged. "I don't imagine a bit of churching would hurt me much." *But it sure will come as a surprise to my customers*, he thought.

The rest of the meal passed uneventfully, with the reverend asking no embarrassing questions about the bed or anything else. Finally the older man prepared to leave, and Henry Lee gratefully waved good-bye to him, admonishing him not to linger so that he'd be home before it was too dark.

Hannah stood beside her husband as they watched her father headed toward the west, his horse at a clipped trot, as he slowly disappeared out of sight into the gray prairie evening on the other side of the creek. Unthinking, Henry Lee put his arm around Hannah's waist. She looked up at him and smiled shyly. Her eyes held him entranced for a moment and her lips seemed to part in invitation. He wanted to pull her into his arms and scorch her lips with his own. She was his wife, lawfully his own, but in fact she was another man's. Remembering, he pulled away from her.

"I'll be moving my things into the workroom for the time being," he said gruffly.

SEVEN

Zanola Little was the proprietress of the converted barn that was the dance hall in Sandy Creek. Elijah Brown, the community's religious leader, described it in one of his sermons as "a den of corruption in the midst of God's children." God's children, for the most part, were very willing to spend their one carefree night of the week laughing, dancing, and drinking moonshine whiskey in that corrupted den.

Zanola was, for six nights a week, a hardworking black farmwoman trying to make it on her own in the new territory. But on Saturdays, she opened up her barn to the neighbors. They could play their own music, dance, or just sit and talk, and it didn't cost them a thing. If they wanted to drink whiskey they had to buy it from her. She made enough, on the whiskey alone, to keep the place open and herself comfortable. The whiskey was very important and this afternoon she was a bit concerned because her supply was very low.

Her whiskey man should have shown up yesterday. Sometimes he came late, but he always came. He was very dependable, and she knew she shouldn't worry, but she'd heard a rumor in town that troubled her.

It was said that he had tied the knot with the preacher's daughter over at Plainview. He'd been caught messing with her by the preacher himself, and there was nothing to be done but marry up. That kind of bad luck had happened to other men before, but the fact that she was the preacher's daughter and, according to the rumor, not even the young, pretty one. All this boded no good as far as Zanola was concerned.

What she'd heard about Hannah Bunch was that she was plain, hardworking, a dutiful daughter, and a God-fearing church member. Zanola was certain those would be great characteristics for a farmer's wife, but wholly unacceptable in the wife of a moonshiner.

For all that folks said you couldn't change a husband, Zanola thought women have too much influence on their men. She worried that sharing his bed with a God-fearing woman might lead the best whiskey man in the territory to do some God-fearing himself. As she swept out her barn, preparing for the evening ahead, she kept glancing down the road, shading her eyes from the sun as she waited for the whiskey man.

When Henry Lee finally arrived, well before her customers, Zanola was very relieved to see him.

"Good afternoon there, Mr. Henry Lee," she greeted him, "I was getting plumb worried that you weren't about to show up."

Henry Lee was surprised. Laughing he jumped down from the wagon and gave her a boyish grin.

"I'm sorry that I couldn't make it over yesterday, but I'd never let the folks in Sandy Creek go thirsty on Saturday night," he teased her good-naturedly.

The small community of former slaves of the Creek Nation was nestled on the banks of a tributary to the Cimarron River. When the Dawes Act divided tribal lands into individual allotments, the blacks, as members of the tribe, were granted acreage of their own and lived relatively free of outside interference.

Growing up only a few miles away, Henry Lee had known the residents of Sandy Creek most of his life.

"We've been doing business together for a good while now," Henry Lee told the woman. "You know just about everything there is to know about me, and when I say that I'll be here, I will."

"Yes, that's true," Zanola said looking him over. "But that was in the past. I don't know what you're going to be like now that you're a married man."

There was an unspoken question in her statement and Henry Lee was taken aback. It was the first time he'd been referred to as a married man, and it didn't sit as well with him as it should have. He hadn't thought that the word would have made it down here so fast. He almost wished that none of his customers would ever know. But in the territory gossip flew around like a whirlwind.

"You heard about that, did you?" he asked, as he thrust his hands into his pockets.

She squinted at him and grinned. "It's the truth then?"

He nodded affirmatively.

"And it's really that preacher's oldest daughter, not the pretty one?" she teased.

Henry Lee felt a spark of indignation.

"Hannah is plenty pretty enough. Why, that sister of hers is just a flighty child."

Zanola's face broke into a wide grin and she laughed and shook her head. "Lord, boy," she told him, "you done got it bad, don't you."

"What do you mean?" he asked, eyes narrowed.

"That little gal done got you wrapped around her little finger. Well, I'm hoping that before you get out of the business you teach somebody how to make that fine whiskey of yours. It goes down smoothest of any in the territory."

"What are you talking about?" he asked her, genuinely confused. "I don't have any plans of getting out of the whiskey business. What would make you think a thing like that?"

"That little gal don't think much of the whiskey making, I'd be betting. And I'd wager she's already planning to turn you into a respectable farmer."

"She's not turning me into anything," he retorted. "I like my life just like it is, and I get all the respect I need. Like you said, I make the smoothest whiskey in the territory. You know me, Zanola, no woman is going to be giving me orders."

Zanola looked at him speculatively. "You saying that she don't mind that you make your living from whiskey?" Henry Lee considered lying, but decided that it didn't matter enough to lie about.

"She doesn't know."

"She don't know you're a moonshiner?" Her voice was disbelieving.

"That's right," he answered, smiling. "Nobody's told her and she hasn't asked, so I guess she'll just go on not knowing how I manage to put meat on her table."

Zanola shook her head. "You ain't going to be able to keep it from her. Somebody's going to tell her and then what are you going to do?"

"She won't be running my life," he assured Zanola. "She's got herself one lucky deal with me, and she won't be trying to do anything to mess that up."

"Good Lord, Henry Lee," she laughed. "You must think yourself some kind of man, doing the little white girl such a big favor!"

Henry Lee had been thinking about the baby in her belly, but he wasn't about to tell anyone about that.

"As you said yourself, Zanola, she's plain and past her prime and she's not so straightlaced as you think. Them church women got needs, too."

"Oh, Lordy! Don't I know it," she exclaimed laughing loudly, "I'm a churchgoer myself, and if I was twenty years younger, I might give you a long look or two myself."

Henry Lee laughed in reply. "Forget that twenty years, Zanola," he teased. "You start giving me long looks and I'll be looking right back!" This flirty, light conversation came so easy to him with Zanola and with other women, and for a moment made him wonder why he had never really tried his charm out on Hannah. Somehow she seemed different from other women, but he couldn't understand why.

He shrugged. "It's time I had a woman to clean and cook and do for me. She'll serve well enough for that."

"What about your bed?" Zanola nearly cackled. "Ain't it time you had a woman in your bed, too?"

"I've always had that," he teased mischievously.

"Ain't that the truth," she said joining him in laughter. "But now that you're a married man, you'd best keep your eyes off our pretty girls tonight."

"Now, Zanola, you know there ain't a one of them wedding vows that says you can't look!"

Hannah spent her evening alone not very differently than she did her day. She continued working outside until nearly dark. Fixed herself a bit of supper, cleaned everything that she could think to clean in the house. Still she found herself with time on her hands.

She decided that being alone would give her an opportunity to take an all-over warm bath in the kitchen. It was, after all, Saturday night and she wanted to look her best for church tomorrow, especially if Henry Lee was going to take her.

As she trooped back and forth to the creek to fetch water to heat she imagined herself in church beside him. They would hold the hymnbook together and their voices would blend as they sang. Everyone would be surprised to see that he attended with his new wife. And all the unmarried girls in town would be envious of the new bride, whose handsome husband obviously doted on her.

It was a wonderful fantasy, but as she sank her tired body into the gloriously warm water reality intruded.

The reality was he did not dote on her. In fact he had moved to the workroom. He'd taken all his tools and wood out to the shed and set up his bed. He'd brought in a small table to hold his wash pan and his lamp and he'd nailed hooks up on one wall to keep his clothes. Hannah had stuffed him a tick for a mattress and he seemed quite content to take up residence in the next room.

She knew that married people slept together. Her parents always had, it was a part of being married, the part that all the girls giggled about. Why Henry Lee had decided not to share her bed was a mystery to her.

They didn't know each other very well and perhaps he was shy. She certainly must have frightened him with her behavior the first night. She still didn't understand how she could have acted that way and felt embarrassed and humiliated that it had happened. At the same time, she secretly wanted it to happen again. Just thinking about it made her feel strange. Her stomach seemed to have little swarms of butterflies in it, and she had to try harder to breathe. Her breasts tingled with the memory of his hands upon them. And in the hollow of her womanhood, she felt an emptiness that was inexplicable.

She closed her eyes and imagined him coming home right now. He would walk in the back door with that same look he had had that night. He would see her here in the bathtub, slick and wet, and would kneel down beside her. He would grab her hair and twist it around his hand, forcing her mouth into his control. He would kiss her lips and then her neck and her throat. Then his lips would touch her breast.

Abruptly she sat up in the tub. What would happen after that she didn't know. And suddenly the idea that he might come home and find her here in the tub was very frightening. She quickly finished scrubbing herself, washed her long hair, standing up to rinse it with a bucket of clean water, and climbed out to dry off.

After dressing for bed, throwing out the bath water and braiding her still damp hair into one long braid, she put out the lamp and went to bed. She had no idea what was happening in her marriage, but she wished that Henry Lee would come home. She felt safer when he was there. She wasn't really afraid, she assured herself, she just liked having him around. She slipped off to sleep dreaming that he was lying beside her.

The man of Hannah's dreams was at that moment sitting in a dark corner of Zanola's barn listening to strange soulful music that was unique to the Negroes. He had always liked this music, it had made him want to laugh and love and put his arms around the pretty available girls. Tonight it was having an unusual effect on him. It seemed almost sad and he wanted only to sit in the corner alone. So he sat quietly drinking his own whiskey, something Henry Lee rarely did. He didn't indulge himself often. Occasionally, out with friends, he would drink a bit, but rarely to excess. Living with his father had shown him what whiskey could do, and he had little tolerance, and no sympathy, for drunks. He liked to be in control. But, as he sat in the corner at Zanola's, he was slowly, steadily drinking himself beyond restraint.

Several Sandy Creek residents had stopped by his table to congratulate him on his recent marriage. Everyone wished him well, yet it was clear they were curious about the details. The pretty young girls who always flirted and danced with him tried to tease him about his newfound marital status, but his distant attitude, mixed with his alcohol consumption, discouraged any further approach and fueled rumor that he was not completely happy with his shotgun wedding.

Toward midnight, with the help of Zanola's right-hand man, Jones, he got back into his buggy and headed toward home. He gave the horse its head and let him find his own way. Zanola wasn't too worried about him, thinking that the distance to be traveled and the night air would clear the whiskey vapors from his brain. She would have been more concerned if she'd known that he had stowed a jug of moonshine under the buggy seat and before he was even out of sight he had continued imbibing.

Henry Lee was not exactly sure why he was drinking. The situation with Hannah really shouldn't bother him so much. It wasn't as if he was in love with her. She would make a good wife and would give him a respectable position in a community that did not hold whiskey men in great respect. He would see that she didn't shame him with other men and once she'd birthed her current burden, he would have no problem bedding her. The passion he had unexpectedly discovered in her was pleasant to contemplate.

He wanted her to be happy, too. He had traded the whiskey for bushels of corn, beans, peas, and potatoes instead of his usual cash. He wanted to please her and let her do for him the way she felt a wife should. He didn't think that she deserved to be punished forever. He wanted to let her be a real wife and have a husband that would take care of her. He was not like Skut, he reminded himself. He was strong enough to appreciate a good woman. And there was time for him to have children of his own.

What Zanola had said, about him giving up the whiskey business for her, bothered him more than he cared to admit.

He was proud of his business and proud of the whiskey he made. The idea that a woman, any woman, could make him give that up was ridiculous. Or was it? She had already managed to force him, a man she hardly knew, to marry her and to agree to give her bastard child his name. If she could do that, getting him to become a full-time farmer might be easy.

That angered him. By God, he had never let any woman run his life; he had always set the rules. Women were convenient and warm and eager to please him, or he didn't bother to give them the time of day. He had never had any patience with men who allowed females to control them by holding back or giving favors, to get what they wanted. If Hannah could control him, then he was less a man than he had thought.

With that in mind, he drank deeply of the fiery liquid in the earthenware jug. It was strange to think of Hannah as one of those cold, calculating women. Those women always seemed overtly sexy and used their bodies like weapons.

And yet, although he knew Hannah was experienced, she did not seem to be very aware of her body. Perhaps it was just more of her subterfuge.

He gazed down the road into the darkness, but in his mind he looked at her. He imagined her face, soft and smiling, but with a strength that made her seem more womanly than girlish. Her hair, its curls forced into the severe style she always wore, could be evidence that she was not all that she seemed. And her body. He imagined that lush, bountiful body and it flamed his imagination. That fire quickly spread to his groin. In his mind's eye he saw her again before the fire, the light shining through her gown, leaving no doubt about the generous warmth of her thighs and the shapely curve of her legs. He saw himself pulling her down onto the table, as he had wanted to that night. Resting himself between the soft strength of those thighs as her legs wrapped around his back, urging and begging him closer.

Adjusting himself on the ungiving buggy seat, he shook the lustful images out of his brain. He told himself that his train of thought could lead only to frustration or self-debasement. He drank deeply and thought that the next several months couldn't possibly pass quickly enough.

Hannah awakened to the sound of someone falling in the back door. The clamor of someone tripping over the milk buckets, knocking over a chair, and falling onto the floor was followed by a familiar voice uttering a very unfamiliar expletive.

Quickly lighting a lamp, Hannah went to investigate. Henry Lee lay sprawled, facedown in the middle of the room, moaning. A stab of fear ran through Hannah's heart. He'd injured himself. Hurrying to his side, she set the lamp on the table and dropped to her knees beside him.

"Henry Lee! What happened? Are you all right? Can you move?"

Henry Lee, who was not precisely sure what evil monster had thrown a bunch of buckets and a chair at him, moaned a little, feeling the pain in his shoulder where it had hit the table.

As Hannah stood above him, her eyes were huge with worry and her face reflected a tender concern Henry Lee had never seen before. Her hair lay in a long honey-colored rope beside her sensitive throat, past the darkened nipple clearly visible through the thin cotton gown, to her surprisingly narrow waist. Henry Lee wanted to climb that rope, leaving a trail of kisses along the way. Her anxious breathing drew his attention back to the rise and fall of her breasts. Unbound and pointing impudently upward, he tried to compare them to something familiar. They were definitely bigger than peaches, but not like melons. With a sigh of contentment, he decided no plant or tree could produce a fruit so desirable to taste. The light from the lamp framed her face and gave her a kind of halo. That was who she was, an angel, he thought. But not one of the psalm-singing ones, a flesh and blood one that made fire run in his veins.

"Oh, my Hannah," he said, his voice slurred. "Are you an angel of mercy or a hot-blooded wench come to tempt me into your flame?"

The undeniable odor of drunkenness assailed Hannah's nostrils and made her both angry and afraid. She was angry that he had left on business and had obviously decided to get himself drunk instead. And she was frightened also. She had seen men drunk on the street in Ingalls, but she had never actually been close to one. She wasn't sure what to expect. She'd read tracts from the Temperance Society where women described in detail how their drunken husbands would rage at them and beat them.

She decided it was best to treat him as she would a wild animal. Show no fear and take charge of the situation.

"You are drunk."

Henry Lee's smile deepened. "That I am, Miss Hannah, a drunker man I have never seen. Well, maybe I have, but I can't seem to remember it right now."

Because he didn't seem angry or vicious, Hannah relaxed somewhat and took courage.

"Do you need me to help you up? You seem to have fallen."

"Damn furniture, ought to have enough sense to get out of the way, that's what I think," he replied.

"Let me help you up." She moved her arms under his shoulders to lift him, but to her surprise he wrapped his arms around her and pulled her close.

"I'm not so sure I want to get up. This seems like a pretty good position to me." He pressed her delicious bosom against his chest, feeling the hard tips of her nipples like twin peaks of fire, searing his flesh.

Frightened by his sudden movement, Hannah tried to pull back; instead she found herself held firmly against him. The closeness of his body was having the same embarrassing effect she had suffered the other night, and she knew she must stop this before he became disgusted with her again.

"Let me go, Henry Lee, I want to get up," she demanded.

"In a minute," he replied lazily. "I just want to feel you against me for a minute. Just want to share a little heat." His mouth wandered to the throat he found so tempting. "I just want a little taste of what it would be like to husband you."

When his lips made contact with the sensitive flesh beneath her ear, a sharp cry escaped from her lips. It was happening again, he was touching her and making her feel all liquid and molten inside. His mouth was firm and insistent against her skin, and blazed a path from her neck to her lips.

His kiss was not gentle, but hot and demanding. With a gentle sucking pressure on her mouth he forced it open and then his tongue was inside, exploring the depths of that hot cavern, as if to show her how he would like to explore another.

His tongue so shocked Hannah, that she squirmed in fright. Her squirm only pressed her more closely against him, and in answer he moved slightly pulling her down full length on top of him. With a groan he slid his hand down her back to cup her much admired bottom.

He pressed her against his rock solid erection and the feeling it evoked in Hannah took her breath away. She was quickly losing touch with reality and could no longer think about what she should be doing, getting away. Instead she found herself doing what she wanted to be doing, kissing him back.

Her lips sought his with the same hunger he had felt and experimentally she pushed her own tongue into his mouth. The surge of fire that action brought to her body caused her to squirm toward him again. Not to get away but to get as close as she possibly could.

As he pressed her bottom firmly down, matching her hot aching pit with his correspondingly heated member, Hannah could not stifle the cry of pleasure that blended in their mouths. Her breasts seemed to swell and burn and she sought his hand to comfort them.

When she brought his hand to her breast and pressed it against her, Henry Lee shuddered at his lack of control. Groaning, he quickly rolled her over on her back. Spreading her legs with his, he was only restricted by the tangle of her nightgown. His mouth left hers and in a chain of fiery kisses he headed determinedly to the breast she had so generously offered.

Freed of the glorious wonder of his mouth on hers, Hannah began to hear strange whimpers of pleasure that were barely recognizable as her own. As Henry Lee fastened his wonderful mouth on the aching peak of her breast, she cried out in passion and confusion.

"Oh, Henry Lee, my God! What are you doing to me!" Arching her back to give him more access, she pressed her womanhood more firmly against the long length of his manhood. "Just don't stop!" she begged, "please, don't ever stop."

Her hot pleading fired Henry Lee beyond tenderness as a red haze of lust filled his eyes. He could no longer bear the thin sheath of cotton between his mouth and her breast. Grabbing the modest cotton gown at the neck, he ripped it open, laying Hannah bare to his gaze.

The jerk of the resistant material and the wild sound of it tearing its way to her nakedness was deafeningly loud, drowning out the moans and breathing of a moment before.

Their eyes met as if they were just realizing what was happening. In Henry Lee's, Hannah saw a strength, a drive, that she didn't understand or know. In Hannah's, Henry Lee saw passion mixed with confusion and fear. In that instant the confusion and fear seemed to overtake the passion and to blot it out completely.

His eyes dropped to the view he had ripped her

gown open to see. Her beautiful breasts lay bare, heaving with her labored breathing, and damp from the attention he had lavished upon them. She flushed with embarrassment and he realized that in his drunken lust he had treated her roughly, like a common tramp, and she had refused him nothing.

Cold-sober now, Henry Lee pulled the torn remnants of her gown together to cover her.

"Hannah," his voice was a hoarse whisper, "have I hurt you?"

"No," she answered a little shakily, not quite able to look him in the eye, "I don't think so."

He rolled off her and sat up. She too sat, crossing her arms against her torn bodice. As their breathing returned to normal, they both stared straight ahead not daring to look at each other.

"Hannah," he said finally, "as you said yourself, I'm drunk. I don't usually drink and I swear I won't again. I would never do anything to hurt you. I hope you know that."

"It didn't hurt exactly," Hannah told him, trying to understand just exactly what she was feeling.

He looked at her quickly, but she could not meet his glance.

"I want to have you as my wife, Hannah. I want you to take my body, like you've taken my name. But I want you in my bed and willing, not on the floor where I've dragged you."

Henry Lee ran a distracted hand through his hair as if trying to reason out the unreasonable. He never lost control with women; he always knew what he was doing. Twice now he had lost his head with his new wife and he couldn't understand it. He made a rational decision about their future together. He needed to stick to that arrangement and not allow the crazy heat of passion that she seemed to generate in him to threaten their potential for happiness.

"Hannah, we've got a lot of things going against us. If we are going to have any kind of marriage at all, we're going to have to give ourselves the best chance possible."

He hesitated, trying to think of the right words. She was so vulnerable now, he didn't want to hurt her, but he had to say it outright so that she would understand. "I think we should wait to share our marriage bed until the reason for our marriage is behind us." Hannah looked at him surprised. He met her gaze and added as gently as possible, "People make mistakes and I don't hold you in contempt for yours, but I think we should wait until it's no longer an issue."

EIGHT

Flat one by six pine planks stretched between kitchen chairs, barrels, and stools, forming makeshift pews in the new Plainview Church. Hannah and Henry Lee had been the last to arrive and found themselves sitting front row center as the service began.

Hannah's whimsical notion of the night before, of having everyone in the church looking at the two of them, was a lot less enjoyable in fact than it had been in fantasy. The whispers had started up the minute they walked in the door. The knowing glances and speculation brought out Hannah's natural shyness and made her long for the days when she was unnoticeable in this congregation.

It didn't help that Henry Lee looked his worst. His face was drawn, lined, and tired, and he seemed to have almost a greenish cast to his complexion. She knew he was ill from the liquor when he refused even coffee for breakfast. Why he had insisted on coming was a mystery.

Hannah had given up on sleep at dawn and had dressed and readied herself for church, planning to attend alone. She looked forward to it. The time alone on the road and the communion with heaven at the church surely would calm her and give her peace. She was very concerned about the events of last night. She was surprised at what she was learning about herself, about the depth of her own passion, and the strange mysteries of her own body. She needed time to sort out what was happening, and she had hoped to have that time this morning.

She encountered her first obstacle when she found that she could not seem to harness the team. Her father had always taken care of the horses, and now she wished she had paid more attention to how it was done. After several unsuccessful attempts, she decided that her only options were to stay at home or to get Henry Lee to help her.

Her first timid knocks on his door produced no results. Ultimately, she was pounding the wood to get his attention. When the door was finally wrenched open, Hannah was momentarily frightened. He looked rumpled, sick, and angry.

"I'm so sorry to wake you, Henry Lee."

He waved her apology away. "You need something, the house on fire, what?"

She steeled herself against his bad temper. "If you could hitch up the buggy for me, I'll be on my way and you can lay back down again."

He ran his hands across his face and through his hair as if trying to rouse himself.

"You should have woke me earlier. Give me a couple of minutes to clean up and dress and I'll hitch up the buggy and take you."

"Oh, you don't have to do that! I can drive myself, I really am very good at handling a team," she protested.

He walked over to his wash table and poured the water from the pitcher into the bowl. Hannah watched as he splashed the cold water over his face and head and managed to get a good bit of it spilt on the washstand and floor.

"I said I would take you, and I will take you."

His firmness brooked no argument.

"Would you like me to fix you some breakfast?" she asked innocently.

He shuddered. "Don't you dare!" he answered. At first his voice seemed angry, but then he was almost laughing. "Did you unload the buggy? You can start that while I get dressed. Just carry the lighter things, I'll get the heavy sacks myself."

Hannah had been delighted to discover the fresh veg-

etables in the buggy. At least he had not lied to her when
he said he was going to Sandy Creek on business. He
must have gotten himself drunk later. Glancing at him
now as the sunlight streamed in through the window of
the new church, bathing his face, she wondered why anyone drank if this was the consequence.

As they stood together to sing a hymn, Henry Lee
wondered the same thing. He felt terrible, of course, but
worse than that he remembered the night before vividly.
He didn't try to sing. He didn't know any of the words
yet it was such a pleasure just to stand next to Hannah
and listen to her wonderful rich voice that seemed more
suited to a beer hall than the House of the Lord. She was
such a prize and he had frightened and embarrassed her
last night.

When Skut would get raving drunk he never seemed
to remember what had happened. For once, Henry Lee
wished he was more like him. He hated the memory of
his drunkenness. He hated wondering what Hannah
must think of it. She had not even wanted him to drive
her to church today. Perhaps she was ashamed to be seen
with him now. Well, ashamed or not, he was her husband
and nothing was going to change that.

When the hymn ended, they seated themselves on
the rough pine planks. Henry Lee found it pretty uncomfortable. He had planned to wait until the long dark days
of winter to make the pews for the church. But, after
sitting for a few moments he revised his plans to a bit
sooner.

Bowing his head as instructed as he listened to the
soft drone of Farnam Bunch requesting guidance from
God, he became increasingly aware of the proximity of
his wife. With his eyes closed he could smell her. It
wasn't the kind of smell he usually associated with
women. It was neither the cheap overwhelming perfume
of the women of ill repute or the typical lavender sachet
of more discreet ladies. She smelled of sunshine and plain
soap and woman. He realized that he remembered this
smell from the night before. Sprawled on the floor, the

scent of her had assailed his nostrils and now beside her in church the same scent caused an immediate reaction in his body.

He quickly opened his eyes as if his sense of sight could cancel out his sense of smell. Looking at Hannah's strong, sturdy hands lying calmly in her lap gave him back his control. She had the hands of a working woman. Callused and rough, her hands reflected the work she did. The work she did, now, in his house. He remembered his mother's wedding ring that had not fit on her finger. He had forgotten that he'd given it to her. He was sorry she couldn't wear it and decided that next time he went to the city he would have it made to fit her. It was tangible evidence that she was his. He liked knowing that, and for some reason he now wanted everyone to know it. He wanted all these people to think of her as Mrs. Watson, not Miss Hannah.

Henry Lee felt an unexpected surge of pride in his new wife. She was a fine, decent Christian woman. The kind that any of these farmers would not have been ashamed to call his own. And she belonged to Henry Lee Watson. Sure, she'd made a mistake, Henry Lee was not about to forget that, but hadn't he made plenty in his life? He speculated that most of the good Christians now in the church had probably made a mistake or two themselves.

Feeling somewhat better, he caught Hannah's eye and gave her a hopeful smile. She returned his smile with a shy one of her own and lowered her eyes discreetly before returning her attention to the preaching.

Henry Lee watched her for another minute, before he too gave polite attention to Reverend Bunch.

Hannah was both anxious and encouraged by what had happened last night. Certainly, it was all very frightening, having him hold her and caress her like that. But it was exciting too, and she realized that she was anxious for it to happen again. At least she had learned why Henry Lee wasn't sharing a bed with her. The trick she had played was terrible and Hannah understood that it must be difficult for him to forgive something like that. At least he was willing to try to forget it, and planned to have a real marriage with her. She wondered longingly how much time it would take for him to get over it. If last night was any indication, surely it wouldn't be too long.

After the service, Hannah found that getting out and to their buggy was somewhat like running the gauntlet. Everyone in the community wanted to ask a question or wish them well. Nearly all commented on Henry Lee's first attendance at church. Hannah was embarrassed for him, but he seemed to take it in good humor. "Can't have my wife attending church without me," he told Mason Dillary. "She might see some other fellow and never come home."

Laughter followed in their wake as Henry Lee made joke after joke about his appearance at the Sunday service. When they finally reached the buggy, and Hannah was about to climb inside with great relief, she heard her father's voice behind her.

"Violet's cooking up a big Sunday dinner for you two, and she just won't take no for an answer."

Hannah felt drained and wanted to beg off, but Henry Lee seemed delighted to be staying for dinner and quite willing to stand and talk to the neighbors indefinitely.

"Henry Lee," Hannah called to him, "I'll just go and help Violet, she'll need me." Henry Lee nodded and Hannah quickly made her exit before anyone else had the opportunity to object. Practically racing down the hill to the house, she arrived in the kitchen just as her stepmother was stoking the fire in the stove and pulling on her apron.

"You didn't have to hurry, honey," Violet told her. "I've been learning to get these meals by myself and I'm doing better all the time. You should have stayed to visit with your friends."

"My friends are a bit nosy for me, these days," Hannah answered bluntly.

"I see," her stepmother said, "I guess I remember that. Being first married and being a bit shy, wanting to keep your happiness to yourself for a little while." She smiled nostalgically. "Yes, I think I remember that."

Respecting each other's privacy, the two worked together companionably and in a short time two chickens were delicately fried. Yeast rolls were beautifully browned and piles of greens, potatoes, and crowder peas vied for room on the kitchen table among the pickled beets, chow-chow, green onions and sliced tomatoes. Myrtie came in from the cellar bearing a crock of fresh cottage cheese and then laughingly called the men to the table.

"You best make your way to the table, Hannah hates to serve up Sunday dinner late, and there's always the chance that she'll just throw it out."

Henry Lee shot his new wife a comical expression, as if he feared her wrath.

Hannah lingered, helping Violet get everything onto the table, until her father insisted that she take her place beside her husband.

"Henry Lee, you just sit right here and Hannah, put that away now and come join your husband."

"That's right," Violet insisted, taking the vinegar bottle from Hannah's grasp. "You are a guest today, so try to act like one," she teased.

As was their custom, the family joined hands to say grace. Placing her hand in Henry Lee's sent a shock wave through Hannah's body, followed by a vivid memory of his caresses and kisses of the night before. Desperately, Hannah tried to refocus her mind upon asking blessing for the food, but unerringly her thoughts flew back to the touch of Henry Lee's hand on her breast and the relent-lessness of his mouth on hers. When her father finally pronounced amen, Hannah quickly pulled her hand away, but she had no control over the flaming roses that brightened her cheeks.

Henry Lee, who seemed totally recovered from his illness of the morning, ate heartily and complimented Violet outrageously on the meal. He seemed more the self-assured, jovial man that Hannah thought him to be before their marriage. He seemed to be almost flirting with Myrtie, who was glowing from the attention.

When Hannah's stepmother offered him another yeast roll, he took two and revealed that he was partial to them.

"Next time, I'll make a double batch," Violet proclaimed, "and you can take the rest home with you."

"Oh, no, ma'am," he said, winking at her. "Don't put yourself out like that. I certainly haven't been suffering from lack of good cooking."

Henry Lee gave Hannah a quick smile as he slathered butter on his roll. "These are surely mighty fine eating, but my Hannah makes the finest light bread I've ever tasted. I consider myself a fortunate man."

Hannah was nearly dumbfounded and extremely pleased with the compliment. Henry Lee had praised her cooking before, but the tone of his voice today seemed to indicate a satisfaction that went further than a good meal. Suddenly, when she was surrounded by her family, he became charming and complimentary. She wondered if he was playing up to her parents, seeking their approval. Did he really care what her parents thought?

What Hannah's family thought was all to Henry Lee's credit. They had both been very uncertain about the potential outcome of such a mismatch, but what they were seeing appeared to be two people who had strong feelings for each other.

Reverend Farnam was reassured that Henry Lee seemed to have a pretty good head on his shoulders, and was as straightforward and honest as a man could be in his profession.

Violet was thinking that the roses blooming in Hannah's cheeks left no doubt that she was loved and cared for by this man.

Myrtie just thought they were the most handsome couple she had ever seen, and she dreamily anticipated a man just like Henry Lee to come along and marry her also.

"I very much enjoyed your sermon today, Papa," Hannah said, breaking up the silence at the table.

The preacher accepted her compliment with a nod. "Hannah has always been partial to the Old Testament," he explained to his son-in-law, smiling. "What about you, Henry Lee?" he asked. "What did you think of my sermon?"

Henry Lee studied his plate, casually moving around the remains of his potatoes.

"It was the first time I'd heard you preach, Reverend," he replied. "You have a fine speaking voice and that is for sure."

Farnam Bunch immediately noticed his son-in-law's hesitance.

"What about the subject? What did you think of the story of Cain and Abel?"

Henry Lee looked the preacher straight in the eye for a moment, as if deciding what and how much to answer. Then with an affirmative nod he decided to speak his mind.

"Truly, Preacher, I have never liked that story," he said. "I know you preachers always talk about the sin of one brother slaying the other. That's pretty bad, I've got no argument with that. But the part that bothers me is where that jealousy began."

Hannah listened avidly, curious about the workings of her husband's mind.

"Here you have two hardworking men," he went on. "One of them raises sheep and the other is a farmer." Henry Lee rubbed his chin and leaned closer to the preacher as if trying to more clearly express his point. "For some reason God decided to prefer the results of one man's labor over that of the other man." Henry Lee shook his head in disbelief. "I can't for the life of me understand why God could not accept the offering of both men. A man who takes pride in his work ought not to be scorned because of his choice of occupation."

Reverend Bunch smiled tightly. Hannah, however, did not recognize the undercurrents between her father and her husband. She was surprised that Henry Lee had given so much thought to the sermon and she could see the point he was making. It did seem unfair that God

would choose the offering of the shepherd and reject that
of the farmer. However, she had learned through her own
mistake in thinking what was good for Ruth and Boaz
was good for herself and Will Sample. The Old Testament
contained many passages that were open to misinterpreta-
tion. She wanted to explain that to Henry Lee.

"I know that it seems unfair," Hannah said. "But the
point of the story really has nothing to do with occupation. Some sacrifices were more acceptable to God than
others, but we don't need to offer sacrifices these days,
so it is no longer important."

"I wouldn't say that it's not important," her father
interrupted, but Hannah ignored him and continued.

"All work done with diligence and care is acceptable
to God. People sometimes put more value on some kinds
of work than on others. They may think that the preacher
or the doctor has more favor in God's eyes, but the truth
is that the Bible says that God himself 'established the
work of our hands,' so that whatever our talent is, if we
do it to the best of our ability, God is pleased."

Hannah's smile was so loving and kind, it was difficult for Henry Lee to look at her. It was no longer a bit
funny that she didn't know about his whiskey business.
He wished that he had told her the first day.

Henry Lee glanced over at the preacher to see him
studying his daughter. He wondered if her father was
going to correct her. To tell her that God could never be
pleased with a man who made his living with whiskey.
The reverend, however, held his peace and changed the
subject.

"Well, Henry Lee," Hannah's father asked, "what do
you think of the new church you built?"

"I believe it will hold up through the winter," he
teased. "But those pine planks could make even the best
of sermons seem a mite long."

The reverend laughed at his son-in-law's frankness.
"I doubt you're the only one with those sentiments. We'll
all be anxious for winter to come so that you can get
started making those pews for us."

"I'm thinking about starting them a bit sooner than

the winter," he told them. "Sure, I won't be able to work steady on them this time of year, but I may be able to get a few done."

"That would be wonderful," Violet exclaimed. "It will make it seem more like a real church."

"I'm thinking to make a trip over to Sallisaw to visit the lumber mills and talk to some of the furniture makers. I'd like to find out what they have to say. I don't know too much about this. I taught myself to work the wood, but there are a lot of things about it that I still don't know."

"You're going to Sallisaw?" Myrtie's eyes were as big as saucers. "Will you take the train and everything?"

"Of course," he said, smiling at her charming sense of wonder. "What good is it to have trains, if you don't ride on them?"

"Oh that's wonderful," Myrtie said. "I've never ridden on a train, but I think it would be glorious." She flung her arm dramatically, barely missing the gravy bowl, but continued without noticing. "Does Hannah get to go with you?" she asked excitedly.

Hannah blushed with embarrassment. She quickly began assuring Myrtie that she had too much to do and that it would not be possible for her to go, when Henry Lee cut into her explanation.

"Of course Hannah will go," he told them. "It wouldn't be very much fun to go on a trip and leave my bride at home."

Hannah blushed at his words. Henry Lee made it sound like a wedding trip and she was sure it wasn't that, or maybe it was. She wondered if he had decided to forgive her for the trick and make her his wife in fact. A tiny flutter of anxiety and excitement skittered through her mid-section. She hoped that it was true, and that he would finish the wonderful journey that he had started last night.

The talk around the table about the upcoming trip continued, but Hannah didn't have a word to add. She was lost in daydreams. She imagined being beside Henry Lee on a train around strangers. Everyone who saw them would know they were husband and wife and none would guess how it had happened. They would all think that the handsome man beside her had married her for love. She suddenly realized how badly she wished that it were true. Involuntarily, a sigh escaped her lips. All eyes turned in her direction.

"Well, Henry Lee," her father said, "it seems we are boring your bride with our conversation."

"Oh no," Hannah insisted, "I was just woolgathering a bit." She felt Henry Lee's eyes upon her, questioning and curious.

"What kind of wood are you thinking to use?" Farnam asked him. "You think pine or maybe oak?"

Henry Lee chewed slowly. "I truly haven't decided," he finally answered. "I sure like the look of walnut, but it'll take a lot of wood. I might use walnut for the places that get the wear and a soft wood like pine or spruce for the underpinnings. It really depends on what size you want, I guess."

"What about the size?" the older man asked. "We just want what fits comfortably in the church."

"That's not what I mean," Henry Lee explained. "Do you want five long benches, where you get in and out on the sides. Or more like the big city churches, ten short benches, five on each side, with the aisle running straight down the middle."

"Which do you think?" the preacher asked him.

"Well," he answered thoughtfully, "five long benches would be the quickest, cheapest, and the most practical." He glanced over at Hannah to see her reaction. "But the aisle up the center would sure be prettier. It would make a person feel welcome the minute he stepped in the door."

"Oh Papa!" Myrtie exclaimed, "you've got to have an aisle down the center for weddings. You can't have the bride just walk down one side of the church!"

The reverend smiled at his youngest daughter indulgently. "We could do all the weddings like your sister's. Just move the benches out altogether, let everybody stand, and the bride can walk wherever she pleases."

"Oh Papa, you're impossible," Myrtie complained. "I think your daughters are right," Violet said. "It will look more like a church with an aisle up the center. And it will be easier for the sinners to make their way down to the front. I think you should consider it."

The preacher ran a hand through his hair thoughtfully for a moment. "How much more do you think it will cost?" he asked Henry Lee.

Henry Lee considered for a bit, glancing over at Hannah again as if weighing a decision concerning her.

"How long you been preaching here, Brother Farnam?" he asked.

"About five years," he answered. "What does that have to do with it?"

"Well, Reverend, I'm a little bit behind on my tithe. I'm thinking that the cost of the pews for the new church might begin to catch me up a bit."

Henry Lee glanced over at Hannah for her approval and saw that she was both very surprised and pleased.

"Now, Henry Lee," Hannah's father replied shaking his head. "I couldn't let you do that, it's too much."

Henry Lee felt a lump of cold dread settling in his stomach. To be refused his offer of charity would be unbelievably humiliating.

"Couldn't or wouldn't?" Henry Lee asked him. "I want to do it, Reverend, unless you don't think the fruits of my labor are acceptable in God's house."

It was a direct challenge to his father-in-law. Like Cain, Henry Lee was presenting his offering. Would the preacher think that money earned making and selling whiskey was unfit to be used to adorn the church?

Reverend Bunch only had to think for an instant. It was his belief that God looked past the man that people see and saw straight to the heart. Somehow the reverend knew that Henry Lee's heart was in the right place.

"Henry Lee, speaking for the whole community, we very gratefully accept your generous gift of time and money for our church."

NINE

The midmorning sun peeped into the cave where Henry Lee had located his still. The barrel of sweet mash he'd made in the sunshine behind the pigsty now sat next to the spring ready to be worked. Henry Lee was so familiar with the whiskey-making process that he didn't have to give it a lot of thought, but today he was unusually distracted.

Since the discussion over Sunday dinner, he had continued to feel like a liar and a hypocrite. He knew now that he should have told her right away about what he did. He suspected that she would be angry at first, but she'd just need time to get over that. What she wouldn't get over was hearing it from somebody else after having made a fool of herself.

He was very grateful that her father hadn't given him away. He'd always thought the preacher to be an honest and fair man, now he decided that he also excelled as a father-in-law.

Thinking how fortunate he was in his choice of relatives, Henry Lee gently set the barrel on the washbench next to the spring. The sweet water, chilled from its hiding place in the ground, flowed out of the wall down into a sparkling little pool about the size of a small washtub. Then it seeped back into the ground beneath the pool, to reemerge near the base of the bluff where it joined the creek. It seemed tailor-made for the needs of a moonshiner and Henry Lee was more than happy to take advantage of it.

He cautiously loosened the top of the barrel. The content, now fermented to a sugar, was a potent material. As he carefully lifted the lid he moved back away from the fumes. The aromatic substance gave him a headache when he worked with it, and he knew the concentrated effluvium in the barrel could be dangerous.

The sickly sweet smell of the fermented mash permeated the cave. Henry Lee stepped out to the ledge area for some fresh air.

Gazing down at his cabin, he saw Hannah outside gathering wood for the stove. He enjoyed just watching her. Even from this distance he could distinguish her purposeful stride. It seemed she never sauntered or rambled, she was always headed in some direction. Always busy making his house more of a home. He glanced down at his shirtfront and ran his hand along the sleeve. It was strange how she made his old work shirt look and feel better than some of his dress shirts. It was easy to tell that she took pride in the way she kept house, the way she cooked, the way she laundered the clothes, and her skill with a needle.

He smiled thinking of what she had said on Sunday. At the time, he had been mostly concerned about her finding out about his moonshining, but now he was able to remember more of her words. That all work was important work. He was sure that she must believe it, as he watched her head into the cabin with an armload of wood for the stove. She worked practically every minute of every day without a sigh or complaint. Things needed doing, so she did them. She didn't expect a good life to be handed to her on a platter. She meant to build that life herself, brick by brick. He continued watching the house, as if he could see her inside, and he smiled to himself. Many times he'd felt pride in his own work, a sense of accomplishment at what he was able to do on his own. This sense of pride in someone else's work was a new emotion.

While he watched the house, a trickle of sweat headed down the back of his neck and he swatted at it with his handkerchief. As hot as it was outside today, it must be intolerable in the house, cooking.

Hannah was, at that moment, thinking almost the same thing. She piled the load of wood in the crate near the stove and wiped her brow. She should have set this all up outside, she realized, but she would have needed help moving the table and equipment and she hadn't wanted to bother Henry Lee. It wasn't that she thought he wouldn't want to help her. She just wanted to do things by herself, to show him how much she could accomplish without troubling him.

The bushels of vegetables that he'd brought from Sandy Creek would have to be cooked and canned, so as not to spoil. Currently sitting on the stove was a huge caldron of black-eyed peas simmering in a little fat back and filling the air with fragrant steam. At the table, she was using a knife to scrape the kernels off the ears of corn. With a little luck, the corn would soon be meeting the same fate as the peas. Off to the side sat the jars and lids. She had started boiling them this morning, and now as they cooled, they awaited the contents bubbling on the stove.

Singing softly as she worked, she thought about last summer when she'd done this with Violet and Myrtie. Canning had been both a trial and an adventure. She hadn't been sure about taking charge. It was obviously the job of her stepmother. But Violet had been as willing to take her orders and to follow her directions as Myrtie. When Violet had started to remove the jars from the scalding water and set them to dry, Hannah had stopped her.

"You'll burn yourself," Hannah had told her, "let me do it, my hands are rougher than yours."

Violet had laughed. "Gracious, Hannah," she'd said. "A woman ten years younger than me could not possibly have rougher hands." Hannah remembered, however, that Violet had smiled. She had been pleased by her stepdaughter's accidental compliment.

Hannah glanced down quickly at her own hands

now. They were large, with long fingers and tidily kept short nails. There was no wedding band, she thought sadly, thinking of the tiny delicate ring that wouldn't go past her knuckle. She had never thought much about having pretty hands or wearing a ring. It had never seemed important. Somehow, now she thought it was. She recalled glancing up in church to catch Henry Lee looking at her hands. What had he thought? Was he still sorry that she forced him into marriage? Had he wished she were prettier?

She blushed with pleasure as she thought back on the night he had come home drunk. She was still embarrassed and amazed at the feelings Henry Lee could invoke in her. She remembered the look on his face when he had exposed her breasts. She crossed her arms in front of herself as if to shield herself from his eyes. She wondered why she had not felt the need to do so that night. Somehow it had seemed so wonderful to be exposed to him. She wanted him to see her. She wanted him to want her, to touch her again like he had that night.

Her body was suddenly suffused with a quivering warmth that was part remembrance and part anticipation. She was tempted to give into the feeling, but quickly shook it off. She had work to do and no time for daydreaming, no matter how pleasant.

Henry Lee worked steadily in the cave, breaking up the sweet mash with warmed spring water. It was very important to thin the mash thoroughly or it wouldn't ripen. The smell and the feel was reassuring. It seemed that this was to be an especially good batch, which pleased Henry Lee more than it should have. He had come to think of it as the "wedding whiskey" and somehow he thought having it turn out well would be a good omen for his marriage.

When the sweet mash was finally a consistency that met Henry Lee's expectations, he carefully smoothed it back into the barrel. It should not be packed tight, but with just enough room to breathe. Like a mother tucking in her little ones, he carefully sheltered the mash with two inches of rye malt to seal off the air. He covered the barrel and breathed a sigh of personal satisfaction. It would take several days for the sweet mash to sour. The sugar in the fermented corn would turn into alcohol and carbolic. Henry Lee knew that all that was needed now was patience. When the barrel began to sound like rain on the roof or side pork frying in the pan, it would be time to start it cooking.

He was whistling as he left the cave. Out of the corner of his eye, he saw three riders approaching in the distance. Although he couldn't make out the faces, he could see that they were Indian, and that meant they'd come for whiskey. Henry Lee hurried, hoping that they would not state the nature of their business to Hannah before he could get there. He had to tell her himself; he couldn't let her hear it from someone else.

Hannah had the corn cooking on the stove and had filled almost a dozen quart jars with black-eyed peas. The jars cooling on the sideboard with the lids carefully setting askew gave Hannah such a sense of purpose and accomplishment that she no longer minded the intense heat of the kitchen.

She set aside a bowl of the black-eyed peas to feed Henry Lee his noon meal and had just begun to stir up a batch of cornbread when she heard the approach of horses outside. Thinking that it might be her father again, she left the cornbread makings and hurried out the door.

Hannah was slightly startled to see three Indians in the yard, but recovered herself quickly. She was not a fearful woman or easily intimidated. She was, after all, living in the Indian Territory, right in the corner of the Creek Nation. She should expect to see Indians, although none had ever ventured into her yard at Plainview Church. As a preacher's daughter, she'd been taught that there is no such thing as a stranger, only potential converts.

She called out a pleasant "good morning" as the three men stopped to observe her. They were all of middle years, but the one who seemed to naturally take the position of leader was somewhat younger than the other two. Although they were big men, with their rounded faces and somewhat rotund bodies they did not seem at all menacing.

They just sat on their horses and stared at Hannah for a few excruciating minutes as she became more and more uncomfortable. Finally the leader spoke up.

"I want to see Watson."

Hannah felt herself relax. Obviously the men were here on some purpose and not just wandering about, preying on unsuspecting households. She opened her mouth to tell them that he was working out in the fields somewhere, when suddenly Henry Lee emerged from among the trees.

"Good morning!" he called out as he hurried to meet them. Hannah saw that he was very anxious to see the visitors and she assumed that they were friends.

"It's good to see you," Henry Lee told the visitors as he urged them to dismount. As the Indians loosened the cinches on their saddles to give their horses a rest, Henry Lee shook the hand of the leader and spoke to him.

"Harjo, I was wondering when you'd show up," Henry Lee said to the leader and then glanced back at Hannah. He needed to get these Indians away from Hannah before they said something to give him away.

"Come down and take a look at my hogs, they are better looking than any in the territory."

If the leader seemed a bit taken aback by the offer to view the hogs, he covered it admirably and motioned to the other two to follow as he walked with Henry Lee.

As they moved away, Hannah couldn't help but notice the limping gait of the leader. On horseback he looked completely in control, but moving on his own two legs was obviously awkward and uncomfortable.

Hannah felt an immediate surge of sympathy, followed by starry-eyed admiration for her husband. Again, he had surprised her. Most men were hesitant to socialize with the lame or afflicted, as if those "thorns of the flesh" might be contagious. Her husband, however, chose his friends where he would. Proudly, she acknowledged that he was a man of deep feeling and open mind.

If only the people in the church realized what a fine man he was. She was sure the only reason he had not become a part of the church community in the past was because of his own modesty and his family background. He had been simply keeping his light under a bushel. She remembered only a short time ago she had considered him totally frivolous. It was obvious she and the rest of the community were going to have to dig a little deeper to discover what a fine Christian Henry Lee Watson was.

Satisfied, Hannah returned to the kitchen. If Henry Lee had three friends visiting, she certainly wanted to offer more than just black-eyed peas and cornbread. She resolutely commenced dinner preparations.

As the men approached the pigsty, Henry Lee turned to Harjo.

"So, how much whiskey are you looking to buy?"

The Indian looked at him with an amused question in his eyes. "Maybe I'm not here to buy whiskey. Maybe, I've come to look at your hogs, Whiskey Man."

Henry Lee felt a flush stealing up his cheeks. One problem he had never suffered was shyness, but it was embarrassing to be caught in such a fouled-up concern.

"I recently got married," Henry Lee stated, not quite able to look Harjo in the eye. "My wife is a very religious woman, a preacher's daughter." Henry Lee began to rush his words as if saying them more quickly would make them easier.

"She doesn't know that I make whiskey, and probably wouldn't approve if she did." The Indian stared at Henry Lee as if he expected him to say more.

"I would appreciate," Henry Lee said, "if you wouldn't say anything about whiskey around her. And please, don't call me Whiskey Man. I'm going to tell her myself, I just haven't got around to it yet."

Harjo continued to remain totally still and to stare at Henry Lee for nearly a full minute, then he suddenly howled with laughter. Turning to the other two men he quickly translated Henry Lee's words into the Muscogee tongue and all three began laughing uproariously. Their laughter was contagious enough to bring a smile to Henry Lee's face, though he no longer found his situation particularly amusing.

As Harjo took a short breathy break in his laughter he said to Henry Lee, "Whiskey Man, you have what all men want, a woman who believes all the lies that you tell her."

That brought fresh laughter to the group and even Henry Lee joined in half-heartedly, but he was bothered by the implication. He had lied to Hannah. She had lied to him also, but for good purpose, his conscience argued, to give a child a name. He had lied out of spite.

Henry Lee gathered up the jugs of whiskey for the three and together they walked upstream about a quarter of a mile and hid the jugs in the bushes. The Indians continued to laugh at Henry Lee's painstaking attempts at subterfuge.

They headed back to the house and Harjo turned serious as he spoke of the news from the Indian Territory. Now that it was flourishing, Indian politicians were talking about entering the union as the forty-sixth state.

"It's to be an Indian state," Harjo told him, "a land for Indians controlled by Indians."

"It sounds too good," Henry Lee warned him. "Do you think it can really happen?"

The Indian shrugged. "First they have to write a constitution, then the people in the territory have to vote. After all have agreed, only the President of the United States can stop it."

"Would he be on our side?"

"Who knows?" he questioned abstractly. "But change is already in the wind. The big men are trying to put on a very civilized appearance for the lawmakers in Washington."

Henry Lee nodded. Corralling crime and corruption until after the declaration of statehood had been passed would be very important to the territorial leaders.

"So many people still think of us as the "wild Indians," Harjo complained. "It's almost impossible to make the folks back East understand that in the territory, Indians are better educated and more financially independent than their white neighbors."

Henry Lee nodded understanding. "And the outlaw problem hasn't helped us," he said. "Washington believes the Nations have a tolerant attitude toward crime, just because every thief and murderer from the surrounding states chooses to hide out here."

"That's right," Harjo agreed. "Winning over the Congress would mean cracking down on crime. And that means the Federal marshalls."

Rolling his eyes, Henry Lee said in disgust, "The Federal marshalls, out of Fort Smith, act like the people of this territory are either naughty children or dangerous madmen."

Harjo was not totally in agreement. "You have to admit," he told Henry Lee, "that when Hanging Judge Parker ran the court, the tradition of swift and severe punishment for lawbreakers kept the criminal element either in hiding or on the run. The marshalls have done a lot of good, ridding the territory of the worst of those mongrels. Chasing down and rooting out the gunslingers and outlaw gangs has brought us a long way toward catching up with the rest of the country and preparing the Nations for the new century."

"Now, Harjo," Henry Lee said shaking his head. "You make it sound like the marshalls are a bunch of starry-eyed heroes. Most I've met are just regular family men, who needed to make a living. And getting shot at by professional gunfighters and train robbers for lousy pay is not what most of them want to do. They'd rather earn their money arresting counterfeiters, con men, horse thieves, and poor hardworking whiskey peddlers, like myself."

The last was spoken with a laugh and Harjo slapped his friend on the back.

"That's another problem," Harjo declared. "The law concerning selling intoxicating beverages to persons of Indian blood is unjust and should be changed."

"It's not going to happen," Henry Lee told him. "Those lawmakers in Washington are convinced that alcohol makes Indians prone to riot, assault, and murder. And the more they try to tell Indians they aren't allowed to drink, the more young Indian boys are going to decide that drinking illegal whiskey is the way to prove their manhood."

Harjo nodded in agreement. "The young men think that spending time in jail is a symbol of courage, just like bringing down their first deer."

"It's a shame," Henry Lee admitted, then added sarcastically, "but, as far as my business is concerned, I couldn't have asked for a better law. As long as whiskey is illegal for the red man, I will be making a dang good living."

The two men could only laugh at the absurdity of the law.

"The marshalls are raiding the whiskey once again," Harjo told him. "Last week they pulled in Pauly Archambo." He said, shaking his head sadly, "Broke Pauly's still to pieces. Now he waits and rots in Fort Smith jail. They say he may do ten years at hard labor."

Henry Lee nodded solemnly. He had always been aware of the risks of his business. It kept the price of whiskey high and the competition manageable. He had never worried much about it before. He knew if he were caught he would do his time and start over when he got out. Now, he suddenly realized he had new responsibilities to concern him. What would happen to Hannah if he went to jail? And the child she carried, how would she manage to provide for the child alone?

Harjo turned a stern look to Henry Lee. "Be very careful, Whiskey Man. I don't want that to happen to you."

His concerned visage was suddenly replaced by a smile. "You make the best whiskey in the territory, you do us no good in jail!"

The two laughed and Henry Lee forced his darker thoughts to the back of his mind. "Do you think statehood will be a good thing for us?"

The Indian considered for a few minutes. "Maybe," he answered finally. "Washington is always chipping away at our rights. Every time that Congress seems to notice the 'I.T.' they try again to break down the working, prosperous Indian nations."

The two men stood still as Harjo allowed his gaze to wander across the horizon, as if memorizing the land in case it disappeared.

"Dissolving the nations of the Five Civilized Tribes, dividing the land into pieces for each member, has turned brother against brother and fathers against sons. Those who see down the long road know that breaking it up into allotments that can be bought by white speculators is like a cancer eating away at the body of the nations."

"That's true," Henry Lee admitted. "Think of when they paid the Cherokees for their western holdings, giving little bundles of cash to everyone right in the middle of town at high noon. Fast-talking white men swarmed like wasps after a rainstorm. A whole lot of Cherokees went home that night with no more than they had that morning."

Harjo shook his head sadly. "I don't know what we will become. My children grow up in a world that has nothing of their grandfathers. They cannot learn the old ways, because they must live in the world of the whites. I understand this," he told Henry Lee, "but I cannot like it."

Harjo shook his head, as if shaking off the gloomy thoughts, and cracked a smile at Henry Lee. "So, my friend, I drink to forget," he said mischievously. "And that is good news for my friend the whiskey man."

By the time they reached the cabin, the two men had exhausted the subject of territorial politics. Harjo and his companions were anxious to get on their way, pick up their whiskey and begin what they hoped to be an exciting period of drunkenness. As they approached the split rail fence where their horses were tied, Hannah came out of the house and walked down to them. Her hair was more tidy and she'd put on a clean apron. Her smile was so warm and friendly that the men were slightly taken aback.

"I've got your meal ready to serve," she announced. "But it's so hot in the kitchen. I've spent the whole morning canning," she told them, gesturing to her appearance as if she needed to make some sort of apology. "If you would like, we could move the table out under the tree here and I could serve you outside." She looked at her husband for approval.

Henry Lee was so surprised at the idea that she would serve a meal to his customers, that at first he only stared at her. Quickly recovering himself, he assured her that an outdoor luncheon would be perfect and enlisted the help of Harjo's two companions in moving the table.

The meal Hannah set before the men was a virtual banquet. The Indians, who had been anxious to get on with their planned amusement, had grumbled among themselves about having to eat a meal they didn't want, just to keep the whiskey man's wife from finding out his business. However, when they sat down to a feast of territorial delicacies, they quickly changed their minds.

The men ate eagerly and even accepted second helpings as Hannah, fighting off her tendency toward reserve with strangers, endeavored to be charming and gracious to Henry Lee's friends.

She wondered what they thought of her. How had Henry Lee explained his sudden marriage? She hoped that he had not told them about the trick she had played. Immediately after having that thought she discarded it. Henry Lee was a man with honor. He would never embarrass his wife in such a way. She was certain that no matter what he had told them, it would not have been anything unkind.

Henry Lee was inexplicably pleased with the meal she had prepared. She always fed him well, of course, but this was their first company dinner. He knew it was no small task to kill, clean, dress, and fry three chickens in such a short time. It was important, among farming people, for a man's wife to set a good table. It meant that the man was a good provider and enhanced his reputation. Henry Lee instinctively realized that somehow Hannah was paying him a very high compliment and he wanted to return the favor.

"My wife is a pretty fine cook, wouldn't you say?" he prompted Harjo.

The Indian smiled broadly and wiped his hands perfunctorily on his napkin. "Wish you could teach my wife to cook like this."

Hannah blushed with pleasure at the compliment and Henry Lee beamed with pride in his new wife.

"Mr. Harjo," she asked him politely, "do you and your wife have children?"

"Yes, ma'am, we've four."

"Girls or boys?"

"Three boys and a girl."

"Oh, I know she must be special to you," Hannah continued. In her nervousness, Hannah found it difficult to meet the gaze of Henry Lee's friends. Even as she talked to them, she kept her eyes either on her plate or on Henry Lee. She would look quickly in the direction of the guests, but her glance didn't linger there, afraid of what she might see. She was afraid that they might wonder at Henry Lee's choice of bride.

In fact, her shyness was working in her favor. The Creek men and women normally did not look each other in the eye unless they were married. The straightforward gaze of white women was usually disconcerting. This white woman married to the whiskey man, however, seemed modest and unassuming and she certainly set a good table. While Hannah might have thought Henry Lee's friends were surprised at his choice of wife, Harjo was actually thinking that it was obviously a love match. The two seemed well suited to each other, and the way the eyes of each seemed to be drawn time and time again to the other, no other explanation was necessary.

"My daughter is nearly grown now," Harjo told her. "She will soon marry and leave for her own home."

"Are your sons still at home?" she asked.

"They are all married, except the youngest," he answered. "That one is at Bacone School."

Hannah had heard of the Bacone School, an Indian college of higher learning in Muskogee.

"So you are a Methodist?" Hannah asked.

Harjo was somewhat taken aback. He hadn't really ever thought of himself as anything but Creek.

"I guess that I am," he replied feeling a bit sheepish. "At least my wife and family are, I guess that makes me a Methodist, too."

Hannah smiled tolerantly. "I think that Henry Lee thinks the same thing about being a Baptist. I guess your wife and I have something in common. We're both going to have to work harder to bring our husbands into the fold."

The two men looked at each other, slightly embarrassed.

"It looks to be a lifetime of work, ma'am," Harjo told her.

Hannah laughed. It was a deep, throaty sound that Henry Lee found immediately disturbing. It set his pulse to racing and he was surprised to feel it spread a familiar warmth in the region of his lap. He quickly looked over at the other men. Had her sexy laugh had the same effect on them? They seemed not to have noticed.

Harjo noticed the whiskey man was obviously very taken with her and a bit jealous to boot. He smiled to himself remembering the early days of his own marriage, when something as simple as his wife's laugh could get him as hard as a brick. Right now, however, all he felt was the numbing pain of his bad leg going to sleep.

He got up from the table and grabbed up a washtub that was leaning against the house. Bringing it back to the table, he resettled himself propping his bad leg on the tub to elevate it.

Hannah watched his actions sympathetically, chiding herself for not thinking of his comfort earlier.

"How did you injure your leg, Mr. Harjo?" she asked.

The table was suddenly completely still. Even Harjo's companions, who ostensibly did not speak English, were frozen in place waiting to see their leader's reaction.

Hannah immediately realized that she had made a mistake. Despairing at her clumsy attempt at being Henry Lee's hostess, she tried to apologize. "Forgive me for prying, Mr. Harjo," she said. "It is truly none of my business."

Harjo, who had in his youth decided that the best way to handle his disability was to knock the teeth out of anyone who mentioned it, decided to make an exception in this case. He found he liked the wife of the whiskey man and her question seemed more concern than curiosity.

"It was not injured, ma'am," he told her. "I was born with a leg shorter and crooked. The birthing woman told my father that I would never walk."

"Well, you have certainly proven her to be wrong, haven't you." Hannah's smile was contagious and Harjo felt himself beginning to trust this woman.

"When I was a boy," he said, surprising himself at his candidness, "the other children called me 'Gimpy-Harjo.' I got in the habit of shutting their mouths with my fist and now no one ever asks me about my limp."

Hannah laughed again at his self-deprecating humor, and Harjo glanced at his friend the whiskey man. It was a pleasure to give Watson another jolt of his wife's laughter.

For dessert, Hannah brought out a green tomato pie that she had thrown together while cooking the rest of the meal. She wished she had blackberries, or something else just as sweet. Her next project, after the canning, would be to scout out the area to see what kinds of fruits and herbs were growing nearby.

The green tomato pie was still very hot from the oven and came oozing out of the neat little triangles that she had cut. She was disappointed at this unattractive complication, but the men attacked the tart treat as if it were ambrosia.

The three men, formerly so anxious to get their liquor and head out, sat contented now, leaning back in their chairs, hands across their bellies. Harjo thought he might simply stay the afternoon and help Henry Lee with his chores, maybe take a nap in the shade of the red oak.

Then he remembered how short a time the couple had been married and the reaction that Henry Lee had suffered just hearing his wife giggle. Nodding his head wisely, he knew that Henry Lee undoubtedly would find a delightfully cool, shady spot by the creek and spend the afternoon loving on his pretty wife in thanks for the wonderful meal. Yes, he thought, that was probably what his friend had planned. So he and his companions would get their moonshine and go see what kind of fun they could stir up.

Harjo thanked Hannah profusely for the meal and surprisingly agreed to return at a later date with his wife. He wondered what kind of tongue-lashing he would get from his woman for bringing her to a moonshiner's house. But, he thought to himself, if the whiskey man can keep his moonshining business from his own wife, Harjo ought to be able to keep it a secret from his.

As they were recinching the horses Harjo warned Henry Lee again. "Remember what I said about the marshalls. It will be very hard to keep your livelihood a secret from your wife when she is dragged into court beside you."

"I'm careful," Henry Lee replied, a bit defensively. "I always know who I'm selling to and my still is well hidden."

"Just don't trust everyone that you know," Harjo cautioned. "There is money to be made from helping the marshalls, and people who would sell their grandmothers if the price is right."

Henry Lee nodded in agreement. "I will watch it closely for a while."

"If I hear anything about you, I will get word to you as best I can."

"I appreciate that," Henry Lee said, shaking his hand.

As the three rode off, Harjo waved to the house. Henry Lee turned and saw Hannah standing by the back door. She had cleared the dishes off the table and was shaking out the tablecloth as she watched the men ride away.

Henry Lee felt a surge of pride. She was the kind of woman any respectable man would want. And he decided that even being unrespectable, he wanted her, too. In fact, he wanted her right now.

He started walking toward her. She's my wife, he told himself. I'll just walk up there, pull her into my arms and kiss her. Then I'll unbutton her dress and find those luscious white breasts and I'll suck and tickle them with my tongue till she begs me to get between her legs. Then I'll show her more pleasure than any man before who's ever touched her.

As he reached the table, the crux of the problem was back again. Other men had touched her. She carried evidence of that touch in her belly right now. She looked so clean and sweet and so loving. But she had looked that way for other men, and other men had suckled her breasts and delved between her thighs. His hurt flashed as hot as his lust.

"I'll move this table back in the kitchen," he told her gruffly.

Hannah heard the anger in his voice. What had she done wrong? She had tried so hard to please him. She thought the meal she'd served was well received and appreciated. She had tried to make the small talk interesting. Even when she had inadvertently upset his guest by asking about his leg, she had managed to smooth it over. What could she have possibly done to upset Henry Lee?

"Thank you," she replied, wishing that she could lay down somewhere and just cry.

TEN

B y Saturday, Hannah had simply decided that understanding Henry Lee Watson, and his strange flashes of temper, was something that would come in time. Just like love, she thought to herself, it will come in time.

She was scrubbing carrots in a dishpan when this thought occurred to her. It stopped her in her tracks. She realized that it was not enough for her, anymore, to just make a good home and have a working marriage. She wanted her husband to have some real feeling for her. It was even worse than that, she realized. It wasn't an abstract thing like "her husband," she wanted Henry Lee Watson to have some real feeling for her. If only she'd known where she was heading before she'd conceived this ill-fated scheme. She had always believed herself to be totally practical and free of silly romantic notions. She hadn't really known herself at all.

Hannah found her eyes gathering up with tears at the hopelessness of the situation. No matter how well she cooked or how clean she kept his house, Henry Lee would not be falling in love with her. Men might feel grateful to cooks and housekeepers, but they fell in love with women that were beautiful.

Hannah looked down at herself in despair. She always told herself that she was above personal vanity, and she'd never really tried to be anything but clean and neat. Now she began to wonder if it were possible to make herself prettier. She could never be beautiful, of course, but maybe she could be pretty enough for a man to love.

Her mind whirling at the possibilities, she began planning what she would do to change her looks and wanted to hurry into the bedroom immediately and have a look through her belongings. She did, however, maintain the good sense to finish the carrots and put them on to cook, before she allowed herself the luxury of personal adornment.

Henry Lee carefully loaded the back of his wagon with whiskey. He'd checked on the wedding batch, still in the barrel, and knew that it was almost ready for cooking. Once that started, he would have to stay right with it until it was done. He would make one more round tonight, selling his whiskey before he was stuck at home with his still for a week.

He expected to begin the distilling tomorrow, as soon as he got Hannah home from church. He rolled his eyes heavenward, imagining what the good Lord must be thinking about a moonshiner who plans to start up his still only after he'd attended church services.

He pulled an old brown tarp out of the shed and carefully covered the jugs. That would not keep lawmen or thieves from finding out what was in the wagon, but he might be able to keep Hannah from knowing.

He knew that he was going to have to tell her soon. He just couldn't figure out a way to do it. Maybe he'd tell her tomorrow on the way home from church. She'd be all happy from visiting her family, and maybe he could make her understand that it was just like she had said. All work, done to the best of one's ability, is valued in the eyes of the Lord.

Hannah sat in the bedroom taking stock of her attributes in the small hand mirror she propped up against the wall. She had stripped down to her chemise and removed her breast binder. She was considerably more comfortable this way, she told herself, not allowing her mind to dwell on Henry Lee's obvious appreciation of her bosom on the two occasions that he had touched her. She wondered if the binder was really necessary. She knew that a good many young women did not wear them. She also knew that a lot of young women put starched ruffles on the bodice of their chemises to make themselves look bigger. It was just the way of nature that those less endowed would try to look more so, and those more endowed would try to look less.

Hannah thought that perhaps she needn't try to look less anymore. Standing at an angle she tried to view the profile of her natural bosom in the glass. It did stick out a good deal, but it wasn't vulgar, she assured herself. Of course, her practical side remembered, going without the binder would mean that all of her dresses would have to be let out in the bust. She didn't have so many clothes that it would be an impossible task. She could do one dress every evening. That wouldn't take away from any of her other work.

Having made the decision and giving herself one last proud glance at her newly-discovered physical attraction, she sat back down in front of the mirror and examined. her face. Her gray eyes, plainly fringed with light brown lashes, did not seem to hold much promise. Her nose was neither too long nor too short, she looked at it straight ahead and from the side. It was a perfectly all right nose, she thought, but it was only a nose. Her mouth was a little too wide and when she smiled, a slight gap showed between her two front teeth. She shrugged, at least they were all there, all white and all straight, she consoled herself. Her complexion was a little rough, she thought. The flawless white skin of the legendary beauties of the day was impossible to maintain on the prairie. Fortunately for Hannah, she had never seen a legendary beauty and thought her face to be reasonably attractive.

After staring for a few moments at the arch of her eyebrows and the curve of her jaw, she had an idea. Undoing the tightly coiled braid at the nape of her neck, she quickly took the braid out and allowed her natural curls to frame her face. The difference was amazing. The curls seemed to give her face a youth and vitality that was lost in the harsh lines of her normally severe hairstyle.

She loved the way it looked, and examined it from all directions. This was her best feature, she was sure. But a woman could not go around with her hair unbound. It just wasn't done. She might get away with going about with her natural bosom, but to leave her hair loose was just not going to be possible.

She leaned way back, trying to get a better view of how she might look at a distance. Perhaps, she could leave it loose just around the cabin so that Henry Lee could see it. He would wonder at that, of course. She thought that maybe she could have it loose, seemingly by accident, and then he would see it. Maybe when he came in to eat, she would act as if he had surprised her and flutter around with it hanging loose while getting him some food.

She let her mind drift over the plan. Suddenly the expression on her face hardened and she grabbed her riotous curls and began roughly to rebraid them in her usual severe style.

"No more tricks!" she exclaimed out loud. She was not going to be dishonest with Henry Lee again. If the fiasco at the wellhouse had taught her anything, it was that tricks can have a way of backfiring.

She scolded herself for being foolish, sitting around trying to make a silk purse out of a sow's ear, while there was work to be done. She grabbed her dress off the bed and started to put it on, when she caught sight of her breast binder. She picked up the binder, holding it for a moment, then she carefully folded it and placed it in the bottom of her trunk. Pulling her sewing basket from under the bed, she began taking out the darts in the bodice of her dress.

When Henry Lee came in for his noon meal, he felt slightly ill at ease. He didn't know exactly how he would tell Hannah that he was headed to Ingalls. He wished that he had a surefire excuse for going there other than the truth. He didn't want to explain too much. The more lies he told the worse things would be ultimately. He would tell her tomorrow, he decided. This whole thing was just getting too complicated to handle.

Hannah was just as uncomfortable with Henry Lee. In her newly-altered dress and her natural bustline, she felt like a spectacle. She tried to keep her back to him as much as possible while she was finishing up the meal. Henry Lee, who had his own problems on his mind, hardly noticed. Finally, Hannah knew that she couldn't delay any longer. She had to face him. Gathering her courage she picked up a bowl of green beans and new potatoes and turned to the table. Unfortunately, Henry Lee was just taking a sip of his coffee. When Hannah turned to face him his eyes were immediately drawn to the undeniable sudden change in his wife's anatomy and his response was to abruptly inhale the coffee. Gasping and choking for breath, Henry Lee recovered himself as Hannah hurried over to him patting him on the back. Her face flamed red with embarrassment and she fervently wished that the floor would suddenly open up and allow her to fall in. It did not, however, and she was forced to sit down and eat with Henry Lee, while pretending that nothing out of the ordinary had occurred.

Henry Lee, for his part, tried very hard to keep his eyes solely on his wife's face. It was such a shock. He realized that she must have been wearing a binder. A lot of women did. He had never cared for the practice himself. He should have realized before that she was bigger than she normally appeared. His memory of her bared breasts as they had lain together on the kitchen floor was disturbing and forced Henry Lee's glance back to Hannah's shapely contour.

He wondered why she had decided to go without the binder. Obviously, it wasn't an accident. She was as aware of the change as he was. Maybe it was the heat. The heat today was tremendous. But, he recalled, she had worn it all during the canning when the kitchen must have been twice as bad as it was now.

The baby, of course, he suddenly realized. Her body was undoubtedly changing. He knew enough about pregnant women to know that their stomachs weren't the only part of their bodies affected. He remembered his mother complaining of soreness in her breasts as one of the first signs of carrying a child.

Apparently, Hannah's breasts had bothered her enough to make her leave off the binder. He felt a strange need to comfort her. He hated the idea that she might hurt or be in pain. Now she was embarrassed because he'd acted like such a fool when he'd seen her. He wanted to take the embarrassment away. He wanted to get her mind on something else.

"I'm going to Ingalls this afternoon," he said bluntly. "I won't be back until real late, like last time I went out."

Hannah's face must have revealed her distress at the memory of the last time Henry Lee came home late, because he quickly hurried on, "I won't be drinking tonight, Hannah. You needn't be worrying about that."

"Oh, I wasn't," she said, truthfully. She was not worrying, she was almost hoping.

"I'm not really a drinking man," he said, wanting to explain, wanting her to understand. "My father was a drunk, I know all about trying to live with them. I won't put you through that, Hannah, I hope you know that."

"I know," she answered quietly.

The lull in the conversation lengthened as both carefully avoided the eyes of the other and studiously involved themselves with the food on their plates.

Henry Lee was trying not to think about Hannah's bosom, when he suddenly thought of a good reason to go to Ingalls.

"I'll be checking on the trains for our trip to Sallisaw," he told her, quite elated at his own inventiveness.

Hannah looked up at him, surprised and pleased.

"You truly don't have to take me with you, Henry Lee. I know that Myrtie sort of pushed you into that. It's such an expense and I'll be happy to stay here."

For an instant, Henry Lee was tempted. Not for the expense, money was not really a problem, but for the freedom. He would be gone two nights, he could stay in Muskogee and have himself one heck of a good time.

There were whores in Muskogee that were so hot they could scorch the hair off a man's chest . . .

"No, I want you with me," he said firmly, to convince both of them. "You can help me pick out the wood and it'll do us both good to get away for a few days and see something new."

"What about your pigs?" she asked. "There won't be anyone here to take care of them."

"Jones from Sandy Creek is always willing to watch things for me around here and I can let them out to forage. They do pretty good for themselves when I'm gone. They eat those acorns from the red oak and then go about distributing new red oaks all over the farm."

Hannah blushed at the indelicacy of this statement and then couldn't seem to stop herself from giggling. Her laughter warmed Henry Lee and made him glad that he had decided to take her with him.

A light summer rain shimmered down outside Hannah's window as she awakened early on Sunday morning. With a groan of pain, she rolled over onto her back and clutched her belly with her hands. She was one of those lucky women whose monthly visit of Eve's curse was never a surprise. Several hours prior to its onset, Hannah would fall victim to terrible cramps that would have kept a lesser woman in bed for the day. Hannah was, however, made of sterner stuff and considered the pain an annoying nuisance. This morning she wished that she could simply lie abed for a few hours and give in to self-indulgence. But it was Sunday morning, and to her knowledge, the only valid excuse for missing Sunday church service was death, and then only if it were your own.

Shaking off the desire to wallow in her own discomfort, she rolled out of bed. Searching through the drawers and petticoats among her clothing, she found her monthly paraphernalia and began girding herself for the onslaught of nature. The belt fit around her waist, secured by hook and eye. Running from the center front, through the legs and up the back was a snugly fitting, three-inch-wide band. The interior of the band was constructed to form a natural pocket to hold securely the folded strips of cheap cotton. When she had assured herself that she was properly prepared, Hannah completed her toilet, allowing herself only an occasional groan at the pains of being a woman.

Henry Lee, in contrast, felt wonderful this morning. Even the morning's rain could not dampen his enthusiasm. His trip to Ingalls had been very profitable. Word had spread of the demise of Pauly Archambo's still, and private citizen and saloon keeper alike were willing to pay premium prices for the commodity they feared to be in short supply.

Henry Lee had been able to get a third more than his usual price for whiskey with promises to buy much more. He had returned home with his pockets bulging with money and a spring in his step. He removed his strongbox from its hiding place in the floor near the fireplace and added his profits to the already generous pile of U.S. currency and gold. As long as the shortage kept up, his financial picture could only get better.

Henry Lee, of course, had no intention of alleviating the shortage. Keeping the price of whiskey high was to his advantage, and he fully intended to enjoy it for as long as it lasted.

The whiskey problem had had another pleasurable consequence for Henry Lee. The shortage overshadowed the story of his hasty marriage to the Plainview preacher's daughter and he was not forced to parry many personal questions.

With things going so well for him, he'd decided to definitely tell Hannah about his business interests. He had convinced himself that Hannah's practicality would win out over any silly beliefs in the intrinsic evil of strong drink, and that she would ultimately be pleased at Henry Lee's obvious ability to provide well for her and her child. His business was becoming more successful, and he wanted to share his excitement with his wife.

As he came in from the barn, he heard Hannah before he saw her. She was making quiet groaning noises and as he watched her through the door, it was evident by her slow, unenthusiastic movements that she was not feeling very well. Henry Lee felt an immediate concern for her. What if something was wrong with the baby? The nearest doctor was in Ingalls and he hadn't given a thought to who he would call upon to help when the baby came. He didn't know any midwives, and he hadn't asked.

"Hannah, are you all right?" he called to her through the screen.

Hannah was startled and blushed. It was bad enough to have these periodic cramps, but for someone else to know, especially if that someone was a man, was horribly embarrassing.

Not quite able to meet his eyes, she answered, "Oh I'm fine, Henry Lee. Just feeling a little bit lazy this morning."

Henry Lee didn't believe her. He had known her only a couple of weeks, but he doubted that there was a lazy bone in the woman's entire body. She seemed always energetic and busy. Something must be wrong.

It was then that Henry Lee noticed the bodice of her dress. He cursed under his breath as he realized that she had retrieved her breast binder and was once again flattened down to a woman half her size. Obviously she had not been able to forget the embarrassment he had caused her yesterday and now she was willing to be in pain rather than draw attention to herself.

This lovely woman was suffering pain because he had acted like such a fool. He wanted to apologize, to tell her that she was free to go unbound and that he would not look at her like that again. Of course, he would look at her, he was looking at her now, but he would sincerely try to keep his eyes on more appropriate areas.

Sitting down to breakfast, Henry Lee went over several plans for explaining to her that she needn't bind herself on his account. He sighed in frustration that a man had to choose his words so carefully when talking with a decent woman. With whores and dance hall girls a man could just say whatever he felt like saying, but with a woman like Hannah, Henry Lee knew that he would be expected to mind his tongue. He should just tell her that it was unnatural and surely unhealthy. He knew, however, that ladies never use the words breast or bosom in mixed company and he wasn't sure how in the world he was going to talk about something without ever mentioning it.

Hannah ate her breakfast in silence, not giving a thought to her bound bosom. She had not remembered to alter her Sunday dress, so she was forced to wear the binder again. She hardly noticed it, however. All her focus was on the twisting, shuddering ache in her lower abdomen. She wanted to just lean over and wrap herself into a tight ball to hold back the pain, but it was imperative that she not make a scene in front of Henry Lee. She wondered briefly if all women continued to hide from their husbands the fact of their normal body functions throughout their marriage. Practically speaking, Hannah thought that was ridiculous. But the idea of actually discussing "the curse" with a man was too humiliating to even be considered.

The rain had let up by the time the two were climbing into the buggy. Henry Lee solicitously covered Hannah's lap with the folded tarp, so that a sudden downpour would not catch her unaware. At the last minute he grabbed up his tool box from the shed and set it beneath the buggy seat.

"I thought I'd take some measurements while you are visiting after church," he explained.

Hannah almost sighed in despair. The last thing that she wanted to spend time doing today was standing around visiting while she waited on Henry Lee. She smiled courageously, however, and silently prayed that he would not take too long.

As the buggy made its way gingerly through the soggy roads, Henry Lee decided if he couldn't actually relieve her pain, the least he could do was to take her mind off of it. He decided to tell her outrageous stories about outlaws and Indians in the territory. Turning on the charm, he was determined to get his new wife to laugh, or at the very least, to smile.

"Let me tell you about the time I met Little Breeches," Henry Lee started. The female outlaw, Jennie Stevens, was a diminutive young woman who had ridden with the Wild Bunch, Dalton and Doolin's infamous gang of bank and train robbers.

"You met Little Breeches?" Hannah asked, immediately distracted.

"Yes, ma'am," he answered, "she was sitting as close to me as you are right now." Actually, he thought, she had been a good deal closer. The amoral little tramp had come on to Henry Lee like wax on a hot stove.

"Was she pretty? What was she like? What did she say?"

Hannah's innocent curiosity pleased him and he wanted to tell a good story that would hold her interest. The actual truth, that the vicious little bandit supported herself, before her arrest, by "unlawfully dealing in ardent spirits in Indian Territory" and that a good portion of those ardent spirits were purchased from Henry Lee Watson, was not a story he thought Hannah could appreciate.

"She wasn't ugly," Henry Lee told her, "but I wouldn't have said she was a pretty woman. She was so tiny, she barely came up to my chest, with such little hands and feet, it was hard to imagine her out robbing and killing. She dressed in men's clothes, said she felt more comfortable in them. And she said that you couldn't strap a six-shooter to your leg if you were wearing a skirt."

Hannah laughed and blushed at that. Why would a woman want to strap a six-shooter to her leg!

"She chewed tobacco," Henry Lee told her, his eyes sparkling with amusement. "She used to see how far she could spit and challenge the men around to outdistance her."

As they drove through the damp, gray morning, Henry Lee continued to elaborate on his story, entertain-

ing his new wife and enjoying the melodious sound of
her throaty laughter.

Henry Lee told her about his trip to Ingalls. He
wished he could tell her about his business success, but
decided that would have to wait.

"I got the tickets to Sallisaw," he stated matter-of-
factly.

Hannah immediately put aside her discomfort to rel-
ish the excitement.

"When are we going?" she asked, her voice almost
childlike in its eagerness.

"A week from Thursday," he told her. "We'll pick
up the Atchison, Topeka and Sante Fe to Tulsa, then
switch to the Katy to Muskogee." Her enthusiasm seemed
to be infectious and Henry Lee found himself smiling and
eager. "We'll spend the night in Muskogee and then take
the Iron Mountain to Sallisaw early in the morning and
back to Muskogee that evening to spend another night
before heading home."

"We're to spend two nights in Muskogee?" Hannah
asked almost in awe. Henry Lee couldn't help but notice
her amazement and was suddenly very pleased that he
had insisted that she go with him.

"Where will we stay?" she asked. "Do you have
friends in Muskogee?"

Henry Lee did have a few friends there, but none he
would risk introducing to his wife. The wheel of the
buggy hit a rut and Hannah was thrown up against him.
Henry Lee put his arm around her waist to steady her
and then liked the feel of it so much that he kept it there.

"We'll stay in a hotel," he said. "The Adams was the
best, of course, but it burned down in the big fire of
eighty-nine. Nearly the whole area down by the Katy
went up in smoke, but they've been rebuilding like crazy,
and I'm sure that we'll be able to find a nice new place
to stay."

Clearly enjoying himself, Henry Lee offered her a
self-satisfied grin and began to reminisce about other
times he had stayed over in Muskogee.

"I used to stay at Mitchell's Hotel 'cause it was clean

and cheap and the food was edible. But one night I was there with some friends, and they convinced me that I should stay at Strokey's. They said that they always stayed there, because they liked it better than Mitchell's." Shaking his head and laughing Henry Lee continued, "It wasn't until late that night that I found out why they preferred it. Mr. Strokey was not too particular about the cleanliness of his sheets, and he let the cowhands all sleep with their boots on. Muskogee was a rough town and no one wanted to be caught barefooted!"

Hannah giggled at the image of Henry Lee, whom she already knew to be fastidious, sleeping in a bed wearing dirty boots.

Her laugh had its usual effect on her husband and he smiled down at Hannah as if she were the most entertaining and attractive woman he had ever come across.

Henry Lee's well-practiced charm was heartstopping for an inexperienced woman like Hannah. In the damp, gray morning chill, she felt inexplicably warm.

"I didn't hear you come in last night," she said a little breathlessly. "You must have been very quiet."

"When those chairs don't jump in my way, I'm like a little mouse," he teased. "Though I was a mite tempted to fall down on my face, just for the pleasure of having you rescue me."

Hannah blushed at the way that he drew out the word pleasure as if it were five syllables long. She had wondered if he really remembered pulling her down to the floor with him. Obviously he did, and if his current boyish grin was any indication, he remembered it fondly.

Hannah was still slightly flushed when they reached Plainview Church and Henry Lee was feeling expansive. He was a successful businessman, a contributor to the church, and the contented husband of a terribly respectable woman with a throaty laugh and a marvelous bottom.

After securing the buggy, the two walked through the crowd gathered outside. Henry Lee stopped and spoke to each and every one, admiring a baby here and flirting with an elderly widow there. It came naturally to him, making friends in the crowd. It was the one useful thing he had learned from Skut Watson. As a businessman, he made himself welcome wherever he went.

Hannah, who was once again being bothered by cramps, did not linger with her husband but continued on toward the church, wanting nothing more than a place to sit down. She went inside, but the sanctuary was still empty. Deciding that sitting in the church alone would make her look unsociable, she started to return to the yard when she heard two women talking on the steps.

"He is such a personable young man," Flora Maycomb was saying to Maude Ruskin, "it's such a shame. Think of the good work he could do if he were in the Lord's service."

"Don't you be getting soft on me, Flora," her companion warned. "Putting perfume on cow manure doesn't make it something you want to bring in your house. Just because Reverend Bunch has let his foolish daughter marry up with him doesn't mean he's still not the Devil's right-hand man in this territory."

Hannah could not stifle the gasp that escaped her lips. The two women turned and stared dumbfounded. Both had been the recipient of numerous acts of generosity from the Bunch family and they both stood, embarrassed that their loose tongues should be overheard by Hannah.

Hannah was more than furious, she was outraged that these supposedly upright, decent women could judge a fine man like Henry Lee. Just because he did not attend church on a regular basis did not in any way make him the Devil's right-hand man and Hannah had half a mind to tell them so. But she decided to let the silly women stew in their own narrow little prejudices.

"Excuse me," she said pushing past them to join her husband.

Through the entire church service Hannah managed to maintain her righteous indignation. She was so angry at those spiteful women, she couldn't even hear a word her father was preaching. She glanced numerous times at Henry Lee and he would meet her look with a quiet smile.

Each time she became more incensed that such a fine man should be the subject of backbiting in her own father's congregation. She wanted to avenge him. She wanted to make it up to him. She wanted to protect him. All her instincts as mother, sister, daughter, and wife merged into one cord of strength that now bound her to her husband. When he was welcomed, she was welcomed. When he was respected, she was respected. And when he was insulted, she was insulted. She wasn't exactly sure when this bond had occurred, but it was firmly in place and she felt no need to tamper with it.

By the time the service ended she was in a boiling rage and could barely offer a civil word to anyone. Her sister-in-law Earline couldn't even divert her with the baby. Hannah was angry at the whole congregation. Not one of them—except her father of course—had ever tried to get to know Henry Lee. He had not, to her knowledge, ever been invited to participate in church activities. Hannah was certain that this slight was merely because he wasn't one of them. He was a mixed breed; he hadn't come from Kansas to raise corn or wheat, so he obviously was undeserving of the comforts of the Lord's house!

She briefly thought of her own past opinion of Henry Lee. She had been wrong, dreadfully wrong. But now, shown the error of her ways, she had every intention of seeing that the rest of the congregation followed suit.

Henry Lee was completely at a loss to explain Hannah's behavior. It was obvious to him that she was mad as a wet hen about something, but he didn't know what. As he hurried through his measurements, it occurred to him that someone must have told her about his whiskey business. That was really the only thing that it could be. However, she didn't seem to be mad at him. All through the church service, each time he looked over at her, they shared a smile. It was possible, he decided, that she had learned the truth, but remained on his side. The idea that she knew all, understood, and he would not have to tell her, lightened his work and hurried his step. He could hardly wait to get back to the buggy.

They quickly took leave of the family and headed out.

Hannah's mind was overflowing with plans to prove to the congregation that her husband was a finer man than any of them.

The rain had disappeared and the sun was peeking through mountains of thick fluffy clouds. Henry Lee smelled the soft sweet smell of the prairie after a good rain. It made him feel happy and alive and he wanted Hannah to feel the same way.

They rode along in silence as Henry Lee waited for Hannah to bring up the subject. As the miles passed, the anticipation got to be too much and he decided that he must get her talking.

"Well, Mrs. Watson," he said turning to her and gesturing to the heavens, "the storm clouds seem to have left the sky, but it looks like they found a home in your eyes."

Hannah had the good grace to blush.

"On a beautiful day like today," Henry Lee continued, "a pretty woman such as yourself should be smiling and singing and the like. Have I done something to make you look as if you've been eating persimmons?"

"I like persimmons," she answered smiling for the first time. "Sometimes sour tastes better than sweet."

"I'm learning that," Henry Lee answered. "Your green tomato pie was as good as any apple or peach I'd ever eaten, but there wasn't a bit of sweetness to it. Kind of like your temperament this morning," he teased. "Are you still feeling poorly?"

Hannah's cheeks burned as she assumed that he referred to her monthly indisposition.

"I'm feeling much better now," she answered truthfully and deliberately changed the subject. "I overheard some gossip at church and it put me in a bit of an uncivil frame of mind."

Henry Lee steeled himself for her reaction. She *had* heard about his business, he wished again that he had already told her himself. At least, if she was going to cause trouble about it, he would have been more prepared.

As a part of his business, Henry Lee had dealt with

his share of angry customers who were priced out, delivered late, or otherwise dissatisfied with his whiskey. He decided to handle Hannah the same way he did them. Let her yell and complain all she wanted, he'd keep his voice low and agreeable and eventually she'd talk herself out. She had a right to be angry, but she'd come around after a bit and see that the business would be good for her and their family.

"Tell me what happened," he said gently.

"I just get so mad sometimes," she explained. "Some people are just irredeemable hypocrites."

"Oh?"

"Well." Hannah reconsidered. "They might not be irredeemable, but they certainly are beyond my forgiveness today."

Henry Lee took a deep breath, hoping for the best. "What did these unforgivable hypocrites do?"

Hannah didn't want to embarrass Henry Lee or make him feel unwelcome in the church, but she wanted him to know that the opinion of some was not her opinion, and that she intended to change the opinions of all. She decided to modify the truth so as not to hurt his feelings.

"I overheard two old gossips commenting on how you weren't a regular churchgoer before we married, and suggesting that you are more of a sinner than they."

Hannah missed the conflict of emotions that raced across Henry Lee's face as she continued. "The problem is that they really don't know you. To them, just because you didn't live in Kansas or Nebraska with the rest of us, you are somehow suspect. I have come to know you, in the last few weeks, and I know that there is no question that you are a fine, respectable Christian man. Why you weren't accepted into the congregation immediately is a complete mystery to me!"

Hannah turned to him and smiled brightly. "I don't want you worrying about a thing, I'm going to straighten everything out. I intend to tell each and every person in that congregation what an upstanding gentleman you are. Why, most of them wouldn't dream of trading with the Negroes or having friends visit who are Indian or crippled. You are a better Christian than all of them, and I definitely intend to tell them so."

Had she turned to glance at her husband at that time, she would have seen his look of horror. Not only was she unaware of the truth, she was forming plans to make herself look like the biggest fool in the Twin Territories. "Hannah, I don't think you should do that."

"Oh, yes, I should!" she insisted. "It's the truth and it's time people knew it. Why, I admit myself, that before we married, I thought you were some kind of ne'er-do-well. I never heard anything good about you. The way people talked I thought you spent all your time going to parties and such."

Henry Lee was stung with her confession. She had thought him worthless, good enough to give her child a name, but nothing more. She'd married him so her sin wouldn't taint any of those fine men in her church. His hurt hardened into anger. If she thought those women at the church were hypocrites, she was certainly the pot calling the kettle black.

"Hannah, I don't care what those people think of me." His jaw was set stubbornly and his speech defiant. "I know what kind of man I am, and I've learned to let the judgments of other people wash right over me. If those church people learn to accept me as I am and respect me, well that's fine. If they can't do that, well that's fine too. I'm not going to let you try to make people accept me. That's not my way. Understand this," he finished with an undertone of anger, "I am what I am and I don't care what they think."

"But," Hannah argued, "I care what they think. They've been my friends and family all my life and I want them to like my husband."

"Oh, I see," he answered, allowing the sting of his anger to surface as he passed the reins into one hand and ran the other distractedly through his thick black hair. "You don't care for *my* sake, just for your own. You want a respectable husband! Well, maybe you should have made your wedding plans a little bit more carefully!"

Hannah was surprised at his anger and embarrassed

that he'd brought up that awful trick she had played in the wellhouse. She couldn't understand why he'd lost his temper. All she wanted was for the church people to be able to appreciate him. Why did he seem so intent on maintaining a reputation that he didn't deserve?

"I'm not thinking of myself, Henry Lee," Hannah insisted as she tentatively reached out to touch his sleeve. "These people are wrong about you and they need to see the error of their ways. I fully intend to explain, very lovingly, that the congregation has not been as neighborly or as generous as you deserve."

"No," Henry Lee's voice carried authority, "you will not speak to anyone about me at all. I forbid you to discuss me with the congregation of Plainview Church or with anyone!"

Hannah was shocked at his vehemence. "Surely you don't mean to forbid me, Henry Lee?" she asked, removing her hand from his coat and laying it primly in her lap. "I'm only doing my Christian duty."

"Your duty, Mrs. Watson, is to follow the wishes of your husband. I have said that you will not discuss it and you will not discuss it."

Hannah was stunned into speechlessness.

Henry Lee drove into the yard rushing his horses and with his anger barely under control. Pulling up to a stop near the back door, he quickly pulled on the hand brake and jumped down from the buggy. Reaching up to Hannah he grabbed her around the waist and set her on her feet with more force than was actually necessary.

"And another thing," he said in the same harsh demanding tone. "I don't want to see you in this ridiculous breast binder again. It makes no sense to torture your body because you're afraid that your husband might get a good look at you!"

ELEVEN

Henry Lee Watson handled his outbursts of temper by busying himself with something else. Hard work was his solace and he indulged wholeheartedly in it after their return from church.

He had planned to start cooking the mash, but the calmness and patience necessary for good whiskey making were lacking in his current mood. His mother had always said that when she was angry or sad, you could taste the bitterness in the food she cooked. Henry Lee figured the same would undoubtedly apply to moonshine whiskey. With his blood all riled up and pounding through his veins, he wouldn't be able to take the time and care that made his corn liquor so fine.

With that in mind, he spent the afternoon doing a task that flourished with anger, chopping wood. He needed to sweat and pound that inanimate stump to release the choler that was churning inside of him.

Her former opinion of him rankled, but more than that he was angry at himself. He knew why she had married him. He should be beyond being bothered by it. He didn't want her child to be an ever-present barrier between them. The child existed, the child was not his, she married him to give the child a name. Knowing the facts, it was past time to let that anger go. He remembered how it was with his parents. Whenever they fought, whether it was over money, or his father's drinking, or predicting the weather, no matter how the argu-

162

ment started, before it was over Skut would bring the circumstances of Henry Lee's birth into the fray.

As Henry Lee plowed through a piece of post oak, he remembered his father's angry words. "I'm saddled for life with some soldier boy's mixed breed brat 'cause Miss Molly couldn't keep her damn drawers on."

Even in retrospect, Henry Lee still burned with the embarrassment and humiliation. A lowlife like Skut Watson felt free to look down on him because his father was just some man that got between his mother's legs.

Slamming the axe down and through the wood he swore to himself Hannah's child would never suffer as he had suffered. That child would never know that Henry Lee was not his father. He would talk to him, teach him what he knew about whiskey and wood. Show him how to plow a straight furrow and judge a good horse. The child would never hear a word of doubt about his heritage, unless Hannah told the child herself.

The idea that she might do that, that she might think that the child would rather know himself fathered by someone other than Henry Lee momentarily rekindled his still glowing anger. No, he decided, Hannah wouldn't do that. And he would be such a good father to the child, Hannah would see that she had made the right choice. She would just have to learn to stay out of things that didn't really concern her. And she'd have to learn to live with a man who made his living with moonshine whiskey. If that didn't suit her, it was just too bad. Angry she was bound to be when she found out, but she'd adjust. Henry Lee just wished that she already knew. But in his present mood, he'd botch the entire confession.

Sunday dinner in the Watson household was uncustomarily quiet. Henry Lee noticed both the sumptuously prepared meal and the mild-spoken and demure wife with the enticingly curvaceous figure. He realized that Hannah was making every effort to placate him. He wasn't sure if he should thank her or apologize. In the silence between them, Henry Lee concentrated on the making of the whiskey. That was something that he understood. Whiskey making was an art, but it did not demand self-assessment, and it never got its feelings hurt.

Tonight he would begin the distillation process. The mash had to cook over an even, gentle fire for three or four days and would have to be watched almost constantly around the clock. The fire must be kept hot enough to make the vapor without cooking down, but not so hot that it carried too much steam or it might scorch the mash. In the extreme heat of the still, pressure built up fast and the danger of explosion was very real.

Normally, he would take his supplies up to his cave and just live there until the whiskey was done. With Hannah here, she would expect him to come for meals and to sleep in the cabin at night.

He had no idea what kind of excuse he could use for his absence. At least they weren't sharing a bed, that would have made it even more difficult to explain.

Getting up from the meal, he complimented and thanked her politely, and then brought her a bolt of sturdy cotton calico in a dark blue print.

"I got this for you over at Ingalls. I was figuring that you'd be needing a new traveling dress for our trip to Sallisaw."

Hannah accepted the material with almost reverence. It looked to be a fine piece of cloth, peacock-blue with a pattern of pale gray, almost silvery, leaves running diagonally from the bias. Although calico did not come as dear as it once had, she knew that her husband must have paid a good bit for it.

"I've got a lot of work to do around the place, if we are going to be gone for three days," Henry Lee told her. "I'm going to rig you up a dinner bell out here on the back step. When you've got a meal ready, or if you be needing me for something, you just clang that old bell a few times and I'll be right here."

"Of course," Hannah answered, wondering what kind of work he would be doing, and why he wasn't asking her to help out.

"With the heat being like it's been," he went on,

turning slightly away so that he wouldn't have to actually look her in the eye, "I've been thinking to set my bed up outside somewhere."

"You're going to sleep outside?" Hannah was incredulous.

"Can't draw a decent breath in the house this time of year," he explained lamely. "But don't you worry for a minute. If you need something, you just bang on that dinner bell and I'll be down here in a flash. No need for you to be afraid around here."

"I'm not afraid of anything," Hannah said. But she had run her husband out of his own house, and that was the thing that frightened her most.

It was late in the evening before Henry Lee got the still operating. The big copper pot, looking much like a giant teakettle, sat on a grate above the fire. He filled the pot with the sour mash and sealed the lip on with putty.

Attaching the extra long teakettle-like spout to a long spindly copper coil called a worm, Henry Lee ran it from the still and into a half barrel placed so that the cool water from the spring would pour over it. From there the coil wound its way into a large earthen jug.

As the mash cooked, the alcohol vapor would escape by flowing down the worm. As the vapor passed through the cold coil it would condense into liquid and drip into the earthen jug.

The drops arriving from the wedding batch were still singlings, and singlings were not fit for drinking. In some cases they were outright poison. The still would be cleaned and the singlings would be run through another time to make doublings, or drinking whiskey.

Although it was necessary for the distiller to be at the still constantly to ensure that nothing untoward happened, there was not really a great deal of work involved. All he did was watch the fire and listen to the liquor drip into the jug.

To pass the time while cooking the wedding batch Henry Lee had brought to the cave half a stack of cut pine lumber. He was going to attempt to copy a piece of

furniture called a Dufold that he had seen in the Sears &
Roebuck catalog.

By day the Dufold looked like a settee, totally innocu-
ous. But at night, the back folded down and the seat
folded out to form a bed. Henry Lee had decided that this
would be ideal for his room at the cabin.

He was still embarrassed that Hannah's father had
seen him bringing his cot into the house. He couldn't
imagine what the preacher had thought, but no one else
was going to suspect a thing. The Dufold would ensure
that.

He examined the pictures closely in the light of the
fire. It would take some hardware and more upholstering
than he was wont to do, but he thought he could build
it—and for a lot less money than they were asking in the
Sears & Roebuck catalog.

Hannah also spent a very productive evening. She
had taken a small corner of the pretty calico and was
soaking it in a pailful of water and a teaspoon of sugar of
lead, to make sure that it was colorfast. Then she'd
searched through her sewing chest for the perfect pattern.
The bolt was a good dress length with enough material
for two waists and a skirt. Since the bodice of a gown
wore out more swiftly than the length, it was common-
place to make a dress last twice as long by having the
skirt do double duty.

The style she selected for the skirt looked somewhat
plain from a distance, but it was slightly gored and fit a
bit snugly at the hips, flaring at the hemline. The waist
was gathered, but most of the fullness was concentrated
on the sides and in the center of the back, where a small,
soft pad could be inserted for a hint of a bustle.

It was an extremely flattering shape, and Hannah,
who had never cared much about her clothes other than
their cleanliness, was suddenly excited about wearing it.

For the bodice she picked out a mannish new style
with pleats over the shoulders and a tailored collar. It
would need a silk tie of sorts and Hannah rifled through
all her scraps and ribbons trying to find something that

would make the right contrast. She'd almost given up when she remembered her straw bonnet.

Quickly shifting through the boxes and wrappings she pulled it out and removed it from its tissue protection. It had come from the Montgomery Ward catalog. Myrtie had seen it and just couldn't live without it. She'd pestered her father until he finally agreed to put it in the next order that he sent. When it came, she had been heartbroken. It hadn't occurred to her that her coiffure would never fit under the tiny little headpiece. After several days of experimentation she'd finally given up and handed it over to Hannah whose severe hairstyle could be accommodated by the stylish lacing of straw.

Hannah had hardly worn it. It was saucy and attractive, but it sat back, framing the face, and didn't shade one ray of midday heat. The purpose of a bonnet was to keep the sun off a woman's face, and Hannah had no use for anything that didn't do its job.

Laying the silk trim tie ribbons against the calico now, a pleased smile broke out on Hannah's face. It was absolutely perfect. The pale blue silk turned silvery next to the calico. A modiste couldn't have made a better match.

With a cheerful little laugh, she started to remove the trim from the bonnet, but stopped herself to try it on one more time. Hurrying to the mirror, she admired herself. It wasn't really such a bad little hat. It gave her face some of the same fullness she noticed when she'd had her hair down. Perhaps she shouldn't discard it?

She thought about how smart the silk ties would look with the tailored bodice. When the solution came like a flash of inspiration she giggled out loud. She'd use the silk for the necktie and re-trim the bonnet in the matching calico.

"Those Muskogee ladies will think I'm from St. Louie!" she warned her mirror with a laugh.

After two days of seeing Henry Lee only for a few minutes at mealtimes, Hannah had begun to believe that perhaps Henry Lee actually did despise her, even though he'd bought her the gift of calico. For breakfast, dinner, and supper she would clang the bell by the back step and within a few moments he would arrive to eat. Rarely did he say more than a couple of words; he wolfed down his food and headed back out the door.

She had tried to draw him into conversation, but he would not be drawn. She asked numerous ridiculous questions for which she already knew the answers, in the hopes of involving him in the house and yard. He simply replied that she should do what she thought best, and seemed unconcerned that she was suddenly helpless and without opinion.

Henry Lee's concentration was obviously focused elsewhere. Where she did not know.

When she heard a horse arrive in the middle of the afternoon on the third day of Henry Lee's withdrawal, she was just grateful to have someone to talk with.

The news, however, was not good. The visitor was Young Newt Hensley, Newton's second boy and a member of Elijah Brown's Negro church. Old Man Hensley, Newt's grandfather, had passed away that morning while hoeing weeds in the garden. Young Newt was sent to see if Henry Lee would make the old man a coffin.

"Pa says pine is all right," he told Hannah. "He don't want nothing too fancy, but he's just no good with carpentry and he wants Granddaddy to rest in a good strong box."

Hannah watched the boy take a deep swallow, trying to control the grief that trembled in his lower lip and moistened his eyes, but wisely refrained from comforting him. After raising her brothers through those difficult in-between years, she learned that doing and saying nothing was sometimes the best course of action.

"You had best talk about what you want with my husband," she told him. Clanging on the dinner bell several times, the two waited by the back step. Hannah brought the boy a bit of light bread with jelly to eat.

"Would you mind eating up some of this?" she asked hoping to take his mind off his troubles. "I suppose I just made too much of this bread this week and if somebody doesn't eat it up, it will just go to waste."

The boy took the bread with a nod agreeing to help her get rid of it.

"Those no-account chickens were thinking I'd be giving it to them, but we've fooled them, haven't we." The note of exaggerated conspiracy brought a hint of a smile to the young man's cheeks.

When Henry Lee approached at a hurried lope, she left the two to discuss business between themselves.

Henry Lee had made plenty of coffins in his lifetime. It wasn't a very pleasant job, but he knew from experience it was easier if the coffin was not for your own kin. He didn't really want to take the time out to do it, but just that morning he'd finished the singlings, so he could leave his still cold and start it up again when he returned. The young boy's earnest attempt to act the man of business touched Henry Lee and he promised to make the coffin that evening and bring it over before the funeral in the morning.

As Young Newt rode off, Hannah emerged from the house.

"Are you making Mr. Hensley's coffin?"

"Yes," he replied raising his arms to stretch high over his head and yawning. He slept only in bits and starts during the distilling and after two days he was feeling pretty worn out.

"I told him that I would make it this evening and bring it over in the morning before the funeral."

"Good. I felt so sad for him, death is so hard to understand when you're young."

"Yes." Henry Lee nodded and the eyes of the two unexpectedly met. He shared a gentle smile with her.

"I was about his age when my mama died," Henry Lee said and then remembering what Preacher Farnam had told him added, "You lost your mother back then, too."

As their eyes held, they each were suddenly aware of the other in a new way. Able to see the hurt, the fear, the unreasonable confusion of suddenly having the focus of youthful existence cease. They could both remember that childhood vision of the future as an empty blackness.

They had looked around for a word of comfort, only to find that they must face their grief alone. Each had decided to persevere, to relinquish childhood, in order to fulfil the day-to-day tasks of life, to accept the numbness of the moment, and do what had to be done. The shared memory of that suffering built a tenuous bond between the two and as Henry Lee reached to take her hand it whisked away the troubles of the past few days. Neither of them had ever shared that feeling of cold empty anger that had ravaged their innocent dreams. Now, with a look in each other's eyes, they saw a mirror image of the devastation each had faced, and the triumph each had achieved. And their joined hands were the first link either had ever allowed for sharing that heartbreak.

Henry Lee saw Hannah as she was, compassionate and resolved. Willing to take on the sorrows of others because she felt herself more able to bear them. Her strength didn't stem from an indomitable will or an inflexible nature, but from the need to be strong, to be constant and unshakable for those around her.

Hannah suddenly understood that Henry Lee's light and frivolous nature was the brightly shining paper and ribbon on a package that contained immutability, intelligence, and a determination to succeed, not despite his heritage, but rather because of it.

The two stood transfixed, stunned by the sudden insight into the soul of the other and the knowledge that the ground they were treading was, for the moment, not a solid firmament.

Henry Lee looked away first, almost embarrassed by the depth of feeling that had come upon him.

"Guess I'd better get started if I intend to finish before dark." He turned away, not quite sure how to take leave. Glancing back he saw her smiling at him. Smiling and something else . . . something more . . . but Henry Lee could not imagine what it was.

Hannah, for her part, didn't know what it was either. She was aware that her spirits had lifted significantly and that there didn't seem to be any logical explanation for it. She chided herself that she should be thinking about the

poor Hensley family and their grief. But every time she
tried to think of the Hensleys, Young Newt's face would
suddenly turn into a young Henry Lee. And he would be
looking at her that way, the way he had looked at her
outside. As if they could see inside each other's hearts.

When Henry Lee came in for supper, the heat from
the kitchen was overpowering and the smell of fresh
baked bread was in the air.

"You're baking bread this late in the day?" he asked
Hannah, knowing that the hot task was usually reserved
for early morning.

"I've made some yeast rolls for the Hensleys," she
answered. "You know how it is at funerals, so many people to feed and the family has neither the means nor the
stamina to feed them all."

Henry Lee smiled. She tried to make her actions seem
so efficient and practical, he thought, when really she's
so very sad for them.

"I don't really know much about funerals. I usually
just deliver the coffin and leave," he told her, prudently
not mentioning that liquor was another commodity that
he frequently delivered to the mourners.

"Well, we certainly don't have to stay if you don't
wish," she said. "But I would really like to take the rolls
and offer my condolences."

"You're going with me?"

Hannah's answer was wary. "If you prefer that I
don't, I . . ."

"No," Henry Lee assured her. "I just hadn't thought
about it, that's all. Of course you'll want to go," he
answered, thinking of her tender heart surrounded by
such a tough, practical facade. "And we can stay for the
funeral if you like."

After supper Henry Lee finished varnishing Old Man
Hensley's coffin.

His Dufold was finished enough to take down to the
house. And setting it up in the workroom, Henry Lee
tried every possible method to become comfortable. But
the strange interlude between himself and Hannah on the

back step had him as jumpy as a saloon girl at a Sunday School convention. He felt exposed and yet he didn't feel threatened.

He began to question the wisdom of waiting until after her baby was born to make her his wife. He didn't think it would bother him anymore to bed her. He chuckled to himself. No, it wouldn't bother him one bit, he wanted to bed her and he was only fooling himself if he tried to say otherwise.

Maybe it was even the right thing to do. Maybe after sharing her bed for the next six or seven months he wouldn't be able to imagine the child being any other than his own.

In a few days they would be in Muskogee. It would make perfect sense for them to share a room, and to share a room meant to share a bed. They would make it like a real honeymoon. A time away from the everyday problems of their lives to devote to each other and the commitment of marriage. Henry Lee was not too familiar with honeymoons, but he knew that being alone with a woman for three days and two nights could bring a good deal of understanding. He smiled to himself, it could also be a good deal of fun.

TWELVE

I t was a terrible day for a funeral. The trees rustled with a gentle whisper, the birds sang, and bees droned lazily in wildflowers by the roadside. The bright blue sky was powdered with high cirrus clouds that sauntered across the top of the heavens, with a cool northerly breeze making the morning seem fresh and springlike. In short, the weather was the antithesis of the mournful reality of death.

The Hensleys lived a good distance from Henry Lee's place, so they started out early to arrive at midmorning before the majority of the mourners. Although Henry Lee's wagon was well-sprung, it was not as comfortable as the buggy. In addition to the jostling, there was no top and Hannah didn't own a parasol, so she was forced to wear her bonnet down close, with the brim shading her eyes from the hot sun. It certainly would not do to show up at the funeral with a bright red nose and too much sun in her cheeks.

The wagon held the coffin. In the bright sunlight it was polished and pretty. Almost too pretty, Hannah thought, to put into the ground. There was also a caldron of butter beans cooked in fatback and a big basket of Hannah's yeast rolls. This made up her contribution to the funeral dinner. How food and funerals had become so closely tied in the communities of the prairie, Hannah did not know, but having a funeral with no dinner was tantamount to not saying words over the grave. It was as if the deceased was not much missed or deserving of the grief of the survivors. It was the responsibility of a preacher's wife to organize the dinner and Hannah, as her father's daughter, had instigated many a funeral meal and she knew that Reverend Brown's wife would be grateful for her help.

Lost in her own thoughts, she was unaware of Henry Lee's preoccupation. He had spent most of the night pacing his room and planning his future with Hannah. Now in the morning sun, he felt somewhat foolish. She was his wife, she'd made this bargain of her own free will. He had never wasted so much time and worry over a woman before. Of course, he'd never really had one that was his very own.

As he pulled his wagon into the shade in the Hensley's yard, the family began filing out of the house. Henry Lee helped his wife down from the wagon seat and then reaching into the wagon bed he retrieved the basket of rolls and handed them to Hannah. He carried the heavy kettle of butter beans himself, until they reached the porch where Young Newt relieved him of his burden, leaving Henry Lee standing on the porch with the menfolk, Newt Senior, his two brothers, his sister's husband, a couple of male cousins, and Reverend Brown.

"Good of you to come, Watson," the preacher told him, shaking his hand.

"Glad to do it." Henry Lee turned to Newt and his brothers. "I'm real sorry about your father. I didn't really know him much myself, but I've heard it said that he was a fine old gentleman."

His condolence conveyed sincerity and was gratefully accepted by the men. Hands were shaken all around, and when Newt took his he grasped it affectionately.

"I appreciate you making the coffin, Henry Lee," Newt said, "I can put together a bench or a chicken coop, but you got a way with wood that is mighty fine. I want my daddy to have the best."

"I know you do, Newt. And I think you'll be pleased." He gave him a hearty pat on the back. "Why don't you come on down to the wagon and have a look. If it suits you we can take it into the house."

As they headed back out into the yard Young Newt ran out to join them. In the clumsiness of his youth he allowed the screen door to slam loudly, which drew an immediate look of rebuke from his father and uncles. Henry Lee gave the young boy a private little smile of courage. The boy returned it shyly, grateful.

As they gathered around the wagon, Henry Lee drew back the tarp that protected the coffin from the sun and the dust. There was a moment of silence as each man realized how final today's events were.

Newt ran his hand over the beautifully finished wood with genuine tenderness. His reverence disconcerted Henry Lee, because he understood it. He quickly averted his eyes.

"This is very fine," Newt said at last. "It may take a while for me to pay you what I owe for this, Henry Lee, but it is what I want my daddy to have."

"It's only pine," Henry Lee said, wanting to quickly dispel any misconception about the price. "That's what the boy said to use. I just rubbed it up a little and put some roseberry shellac on it. Five dollars ought to cover it, pay me whenever you have a mind to."

Newt clasped his hand again. "I'm grateful."

They all stood together for another couple of minutes, exchanging small talk. It seemed strange to Henry Lee that no move was made to take the coffin into the house. It was as if they were collectively waiting for something to happen.

Finally, after an embarrassed glance toward the preacher one of Newt's brothers asked, "You got a jug on you, Henry Lee?"

Henry Lee glanced quickly at Reverend Brown. To his credit the preacher hurriedly masked his shocked expression and excused himself. Suddenly Henry Lee had an inexplicable wish that he were not in the whiskey business.

"We're not really drinking men," Newt explained,

"but when things like this happen, well, it just seems like a little snort would help a lot."

"I'm sorry," he began lamely, "I don't have a drop with me. I . . . I mean my wife . . ." Henry Lee didn't really know what he had planned to say, but whatever it was it didn't come out.

Newt raised his hand. "I know what you mean," he said. "My wife wouldn't approve neither, even if it does help. Somebody will show up with some sooner or later and if they don't, well, we'll just get through this the best we can."

Henry Lee nodded, thinking he was a hundred kinds of fool for forgetting. He was in the whiskey business, how in heaven's name could he have missed this opportunity?

"We best get this thing into the house," one of the cousins suggested.

Henry Lee and a couple of the younger men carried the coffin into the front parlor. Two dark-skinned women, who were sitting with the body, scurried away when the men arrived.

The old man was laid out on two boards strung between a couple of ladder-back chairs. The men set up a couple more chairs and placed the coffin between. Henry Lee opened the coffin and placed the lid standing on its side in front of it. This hid the chairs from view and gave the viewer less of the sense of a box.

"I'll send one of the women to lay him out again," Newt said retreating from the room. He was quickly followed by his brothers, cousins, and his brother-in-law until there was no one left except Henry Lee and Young Newt. Henry Lee wanted to leave also, but the body couldn't be left unattended and he didn't have the heart to leave Young Newt alone. The two stared at each other for a couple of minutes, the inactivity making them feel uncomfortable.

Henry Lee looked down at the body of the old man. He looked somewhat familiar, but he couldn't remember actually seeing him alive. He reached over and touched the white material that lay between the old man's body and the boards.

"Are they going to bury him with this tablecloth?" Henry Lee asked the boy.

"Yessir," he answered. "Mama says it was a wedding gift that he and Grandmama got when they married, and he ought to bring it up to heaven when he meets Grandmama."

Henry Lee nodded, understanding the strange blending of religion and superstition.

"I think the two of us can lay your granddaddy out just fine and save the womenfolk some grief."

The youngster nodded, soberly.

Henry Lee wrapped the body with the ends of the tablecloth and told Young Newt to grab his legs. The man weighed very little in his old age and was rigid as a load of kindling. It wasn't difficult for the two of them to lift him off the boards and up into the coffin. He unwrapped the body and carefully arranged the excess material of the tablecloth around it, making sure that none of the rough wood of the coffin interior was visible. When he assured himself that there was nothing more that he could do, he picked up the boards laying between the chairs and set them aside.

Newt's wife entered looking overworked but stoic. She was flanked by Hannah and another woman. Henry Lee glanced at his wife, as if to gather strength, and then grasped Mrs. Hensley's hand.

"Mrs. Hensley, I'm so sorry for your loss," he said glancing at his wife from the corner of his eye. "Young Newt and I went ahead and laid Mr. Hensley in the coffin. Come see if there is anything that we've neglected."

They made their way to the side of the coffin where Newt's wife looked down at her father-in-law and gently smoothed his hair.

"He looks right peaceful, don't he?"

The others agreed with her.

She turned to her son. "You and Mr. Watson done laid him out like this?"

"Yes, ma'am," the boy answered, a bit unsure.

"Thank you," she said to Henry Lee and then gave a gentle motherly hug to Young Newt, who beamed brightly at having finally done the right thing.

The afternoon sun blazed down on the gathered mourners at the grave side. Henry Lee and Hannah stood together as Elijah Brown gave the eulogy for the old man. The deep and melodious voice of the preacher was a comfort to those gathered.

"Brother Hensley loved these prairies," he said. "He started up his first place not far from here. He tried three different times to make a go of it in different parts of the territory, before he finally came down here to Sandy Creek with his son."

Many of those gathered had lived a similar life, moving from one place to another hoping to have better luck at the next plot of ground.

"All that time, all his whole life," the preacher went on, "Brother Hensley was looking for a home."

There were nods of affirmation from the family and friends.

"He was looking for a home!" he repeated loudly. "He was just looking for a home."

His voice became quiet, just above a whisper. "And yesterday, brothers and sisters, he found a home in heaven at last."

"Amen!" was heard from one listener.

"Hallelujah!" from another.

Old Man Hensley's daughter began sobbing loudly and was comforted by Newt's wife.

Hannah couldn't stand to look at them, so she stared at the coffin as if in a trance and took her mind elsewhere. It was a trick she had acquired years ago. Funerals always reminded her of her mother's death, and as a member of the preacher's family, she had to attend a good many of them. She had learned when still in her teens to allow her mind to wander to the necessary tasks to be completed. It was impossible to think of two things at once. If she thought about the practical details, her mind had no room for the pain.

She quickly made inventory of the last few hours. She had never worked with these women before, but found them much like the women in her father's congregation. Their ways were different from Hannah's, but everything had got done. It was not how Hannah would have done it, but then her way was not the only way.

It was nice, however, not to feel the burden of responsibility. For Hannah, this was the first time in a very long time when the congregation did not turn to her automatically to organize things. It enabled her to spend more time comforting the family.

They were holding up very well, she thought. And she was glad she had been there for Newt's wife, who seemed to be carrying the rest of the family and needed a strong shoulder to lean on herself.

It was still hard for her to believe that Henry Lee had put the man in his coffin and arranged the body. Newt's wife's relief had been blatantly obvious. And Young Newt's face, when he saw that he had pleased his mother, was something not easy to forget. Henry Lee had done that. Her Henry Lee. Without prompting, or previous experience, he had instinctively known how to help. Even her father, who Hannah had always considered the closest thing to a saint on this earth, would never have known to do that. It was just more evidence of the goodness and depth of her husband's nature.

Hannah was aware of Henry Lee at her side, and in her ruminations upon his decency and kindness she reached over and took his hand. His warm, calloused fingers felt perfectly matched to her own. She looked up at him to find him looking at her. His deep blue eyes searching her own, as if to read what she was thinking and feeling. Yet it seemed he must already know. They felt the same way. In this they were one.

Continuing to gaze at each other, they both suddenly became attuned again to what the preacher was saying.

"After Brother Hensley's wife, Mattie, died," he was saying, "it was almost as if a part of him died with her. Oh, he wanted to be here, to watch his grandchildren grow up, to see the community prosper, just to watch the sunrise every morning. But a part of him wanted to be with the woman that he loved, the woman that he had committed himself to all those years before. The woman that had shared his life, through better and worse, richer and poorer, sickness and health, only death could part them."

There seemed to be a flow of energy racing back and forth between Henry Lee and Hannah, connected by their hands but also by their hearts, as they heard the preacher speaking the words that they had so recently said to each other. When they had made those vows, neither had understood the depth of their meaning. Now as they stood at the site of the newly-dug grave, both silently reaffirmed that their lives were irrevocably entwined.

Reverend Brown closed his Bible quietly as he concluded, "Death no longer parts our brother from the woman he loves. They are together again in paradise."

The movement around them broke the trance between the two and Henry Lee moved to pick up one of the ropes to lower the coffin into the ground.

As the preacher committed the body to the ground, Henry Lee returned to Hannah's side and took her arm. He felt a sense of pride and ownership, this woman was his, all his and would be forever. Hannah thought she finally knew what it felt like to be married.

A few days later, she wasn't sure that she hadn't imagined the feeling. The day of the funeral they had been so close. During the drive home that evening, Henry Lee had actually put his arm loosely around her shoulders as he asked concerned questions about how she was feeling and if she was tired. Hannah was sure now that things were beginning to work out between them.

But when they arrived home, as late as it was, Henry Lee immediately changed into work clothes and grabbed up his bed roll telling Hannah he would be sleeping outside and would see her at breakfast.

He had been true to his word and the next day, Hannah saw him only at meals and he seemed to be very rushed and distracted. He barely spoke to her. With the date of their trip rapidly approaching, he did remind her to have her things ready, but he needn't have bothered. Her new dress was finished and she had already picked through the nicest of her clothing to take in her satchel. There was always the possibility of becoming ill or injured among strangers. If it became necessary for a strange woman to take care of her, she wanted her unmentionables to be her best.

Henry Lee's defection preyed on her mind incessantly. She wanted to please him, to do something to make him want to return to the cabin. She tried to make his home more inviting, a crocheted doily here and a vase of wildflowers there. She made a tick for his Dufold and used the leftover blue material from her new dress to upholster it. He had seemed very pleased and complimented her on the quality of her workmanship, but quickly hurried back out. But mostly she appealed in the manner she thought most successful. She cooked.

Devoting an unreasonable amount of time to the task, she made Sunday meals three times a day, trying to capture his attention. He ate like a man starved and seemed totally delighted at his good fortune, but never once did he linger at the table.

This failure only spurred Hannah to new heights of culinary excellence. So, when she was tramping through the woods trying to capture a thieving pig who had run off with one of Henry Lee's shirts from the wash, she was delighted to discover a blackberry thicket just ripe and ready to pick. It might be possible, she determined, to win her husband with a blackberry cobbler.

In midafternoon, when all the washing was hanging out on the line and the work caught up, Hannah dressed in her oldest, shabbiest dress. Blackberry picking was a thankless task, and the millions of thorns that grow from the branches of the thicket often made it a painful one. But Hannah was confident that a blackberry cobbler would do for her marriage what her desire for her husband's attention could not.

*   *   *

As Hannah carefully picked berries, Henry Lee sat
working in the cave watching the steady drip from the
still. He poured some of the finished brew into a mason
jar and after fastening the lid, he shook it thoroughly.
Holding it up to the light he examined the bubbles that
had formed at the top of the liquid and a smile broke out
on his face. They were the exact size of #5 shot. The
proof was perfect.

He had laid out some poor quality knotty pine and
was busily working on another coffin, not nearly so fine
as the one he'd made for Old Man Hensley.

Henry Lee had decided since whiskey was in short
supply, selling some whiskey right in the middle of the
territory could bring him double price. He had to pass
through Muskogee anyway, so there was really no reason
not to make the trip profitable as well as fun.

His idea for a coffin, Henry Lee thought, was
inspired. Harjo had a brother-in-law who ran an under-
taking business in Muskogee. It would not seem strange
at all for an undertaker to pull a wagon up to the train to
retrieve a body. And no federal marshall would be anxious to inspect a coffin that had been riding in the hot,
steamy baggage car for several hours. Henry Lee smiled
at his own cleverness. He figured he could easily ship
thirty-eight gallons of whiskey in the coffin and it still
wouldn't be much heavier than a good-sized corpse.

He would send a wire to the undertaker saying that
Harjo's body was being shipped to him on the Katy. Since
he would know that his brother-in-law was not dead, the two
of them would pick up the coffin and hold it for Henry Lee.

It was a good plan, he thought. The only tricky part
would be explaining to Hannah why he was shipping a
coffin to Muskogee, but since she knew that he made
coffins, she might not be too suspicious about hearing an
undertaker in Muskogee had requested one.

He was proud of his business acumen and wished he
could share his accomplishments with Hannah. He was
not ready yet, however, to tell her about the whiskey. He
felt that he knew her better now, and was sure that she
would grow accustomed to his line of work, he just didn't

want to cause trouble before they took their trip. Once they were really man and wife, once he'd pleased her in his bed, she'd come around soon enough. A devilish smile crossed his face thinking of pleasing her. A few weeks ago he would have questioned whether churchladies could enjoy the marriage bed. He was sure that Hannah could. She compressed all her feelings, all her passion into a tiny hard knot that she held close to her heart. Henry Lee knew that if he ever broke through and released all that pent-up emotion, she would be pleased indeed.

Shifting position to accommodate the ache that had developed in his groin, Henry Lee smiled to himself. He was the man for the job. The same thoroughness and attention to detail that characterized his woodworking and whiskey made him a lover that women did not soon forget.

It wasn't that he needed to prove himself or gain admiration, Henry Lee simply enjoyed loving a woman, making her forget who she was, or where she was, having her drop all pretenses and coyness and become only female, so that he could be only male.

That's what Henry Lee wanted to happen between himself and Hannah. He wanted her mindless and straining beneath him, her pretty, hymn-singing mouth covering his body with desperate kisses. He'd take her mind off his occupation for sure. And she'd never have another thought for the man who had fathered her child. He'd keep her so satisfied she'd get down on her knees twice a day to thank the good Lord for allowing her to spend her life in Henry Lee's bed.

Henry Lee tried to shake his lusty thoughts out of his head and concentrate on the task at hand. Just two more days, he promised himself, and he'd never spend another night without her beside him.

Hannah's progress through the blackberry thicket had filled up one bucket and was working on the second. There were plenty of ripe berries here for as many pies as Henry Lee could eat and plenty of jam to keep for the winter.

She wondered why Henry Lee hadn't mentioned the thicket. Having such a fine one on one's property was tremendous good fortune. Her father was incredibly fond of blackberries and there weren't any within miles of his home. Hannah had tried once to cultivate a thicket, digging up a small bush near the river, but although it grew pretty well for a while, it never bore any fruit and Hannah had finally given up on it. She would have to save some for Violet to make a pie for her father.

As the time passed Hannah tried to hurry. She wanted to pick all that were ripe, before the birds got to them, but she also wanted to have time to fix Henry Lee a cobbler for his supper tonight.

Reaching deep into the thicket, she encountered something unexpected. A webby pouch hung, as ripe as the berries, within the thicket. When her hand brushed against it, she inadvertently punched it open. Jerking her hand back quickly, she saw the silky evidence of the remainder of the spider's nest on her fingers, and in horror she watched as hundreds of tiny spiders scrambled into the world and raced up her arm.

The blood drained from her face as a wave of cold terror, fear, and nausea swept through her. Dropping her bucket, she began screaming hysterically as she tried to wipe away the unending stream of spiders as they doggedly pursued shelter up her shoulders, across her chest, down her waist, and in her hair.

Hannah's scream made Henry Lee's blood run cold. Without thought he raced out of the cave and jumped from the ledge hitting the ground at a dead run. He had no weapon, but he ran without caution, mindlessly he raced toward the sound of his wife's terror. When he reached the backside of the hogpen, he realized that the screams were not coming from the house. He quickly grabbed up a singletree leaning against the barn and raced into the woods.

The territory wasn't bear country and few animals in the wild were threatening to people, an occasional cougar or perhaps a rabid bobcat were the only dangers that Hannah might not be able to protect herself against. He hoped it was neither of those since her screaming would undoubtedly frighten the animal and make the situation worse. When he found her she was still screaming, slapping at her arms and face, pulling at her sunbonnet and hair, she was so pale she looked near to fainting. When he saw the tiny spiders scurrying down her skirt, he understood what was happening. Dropping the singletree, he began helping her brush away the frightening little varmints. She was shuddering as if freezing as he wiped her skirt and her arms, she pulled at her hair which was now loose and wild and then began crying in panic. They seemed to be everywhere as he frantically swept at her arms and clothing. She seemed most frightened by the ones crawling in her hair, and Henry Lee untied her bonnet and threw it behind them; grabbing handfuls of those loose honey-colored tresses he shook them like flags in the wind as Hannah clawed at those racing across her face and neck.

"Down my back! Henry Lee, they're crawling down my back!" she screamed.

Henry Lee turned her around and assessed the situation immediately. Without thought he grabbed the back of her dress and ripped the cheap cotton to the waist; jerking down the back of her chemise, he quickly located and disposed of the one crafty little spider who had found his way there. Raising her hair and wiping her neck and bare shoulders, he assured himself that that was the last of them. For good measure he checked her arms and skirt again thoroughly for any villains that might have got away.

She was still crying. Tears coursed down her face in streams and she was trembling so hard that Henry Lee wondered if she would be able to stand. Instinctively, he slipped an arm behind her knees and grabbed her up to his chest and carried her out of the woods.

Her arms around his neck, she held him as if he were her last hope and soaked the front of his work shirt with her tears. When he reached the edge of the woods he headed up the small rise. In the shade of a catalpa tree, Henry Lee sat down on the ground, still holding Hannah to his chest, and began to rock her as one would a baby, whispering and crooning in her ears that she was fine, the spiders were gone, she was safe, and he would take care of her. He planted gentle kisses on her hair as he tenderly stroked her bare shoulder and arm.

Henry Lee thought that she had never been so beautiful. Her hair was untamed and everywhere. Who would have thought that neat little braid held such wild curls? The hair seemed to soften her face making her look like a little girl, so exposed, so trusting.

As she quieted, Henry Lee found himself unwilling to loose her. He cuddled her more closely, listening to her breathing and the pounding of her heart. The feel, the smell, the closeness of her was arousing. He felt the usual reaction rising in his trousers. The skin that he had laid bare now tantalized him. His lips could almost taste the creamy shoulder that lay before him, beckoning him to kiss it. But he waited. She was so vulnerable, he wanted to go slowly so as not to frighten her again.

When the last quiet, hiccuping sob ceased, she continued to sit on his lap allowing his arms to protect her. She was embarrassed by the way she had acted. Grown women did not become hysterical over a few spiders, she told herself. But, even as she thought of the spiders crawling all over her, another involuntary shudder went through her. When finally she spoke, her voice was hoarse from screaming.

"I don't know what came over me," she began, "I'm not a flighty miss who screams at every little thing."

She would have pulled away from him then, but Henry Lee continued to hold her. Not with force, he simply did not relinquish her and she was not willing to try harder. She merely righted her clothes as modestly as the torn cloth would allow and rested against him.

"I wanted to do something special for you," she told him. "I saw those blackberries and I wanted to make you a blackberry cobbler. I make a wonderful blackberry cobbler, it's my father's favorite."

"That's real sweet of you, Hannah darlin'," he told her, snuggling closer. "You already fix me the finest meals in the territory, there's no need to go to any extra bother."

"But I wanted to!" she insisted. "I know you'll just love my blackberry cobbler."

"Hannah," he said to her softly. "I truly do not care for blackberries at all. Those pesky little seeds bother me and I can't bear to have the nasty stuff in my mouth."

Hannah stared straight ahead for a minute in abject shock, then suddenly a tiny giggle began working its way up through her middle until it poured out of her in gales of laughter. Henry Lee couldn't help being drawn to the contagious sound and the two sat there holding each other close and laughing uproariously.

"I can't believe that I made such a fool of myself trying to impress you. I wanted you to see what a competent wife I can be, going out and finding berries on my own to make you a pie. And what I ended up doing was showing you that I can be as foolish and spooky as a schoolgirl, while trying to make something for you that you didn't even want!" She shook her head in self-disgust.

"It's all right," he said to her in a voice just above a whisper. "Nobody would want those creepy varmints all over them. You don't have to pretend with me, Hannah. You hate bugs and lizards and such, that's fine. You don't have to be brave and sensible about such nonsense. I'm here for you, Hannah. I'll slay all your lizards and chase away the spiders forever."

He felt her smile against his chest.

"Well, it's a good thing, Henry Lee," she teased. " 'Cause you sure can't accuse me of being brave and sensible when I'm screaming like a pig with his tail caught in a rat trap!"

Henry Lee laughed. "Now, Hannah," he said, pretending to be stern, "I'll have you know that my pigs have got a lot more gumption than to squeal at a mess of baby spiders. And even if they did, they could never sound as wild as you did. Why, when I heard you, I thought some giant gator had swum up from Louisiana and grabbed you by the foot to take you home to feed his wife and young 'uns."

Hannah pulled away enough to look at him, she was smiling.

"I bet I did make you think something terrible happened, for you to come running up with a singletree in your hand. It's a good thing that you didn't try to beat off those spiders, you would have killed me for sure."

Henry Lee turned her about halfway around and raised his knees, which had her looking almost straight into his eyes, and seated right on top of where she could do the most good.

"Didn't I tell you the story about the man who was arrested for killing his wife?" he teased her.

Hannah shook her head, smiling and expectant.

"Well, when they took him before the judge and the judge asked him what he had to say for himself, do you know what he said?"

Hannah didn't.

"He said, 'Judge, if I can't kill my own wife, whose wife can I kill?' "

Hannah gave him a look of mock disgust and playfully punched him in the ribs.

"That's a terrible story!" she said giggling.

Henry Lee was laughing, too. And then he reached up and gently combed his fingers through Hannah's hair. They both sobered immediately as Henry Lee brought a hank of it to his lips, never taking his eyes off Hannah's face.

"Your hair is so beautiful," he whispered. "It seems such a shame to hide it from me."

"I never meant to hide it," she replied so quietly he barely heard her.

He brought the hair to his lips again, still gazing at her, then he rubbed his cheek with it. Slowly he began gathering it into his hand, pulling her closer and closer by inches until she could feel his breath on her face. He kissed the hair he still held in his hand in reverence, then he brushed her own lips with the kiss he had left on her hair. Hannah, wide-eyed, opened her mouth to speak, but when Henry Lee saw her lips part, he couldn't hold back any longer and he turned his head slightly to capture her mouth against his.

He felt, more than heard, her tiny gasp of surprise and pleasure. He deepened the kiss slightly, drawing her into his arms tightly until he could feel her nipples hardening against his chest. She returned his kiss timidly, as if she was unsure how to please him. But please him she did. He let his tongue leisurely drift along her teeth until she opened for him, he entered her mouth teasingly, gauging her reaction. He felt her jerk slightly in fear and immediately retreated. He would not press her, he could kiss her elsewhere and come back with his tongue when she was more ready.

He trailed a fiery path of tiny kisses along her cheek, to her ear and down her neck. Reaching the sensitive skin at the base of her throat he gave her a tender little love bite. She gasped his name and he smiled against her creamy flesh.

"You like that, Hannah darlin'?" he whispered into her bare skin. He grasped her breasts in his hands, weighing and kneading the generous orbs. The front of her torn dress slipped lower, but she was beyond noticing.

His hot breath raised gooseflesh on her naked shoulders and he went after that rough smoothness with his teeth and tongue until she was squirming against him, simultaneously easing and fanning the fire between them.

Henry Lee was at cross purposes with himself. He couldn't reach Hannah's bosom to taste the hard pouting nipples he held in his hands, but he was unwilling to give up the pleasing pressure of her luscious bottom against the evidence of his lust.

Compromising, he released her breasts and planted his hands firmly on the ground beside him. He raised his buttocks off the ground, bringing Hannah's bosom within the reach of his mouth. Hannah's eyes opened wide at suddenly finding herself in midair, and when she saw where Henry Lee intended to put his mouth, she arched her back toward him, offering herself eagerly.

Henry Lee grasped the edge of her chemise with his teeth, pulling it down just enough to bare her left breast. He looked up into her eyes and watched her watching him. Hannah was not sure that she could breathe. Her naked breast seemed inordinately exposed in the dappled sunshine of the shade of the catalpa tree and in sharp contrast to her husband's thick dark hair and tan skin so close by. She looked into the depths of his blue eyes, now flashing with desire and firing her own. Her hand moved to his hair and gently clutching a handful, she brought his mouth to her breast.

Henry Lee wanted to savor the taste of her. He would not be greedy with her offering. For a moment he simply held his mouth close to the thickened pulsing crest, teasing it with his hot breath, until he heard a plea from Hannah's lips that was as near pain as it was pleasure.

He traced the edges of the circle surrounding the peak with his tongue, before popping the distended nipple in his mouth. He suckled gently, then with more force as her breathing quickened and she strained against him. He grasped her nipple gently with his teeth and then used his tongue to lash it back and forth. Her squirming reaction threatened her precarious perch and Henry Lee immediately released her breast and lowered himself to the ground.

He was full, hard, and ready and her wiggling bottom wasn't doing anything for his control. He brought his mouth to hers and rolled her on her back. Jerking her skirt up past her knees, he ran his hand slowly up her cotton stocking, finding the tender exposed flesh between her garter and her drawers. Hesitating there, to give her time to reconcile herself to his touch, he raised his head and gazed into her partially closed eyes.

"Open your mouth, Hannah," he whispered. "I want to kiss you with my tongue."

Her eyes widened in surprise, but Henry Lee saw the

glaze of desire in them, and when she eagerly complied Henry Lee roughly thrust his tongue into the depths of her sweet mouth.

She tasted good. She tasted so good. Nothing that he had ever tasted was better than her. He never wanted to taste anything else. He explored deeper and deeper, tempting her throat, fencing with her tongue. She was like his whiskey, warm and smooth.

Whiskey! His mind screamed at him. The whiskey must be burning up, either that or spoiling.

To hell with the whiskey! he told himself angrily. He slid his hand up to the apex of her drawers covering her aching mound. She jerked spasmodically at his touch causing him to groan into her mouth.

You never let your whiskey ruin! His mind kept admonishing him.

Forget the whiskey! He fought back. Hannah opened her thighs to him and he could feel the heat and wetness through her drawers.

It's the wedding whiskey. The voice got through. If he let the wedding whiskey ruin, it might ruin the marriage.

He told himself that it was superstitious nonsense, but he knew he didn't want the wedding whiskey to ruin. It was a symbol of too much.

With a groan of pure agony, Henry Lee pulled away from her. He stared down at her, she was flushed from her cheeks to her waist, her eyes were hooded and sleepy with desire. Her breathing was quick and short. His hand still covered her feminine mound and she was pulsing and hot against him. No man could leave a woman like this. It couldn't be done. You couldn't just roll off and walk away. It was impossible.

Henry Lee thrust himself away from her and lay beside her on his back, shading his eyes with his arm as he waited to get control of his breathing.

Hannah lay beside him, shuddering in desire. What had happened? Why had he stopped? Her whole body seemed to be throbbing and the ache between her legs had turned from pleasure to pain when he had taken his hand away. Instinctively she dropped her own hand to that boiling fire, but it was not the same. Suddenly realizing what she was doing, she pulled her hand away, ashamed that she had touched herself.

Henry Lee saw the gesture and whiskey or no whiskey, he would not ignore her need. Turning back to her, he loosened the tie on her drawers and allowed his hand to explore the silky skin beneath. Setting his jaw firmly he determined to ignore the pounding hardness in his trousers. He wasn't about to make her his woman here on the ground, like an animal. But he knew a bit more than most men about a woman's pleasure and he wanted to give it to her.

"Easy, darlin'," he consoled in a whisper. "I'm going to make it fine, real fine. I'm going to soothe this yearning, I promise." He accented his words with tender kisses along her throat and strong skillful strokes of his hand.

"It's like a prairie fire," he whispered against her flesh. "You get ahead of it and start your own flame. When the two fires meet up, they consume each other."

His hand found the soft down covering of her womanhood and caressed it tenderly. He heard Hannah's gasp of desire and felt her pressing eagerly against his hand.

Finding the tiny nub that focused her pleasure, he flicked it leisurely and was rewarded with her cry of delight. Cupping his face in her hands, she pulled him to her. The kiss was neither tentative nor shy and Henry Lee heard only the roaring of his own blood in his ears as he struggled for control.

Hannah's body was about to go up in smoke. She could no longer tell where her flesh stopped and Henry Lee's began. Seeking the hidden wonders of his mouth, she pressed herself against him. She was so open, so empty and he could fill her, she wanted him to fill her.

The heel of his palm pressed with such wondrous effect against the treacherous slope that led to the valley of her womanhood. When his fingers reached that unexplored cavern, she cried out his name.

"Yes! Henry Lee! Oh Yes!" She arched her back

instinctively and spread her thighs for him, begging for the consolation of his questing hand.

"That's right, Hannah," he whispered against her throat. "Open up for me and I'll give you a sweet cure for what is steaming inside you."

Gently suckling her hard, pointed nipple, his fingers teased the entrance to her woman-place and explored it without hesitation.

Pushing eagerly against the pressure of his hand, Hannah incoherently whined her need.

"You are so tight, Hannah," he whispered, his hot words burning the flesh of her breast. "So soft, so tight, oh, Hannah darlin', I'm going to make it real good for you."

As proof of his words he allowed one curious digit to delve inside as his thumb came up to tease the rigid little fuse that impudently peeked out of the curl-covered slope.

No longer able to embrace him, Hannah flung her hands to the ground, digging her nails deeply into the grass as if to anchor herself to the earth. Her head flailed back and forth as mindless, primitive whimpering escaped her lips.

She was trembling on the edge as he nipped the creamy flesh of her bosom and kissed the sting away.

A tremor began growing within her and Henry Lee, feeling it inside her, lavished his attention with renewed fervor.

"Feel me inside you, Hannah," he whispered hoarsely. "Feel me touching you, stroking you. Touch me back, Hannah. Squeeze my hand, yes, Hannah darlin', let me know you like it."

She exploded screaming his name as the muscles that surrounded his fingers contracted in ecstasy.

Henry Lee was watching her as she strained against him, her head thrown back in wanton pleasure. His own body ached with unassuaged need, but a smile of satisfaction spread across his face. He had never felt more a man.

As her passion eased, Henry Lee released her from his intimate caress. Clutching her damp womanly pelt possessively, he was hesitant to relinquish his claim. He pulled her tenderly into his embrace, nuzzling her neck, as he ignored the rock-hard evidence of his own lack of fulfillment.

"Oh, Henry Lee," Hannah's voice was breathless with wonder. "What have you done to me? I never knew anything could be like that."

Pulling back a little so that he could look into her eyes, Henry Lee couldn't keep from smiling in pride.

"There's more, Hannah, so much more." His eyes were alight with mischief. "And I'm willing to teach you everything that I know."

She giggled at his teasing and he pulled her into his arms, pressing his aching manhood against her.

The whiskey. His memory floated back unerringly. He was right to give her pleasure, but his own could wait. His whiskey was going to burn or his still explode if he allowed himself to make his decisions from his trousers instead of his brain.

He pulled away from her before he had time to talk himself out of it.

"I've got a lot of things to do this afternoon, Hannah," he explained feebly. Planting a hasty kiss on her forehead he stood and gave her one last longing look. "I'll see you at supper," he said as calmly as if he'd just chanced to pass her.

Hannah glanced down at her condition and quickly pulled up her chemise covering her naked bosom and thrust down her skirt that was bunched up all the way to her waist, not daring to stop to readjust her untied drawers.

"Henry Lee?" she asked tentatively, feeling both a sense of closeness at what they had shared and estrangement at his sudden erratic behavior.

He heard her confusion and desire in his name and he could not face her. He couldn't look her in the eye.

Turning away from her, he answered simply, "I've got to get back to work."

Hannah sat up stunned and watched him walk away.

Her confusion turned to dismay as she realized that she must have injured him somehow. He was walking strangely, partially bent over, as if he couldn't straighten up.

THIRTEEN

The clatter of the rails and the intermittent, rhythmic motion of the rail car could not lull Hannah out of her anxious excitement. Dressed in her new blue calico and fancy bonnet, she sat next to a dashing, well-dressed man in a brown suede coat and string tie, who just happened to be her husband. Their mood was light and carefree, as if the last few difficult days had not happened.

Not that Hannah had forgot the incident under the catalpa tree. It had hung between them like an inflexible barrier for the last two days. Then this morning when she had awakened just a little before dawn, she found Henry Lee in the kitchen, coffee already made, and in a talkative, friendly mood. A sharp contrast from his previous constant absence and few mumbled words. He'd had the wagon hitched, loaded and ready and his excitement and enthusiasm for the trip was contagious.

She had been somewhat surprised to find a coffin loaded in the back of the wagon. She had been unaware that Henry Lee did that kind of work on the side, but she was very proud. She remembered how pleased the Hensley family had been with the coffin he'd made, and although this one did not seem as nice, she knew his work must be good for him to get requests all the way from Muskogee.

Henry Lee had laughed and joked all the way to Ingalls. He smiled and teased and made outrageous compliments about her new dress and bonnet. It was almost as if, in his time away from her, he had thought up stories and jokes to entertain her. He was well-known for his charm, and this morning every scrap of it was directed toward his wife. Considering the strange situation that existed between them, Hannah couldn't imagine why, but she was not such a fool as to question her good fortune.

Henry Lee's effervescent behavior was partly in response to what had happened under the catalpa tree, but also stemmed from nervous excitement. Never before had he smuggled whiskey so deep into the territory and he found the fear of discovery to be very heady stuff. The stationmaster had looked askance when he had brought in the coffin. Unlike Hannah, who accepted his lame excuse without question, the stationmaster found Henry Lee's story of shipping a friend's body to Muskogee unusual.

Henry Lee insisted that the coffin be shipped on a later freight, rather than in the baggage car of the train that would carry himself and Hannah. If someone did decide to open it, or if it fell and burst open accidentally, he wanted a running start on the law.

He just hoped that Harjo's brother-in-law could be trusted to read between the lines of the telegram that he had just dictated.

COFFIN OF YOUR BROTHER-IN-LAW HARJO TO ARRIVE ON 6:30 KATY FREIGHT STOP WIFE AND I TO ATTEND FUNERAL STOP H. L. WATSON

Outwitting the law was not the only concern that made Henry Lee nervous. Tonight he was going to take Hannah to his bed. Finally. He had spent two days listening to the drip of whiskey from the coiled condenser and planning the total and complete seduction of the woman he'd married. No more crazy loss of control and wallowing with her on the floor or the ground. He was going to make careful, exquisite love with her in the best bed in Muskogee.

Thinking about it, he turned to give her a teasing smile. She looked wonderful in her new dress. He'd thought the bright blue would do more for her than the washed-out pastels or the severe blacks and browns that seemed to comprise the bulk of her wardrobe. Her clothes seemed too matronly, almost as if she had thrown her corset across the armoire years ago. He couldn't imagine why. Twenty-six was not such a great age, and today, smiling and giggling, high color in her cheeks, she didn't look a day over twenty. He vowed that he'd see that she had more clothes that flattered her. Her looks were not typical, but, he decided, she was no less pretty as a result.

Although Hannah had traveled a good bit in the Oklahoma Territory and in southern Kansas, this was her first trip through the Indian Territory and she was both surprised and pleased by the difference in the scenery. While the Oklahoma Territory seemed ideally suited to the growing of wheat and corn, an endless flat prairie resembling what her family had left in Kansas, the Indian Territory was more wooded, hilly and less suited to farm life. As the train wound its way through the hills and valleys beside the Arkansas River, she commented on the contrast. "It's so different from the farmland across the border."

"They sent scouts out here, when it became obvious that the government was going to move the tribes west of the Mississippi. The Indians looked for the type of land that seemed most familiar," he explained. "Woods for game and hills for running streams were more important than being able to plow a straight furrow," he told her. "The Indians never intended to farm in the way that white men did. They lived in Indian towns and hunted game. Their farming was more like a big garden where everyone took a share."

"This land doesn't look very good for farming," Hannah agreed.

Henry Lee nodded.

"They made their choice more on sentiment than good business sense," he said. "My mother was a half-breed Cherokee," he said tentatively, and watched with pleasure as she easily accepted this piece of information. "Mama said that when the scouts saw the foothills of the Ozarks around Tahlequah, it reminded them of the Great

Smokies and so they chose it, even though you can barely grow a weed in those rocky hills!"

The two shared a laugh together. The impracticality of choosing a home based on the beauty of the land, rather than its ability to provide a living, was something that neither would have done. Both of them, however, secretly admired the spirit that maintained the courage to do that.

They arrived in Tulsa a little before noon. They were to change trains with a layover of about two hours. Tulsa was a sleepy little village of a little over a thousand people.

"It's not much of a town," Henry Lee told her as they left the train. "Its only reason for existing is to be a railroad junction for the Atchison, Topeka and Santa Fe and the Frisco."

Hannah glanced around unimpressed by the few little dismal buildings. "Ingalls is more of a town than this," she said.

Her husband agreed. "Tulsa was laid out by the Frisco Railroad Company and is as efficient as a train schedule," he said. "The streets running east and west are numbered, First Street, Second Street, Third Street. The streets running north and south are split down the middle by Main Street, and are called avenues." Gesturing to the dusty thoroughfare they crossed he widened his eyes in sarcasm. "Pretty fancy name for this old cow trail, don't you think?"

Hannah agreed with a throaty giggle.

"All the avenues east of Main Street are named, by the A-B-Cs after cities east of the Mississippi." He pointed eastward and explained, "There's Boston Avenue and Cincinnati Avenue, like that."

Hannah nodded her understanding.

"All avenues west of Main Street are named for cities west of the Mississippi, like Cheyenne Avenue and Denver Avenue." Henry Lee's eyes lit with humor. "The public joke among the men here in town is that no matter how drunk you get in Tulsa, you can always figure out where you are."

Laughing at his joke Hannah asked him, "Well, Mr. Watson, you seem to be perfectly sober today. I suppose you know exactly where you are. But do you know where you're going?"

Henry Lee smiled down at her. He enjoyed teasing her and he was beginning to love it when she teased right back.

"Yes, ma'am. I know exactly where I'm going. I'm taking my bride out for a bite to eat."

"We're going to a restaurant?" Hannah was delighted by the adventure.

"I have some friends who run the best restaurant in Tulsa." With a grin he added, "It's also the only restaurant in Tulsa!"

Marco and Rosa Morelli were getting on in years, but still maintained the love of life and adventure that had brought them from Naples, through New York and Chicago, clear across the plains to this desolate little town. They had tried farming, sheep, and cattle, but had ultimately found their niche in cooking good hot food for train passengers passing through.

"My friend, Mr. Watson!" Morelli called out, raising his hands as a gesture of welcome. "Rosa and I have missed you. You stay away too long."

Henry Lee grasped the man's hand as a screech was heard from the doorway.

"You!" the woman yelled at him. "Don't you know that you cannot live without good food, but do you come in to eat? No, not for months we don't see you, and I ask my husband, I ask him why. Is he hurt? Is he in trouble? What kind of busy does he have that he can't pass this way and let me fix him an antipasto?"

Hannah was taken aback by the woman's strange manner, but Henry Lee didn't seem to take it seriously and grabbed the handsome older woman around her ample waist for a big hug.

"I have been busy, and you will approve, I know," he told her. He turned and gestured to Hannah. "Rosa, Marco, I'd like you to meet my wife, Hannah."

Rosa screamed again and pushed Henry Lee away.

'Why do I waste my breath on a man who lets his wife stand starving in the doorway? Come in! Come in!" she said to Hannah hugging her like a long lost friend and then holding her at arm's length and taking a good long look at her.

"Is she pretty, Marco?" she said in a way that conveyed that she definitely was. "A good, strong girl he picks," she spoke secretively to Hannah touching her finger to her brow, "I knew he was a smart one, learn from my Marco. When you pick a wife, you pick one that don't look like the wind would knock her over."

Rosa placed her hands on Hannah as if measuring the width of her pelvis. "Look at these hips, Marco. The boy will get plenty of babies from this one, no trouble."

Hannah's face flamed scarlet. Such plain speaking was embarrassing, but she could tell the woman had meant her words for the best. Besides, Hannah thought, it wouldn't hurt for Henry Lee to be aware of his wife's more practical advantages. Rosa fixed them a wonderful meal of some of the strangest dishes that Hannah had ever tasted. Everything from the pickled onions, through the spaghetti and on to the dessert custard was unique. Marco gave them lessons on spaghetti twirling and Rosa promised that she would teach Hannah everything she needed to know about cooking for a new husband. When Henry Lee declared that his wife already was the best cook in the territory, Rosa raised her hands to heaven.

"Thank God, at last he is truly in love! When a man believes that his wife cooks best, you know that his stomach has become as blind as his eyes!"

The Morellis were busy serving customers and Hannah and Henry Lee laughed and talked. When the last of the customers had headed out the door the two came and joined them at the table.

"I have a business proposition for you," Morelli told him. "It is something for the future, to set aside now. A young husband like yourself should think of the future, I know. Next time you look, you'll see the house full of bambinos and say, 'How this happen?' " he joked.

Henry Lee gave a startled glance at Hannah. He won-

dered when they would start telling people about the
baby. Morelli was right, the future was here with them
and a good husband and father would be making plans.
"What kind of business do you have in mind?"
"It's not business, not yet, it's *investment*," the older
man told him. "The old Indian whose allotment sets just
south of town here, he comes in to eat Rosa's cooking
sometimes. He tells me he no like to live so near the
town, make him crazy he says. So he go to live nearer
his son. He want to sell his land, sell it fast."
Henry Lee nodded, interested.
"I think I should buy it. The town gonna grow I
think, and it has nowhere to grow this side of the river
except that way."
"Well, if you think you should buy it, why mention
it to me?"
"Ah," Morelli dragged the sound out almost mourn-
fully. "My Rosa and me, we got good sense and hard
work, but we got no money." He gestured comically pulling the insides of his pockets out to show that they were
empty.
"My good friend, Henry Lee, he got good sense and
hard work, too. But, he's got money."
Hannah looked at Henry Lee, surprised. She hadn't
been aware that Henry Lee was doing any better than the
other farmers, but she was proud to hear otherwise. A
fine man like her husband certainly deserved to do well.
Henry Lee saw the look on Hannah's face and immediately worried that she had heard enough to become
suspicious.
"We don't want to bore you ladies with this business
talk," he said. "Hannah, maybe you could get Rosa to
show you the kitchen?"
Rosa wasn't buying any flimsy excuses. "Men!" she
said. "They don't want us to hear their business talk, you
know why? 'Cause we are so smarter than them, and they
are afraid that we will find out!"
Hannah laughed.
"Come, little new bride," Rosa urged her, "I have new

dress I've been making for my granddaughter, you must
see it."

The two women disappeared through the door that
led to the living quarters upstairs and Henry Lee turned
to Morelli.

"How much does the old Indian want?" Henry Lee
asked.

"He is not greedy," Morelli answered. Henry Lee
was sure that even if the city did not prosper and grow
into the land, it was still fairly good bottom ground land
that could be farmed and the trees on it, alone, would be
worth the asking price. Morelli could come up with about
a third of the money needed, if Henry Lee could make
the rest.

"I have a little business deal going in Muskogee,"
Henry Lee said. "I expect to make a good bit of profit
fairly quickly. Tell the Indian he can have his payment in
cash tomorrow, if he'll come down five percent on the
price."

"You can have that money by tomorrow?" Morelli's
face clouded with concern. "It is dangerous to make so
much money so fast, my friend."

"I'm careful," Henry Lee assured him.

"That's good. 'Cause now you have family to worry
about," he said gravely. Then lightening the mood he
added, "And an old business partner who is going to help
make you a very rich man!"

Henry Lee and Hannah were almost late getting back
to their train and had to grab their bags and run the last
few steps. They were flushed and laughing like children
when they finally found their seats.

A stiff matron seated across the aisle gave them a
withering look of disapproval.

"We're on our honeymoon," Henry Lee told her,
loud enough for everyone in the car to hear. Hannah
blushed and lowered her eyes. When she looked up again
in embarrassment, she saw that everyone in the car was
watching them with tolerant approval and smiling at their
private happiness. It must have been contagious, because

Hannah found that she could no longer be embarrassed, she was just too pleased.

They arrived in Muskogee a little after four. The train station, just off Okmulgee Street, was brightly colored and welcoming, and there were so many people coming and going it nearly made Hannah dizzy to watch. In an instinctive gentlemanly gesture, Henry Lee took her arm and guided her through the milling crowds toward the center of town. Hannah stared in big-eyed wonder at all the new sights, but then tried determinedly not to look impressed. She wouldn't want everyone to think she was some country bumpkin who'd never seen a city before.

"Is it always like this?" Hannah asked, as she watched a bright red kerosene wagon inch around the corner, barely missing a bicycle headed in the wrong direction.

"Sometimes it's worse," he replied apologetically, "but only on the main thoroughfares. The side streets are a lot quieter."

A little way further they turned off onto one of the side streets Henry Lee had mentioned, and Hannah had to agree the relative peace and quiet was welcome.

On the corner, only a block away from the traffic and noise of the main boulevards, the Williams Hotel could be entered by climbing three marble steps and passing through a curved archway with real stained glass in the windows.

Henry Lee stopped abruptly on the first step as if gathering his thoughts.

"Is this where we are going to stay?" Hannah asked. To her the hotel looked like a palace. "Are you sure we can afford this, Henry Lee?"

Interrupted from his thoughts, Henry Lee quickly assured her that money would not be a problem.

"Hannah," he went on, his look guarded and his cheeks slightly flushed. "You're my wife, and it will sure look strange to these folks if we sign as man and wife and then ask for separate rooms."

Hannah began a thorough investigation of her hands

ınd fingernails, no more able to meet Henry Lee's eye
:han he was to meet hers.

She had thought it might come to this. In all truth,
;he had hoped that it would. She didn't know why Henry
Lee continued to hesitate to bring her to bed, but she felt
.t was time. After what had happened under the catalpa
:ree, he surely must realize that she would not spurn him.
Her face grew vivid red at the memory of how ready
;he'd been to be a wife to him, right there in the grass
ınd shade of the afternoon.

"Hannah," he said, "it wasn't just foolish talk when
I said this was our honeymoon. I'm thinking that it's high
time that we began to live together as man and wife."

Hannah was not sure if she would ever be able to
breathe again. She wanted this, waited for it, but she now
felt so shy and scared, she had little idea of how to go
about accepting it.

She shyly reached for his hand and still without looking at him she replied, "I am your wife, Henry Lee."

Henry Lee's breath rushed out in a sigh of relief. She
was as eager as himself to consummate their marriage, he
was sure of it. He wanted to explain it all to her. How
he was sure that in the long run it would be better this
way. It would make the baby seem more like his and by
the time it came along they would be comfortable in their
married life. He realized that he no longer cared about
the other man. The sins she had left behind her meant
nothing at all to him, and he was sure that she wasn't
pining after someone else. They would not let the shad-
ows of the past darken their future.

Taking her arm, he escorted her deferentially up the
steps and through the doorway. He thought playfully
about carrying her across the threshold, but decided not
to push his luck.

The lobby was as beautifully decorated and refined
as the entryway and Hannah tried not to gawk at the
finely-made furniture and the rich fabric of the drapes.
The Williams Hotel was very new, and Henry Lee had
heard that it was the hotel currently being patronized by
Kansas City cattle buyers and Washington bureaucrats.

Therefore, it must be very fine indeed. Henry Lee hadn't
even balked at the prices. A man only had a honeymoon
once, after all, and Henry Lee Watson was a very successful businessman.

An attractive young Indian man, dressed in a black
and white checked suit, stood behind the desk. He
politely acknowledged them with a nod as he spoke into
a wooden box on the wall while holding the cylinder
attached to it by a cord, up to his ear.

Finishing his conversation he returned the cylinder to
its hanging spot on the wooden box and offered a rather
insincere apology concerning the bother of modern con-
veniences.

"We'd like a room for two nights," Henry Lee said.

"Your name, sir?" the man asked.

The man quickly scanned his book finding it.

"Yes, Mr. Watson," he said, "you've requested our
best room. That would be the Territorial Suite." He spoke
with bombast and self-importance, dragging out the syllables of each word to its greatest possible length.

"If you would sign the book, sir, I will be happy to
see you and your lovely lady to your temporary
domicile."

Henry Lee was not certain whether he was interested
in a "temporary domicile," but concentrated on carefully
printing the letters of his name on the register. Henry Lee
was too long for him to write, but putting down Watson
was far superior to an X.

"A Mr. Harjo was by a few hours ago," the young
man told him. "He said you'd be coming and he left you
a note." The man reached to retrieve a small piece of
folded paper from a nest of boxes on the wall behind him.

As the man gathered up their luggage and asked
them to follow, he headed up the stairway at the far end
of the room. Henry Lee opened his note and tried to make
it out as best he could. Reading was not one of his better
skills. He had never attended school and his mother's
occasional attempts to teach him were as inconsequential
as they were sporadic. He struggled with the first few

words, then shook his head and followed his wife up the stairs.

The Territorial Suite was actually two good-size rooms facing the tree-lined street. The sitting room was slightly crowded with several spindle-legged chairs, three small tables, covered with crocheted doilies, knickknacks, and pictures in every possible inch of available space. It was altogether too fussy for Hannah's taste.

The bedroom was dominated by a massive four-poster bed that made any thought of furnishings fly completely from Hannah's head. She quickly retreated to the fussy sitting room, making herself useful by rearranging the multitudinous objets d'art.

Henry Lee came in, thanked the young man and gave him a penny. He watched Hannah nervously redistributing the ornaments. "I'll open the window and you can toss all this rubbish out," he joked. She smiled shyly, sharing his amusement, and determinedly stilled her restless hands.

He followed the young man out into the hall and stopped him before he reached the stairs.

"Could you read this for me?" he asked.

The young man seemed somewhat surprised and then with a patrician air, dramatically and loudly read Henry Lee's message.

AM FEELING WELL ENOUGH TO ATTEND THE FUNERAL MYSELF. IT WILL BE TONIGHT. MEET ME AT THE AMBROSIA BALLROOM AT NINE THIS EVENING. BRING YOUR LOVELY BRIDE. IT'S A VERY DISCREET PLACE. HARJO.

Because Henry Lee believed his own lack of education neither to be shameful nor a hindrance, he was not angered or embarrassed by the man's superior attitude. He thanked him, handed him another penny in appreciation, and headed back to his room, pleased.

He found Hannah still standing in the middle of the

sitting room, trying to make country-style order out of the chaos of city fashion.

"You think these city people like all this stuff cluttering up all the time?" she asked him, smiling in mock disgust.

"That's what I've seen," he admitted. "Makes them think they are well-to-do when they have more things than places to put them."

"Seems foolish to me. I want things simple."

Henry Lee walked up beside her; standing as close as was politely reasonable, he reached over and took her hand. He wanted to kiss it, but fearing that boldness would frighten her, merely rubbed the soft skin of the back of her hand against his cheek.

"Maybe, Hannah, we are more suited than we thought."

The slight stubble of his cheek seemed to send little electric shocks down her arms and straight into her chest, constricting it and making it difficult for her to breathe.

Henry Lee saw her reaction and it gave him a strange sense of power and control. He pressed his advantage and pulled her gently up against his chest. There was no pressure or force, he merely held her there, next to him. He could feel her trembling against him, trembling for him. He followed the direction of her eyes and found her gazing at the bed in the next room. It was to be their marriage bed and they both knew it. A tremor of his own fear skittered through his thoughts, quickly replaced by compassion and concern for Hannah. He was the man of vast experience, and no matter what her past, she was not sophisticated or worldly. He would court her tonight, win her and when he took her to him, she would never regret it.

Hannah felt both shy and bold simultaneously. She wanted his touch and was afraid of it, too. At least now she knew that the waiting would be over soon. Tonight they would be man and wife at last. She wanted the waiting to be over. She wanted to find out what the marriage bed was all about. But mostly, she wanted him. She wanted Henry Lee to touch her and kiss her and make her feel again the way he'd made her feel that afternoon under the catalpa tree.

Remembering her own lack of control and the bombardment of sensations that Henry Lee had sparked in her rekindled her fears. Perhaps her eagerness made her seem desperate or unnatural. It was terrible not knowing what behavior was normal for a wife, not knowing what was expected. Henry Lee sensed her apprehension and ambivalence and quickly released her. He was willing to wait, to see her more eager. He had plans to quiet her fears and get her used to his touch.

"Tonight you'll get your chance to show off that pretty new dress," he said.

"Where are we going?" she asked, excited.

"It's called the Ambrosia Ballroom."

FOURTEEN

U.S. Chief Deputy Marshall Tom Quick of the Musko-gee District, Indian Territory, sat in a rocking chair on the upstairs porch of the courthouse. He loved to sit there in the evening with his boots propped up on the railing, and watch the comings and goings on Okmulgee Street. He had seen a lot of things come and go in the twenty-three years he'd been a lawman in the Indian Territory. He'd seen Muskogee when it was nothing but a wide spot in the road. And the folks that were running it these days, he'd seen them when they were still making messes in their knee-pants. Some said that Tom Quick was too old for the job these days, that all he did was sit on that porch and ramble on about the past glory of the marshalls. How quickly they could forget. They'd already forgotten how he'd rounded up Zip Wyatt's gang. How he was in on the killing of Ike Black. And they didn't even recall him running those worthless Caseys to ground.

Once he had known every outlaw in the territory on sight. Now he sat on the upstairs porch and watched for kids stealing apples from the greengrocer across the street.

As he sat, rocking and thinking, his boots tapping out an unknown melody, something caught his eye. A full-breasted young woman in a blue calico dress was walking down the street. She was a welcome sight to Tom who, although he was well past sixty, still had trouble remaining faithful to his long-suffering wife of forty years.

The filly in the blue dress was built just the way he liked. No delicate little princess, but a sturdy, buxom gal that a man could ride half the night without fear of wearing her out. She looked a bit too respectable for his liking, however, and she already had a man with her.

Marshall Quick might well have returned to his thoughts had the man beside the woman in blue not, at that instant, turned to her and smiled. It had been years since he'd seen it, but he recognized that face immediately.

"It's Skut Watson's boy!" he stated aloud, with absolute certainty. The boy didn't favor his old man a bit, but he'd seen him plenty of times as he was growing up and he would have known him anywhere.

He'd had run-ins with Skut Watson practically from the day that he'd come to the territory. The boy's father had been a lazy, drunken, professional liar and cheat. He'd have stole his own grandma's underdrawers if he thought he could make a nickel. The worthless piece of thieving trash had been of so little account as to have been hardly worth the trouble to arrest, except to collect the money for the mileage.

Marshall Quick knew that this whelp was not as bad as the father. But he was a moonshiner and whiskey peddler, that was well known, even if he had never been caught. He made whiskey on a little piece of bottom ground on the edge of the Territory in the Creek Nation. Old Skut had traded his wife's allotment among the Cherokees for that place near the border so he could scurry across to safety when things got too hot for him. The boy continued to live there after the old man died, making his whiskey without interference from the lawmen in Muskogee a hundred miles away.

Tom Quick studied their progress down the street, his hand resting on his chin in concentration. It was pretty easy to figure out what had brought him so close to the law. After the crackdown on moonshiners in the area and the breakup of Pauly Archambo's organization, whiskey was in short supply. Watson had obviously come

here to expand his business and take up where Archambo
had left off.

It was the marshall's duty to see that didn't happen.
Tom Quick was not one of these modern, city-type marshalls, who were thinking that a little moonshine making
or whiskey peddling was more a nuisance than a crime.
He knew what liquor could do in the hands of the red
man. Even among the whites, he personally believed that
the consumption of alcohol was the main reason for most
killings, shootings, rapings, and general mischief in the
territory. And those that made and sold the evil elixir
were as guilty as the perpetrators.

Trafficking in intoxicating beverages had given more
than one outlaw his start on the road to crime. It was his
duty as marshall to find out what the no-account bootleg-
ger was doing in Muskogee, and if he was here to sell
whiskey, Watson was going to find himself behind bars
by nightfall.

As he watched the couple, laughing and cheerful,
make their way down the street, he called out through
the door behind him.

"Wilson! Get me Neemie Pathkiller right away!"

Looking once again on the couple disappearing out
of sight, he focused his tired eyes on the woman's broad
behind. "Maybe she ain't as respectable as she looks."

Hannah couldn't quite believe her good fortune. A
new dress, a handsome husband at her side, and an exciting new city to enjoy them in. Henry Lee was wearing
the suit he had worn at their wedding, but he was not at
all the somber groom that he had been that day. He
laughed and joked and told stories, determined to entertain his wife.

As they slowly made their way down the street, they
stopped to look into the doorways of stores as they
passed. Neither had spent much time admiring store-
bought goods, and now found themselves fascinated by
the abundance of things that were actually available for
purchase. In towns out on the border, only the essentials
of living could be found for sale, and those were usually

at premium prices. But here in Muskogee, where trains came and went in a half dozen directions, every possible necessity and luxury seemed to be readily available in the shops.

They had shopped at the major dry goods store to buy presents for Hannah's family. A trip to the city was a big occasion and everyone would want a remembrance. Next they had made a stop into MacIntee's Jewelry where Henry Lee had surprised her by pulling out of his pocket the wedding ring he'd given her.

"Could we have this sized to fit my wife?"

The jeweler assured them that he could have it done by the next day, and took the measure of the third finger of Hannah's left hand.

As they headed on down the street, Henry Lee's eye was captured by the display window of a saddlery. A fancy, hand-tooled saddle with silver studding sat like a work of art on a sawhorse.

"It is beautiful," Hannah admitted.

Henry Lee smiled at her in agreement. He had never owned a decent saddle horse, considering that a luxury for a man who made his living from a wagon, but he appreciated a thing of beauty and was pleased to share it with Hannah.

He liked the way her mind worked, she thought in much the same way that he did. That made it easier to talk to her. He could just tell her things and she could understand without needing a big explanation.

He wished that he'd told her about his business. Surely, she would be able to understand that, too. But tonight was not the night for confessions. Tonight was strictly for courting. And, he thought smiling to himself, later, for loving.

At supper, Henry Lee was in such a state of agitation, anticipating his plans, that he failed to notice the man eating alone at the table next to him. The man, of Indian heritage but dressed in white-man's attire, was neither short nor tall, thin nor fat, young nor old, handsome nor ugly. He had no distinguishing features at all. It was one of the things that made Neemie Pathkiller good at his job.

Nobody noticed him or remembered his face. That made it easy for him to observe others and remember everything. He had worked for Tom Quick on plenty of jobs. He knew his business and he rarely made mistakes. As he watched the young whiskey peddler at the next table, he knew that this job would be easy pickings. The man was obviously so taken with his lady friend that he hardly knew what was going on around him. Constant vigilance might not be mandatory for cowboys and farmers, but criminals who weren't on their toes filled up jails.

As he saw them making ready to leave, he hurried to get ahead of them. Accepting his change from the waiter he asked, "Do you happen to know the date today?"

The waiter looked up curiously. "Why, it's the seventh I believe, sir."

Taking a bill from his stack of change he handed it to the waiter. "Could you write that date on this bill for me?"

The waiter complied with a befuddled shake of his head. Pathkiller smiled and gave the man another bill as a tip. He knew the waiter would remember the incident and would easily be able to recognize his writing on the bill when the case came to court.

Pathkiller stepped outside and leaned against the building rolling a cigarette as Henry Lee and Hannah came out of the restaurant and headed leisurely down the street. As he watched them he almost felt pity for the young couple, so obviously in love, but he quickly pushed it back. Love was a transitory foolishness that could be deadly for a man on the run.

The Ambrosia Ballroom was a warehouse converted to a dance hall, or as the proprietress Hattie Byron preferred to call it, a salon. Mrs. Byron, whose late husband was killed fighting the big fire of '89, maintained a degree of respectability among the townspeople. But her business—which brought together cowhands, college boys, and ne'er-do-wells to mingle with lonely widows, merchants' daughters, and women of dubious reputation—was viewed by the community with a great deal of suspicion However, Mrs. Byron never allowed the personal morals of her friends and neighbors to deter her in the acquisition of money.

She knew Henry Lee Watson by reputation only, but when a long-legged, darkly handsome young man with a freshly scrubbed farmgirl on his arm arrived, she knew that must be him and promenaded over to introduce herself.

"Mr. Watson." she offered him a bright smile and her hand. Henry Lee took it in his own and began to lift it to his lips. With a sidelong glance at Hannah, he decided simply to shake it. "We are so happy that you've come to our little party." She smiled tolerantly at Hannah. "Is this the new Mrs. Watson I have heard about?"

Henry Lee introduced Hannah and poured on the charm. Hannah was amazed as he put on his positively devastating smile and set out to dazzle Mrs. Byron.

Hannah looked up to see a familiar face. Harjo was dressed like a railroad baron and shiny as a new penny, making his way, with his hesitant limping gait, over to them.

"Watson, my friend, it's good that you came," he greeted, slapping Henry Lee on the back. "And you, ma'am, also," he said bowing to Hannah. "Marriage must agree with you, you grow more lovely each time I see you."

Hannah blushed at the compliment. It still felt strange to be the recipient of such flowery talk, but she was beginning to like it.

"Why don't I take your lovely wife for a spin around the floor, while you two discuss a bit of business," Harjo said taking Hannah's arm and leading her away. She glanced back to see Henry Lee watching her. His eyes were warm with affection, but there was worry also and Hannah wasn't quite sure why.

"I didn't realize that my husband had business with Mrs. Byron."

Harjo raised his brows. Obviously Henry Lee had still not told his wife about his whiskey business. But she certainly was not going to hear it from him. He laughed and brushed off the question.

"A businessman, like your husband, sees every introduction as an opportunity for business," he said to her. "Now let me try out this bad leg on a slow tune so that I don't tread on your feet too badly."

"Oh, Mr. Harjo," Hannah said, embarrassed. "You needn't make the effort on my account. I don't dance, of course, my father would never approve."

Harjo smiled down at her. "But, Mrs. Watson, it no longer matters whether your father approves. You are a married woman now, it's your *husband's* approval that you must seek."

The truth of this statement gave Hannah pause. Of course, it was true. Only her own conscience and the wishes of her husband need concern her. She was no longer the preacher's daughter and if she cared to dance, she certainly had a right to do so.

With a heady sense of freedom, Hannah offered Harjo a bright smile. "How correct you are, Mr. Harjo, I do need only to concern myself with my husband. I assume you know his feelings in regards to dancing."

Harjo smiled at her, liking her tentative steps toward adventure. "Your husband, ma'am, is an excellent dancer and loves to wear the finish off the floor. I think it is safe to say that he would be interested in a woman who could dance a step or two."

"Well then, Mr. Harjo, I'm counting on you to teach me, because I don't know even one step and have never been on a dance floor before."

"You have come to the right man, Mrs. Watson. As a poor dancer with a gimp leg, I have managed to compress dancing into about three easy moves that get me through most music. I will be happy to demonstrate my meager abilities."

The man was as good as his word and a surprisingly talented teacher. The two of them made their way to an uncrowded area of the floor and Hannah discovered that for a man with such a noticeable limp while walking, Harjo danced with a rustic grace. His explanations of the moves were simple and concise, and in only a few moments Hannah found herself dancing, albeit somewhat clumsily, for the first time.

It was fun and free, like the flight of a bird. Hannah twirled in his arms delighted at her newfound abilities. She could not imagine how this could be a sin and she thought it a shame that she hadn't tried this diversion before.

She imagined other women that might have come to this place with her husband. They would be women that he had sought out, women that he had found attractive and interesting. Hannah felt herself becoming jealous of those faceless females. They had received the attention of Henry Lee because he admired them. She received it because she had trapped him into marriage.

She *was* as capable as any other woman, she *could be* whatever Henry Lee wanted. She was sure of it. If he wanted a woman that dressed fancy and danced with him, she could learn to do that. There wasn't anything that Hannah had tried to do in her life that she hadn't succeeded at in some fashion. She didn't expect it to be simple.

After several semi-graceful turns around the floor both Hannah and Harjo were slightly breathless.

"Do you think they might have a dipper of water or such around here?" Hannah asked her escort.

"We can certainly try to find some," he replied, leading her toward the far corner of the room where a stairway could be glimpsed through a doorway.

An Indian man seemed to be guarding the doorway and stepped in front of them blocking the entrance.

"You looking for something?"

"I'm looking for something to drink," Hannah answered before Harjo had an opportunity to open his mouth.

"You got money?"

Hannah was surprised at the question. Water was not usually for sale in the territory, it was considered only neighborly to offer it freely to anyone.

"Mrs. Watson . . ." Harjo began, but Hannah interrupted him. Her thirst should not be quenched at the expense of a friend.

"My husband is over there with Mrs. Byron," she said pointing Henry Lee out to the man. "His name is Henry Lee Watson and I'm sure he will be glad to pay you."

The man looked at Henry Lee and then at the woman and Harjo. He laughed inexplicably. "Yes, I suspect that he is good for the money." He reached back into the doorway behind him and handed Hannah a quart jar, filled to the brim.

"Thank you," she told him primly and turned away with her nose slightly in the air.

"Mrs. Watson," Harjo touched her arm and drew her aside. "I don't believe that this is what you think it is."

Hannah looked at the contents of the jar. Even through the blue glass, it was obviously clear liquid.

"It's not water," Harjo explained, hoping that she was not going to make a scene. "You've just purchased a quart of whiskey."

"Whiskey!" Hannah's exclamation was desperately whispered. She looked at the jar as if it had suddenly turned into a snake, and then quickly looked around to see if anyone had seen her. "Oh my heavens! What will I do? What will Henry Lee think of me?"

Harjo seemed at a loss for words for an instant, then he smiled broadly. "I think, Mrs. Watson, that your new husband is as tolerant of whiskey as he is of dancing."

"Do you think so?"

"I know so."

Hannah considered for a moment, remembering the evening when he had come home liquored up. He obviously had occasion to drink, although he had promised never to get drunk again. She felt a blush spread through her as she remembered his wild behavior that night, how he'd ripped open her nightgown and kissed her with his tongue in her mouth. Did the liquor make him act that way? She had heard that it gave courage, maybe it gave desire also.

Without another thought she slipped the lid off her jar and brought the fiery contents to her lips. She took a good gulp. The liquid widened her eyes and burned her throat, she was shocked at how terrible it tasted.

"It's awful!" she said, surprised. Harjo's mouth dropped open, stunned at her action. The irony struck him as funny and he laughed gleefully at Hannah's dislike of her husband's fine corn liquor.

"I believe it's an acquired taste, Mrs. Watson. Hardly anyone likes it on the first drink, you simply must keep at it," he told her, his eyes shining with wicked amusement.

She took another small drink. It didn't burn nearly so much as the first one.

"My father would definitely not approve of this. Do ladies actually drink this?"

"Oh, yes indeed, frequently. They say it is for medicinal purposes, but they do drink it. Not to excess, of course."

"Of course."

She was silent for a moment, then asked somewhat tentatively, "Do the ladies my husband has escorted in the past usually partake of liquor?"

Harjo thought of the other women he had seen with Henry Lee, high-priced whores and sassy saloon girls all of whom willingly consumed at least their fair share of any whiskey available.

"Well, actually, Mrs. Watson, most of the women he has escorted in the past have imbibed rather freely." Harjo did worry that his friend would not appreciate having his wife classed in the same group with his former girlfriends. "I do think, however, that ladies consume rather sparingly."

"I'm sure," Hannah agreed. They stood together at the edge of the dance floor, Hannah still holding her quart jar and Harjo trying to keep his humor in check. What a great joke it was going to be when Henry Lee discovered his wife, whom he was afraid to tell that he was in the whiskey business, had purchased whiskey from him.

Wisdom, however, being the greater part of valor,

Harjo decided that it was best that he was not present when Henry Lee discovered the joke.

"I do apologize for deserting you," he said. "But I've just seen a friend across the room that I must speak with. Will you be all right waiting for Henry Lee?"

"Certainly," she said. "I'll be fine."

Left to her own devices, Hannah watched the dancers on the floor, some graceful and poetic, others merely exuberant. She felt slightly uncomfortable, and, at a loss as to what to do while waiting on her husband, she found herself taking casual little sips from the quart jar. It gave her something to occupy her hands and a reason to be standing alone to the side. She decided that Harjo was absolutely right. It was an acquired taste. It still burned a great deal, but she thought the whiskey was actually quite pleasant.

In fact, she thought, the whole evening was quite pleasant. She began to sway to the music. She wanted to sing and dance, float around the room. At that she caught herself. "Now Hannah," she admonished herself. "You can't just go floating around the room." The idea was so funny she began to laugh and couldn't seem to stop. Covering her mouth with her hand, as if to lock in the hilarity that was struggling to escape, she hiccupped. With a little polite cough to cover she took a couple more sips from the jar. She looked across the room and smiled at Henry Lee, who was headed her way.

For the first time that he could remember, Henry Lee regretted the time he had been forced to spend on business. Mrs. Byron was a very astute negotiator, and had refused to purchase one drop of corn liquor. She would not be associated with the whiskey trade. She was willing, however, to allow it to be sold out of her back room for a small fee. Twenty-five percent was what she had considered a small fee. Henry Lee had been furious at that offer. Already the liquor was being sold, so he was caught, but he was unwilling to take all of the risk of bringing the whiskey to the middle of the territory and receive the same amount as if he had stayed home. The bargaining had gone on forever and Henry Lee's eagerness to get it over with so that he could be with his wife did not work in his behalf. He finally agreed on fifteen percent, paid in advance, but vowed that he would never take the risk involved to ship into Muskogee again. It just wasn't worth it.

He was surprised to see Hannah standing by herself, with Harjo nowhere in sight. He hurried over to her. When he was only a few feet away, he saw the mason jar in her hand. It stopped him dead in his tracks. He looked her directly in the eyes. She was smiling so warmly, so sweetly and swaying so unaffectedly to the rhythm of the music. It was obvious that Hannah Bunch Watson was tipsy.

Henry Lee had years of experience with inebriated females and knew that any false moves could create an embarrassing scene. Smiling sweetly he moved to his wife's side and took the whiskey jar out of her hand.

"Did Harjo buy this for you?" His voice was so sweet that Hannah missed the undercurrent of anger in it.

"No, you did!" she answered, laughing at what seemed, for some reason, terribly funny. "I told the man that you were my husband and that you would pay him for it."

"Indeed, I will."

He placed the half-empty whiskey jar on the window sill behind him. "Did Harjo share any of this with you?"

"Oh no, he had something else he had to do. I've just been watching the dancers."

Henry Lee nodded fatalistically. A half quart of corn liquor was a good deal for someone who was not familiar with it.

"Have you ever drunk before?"

"Oh no, my father would never have approved." Hannah found that rather funny also. "But it doesn't matter about my father anymore, I only have to please my husband now." She smiled at him so radiantly that Henry Lee's anger seemed to wilt in the face of it.

"Harjo told me that dancing and drinking are diver-

sions that you like. I want to learn to do those things that
you enjoy." She grabbed his hand eagerly. "Come and
let me show you what I've learned already. Harjo has
been showing me how to dance and it is just wonderful."

Henry Lee could no longer remember why he was
supposed to be angry. Hannah's dancing was far from
perfect, but her natural ability coupled with the lack of
inhibition derived from the drink made it easy for Henry
Lee to lead her through several difficult steps. He enjoyed
teaching her and he loved holding her close.

She did not seem frightened of him at all now. He
decided that perhaps Harjo had unexpectedly done him
a great service. They would dance. He would hold her
close. She would grow accustomed to his touch. And
later, when she was still warm and relaxed from the
liquor, he would teach her another dance. One that was
done, prone, on the bed sheets. He smiled and whirled
her around pressing her as close as was decently possible
in public.

Neemie Pathkiller had slowly made his way around
the room watching every possible entrance and exit. It
was clear that both Hattie Byron and Watson thought
themselves so safe that neither was overly concerned with
getting caught. The liquor was being sold, more or less
openly, through the back stairway. He leisurely made his
way to the doorway and spoke to the Indian making the
sales.

"Give me a quart," he told him offering the bill with
the date written across it. Pathkiller took his jar and
moved over to a window near the far side of the room.
He'd already alerted Tom Quick. The marshall and his
men were waiting for a signal from Pathkiller. As soon as
they knew that Watson had picked up the money they
were going to storm the place and arrest him.

Pathkiller watched the couple swirling together on
the dance floor, neither even slightly aware that their
pleasant evening was about to have a very unpleasant
ending. It was almost too easy.

                    *   *   *

For over an hour Hannah had felt like the princess at the ball. And she danced with the most handsome, most dashing, most charming prince who ever lived. She felt absolutely wonderful. Henry Lee held her so close she could feel the heat from his body and more than once she felt his lips in her hair. She wished all the other people could just disappear and she would simply stand in the middle of this candlelit ballroom and hold the man that she loved.

Into her beautiful dream, the man who sold her the whiskey appeared at Henry Lee's side.

"Just want you to know that we can square up whenever you're ready," he told Henry Lee.

Henry Lee nodded and said he would be with him shortly.

"He certainly is concerned about getting paid," Hannah commented. Henry Lee smiled, now amused at what had happened.

"Are you about ready to leave?" he asked, and then pulled her close. Leaning down to whisper into her ear, he added, "We can stay longer and dance if you like, or we can head back to the hotel."

Hannah blushed prettily, but the whiskey had given her enough courage to overcome her natural modesty and she nodded.

Henry Lee led her to the side of the dance floor, and asked her to wait while he went to transact his business alone. Hannah stood for a moment watching the dancing around her, then she noticed her half-empty jar of whiskey sitting on the window ledge. Having been reared with the adage "waste not, want not," Hannah retrieved her jar and finished the contents in one fiery swoop. She batted her eyes to combat the tears. She felt dizzy for the first time and decided that she had better stay close to Henry Lee. She turned and started in his direction.

The Indian counted out Henry Lee's money. "Thirty-eight gallons made 152 quarts, minus the one that your woman took equals 151 quarts sold." "Thanks," Henry Lee said, giving the grinning salesman a cut for his trouble. Taking his money, Henry Lee folded it, carefully attached it to his money clip and slipped it into his inside jacket pocket. Watching from across the room, Neemie Pathkiller immediately went to the window and slammed it shut. Henry Lee had just turned to find Hannah at his side. She was giggling and weaving a bit and he started to make a comment about not leaving a moment too soon when a commotion broke out near the entrance of the ballroom.

"Federal marshalls! Nobody leaves!" came the command from Tom Quick, hidden from view by the press of the crowd. With muttered expletives and cries of feminine alarm erupting throughout the ballroom, the crowd began hurrying in every direction, trying to find an exit. Both the front and rear doors were blocked by lawmen and the crowd surged around them, trying to push a way out. People tried to scramble through the open windows, but their ways were blocked by deputies.

Henry Lee quickly assessed the situation. He wasn't certain they were after him, but it was highly likely. He wasn't about to stick around and find out for sure. He had not only himself to think about, but Hannah too. He could not allow her to be arrested. He scanned the room desperately, then his eyes fell on the stairway where the whiskey had been sold. Grabbing Hannah by the arm he rushed her through the doorway; stopping to close the door, he jerked a spindle from the stair railing and wedged it against the door. It wouldn't stop anyone, but hopefully it would slow them up a bit.

Rushing up the stairs with Hannah in tow proved to be a bit more difficult. With all the excitement going on around her, Hannah had developed a fit of laughter. Henry Lee was desperately fighting to maintain their freedom while Hannah was shrieking so hard with hilarity that she couldn't seem to walk up the stairs and had to be half-carried, half-dragged.

When they reached the top of the landing, he saw only one door and it was locked. Without hesitation, Henry Lee lowered Hannah to the floor and, grasping the door frame with both hands, slammed his foot into the

niddle, breaking the lock. Hannah literally screeched
with laughter at that.

The living quarters of Mrs. Byron were neat as a pin
and lavishly furnished with fancy veneered furnishings
from back East. Henry Lee hardly gave it a glance as he
quickly hurried through the apartment looking for a back
exit. Hannah, however, was impressed. The room was
the most opulent that she had ever seen and in her current state of mind, she saw no reason not to enjoy the
adventure. Plopping herself down on a backless red satin
settee, she put her feet up and struck a pose that she
imagined to be nonchalant elegance. She threw her head
back, trying for a new, more distinguished affectation but
it was too quick a move, and she decided that lying down
might be the best idea after all.

Henry Lee discovered to his dismay that there was
no back stairway and that if they jumped out any of the
windows, they would land in the arms of the lawmen
surrounding the building. There was a small balcony-
porch off the kitchen in the back. It was roofless except
for a series of slatted boards that served to make some
shade without blocking the sun. Henry Lee eyed the
boards and then grabbing a chair in the tiny kitchen he
stood on the chair, testing each one until he found the
piece he wanted. Slightly loose, he was able to easily pry
it off its frame. He pushed it up, onto the main roof.
Pulling himself up through the space he had created, he
looked over the roof. He saw exactly what he was hoping
for. The roof of the next building could be easily jumped
to from this one and on down the street, it looked to be
possible to go forever over the heads of the officers.

Dropping back down on the porch he hurried to
retrieve his wife. Hannah was lying facedown on the
settee.

"Honey," he shook her gently, "don't go to sleep on
me now. We've got to get out of here."

He pulled her up into a sitting position, but she kept
her eyes tightly shut.

"I can't look," she told him.

"Why not?"

"The room keeps spinning around, I've never seen anything like it. I just sit here and the room goes round and round like a carousel."

Henry Lee shook his head in disbelief. What a time for Hannah to take up drinking!

"Come on, sweetheart," he said, lifting her up into his arms. "Didn't I tell you we were going back to the hotel? Well, we are going to take a different route than how we came. One that nobody has ever taken before."

"We're going to be explorers!" Hannah giggled. "We're going to have our own little adventure, how exciting!"

Henry Lee couldn't help laughing with her. "It is going to be an adventure," he agreed. He just hoped it wouldn't get any more exciting than it already was.

Henry Lee stood her up on her feet next to the kitchen chair on the porch.

"Now watch me," he said, reaching up to grasp the roof boards with his hands. "You just get a good hold here, take one step on the ladder back of the chair, then you get your toe in good between one of these bricks and just climb right up through this opening and I'll lift you up."

He proceeded to pull himself onto the roof and then leaned down to help her.

Hannah tried to steady the spinning room and her shaky legs, but the more effort she put into it, the more difficult it became, and the more difficult it became, the funnier it was. She couldn't even seem to stand on the chair. She tried once, twice, three times to stand herself on the seat. She began giggling again and quickly doubled over with laughter. Dropping to her knees she laid her head down on the chair.

"Give me your hand," Henry Lee ordered, leaning as far down as he could reach. But, even as she obeyed, he knew he didn't have enough leverage to lift her up through the roof as a dead weight.

They had wasted so much time, there wasn't even a second to spare if they had any hope of getting away. He jumped back down on the porch. Picking her up in his arms he stood again on the kitchen chair and pushed her upward in front of him.

"Hannah," he barked in a voice that brooked no argument, "you must crawl up onto the roof. I know that you can do it, so do it!"

Hannah immediately responded to the stern tone of voice and actually grasped the boards and began trying to pull herself up. When it was clear that she was making progress, Henry Lee placed his hands firmly on her bottom and heaved her through the roof until only her legs dangled. Grabbing her right foot, he pushed it up until she had her knee on the roof and she could make the rest of the way by herself.

Henry Lee heard a crash and knew that the marshalls had made their way through the door at the bottom of the stairway. Pleading to the Fates for more time, he quickly followed her to the roof.

Hannah had taken the opportunity to lie down again. Henry Lee gave her a quick look and allowed his mind an instant to recall having her luscious behind right in his face and the sight of her long, stocking-clad legs. Then, forcing himself to the situation at hand, he carefully replaced the board that he had removed from the top of the porch. If he was lucky, no one would recognize the significance of the placement of the kitchen chair and would not come searching the roof for them.

Taking Hannah's hand he helped her to her feet.

"Don't give out on me now, Hannah," he urged. "We've still got a long way to go to get to the hotel."

Hannah took a determined breath and the two hurried across the roof of the building to the south side. The next roof was slightly lower than the one on the Ambrosia Ballroom, and was separated by about a yard. It would be an easy jump, Henry Lee thought, even if he had to carry Hannah. He had just turned to ask if she wanted him to carry her when she went flying, jumping the distance with ease and landing on her feet, only to drop to her knees, laughing again.

Henry Lee quickly jumped after her and grabbed her up in his arms. She began spinning around as if she were dancing again, humming the music and laughing and laughing.

"Hannah Watson, you are the laughingest woman I ever saw! You are going to laugh us right into jail in a minute."

FIFTEEN

For Hannah, the experience of running from roof to roof was an adventure the likes of which she had never seen. Sometimes she ran as easily as Henry Lee, feeling the slight breeze of the hot summer evening, and at other times she would get the giggles and Henry Lee would have to pull her behind him. She wasn't sure how much trouble she and Henry Lee were actually fleeing. Obviously, she had broken the law when she'd purchased the whiskey, but she wasn't certain if Henry Lee's comment about jail was a joke or a possibility. The idea that someone would arrest the daughter of Reverend Farnam Bunch was ludicrous. Then she remembered that she was no longer thinking of herself as the preacher's daughter, now she was Henry Lee's wife. Would someone arrest Henry Lee's wife? She honestly didn't know. After all, his wife did spend her evening dancing as carefree as a Methodist. And who knew what to expect of a woman who drank hard liquor? This new Hannah was someone entirely unfamiliar. But she certainly did seem to have a good deal more fun than the old Hannah!

As they came closer to the end of the block, Henry Lee began to search for a way down. Checking back alleys and side entrances, he finally found the perfect escape route at the back of a building near the end of the block. There was a stairway on the alley that served an apartment on the second floor. It was ideal. He lowered Hannah to the landing and then jumped. As he rushed down the stairs, Henry Lee was already plotting a divergent course back to the hotel. They had come this far, he certainly didn't want to be caught now.

As they reached the bottom of the stairway, he heard the sound of footsteps on the sidewalk at the end of the alley. Grabbing Hannah he pulled her with him into the shaded area under the staircase. As the steps seemed to pause, he cautioned Hannah with a finger to his lips to remain silent. In a sliver of moonlight he saw her face, and realized that it was not going to be possible. Just trying to be quiet was slowly but surely forcing up a riot of giggles and even her own hand upon her mouth was not going to be able to hold them in. The footsteps had stopped as if waiting. Waiting and listening. In the quiet night the slightest sound would easily carry to the street. Henry Lee could not let that happen. Without another thought Henry Lee removed her ineffectual hand from her mouth and replaced it with his lips.

If the liquor had sent Hannah spinning before, the tender contact of Henry Lee's lips seemed an overwhelmingly devastating brew. The giggles that were threatening to escape only moments before had dissipated instantly in the onslaught of passion. His warm lips toyed with her own, testing and teaching as they explored. He deepened the kiss and she wove her arms around his neck, eagerly offering him her mouth. There was no shyness in either as they sought knowledge of the other and pleasure for both.

Henry Lee pulled away slightly, only to return with tiny little nips for the corners of her mouth and she opened for him, anxiously craving the taste of his tongue on her own. As he accommodated her, they pressed more tightly together and Hannah felt his rigid reaction against her belly. With instinct as old as time, she pressed against that heated hardness and squirmed in appreciation.

Henry Lee was panting like a racehorse in the last furlong, he wanted her nearer, much nearer and he wanted her now. Grasping her bottom, he raised her up against him so that his aching desire pressed directly against the hot core of her. It felt wonderful and his tongue did a dance in her mouth to demonstrate his admiration. He began thrusting against her, teaching her how it could be with them, giving her a preview of the wonderful dance they could make together. Because she had no ground to brace her, Hannah could only helplessly accept the lusty passion that was being offered.

Aching, straining against each other, the need for closeness, the ultimate closeness, overrode all other considerations. Neither thought of where they were or the danger that was waiting close by.

Henry Lee's arms began to ache with the strain of holding her up and against him, but he was unwilling to let this hot gratification cease. Raising his knee he brought it up between her legs and she willingly opened for him. She straddled his thigh and he braced his knee on the wall of the building. It wasn't as close as before, but he could still feel the heat of her womanhood against his urgent enthusiasm. And his hands were now free to tease and treasure the heaving breasts that pressed so willingly against him. The stiff aching nipples needed attention that only he could give them, and he gladly gave it.

For Hannah it was wonderful. Straddling him somehow shattered all her preconceived notions of how a lady should behave. The inflexible maleness of his thigh between her own seared her with sensuality. She wiggled and squirmed against him, writhing with desire and pleasure that was almost pain. With the whiskey dulling her normal inhibitions, she found herself anxious to spread herself for him. Mother Nature had meant for her legs to be wide before him and she gratefully complied, wrapping her legs around his waist and pulling herself as tightly to him as possible. She wanted him to feel the effect he had on her. It was her last rational thought. Thinking or planning or considering her actions was no longer possible, her total concentration was on the man whose thigh she rode and the feelings that he evoked in her body.

Her enthusiasm was about to unman him. He'd not felt such loss of control since he was a green kid. She was so hot, so hungry, but with no pretense of practiced ways. She wanted him as the mare wants the stallion, with all her being and as nature intended. And the stallion was about to spill his seed too soon. . . .

He pulled away from her kiss, wanting to clamp down on his ardor. To gain control at last, or to get her out of that dress; he was not sure which he wanted, but he knew that another minute like the last would be his undoing.

"Oh God, Hannah!" His words were loud in the quiet night.

He immediately realized his mistake. He had kissed Hannah to keep her quiet and then he had completely forgotten where he was and had cried out her name.

With her still riding his thigh he clasped her to his bosom and tried to listen. Were the footsteps coming down the alley? Had a deputy heard them and even now was coming to drag them off to jail? Henry Lee couldn't tell. The surging of his own blood, the pounding of Hannah's heart, and the mingled panting of their passion drowned out all other sounds.

"Shhh," he whispered to her as he gently lowered her to the ground. She clung to him as he tried to pull away.

"Let me make sure we are safe," he told her and promised to return quickly.

Stealthily he made his way down the alley toward the street where he'd heard the footsteps. With his back to the building, trying to make himself as small as possible, he managed to get a look down the street. It was completely empty. The owner of the footsteps had gone on and Henry Lee had been so involved with Hannah he hadn't even noticed. He shook his head in disbelief and leaned gratefully against the building, trying to catch his still gasping breath. He ran a disgusted hand over his face and through his hair. Here he was in a strange town, with a tipsy wife, who didn't know about his business, selling whiskey to strangers and being chased by Federal marshalls who wanted to put him in jail for years. So what did he do? Well, he nearly serviced his wife in a public alleyway.

Cursing himself in disgust, he hurried back to find

Hannah slumped against the wall. As he knelt down to help her up, she immediately went back into his arms.

"I love you, Henry Lee," she whispered desperately. "I love the way you make me feel. I never thought marriage would be so nice."

Henry Lee could hardly resist her precious declaration and her welcome embrace.

"Oh Hannah," he said, planting a chaste kiss on her forehead as he pulled her to her feet. "You are going to love being married, and I am going to make you the happiest, most satisfied wife in the territories. That is, if the marshalls don't catch us and send us to jail."

The two made their way through the alleys trying not to encounter anyone on their way back to the hotel. Henry Lee had spent a good bit of time in Muskogee and had always thought that he knew his way around, but the alleys and side streets necessary to avoid detection were mostly unfamiliar, and he just hoped that his luck held enough not to get them irrevocably lost.

Hannah seemed to be fading fast. The liquor that had made her so happy earlier seemed to be making her slightly squeamish now. She was weaving and stumbling so badly that Henry Lee feared she would trip over something in the dark and hurt herself. He decided it was best to carry her, although it slowed them down quite a bit. Hannah was delighted with this arrangement. Being right up against his chest, feeling so safe and comforted. It was almost worth the dizzy stomach she was suffering.

Henry Lee actually passed Williams Hotel without recognizing it. Backtracking, he found a service entrance that he gratefully utilized. With Hannah still in his arms, he quietly made his way to the front lobby. The clerk and several other men seemed to be having a poker game in the room directly behind the desk. Henry Lee easily moved past them and up the stairs.

When he finally set Hannah down in their own room and carefully locked the door behind him, he felt such an overwhelming relief that he began to laugh. It started way down in his diaphragm, just a small amusement that worked its way up his chest, gathering momentum until finally he roared with laughter, leaning with his back against the door laughing as if the last two hours were the funniest he had ever lived. Hannah, leaning against him, began to laugh too. She wasn't quite sure what the joke was, but with the liquor still very much singing in her veins, it was not hard to bring back the giggling episodes that had so incapacitated her earlier. Henry Lee looked at her and remembered how he had to drag her up the stairway, and her inability to stand on the kitchen chair became even more hysterical and as his giggling Hannah leaned against him, the two slowly slid down the door until they were half sitting, half lying together on the floor in front of it.

"What are you laughing at?" she asked him, scarcely able to talk through her own giggles.

Henry Lee couldn't answer, he just pulled her close. With strength born of sexual desire, Henry Lee raised himself from the floor and pulled his wife up beside him.

"Can I have this dance, Mrs. Watson?"

Hannah's head was spinning from the sudden movement from sitting to standing, but she agreeably assumed her position as he led her in a waltz. Spinning, spinning, spinning, the room seemed to be going too fast for Hannah. The light seemed to be getting blue, a strange dark unfathomable blue.

She slumped against Henry Lee, getting his immediate attention.

"Hannah! Hannah! Are you all right?"

When she didn't answer, Henry Lee pulled her up into his arms and carried her into the bedroom. Laying her out on the bed, he fumbled with the lamp, finally managing to light it.

She lay completely immobile on the bed, slightly flushed, but basically healthy. Henry Lee put his hand on her head to check for fever. She was cool and neither too dry nor clammy.

He sat stunned, staring at her for a moment until a slight sound escaped her. It was a snore, a very ladylike and dignified snore, but a snore nonetheless.

She'd passed out.

He continued sitting there just looking at her, not quite believing what he knew to be the obvious truth.

Finally the humor of the situation got the best of him.

"I must be born under an unlucky star!" he proclaimed raising his hands in a mock entreaty to heaven. "On the floor, on the ground, in alleyways, she's ready. But when I finally get her to a bed, she passes out!"

He finally stood. Laughing and pacing the end of the room, he remained amazed at his bad luck.

"Henry Lee," he told himself, "this marriage business is more trouble than meets the eye!"

After a few moments he was finally able to accept his wife's unintentional rejection. He tenderly undressed her, trying, for his own sake, not to look at her scantily clad body. When he had her down to her chemise, he carefully covered her with the sheet and took a blanket for himself and headed into the sitting room to spend a miserable night on a too short settee.

Tom Quick was furious. He had orchestrated a huge net to capture an annoying little minnow, and somehow that wily little fish had managed to get away.

The raid on the Ambrosia Ballroom had taken seventeen men to capture forty-six local citizens. Of those arrested, the only charges that could be filed were three counts of "public drunk" and eleven of "consumption of intoxicating beverages." The three drunks were sleeping it off in the jail and the eleven others had paid their fines and gone home embarrassed and angry with the marshall's department. Threats from those arrested but not charged continued to pour in. They had managed to haul in several important local businessmen whose wives were not aware that they patronized Mrs. Byron's establishment, one off-duty deputy marshall, and the legal counsel for the territorial governor.

But they hadn't been able to nail one no-account whiskey peddler.

The talk would start all over again. *Marshall Quick is not too quick anymore,* they would begin to joke. The retirement talk would begin soon. Suggestions that a new leader, a younger man, might be better suited to the job. The citizens would say that the territory no longer needed desperado hunters, but a civilized police force that concerned itself with the rights and property of the citizens of the territory.

Tom Quick had heard it all before. He had fought it all before. And when he'd finally beaten it, he'd sworn to himself that he would never let himself in for that kind of criticism again But now he had. Henry Lee Watson had made a fool out of Tom Quick, and he was going to be right sorry, before it was over.

A light rap on the side entrance got Marshall Quick's attention.

"Come in!"

Neemie Pathkiller slogged through the door looking like he'd been ridden hard and put up wet. He had taken his eyes off Watson during the raid and had lost him in the chaos. It had taken over three hours to figure out where he'd got off to.

"They left over the roof," he told the marshall. "He was the one that went up through Mrs. Byron's apartment. He removed a board from her balcony overhang and they climbed up onto the roof and made their getaway by the rooftops."

The marshall just stared at Pathkiller, boiling with anger.

"You keep saying *they,* are you sure he took the woman with him?"

"Seems likely since we couldn't find her. Also, I leaned on the Indian selling the whiskey. He spoke to the woman and she claimed to be Watson's wife, for whatever that is worth."

"His wife." The marshall considered this new development. "Wonder what kind of woman would marry herself up to a whiskey peddler."

"Slutty little saloon girl, no doubt," Pathkiller offered.

"Did she seem that way to you?"

"No, not at all," he admitted. "I would have guessed her to be the prayer meeting type. But it could be that

Heaven Sent

she's a good actress. She was drinking whiskey like it was water and those Sunday School girls sure aren't known to be partial to it."

"It's certainly worth looking into," the marshall decided. "But right now we've got us a whiskey peddler to find."

"The trail is plumb cold, Marshall. I could never follow him now."

The marshall shook his head in exasperation. "Use your brain, Pathkiller. It's the middle of the night. What would a man with money in his pocket and a pretty woman on his arm be looking for?"

Pathkiller considered for a minute, then a thin smile broke out on his face. "He'd be looking for a bed," he answered the marshall, who smiled back and nodded in agreement.

Fortunately for Henry Lee, Neemie Pathkiller judged all men using himself as a yardstick. When he went looking for a bed, he generally looked for the cheapest in town. Assuming that Henry Lee would also, Pathkiller began a systematic search of the cribs and flophouses. It took time, since most of the proprietors of these establishments were not particularly willing to get up in the middle of the night to discuss who might or might not be sleeping upstairs.

Pathkiller was sure that Watson would not use his own name, so he merely gave a description of the couple. This led to two false leads, where Neemie broke into rooms to find that the "good-looking part-breed and the big blonde" were not the Watsons.

It was midmorning before Neemie worked his way up to the Williams Hotel. The desk clerk was jabbering on the telephone contraption and Neemie had to cool his heels a good five minutes before the man deigned to speak to him.

Pathkiller didn't hold out much more hope. If he'd been Watson, he would have split town at first light. He'd had someone check all the westbound trains, but Watson hadn't left on any of them. It was as if the man had been swallowed up into thin air.

He was not, however, going to stop looking until he had covered every possibility. It was a matter of pride with him now. He had taken his eye off his target and had missed. He would be careful not to make another mistake.

"May I help you, sir?"

"I'm looking for some people. A married couple, should have come in town yesterday or the day before. The man's tall, well-favored, dark, part Cherokee from his looks, and the woman's kinda blonde, kinda brown hair, a big woman but shapely." Pathkiller used his hands to describe the woman's shape.

The desk clerk recognized them immediately.

"Oh, you must mean the Watsons!"

Pathkiller was stunned. "You mean they are here!"

"Well, they aren't here right now. I think I saw them head out a couple of hours ago, but yes, they are still staying here." He quickly checked the register. "Yes, they have their room reserved for one more night."

At 10:30 a.m. Marshall Tom Quick paid a visit to Hattie Byron. Ostensibly, he went to apologize for the trouble and inconvenience the raid had caused her. Actually he was there for information. He'd always believed himself to be very persuasive with the ladies, so with his shoulders dusted and his hair slicked down, he went to find out what the proprietress of the Ambrosia Ballroom knew about Henry Lee Watson.

Hattie Byron was not in the best of moods. And seeing Tom Quick was just what she needed to set her off.

"Good morning, Marshall." Her voice reeked with sarcasm. "I certainly hope that it is a good morning for you, because it has been one of the most terrible that I have ever spent in my life!"

"I'm very sorry to hear that, Mrs. Byron."

"You are sorry to hear it? Why, you should already know it, Marshall. After all it *is* your fault, isn't it?"

The marshall cringed slightly. She was some fiery woman, he thought. He secretly wondered if she was as excitable in the bedroom as she seemed to be in the parlor.

"That is exactly why I came over this morning, ma'am. To apologize for the terrible ordeal you suffered through last night. I can imagine that you are devastated to think that criminal activities were taking place in your own establishment, against your knowledge."

The marshall was no fool. She made money on whatever whiskey was sold last night, but there would never be any way to prove it and she could be of more help working with him instead of against him.

Hattie wasn't about to accept his apology, even if he was offering her a deal.

"You have no idea what I went through, Marshall Quick. First, my business is nearly destroyed. Many of the draperies are beyond repair. Then I am dragged to jail, actually to jail! Where I am forced to sit for hours, until I am finally allowed to come home. I find that my apartment had been broken into in my absence. Now tell me, Marshall, why weren't you busy arresting the person who broke into my house instead of persecuting an honest, hardworking widow woman?"

Her flashing eyes and dramatic gestures intrigued the marshall and all during her tirade he found his gaze drifting to her ample breasts, so decently covered with black brocade.

"Was anything missing in your apartment?" the marshall asked hopefully.

"Not that I've noticed, everything was pretty much in place. But the lock on the door was destroyed and must be replaced."

Tom Quick was grateful she was angry at the intruder. He was more than willing to use it to help his cause.

"Actually, Mrs. Byron, I am looking for the man who broke into your apartment."

He had her attention now. As if suddenly remembering her manners she said, "Marshall, please take a seat.

Let me get you some coffee." She brought him a cup
and a plate of cookies. "Thank you, ma'am," he said,
mimicking a courtly bow.

"I just hate the idea of strangers being in my quarters," she told him. "I want to know who they were and
why they broke in."

"The man we sought in last night's raid is a moonshiner and whiskey peddler from out near the border, by
the name of Henry Lee Watson. Ever heard of him?"

Mrs. Byron was as good a poker player as she was a
businesswoman. "No, Marshall, I can't say as I have ever
heard that name before."

Quick knew that she was lying, a secret shared with
this woman would be a secret forever. He wondered if
she had a man sharing her secrets. If not, he fully
intended to be that man shortly.

"Watson was the only person we were looking for
last night," he said. "Seems he's trying to move some of
his whiskey business down this way and we want to nip
that in the bud."

Mrs. Byron nodded and offered Marshall Quick
another cookie. She was aware of the marshall's specula-
tive interest in her, but business was business. A woman
didn't get ahead in this world by thinking between her
legs instead of between her ears.

"Watson managed to get away from us last night by
breaking into your apartment and getting onto the roof
from your balcony."

"That's impossible!"

"Come let me show you."

The two made their way to the porch where Marshall
Quick located the loose board.

"They climbed up on something, got on the roof and
headed on down the street."

"The chair." Mrs. Byron snapped her fingers. "There
was a kitchen chair sitting right out here next to the wall
and I couldn't for the life of me figure out why."

"Well, that's why, Mrs. Byron. Your burglar is that
whiskey peddler and we intend to get him."

Hattie Byron considered that for a moment. The marshall seemed very determined and if he caught Watson, there was always the possibility that he might implicate her. It was best to cover yourself first and worry about the next guy when you have the luxury to do so.

"What did you say this man's name was again?"

"Henry Lee Watson."

"I believe I have heard of him, Marshall. A handsome, dark-haired man in his mid-twenties?"

"Yes, that's him."

"I did see him here last night," Hattie admitted. "He was with his new wife. I understood this was their honeymoon trip."

"Oh, really?"

"Yes, just a few weeks ago he married a preacher's daughter from over in the Oklahoma Territory."

"A preacher's daughter!"

"Yes." Hattie moved closer as if she couldn't bear to speak such gossip above a whisper. "They say her father caught them fair and square and that there was nothing left for the man to do but marry up in a hurry."

The marshall was really getting somewhere now. If he could keep this woman talking, maybe he could find out a way to get Watson.

"Perhaps we might sit in the parlor and discuss it," he suggested.

"Certainly," she said, turning to make her way back through the house. Hattie could feel the marshall's eyes on her and she turned to catch him watching her behind with appreciation.

Mrs. Byron had heard it said that Marshall Quick was randy as a goat, but very discreet. This could turn out to be more pleasure than business.

SIXTEEN

The early train from Muskogee to Sallisaw was not crowded, but it made frequent stops to deliver mail and pick up milk and eggs from local farmers.

Henry Lee and Hannah sat together, not touching, both lost in the sober recollections of the night before. For all the laughing that was done the previous night, the situation wasn't nearly so funny this morning.

Her head splitting and her eyes blurry, Hannah felt worse than she'd ever imagined possible. Her stomach had been squeamish the night before; after an abrupt emptying of its contents this morning, she felt hollow and achy.

When Henry Lee had awakened her this morning, she'd felt as if her eyelids were nailed shut. She had vivid recollections of the previous evening and she was shocked at her own behavior. Who would have thought that such a small amount of that clear, innocuous-looking liquid could make one act so strange, or feel so bad the next day?

Her behavior, both in public and later in that darkened alley, was personally embarrassing and morally inept. She was the churchgoer, she should be setting an example for her husband. Instead, she proved to be no match for the temptations of the flesh, dancing and drinking. She had wanted to prove herself as sophisticated as a woman he might have chosen on his own. How could she forget that her best features were her strong back and God-fearing heart? She had ignored every lesson her father had ever taught her, defiling her body with demon liquor and degrading herself by her wanton behavior.

Humiliated and ashamed, she decided that a good lesson had been learned. Never again would she compromise with the ways of the flesh. She would remain stalwart and controlled. Now that she was personally versed in the evils of corn liquor, she would use that knowledge to work for temperance in the territory.

Henry Lee was feeling as much regret as Hannah. After the ironic hilarity of the night had passed, he had been chillingly aware that he had placed his wife in danger.

The thought that she might have been taken into custody brought on a cold sweat. A woman like Hannah should never see the inside of a jail. And what would she have said going up before the judge? She knew nothing of the whiskey business, she would be totally innocent. And because of her ignorance, totally humiliated. He shuddered at the thought.

But he gave himself no pats on the back for getting her away, either. Dragging her across rooftops and through alleyways in the middle of the night was dangerous. What if she had tripped and fallen? She might have injured herself, or the baby! What kind of man would put his woman in such a situation? A worthless no-account, he answered himself, eaten up with remorse.

He turned to look at her sitting so stiffly beside him. He had vowed to love and protect her, no matter that it wasn't his idea. No one could have made him marry her if he hadn't been willing. He had wanted to have a decent woman for a wife, but he had proved unworthy of the gift.

Hannah looked pale, drawn, and weary. A wave of unexpected tenderness washed through him. He put his arm around her shoulder and drew her to him.

"Just rest here against me," he said as she started to pull away. "You look so tired, you need a little nap to begin the day."

"I am so ashamed of the way I acted," she confessed.

"I wanted to impress you with how sophisticated and citified I could be."

She hid her face in the front of his shirt, not able to face him squarely and riddled with guilt. Confession was good for the soul, it was said. She intended to be honest about her behavior.

"Mr. Harjo told me that other ladies that you escorted in the past drank intoxicating beverages, and I wanted to prove to you that I was not a bit less worldly than they."

Hannah couldn't see Henry Lee's smile. He was surprised that she chose to apologize. He had expected her first concern to be his part in the liquor raid. But it pleased him that she was willing to go against her own upbringing to try to get his attention.

"Hannah," he whispered gently. "I haven't a thought for any of my former companions. None of them could hold a candle to you, of that I'm sure." He squeezed her shoulder lightly hoping to reassure as well as comfort her.

"Henry Lee, when I think of how embarrassed you must have been, having the marshalls chasing us."

Henry Lee stiffened, waiting for her reaction to the marshalls and his obvious involvement in the raid.

Hannah gave a ladylike sniff, trying to hold back the flood of tears that threatened. "When I think that you might have been arrested and taken to jail because I, so foolishly, wanted to try to pretend that I am something that I'm not. When I think of that, Henry Lee, I just don't know how you can forgive me."

Henry Lee held her in silence for a moment trying to gather his thoughts. Obviously, she thought the whole chase was over her quart of corn liquor. It was more evidence of how naive she was about the whiskey business, and made him feel even worse. He wanted to tell her, he wanted to make her understand. It was important to him that she did. There should be no lies between a man and his wife. He would be honest with her at last. But today was not the day.

He hushed her tears and kissed her lightly on the forehead. He held her close and reassured himself that there would be time enough to tell her later.

*   *   *

Sallisaw was a pretty little community in the foothills of the Ozarks about thirty miles west of Fort Smith, whose citizens were mostly fruit growers. Strawberries and peaches were the main crops, but it was good land, this corner of the Cherokee Nation, and a man could grow just about anything.

As the two stood on the train platform and surveyed the little town, Hannah sighed longingly.

"Do you think we'll ever have real little towns like this out our way?"

Henry Lee smiled at her. He understood her need for community. He felt it too.

"Towns just take time, Hannah. There have been settlements here in Indian Territory for over fifty years. You can't expect Oklahoma Territory to accomplish as much in less than ten."

They smiled at each other, feeling a sense of accord.

"You really think that it will be this way out on the border?"

He nodded, smiling. "Our children will grow up knowing all there is to know about towns."

Hannah blushed at the reference to children. She felt a rush of pleasure at the prospect of having a child of Henry Lee's. In her mind she saw an impetuous toddler in knee pants, thick black hair and shining blue eyes. She wouldn't meet Henry Lee's eyes for fear he would see her longing there.

Henry Lee misinterpreted her evasiveness and thought her to be embarrassed about the child she carried. Pulling her into a deserted alleyway that offered a modicum of privacy Henry Lee pressed her back against the clapboard building and placed his hand on her belly, openly claiming the child for his own.

"I mean all our children, Hannah," he told her quietly, placing a tiny kiss on her forehead. "This one too."

Hannah enjoyed the loving caress but didn't comprehend his words.

"What are you saying?"

His voice soft with sincerity he told her. "The child

that you carry is mine in every way but blood. I'm going to accept him as my own and I want you to know that I won't ever allow him to believe anything else."

Hannah was bewildered as she gazed into the depths of her husband's eyes. "Henry Lee, you are not talking sense. I can't be carrying a child. We haven't . . . well, you know . . . we haven't." Hannah blushed as she attempted to explain her confusion.

Looking at her quizzically, Henry Lee was more specific. "I'm talking about the child you already carry, the other man's child."

"What other man?" Hannah's voice was a little too loud and clearly shocked.

Henry Lee stood stock-still, looking at her. He would have told anyone that he was very good at getting a quick grasp on a situation. But at the present time he was struggling pitifully to figure out what wrong turn he had taken to get to the unfamiliar ground he was now treading.

"You're not having a child." It was a statement more than a question.

"Hannah, why did you marry me?"

She looked at him quizzically for his strange turn of mind.

"We've been through all that, Henry Lee. It embarrasses me to even think about it, I sure don't want to have to talk about it, again. I told you I was sorry. I really never meant to do it to you."

He took her hand in his own and squeezed it gently. "I don't want to embarrass you, Hannah. But I need to know exactly what you were doing in the wellhouse that night. You knew your daddy was going to find us, why did you let that happen?"

She tried to turn away from him. He understood that she didn't want to face him. Pulling her back to his chest, he held her close and comforted her, so she wouldn't have to look him in the eye.

"Just start from the beginning and tell me everything."

Hannah took a deep breath gathering her courage. She didn't understand why Henry Lee wanted her to confess it all at last, but she knew that she owed him this explanation for a good long while, and at least she would be glad to have it over and done.

Henry Lee quietly listened to her story, tiny seeds of joy timidly blooming in his heart.

"Myrtie was near grown and Papa had remarried. I didn't have any reason to be at home anymore. I wanted to marry, to have a family of my own. But I didn't have a suitor. To tell the truth, Henry Lee, I never had one, not even one," she confessed sorrowfully. "But Will Sample hung around the house all the time. I was sure that Will had feelings for me. He was so shy. Every time I would try to talk to him, try to draw him out, he'd get all clumsy and red-faced. I just convinced myself that he wanted to call on me, but that he was too shy to do it."

She pushed an errant lock of hair from her face, securing it behind her ear. "The months were just passing by and nothing was changing, he never tried to talk to me or sit with me, or walk out with me, and I just couldn't wait any longer. I wasn't in love with him, but I knew I could make him a good wife. I can keep a good house, you know that, and I'm a hard worker. I always have been."

Henry Lee listened to her ill-fated plan to trap Will Sample with a smile on his face and blossoming good humor. It was hard to imagine, his Hannah as a manhunter. But it was a sure bet that it took a desperate situation and a lot of Bible reading to turn her into one.

When she finished her shameful tale, she hung her head and spoke pleadingly.

"I know you can't forgive me for mixing you up in this foolish mess."

"Forgive you," Henry Lee laughed and turned her to face him. "I don't want to forgive you, I want to thank you. Believe me, Hannah. I am a much better husband for you than Will. He's a decent, hardworking man, but the two of you together would have made the most boring couple in the territory. You need a man to bring a little sparkle to your pretty cheeks. And I am definitely the man for the job!"

He punctuated his appraisal with a series of feathery love bites to her throat. Chills of delightful fire flew down Hannah's neck as she glanced around to assure herself that no one was looking.

"You're not angry?"

"I'm elated. You won't believe what I thought your reasons were."

Hannah looked at him questioningly and he briefly explained about overhearing her conversation with Myrtie and the conclusions he had drawn.

"How could you think that of me?" Hannah protested.

"I didn't know what to think, it made sense to me. A woman with a child on the way needs a husband and pretty near any husband will do."

Hannah shook her head as if it were too much to grasp.

"And you didn't mind. You thought I carried another man's baby, that I was using you to cover up my own wickedness, and you kept me anyway."

"I was crazy mad at first, Hannah, but I couldn't blame the child, I knew it wasn't his fault. After a while, when I came to care for you, well, I couldn't blame you either."

He lifted her chin and looked deeply into her eyes. He wanted her complete attention. He wanted her to understand what he was saying, so there would never be a question in her mind.

"You are my wife, Hannah. Because of that, your child would be my child, no matter the circumstances."

Hannah felt her eyes welling up with tears.

"You know what I think?" she told him, wiping away the evidence of her emotions with the back of her hand. "I think God was hearing my prayers all along, and he sent you into that wellhouse, just for me."

Henry Lee smiled at her tenderly, not willing to dispute, but wondering if God ever took a hand in the personal lives of whiskey peddlers.

To chase his darker thoughts away, Henry Lee pulled

her eagerly into his embrace, his lips tenderly bearing fire to her blood.

Hannah wrapped her arms around him, tracing the strong, sinewy muscles of his shoulders and back. Kissing him with her tongue, the way he'd taught her, she heard a moan deep in his throat, and felt the reaction of his body pressing against her.

"Hannah darlin'," he said pulling away. "I don't think I can live until this day is over. How many hours is it until we can go back to the hotel?"

Giggling at his tone of desperation, Hannah placed her hand in his, her heart was in her eyes, as they walked down the dusty main street of the sleepy town.

"It's a long time, Henry Lee, but I've got a feeling that it will be worth the wait."

They made one stop at the telegraph office. Henry Lee had promised to send the money for the south Tulsa land to Morelli and he was grateful to get rid of the whiskey profits that he carried. Hannah was somewhat surprised to see such a pile of currency. She couldn't imagine why he had brought it all the way to Sallisaw to send it to Tulsa. As the telegraph operator counted out the cash, neither paid any attention to yesterday's date scrawled in pen across the face of one of the bills.

Feeling uncomfortable under Hannah's gaze, Henry Lee quickly asked, "Which way to the Sallisaw Table Company?"

"Just keep going right down to the end of this street, when the road curves away, that's it," the operator told him, leaning out from the counter and pointing to the west.

Henry Lee thanked him and retreated as quickly as possible, taking Hannah's arm and escorting her outside. He didn't want to make up any false explanations for Hannah, he wanted honesty between them and soon.

"You forgot your receipt!" the man called after them, but they were already gone.

The Sallisaw Table Company was a large brightly painted barn of a place at the edge of town.

Henry Lee, matching his step with Hannah's, gazed

down at her. His eyes dancing with mischief, he relayed the story of the company's proprietors.

"It's owned by two brothers, Hiram and Willard Oscar. But as anyone in Sallisaw can tell you, the Oscars are more than brothers. Shortly after they came to the territory, Hiram married Nellie Winkle, a fine-looking widow a few years older than himself."

Hannah nodded, encouraging him to go on.

"Now Nellie had a pretty little teenage daughter from her first marriage. She and Hiram hadn't been married no more than a year or two before Willard, Hiram's younger brother, and the daughter, Maude, fell for each other and got themselves married."

Henry Lee hesitated in his discourse, allowing Hannah to add up the ramifications of this consequence.

"That made Hiram Willard's stepfather-in-law as well as his brother," Hannah concluded. "And it made Willard Hiram's stepson-in-law, as well as younger brother."

Smiling at her quick wit, Henry Lee continued. "When both Nellie and Maude gave birth not three months apart, the cousins born were also uncle and nephew."

Hannah shook her head in disbelief. "I bet that was prime fodder for gossip for a good long time."

"About thirty years," Henry Lee agreed. "But it wasn't such a bad thing for business. The story was told and retold so much that nearly everyone has heard of the Sallisaw Table Company."

Henry Lee regaled Hannah with the story. "It might have died down just with the passage of time," he said, "but the two boys when they grew up fell in love with identical twin sisters!"

Hannah giggled, her eyes wide with amusement. "Did that make their children double cousins or what?"

"I don't know, but it sure made the Oscar family famous in these parts."

Neither Hiram nor Willard had yet retired to rocking chairs, and both greeted Henry Lee and Hannah in the shade of a young maple outside the building. Hands were shaken all around and the prerequisite discussion of the weather completed, before Henry Lee stated his business.

"I'm hoping to make some pews for a new little church over in the Oklahoma Territory," Henry Lee said. "I need some good lumber, and as much advice as you're willing to give. I know a bit about working the wood, but I'm self-taught and always willing to listen to those that know more about it."

As Willard talked to Henry Lee asking what his ideas were and what kind of lumber he was hoping to afford, Hiram stood back and took the young man's measure. He seemed a straightforward, upright young man and his woman seemed clean and decent, hanging on his every word. He decided that he liked the boy. When Hiram made a decision, it was rarely revoked.

"Come on in here, boy," Hiram called to him. "Let's see what you know about wood."

Henry Lee and Hannah followed the two men into the building. The smell of sawdust was fresh and pungent, but not a pile of it could be seen anywhere. The Oscars were fastidiously clean and knew well the fire dangers posed by their line of work.

The walls and cupboards contained more kinds of saws, chisels, clamps, planes, and calipers than Henry Lee had ever seen in his life and in the corner near the back window was a huge lathe run by a foot treadle. A fine piece of white oak waiting immobile in a vise, a bow saw ready at its side, was prepared to become part of a fancy chair back. A door stood open on the far wall and revealed an open area full of cut lumber of all descriptions and a huge pit saw in the middle of the yard.

Henry Lee felt a surge of excitement go through him and he quickly shared it with a smile to Hannah.

Hiram saw it, and with a nodding smile from his brother, was reassured that he was quite right about this boy.

"Come on now, let's see what you can do. See how much you know then we can figure out what we can teach you."

Henry Lee eagerly handed his jacket to Hannah and

rolled up his sleeves. He felt like a kid who had just been given free rein in a candy store.

Willard drew Hannah away.

"My house is right through the woods there, down that path," he said pointing out the front door. "My Maudey would be mighty pleased to have a brand-new person to gossip with," he told her smiling. "Your husband's going to have his hands full with Hiram, so tell my wife to set a couple more plates for dinner."

Hannah gave one last lingering look to her husband. He was diving into the work with cheerful enthusiasm. Pleased for him, she hummed a catchy tune while making her way through a path of cottonwoods to the house sitting on the rise.

Maude Oscar's kitchen was bustling with activity when Hannah arrived. Children of various sizes and ages wandered in and out as Maude alternately scolded or praised. She seemed delighted at her unexpected company and immediately set Hannah to peeling peaches for canning.

As soon as word got out that Maude had a guest, her mother/sister-in-law, Nellie, showed up and the twin daughters-in-law were not far behind. Daisy and Dulce were about Hannah's age, both pregnant and with toddlers in tow.

"I got a look at your husband down at the shed," Dulce said to her and then expressively drew the attention of the rest of the crowd. "He is some looker, your man! Why, he nearly took my breath away."

"Dulce May!" her sister scolded her. "Don't pay Dulce any mind," she told Hannah, patting her reassuringly on the arm. "She's always looking at the men, it don't mean nothing, it's just her way," Daisy explained to Hannah.

"It never hurts to look," Dulce insisted. "That's all I could do anyhow," she complained, patting her rounded stomach. "My man keeps my belly big as a cow with his young 'uns all the time. The only way I could get a man to look at me these days would be to set my hair on fire!"

Hannah laughed along with the rest, but sensed in

Dulce a free spirit that was not so sorry to be tamed by a "belly as big as a cow."

"When are you due?" Hannah asked the twins.

"I'm expecting mine in about six weeks," Daisy answered, "but Dulce could have hers anytime, and she always does it early!"

"What about you?" Dulce asked her, "Maudey said you was looking pretty peaked when you came in this morning."

"Dulce!" A chorus of disapproving relatives scolded the young woman for her curiosity.

"Oh no," Hannah told them, blushing furiously, "I'm not in the family way."

"You sure?" Nellie asked her. "That's one of the first signs, you know, feeling like to puke in the mornings."

"No," Hannah insisted. "We just got married." She felt a strange sense of pleased embarrassment. "We are kind of on our honeymoon."

"On your honeymoon!" Dulce exclaimed. "And you let your man get away for a whole day to build furniture? I wouldn't let my Jacob leave even to go to the outhouse!"

The women howled with laughter. Hannah covered her face in embarrassment. She had never heard women talk of such things in her life. But then, she reminded herself, she had never been one of the married women before.

She felt surprisingly comfortable with these plainspoken women and she felt safe enough to risk a question.

"It's kind of natural, then, to want your husband to be in bed with you?"

"They ain't nothing in the world more natural!" Dulce insisted.

"You don't think it's unbecoming for a Christian woman to be so . . . so lustful?" Uncomfortable now, Hannah wished she had never brought the subject up.

"Didn't your mother talk to you?" Nellie asked.

"She's dead, and my stepmother did talk to me, but she never said anything about the kinds of feelings I have . . . well, with Henry Lee," Hannah admitted, blushing.

"Honey," Maude said, taking a seat at Hannah's

right, "that's exactly how you're supposed to feel. It makes perfect sense. Why would a woman go through all she had to go through to get a baby, if the making of them was something she hated."

Nods of agreement were seen all around. "God intended for a man and a woman to enjoy the mating, so they'd be fruitful and multiply," Daisy put in.

"Besides," Dulce added, "it ain't fair that only the sinners should have fun!"

Laughter ricocheted through the kitchen again, and Hannah joined in.

The noon meal was served on the biggest table Hannah had ever seen. It was at least twenty feet long, large enough for every person in the family.

"That's one advantage of making your own furniture," Nellie told her. "You can have exactly what you want."

Henry Lee came in with the other men, looking flushed and happy. Woodworking was a hard job, but it was clean, satisfying work. He was basking in the admiration and respect he had received from the Oscar brothers.

"You've a natural feel for the wood," Hiram told him. "You can look at the raw lumber and see what's best to be done with it. That's not something that can be taught." The old man shook his head. "My boys, they work hard and do exactly what I tell them, but they don't have what you and I have. It's a gift, just like singing or playing the fiddle."

The old man's approval lightened Henry Lee's step and working with the Oscars' marvelous collection of tools was sheer pleasure.

Henry Lee was seated next to Hannah at the long table and anxiously tried to tell her all the things he'd learned. Hannah's eyes rarely strayed from her husband as she listened to his animated description of the Oscars' woodshop.

"Hannah told us you're on your honeymoon," Dulce stated, sitting across from Henry Lee and thoroughly enjoying the bright handsome smile he'd been bestowing on Hannah.

Henry Lee grinned, only slightly embarrassed by the personal nature of the question.

"Yes, ma'am," he answered.

At the surprised looks from the men at the table, it was obvious that Henry Lee had said nothing about his newly married state.

"In fact," he went on, "Hannah's daddy is the preacher of the church that needs the pews. I'm kind of making them as a present to my father-in-law for letting me get away with his girl." His joke brought laughter around the table and he smiled warmly at his bride.

In the afternoon Hannah helped Maude carry the dozens of quarts of peach preserves down to the cellar, making room for them among the stacks of canned goods necessary to feed the Oscar clan for the winter. Hannah talked about her own home and all of the things she hoped to accomplish over the winter. It was a surprisingly pleasant experience to be with people who thought of her only as herself and Henry Lee's wife, not as the preacher's daughter.

Henry Lee was also enjoying the unusual circumstance of being neither the son of his ne'er-do-well father nor the whiskey man. He was accepted by the Oscars as an equal and relished his newfound normalcy.

Hiram showed Henry Lee the use of the coping saw and taught him to make fancy scrollwork for decoration.

"You do the scalloping in soft white pine," he told Henry Lee, "then when you put the finish on them, you make them match up to your other wood, like they was a part of it."

The edging and trims were new to Henry Lee and he eagerly absorbed all the information that the old man imparted.

"Back East they are counting on veneers to do everything for them," the older man complained, shaking his head. "But a piece is only as good as the wood and the workmanship, and covering up shoddy work with a fancy top piece is the same as cinching a Spanish saddle on a mule. All that silver looks mighty pretty, but it still ain't much to ride."

By late afternoon Henry Lee had decided on the lumber he wanted for the church benches. Hiram and Willard approved his choice of a fine-grained walnut. He'd use spruce or pine for the underneath parts, as they were softer and easier to work with, but the beauty of the walnut could not be duplicated elsewhere.

"You should be staying the night with us," Hiram told him. "We always got plenty of room, there was no need for you to get a hotel room in Muskogee."

Willard joked, "Now Hiram, you don't expect a man to spend his honeymoon with us. I'm thinking he'll be right grateful to get back to that hotel room this evening." The man winked conspiratorially. "That is, if you haven't plumb worn him out today."

Hiram waved the suggestion away. "He's young!" he announced and proceeded to tell a ribald story about a young man on his wedding night.

Henry Lee laughed good-naturedly, but he was eager to be alone with his wife. He felt good, optimistic about their future. It seemed that after a day with the praise and encouragement of the Oscar brothers, he felt that maybe he did deserve a portion of happiness for his own.

They left on the last train of the day; with well-wishes and hugs all around, Hannah promised that when Henry Lee came again to buy lumber, she would be sure to come with him.

Hiram took Henry Lee aside and told him solemnly, "If you ever are in need of a job, or if I can help you in any way, let me know. You seem like a man who makes his own way, but everyone needs a bit of help now and again."

The couple sat smiling comfortably together for the short ride back to Muskogee. In sharp contrast to the guilt and remorse of the morning, both were in high spirits and talking. The Oscars were definitely memorable and together they giggled over whether the parents themselves could even tell whose children were whose.

Hannah relaxed against Henry Lee's shoulder and he placed a delicate kiss in her hair. She felt it, relished it, but didn't acknowledge it. Henry Lee was eager, but felt no compunction to hurry. They would be back at the Williams Hotel in an hour or so, but more than that, they had their whole lives together before them. It was such a comforting thought that he relaxed completely, closed his eyes and fell into the kind of sleep usually reserved for the innocent.

Hannah felt his body sag against her and knew that he was sleeping. She felt a little bit smug, the man lying relaxed at her side belonged to her. She turned slightly to get a look at his face. Even in sleep, there was nothing boyish about him. His strong jaw, high cheekbones, and dark brows were still tough and manly. Inexplicably, she felt a surge of tenderness for him. Like her, he had never been a child, never known the carefree times of youth. But, unlike her, he hadn't buried his childhood in the rigid codes of adult life, he had simply brought to adult life the laughter and humor of childhood. At that moment, Hannah could not imagine a finer man anywhere. She laid her head against his chest and slept also.

Neemie Pathkiller had waited all day either in or around the Williams Hotel. By now he was angry and frustrated. His greatest fear was that they had realized the danger and simply left their belongings behind as a decoy.

He knew that they must have had contacts in town to do business, but he couldn't track them down. He did know that there was some connection with Charles Harjo, but exactly what the relationship was, he couldn't be sure. He was having Harjo watched in hopes that he would lead them to Watson, but the wily Indian was as cool as Christmas, and thus far had done nothing out of the ordinary.

He had just leaned against the side of the building, preparing to roll himself a cigarette, when he heard running feet coming down the alley.

A young Cherokee boy stopped in front of the hotel, looked the area over closely, and then hurried up to Neemie.

"A man told me to find you and say that they just

got off the northbound Iron Mountain, and are coming this way."

Neemie stared at the boy for a minute with venom in his eyes, making sure that he kept what he knew to himself, then he tossed him a penny.

"Go to Marshall Quick's office at the courthouse. Tell him that the man at the Williams Hotel says 'soon.' "

He silently continued to roll his cigarette, but when he'd finished, his lips curved slightly. So, they had risked coming back. Now he had them.

SEVENTEEN

H annah, her arm entwined with her husband's, made
her way through the streets of Muskogee toward
their personal haven, the Williams Hotel. Their short train
nap had seemed to revitalize them both and they were
bubbling with smiles and enthusiasm.

They had made a quick stop by the jeweler's, and
the third finger of Hannah's left hand now sported the
gleaming evidence of her marriage.

Henry Lee was on his most charming behavior, telling her an amusing story of a haberdasher who tried to
sell his ribbons and ladies' hats by modeling them
himself.

Hannah found herself paying more attention to the
teller than the tale, as she gazed warmly at Henry Lee's
sparkling eyes and flashing smile. Both were consciously
trying not to think about the evening ahead. They were
trying to be satisfied with the happiness they felt together
at the moment, not wishing themselves into the future.

Hannah saw the men step out from the doorway of
the hotel, but until they laid hands on Henry Lee, she
hadn't known to be afraid.

Tom Quick's authoritative voice rang out: "Henry Lee
Watson, by order of the U.S. Government and the Department of Justice for the Indian Territory, you're under
arrest for trafficking in intoxicating beverages!"

Quick allowed the two younger deputies to grab
Henry Lee and cuff him. He wanted to watch the young

whiskey peddler's face as his future took a drastic turn for the worse.

"What are you doing?" Hannah cried out as Henry Lee was pushed up against a wall spread-eagle, and frisked for weapons. Finding nothing the deputies jerked his hands behind him and placed him in handcuffs.

"You are making a terrible mistake!" Hannah told the marshall. "My husband and I are from out of town, we are here on our honeymoon. He's not involved in anything illegal."

Tom Quick glared at the young woman, sneering. Hannah could see that he didn't believe her and turned to her husband to substantiate her assertion.

"Tell him, Henry Lee! This is some terrible mistake."

Henry Lee was facing away from her and did not look her way or say a word. He was numb with emotional pain. *Don't look at me!* his brain was screaming, but he held his peace. He had not protected her after all; she was going to see him arrested, maybe even be arrested herself. A woman like his Hannah should never know anything about jails or the people in them. He turned to look at the marshall. He knew the old man was Tom Quick. They had both been in the territory for a long time. Quick knew all about him, all about his business, and if he had decided to arrest him tonight, he obviously had enough evidence to send him to jail. He felt an ominous sense of doom.

"Let the woman go, Quick!" He tried to make it sound like an order, but he couldn't hide the plea in his voice. "She knows nothing about it."

Hannah heard his words and felt as if the ground she stood upon had been jerked away, but she fought it. Henry Lee needed her and she would not—could not—allow herself to succumb to fear or panic, and she certainly would not be jumping to conclusions.

"Henry Lee could not be involved in anything unsavory, Marshall," she insisted. "He's a fine, upstanding man. You must have him mistaken for somebody else."

Tom Quick was amused. The girl was still fool enough to insist that she knew nothing and Watson was practically begging to confess if he could buy the girl's freedom with it.

"Get 'em both in the wagon," Quick ordered, and the two deputies escorted their prisoners to a police wagon that was parked in the alley.

The wagon was totally enclosed with built-in benches on each side. Henry Lee, with his hands still constrained behind him, was helped in and seated on the left. Hannah scampered in unassisted, deliberately avoiding the hand offered by the other deputy.

The door closed behind them and was barred from the outside. The husband and wife found themselves alone at last, but not where they had both hoped to be.

The only light in the wagon came from several tiny square windows cut in the sides of the walls near the ceiling. They were barely big enough to allow a man's hand through and the light they let in arrived in stripes of blue-gray, painting them both with unreality.

"Henry Lee? Are you all right?" she asked. Her husband still hadn't looked at her.

"That's the question I should be asking you," he mumbled almost unintelligibly.

"I'm okay," she answered, running her hands up and down her arms as if to warm herself in the stifling heat of the wagon. "A little scared, I guess. What is this about? Surely that jar of liquor you bought me last night couldn't get us in this much trouble."

In some strange way, Hannah hoped that it was her fault. She wanted to help, she wanted Henry Lee to look at her again and to smile.

"No." Henry Lee shook his head with a rueful laugh. "It has nothing to do with that. Or maybe it does. That was my whiskey we bought last night." He looked at her then. His eyes were hard and cold, not daring to hope for compassion or understanding, afraid to expect too much from the woman he loved.

"I'm a moonshiner, Hannah. That's how I make my living. I always have. I've never been caught before, but now I am."

"Moonshiner." Hannah said the word as if she had

never heard of such a thing before. Then she repeated it as if getting used to the sound on her tongue. She knew a good deal about moonshiners, selling whiskey to the Indians, leading them into drink and sloth and crime with their wicked, evil brew. There were dozens of them in the border country and she had heard more than one person in the church complain about the danger they posed to everyone. She'd heard much about moonshiners, but none of what she knew related to the man who sat across from her. The man that she loved.

"I realize that you didn't know about this before you married me. I would have told you, had you asked. But you really made your choice without me in on it. I'm sorry, Hannah, but sometimes when you set out to trap a man, you get more than you've bargained for."

Hannah was still struggling with reality. "Does my father know?"

"Yep." He replied shortly, looking straight at her now. She may have seen him bowed, but he wasn't broken and he wasn't about to wallow in shame. "He's always known. Why he didn't tell you, I couldn't say." Henry Lee gave a half-amused shake of his head. "I guess you'll have to ask him. I suspect most everyone at Plainview Church knows," he added cruelly. "I figure that's why it was such a scandal when we up and married. They thought you were much too good to be taking up with the likes of me."

Henry Lee looked away, studying the ceiling of the wagon. Hannah sat stunned, trying to make order out of her mind in chaos. Everything in their marriage was a lie. She had believed in him, trusted him, and he was an imposter. He had shown her a fine, hardworking man and made her fall in love with him. Now she discovered that the man she had loved was not that man at all.

Her rage and hurt began to pile up on her, stinging and burning in her eyes. She had been fooled and made a fool in front of her family and friends. It was almost too much to be borne.

"You lied to me! Everything you said was a lie!"

"Not everything, Hannah." He understood her anger.

He was angry himself. How stupid he had been to bring whiskey right down to the doorstep of the Federal marshalls. When a man got that greedy, he deserved to be caught. But, he added to himself remorsefully, his wife certainly didn't.

"When we were running last night, it was because they were after *you*. They were trying to arrest *you* last night."

He didn't answer; he didn't need to. She already knew the truth.

"All those trips you make in the evenings to trade, you were out selling whiskey! Harjo and the people of Sandy Creek, they're not your friends, they're your customers."

"They are my friends, too, Hannah. It's possible to be both."

"Is it?" Her face was red with anger. "I suppose it's also possible to care about a woman and lie to her at every turn!"

The wagon stopped abruptly and a minute later the door was opened. She didn't refuse help in getting down. She needed someone to steady her now. She was completely off balance.

Henry Lee watched her, concerned. Surely, even old Tom Quick could see she was not the kind of woman that you throw in jail. He would have to do something to get her out even if it meant confessing to everything and more.

They were ushered into a back door of the courthouse, near the area that served as a jail. Henry Lee was led down a long hallway in front of her and Hannah started to follow.

"This way, ma'am." The deputy beside her took her arm and started up a flight of stairs.

"My husband?"

"He's off to the lock-up. Marshall Quick wants to talk to you first, ma'am."

"I need to see my husband!" she said, realizing that it was true, but not knowing exactly why.

The young marshall recognized a woman of quality

when he saw one. Ill at ease and embarrassed, he wanted to be rid of her as soon as possible.

"You can take that up with the marshall, ma'am."

Rounding the corner at the top of the stairs, she was directed to Marshall Quick's office. It smelled of stale tobacco and old boots, and even the open door leading to the upstairs porch didn't relieve the musty, closed atmosphere of the place.

The marshall came in and gave Hannah a slow, deliberate appraisal, and smiled, revealing his personal approval. He admired Watson's taste. This big, buxom gal, all covered up like a schoolmarm, surely was enough to make a man worry himself about getting those clothes off her.

"Ah, Mrs. Watson," Quick said, putting on his best behavior, "set yourself down. You *are* Mrs. Watson, not just calling yourself that?" He smiled smugly at her. "We can find out for sure, of course."

Hannah felt her anger swiftly being redirected at this man. He sat there ogling her, smelling badly, and judging her and Henry Lee, like he was God's archangel.

"I am Hannah May Bunch Watson. I was duly married to Henry Lee Watson in Plainview Church, Oklahoma Territory, on the twelfth day of last month." She bristled with indignation, seating herself as if she were now the one ready to pass judgment. "Please feel free to check up on that. The minister will remember us. He is my father, the Reverend Farnam Bunch!"

Tom Quick did not allow one tiny portion of the surprise he felt show in his face. Hattie had told him that she was a preacher's daughter, but he hadn't truly believed that. There were plenty of so-called preachers in the territory, drunks or con men most of them, and he had assumed that she was one of their gets. However, if she was a real preacher's daughter, a good Christian woman mixed up with a criminal, then he should be trying another tack entirely.

Quick rose from his desk. "Let me see if I can get you some coffee, Mrs. Watson. You've been through a terrible ordeal this evening. It seems like I'm making it worse. Just rest here a spell and I'll see what I can find."

Hannah was puzzled by his sudden shift, but assumed that he had finally realized she was telling the truth.

Left alone, she tried to gather her thoughts. Henry Lee had denied nothing. She was the wife of a moonshiner and whiskey peddler. It was unexpected and unfortunate, but as he had pointed out, he hadn't begged her to marry him. She had forced him into it and she had decided at the time that she deserved her fate. She hadn't known what her fate was to be. But now she did.

There was no way that she could become unmarried. Divorce was as distasteful as crime. They had made this marriage in good faith and they would have to make the best of it, no matter the circumstances.

She would be the wife of a man that had committed crimes. He would have spent time in jail but he would pay his debt to society and be a better man for it. The Bible was a compendium of repentant sinners, there was no reason why Henry Lee couldn't follow in their footsteps.

And he had a wife now, to help him see the error of his ways, and change himself for the better.

To Hannah it was the same as ruining a batch of preserves. You just throw them out and start over from scratch, trying to do it better the next time. If something got broke, you fixed it.

She chastised herself for her earlier anger at Henry Lee. She had only been thinking of herself, when she should have been thinking about him. From what little he'd told her about his life, she was convinced that he had never had any proper guidance, certainly no Christian teaching. She had all those advantages and hadn't she so easily fallen into sinful ways herself?

The fact that he wasn't a worse criminal than this was just evidence that he was an exceptional man, with a shining soul. And right now, that shining soul was suffering. He was somewhere here in this building locked in a cold, dark cell thinking that she hated him. She had to speak to him, and right away.

The door opened and Tom Quick came back in.

"I couldn't find any coffee around here this late in the day. I went across to the drugstore and the druggist gave me this," he said, indicating the bottle of brown liquid in his hand. "He says it's for ladies who are fatigued or distraught."

He handed the bottle to Hannah and she poured some of the foaming elixir into a glass before looking at the label. She read the words "Dr Pepper" and decided to drink it sparingly, fearing it might have the same effect on her as the corn liquor.

As Tom Quick watched her, he plotted his next move. He had checked with the deputy while he was out. They had shucked down Watson and found nothing—no money, no receipt.

The marshall looked across the desk at her and smiled in a way that he hoped would be fatherly and sympathetic.

"I'm sure this has been an awful shock for you, ma'am. Discovering that your new husband is nothing more than a common criminal."

Hannah said nothing but gazed into her glass at the foaming brown liquid.

"Watson has been making moonshine, oh . . . I'd estimate for about ten years or so. Ever since he was a boy, really. He's got a still up on his farm somewhere."

He watched her face, it revealed little more than her own curiosity.

"You been living on that farm?"

"Yes."

"You seen anything that mighta been a still?"

Hannah ran a quick inventory of every building on the farm. She couldn't remember anything that was unusual in the way of farm tools. Nothing she could think of even remotely resembled what she imagined a still to look like.

"No, I never saw anything like that," she answered him, looking him straight in the face.

There was no question in Quick's mind that she was telling the truth. The still must be well hidden, no help there. He'd have to try another way.

"Now, Mrs. Watson." He stood and began pacing back and forth from behind his desk to the door to the upstairs porch. "Your husband brought a load of whiskey from the border down here to Muskogee. We checked with the railroad about your baggage and they insist that you only brought a couple of satchels. Do you have any idea how your husband could have got that whiskey down here?"

"No," Hannah answered truthfully, but as she looked down to take a sip of her Dr Pepper she saw in her mind the wagon loaded with the coffin they sent on the freight train. Her first instinct was to tell the marshall, cooperating with the law was the duty of a Christian. However, she was a practical person, and it didn't seem reasonable to make heroic efforts to help the people who were trying to send her husband to jail. If she just didn't say anything, it wouldn't really be the same as lying.

When she raised her head to look at him, he tried again.

"What about the money? Did you happen to see your husband with a large sum of money?"

Hannah was unable to control the flush that came to her face as she recalled the telegrapher counting the money in Sallisaw.

Quick didn't miss it. She knew something about the money for sure. If she lied and said she didn't, he would hold her in jail until she changed her mind.

Hannah couldn't out-and-out lie to an officer of the law. But there was no commandment that said "thou shalt not hedge."

"Actually, my husband did spend a good deal of money at the Sallisaw Table Company this morning."

"Sallisaw Table Company? You mean the one owned by the Oscar brothers?"

"Yes, that's the one."

Quick had known the Oscar brothers since the day they arrived in the territory. They were as honest as the day was long. What on earth could they be doing mixed up with Watson?

"What did your husband spend this money on?"

"Lumber. I believe my husband said it was walnut."

The marshall looked at her for a long minute, trying to figure out if she was straight or not. She couldn't have made something like this up.

"Excuse me for a minute," he said and left the room. Heading down the hall he called for Pathkiller. When the fleet-footed Indian arrived, he asked quickly, "What have you got?"

"So far, nothing, the hotel room is clean as a whistle and none of the clerks at the telegraph office recognized the description of Watson or the woman."

Quick accepted the bad news with a nod of resignation.

"The woman says they went to the Sallisaw Table Company this morning to buy some walnut from the Oscar brothers."

"Walnut?"

"That's what she says. Nobody'd make that up. Ride over there this evening, before they've got time to get to the bank, and see if your evidence money is there."

Pathkiller crammed his hat back on his head with a look of disgust. This was getting a bit ridiculous for capturing a moonshiner. If he wasn't getting paid expenses, he wouldn't even bother to go.

Hannah was sitting straight and dignified in her chair when Marshall Quick returned. He didn't have much hope of getting more information out of her. She was truthful, but obviously Watson had kept her in the dark.

"Marshall Quick," she asked finally. "Will I be allowed to see my husband? It is really very important that I talk to him."

Quick sat back down at his desk and tried to look understanding. "I've appreciated your cooperation, Mrs. Watson, but I still have a couple of questions."

"Then will I be allowed to see my husband?"

The marshall had hoped to hold that out as a reward

for answering the next question, but given no other real choice, he readily agreed.

"Do you remember your husband talking with anyone, discussing business or money, since you got to Muskogee?"

"The Oscars, of course," she replied easily.

"Anyone else," he pushed. "Can you remember him talking with anyone else."

Hannah thought for several moments. There were only two people that Henry Lee had spoken with last night. She thought of Harjo, teaching her to dance with his bad leg. He had a wife, she remembered, and a son in college and a daughter. She hated to think of Harjo and his family suffering along with Henry Lee. And she was not sure that Harjo was even involved. But she was absolutely certain that the other person he talked with was deeply involved.

"When we went to the Ambrosia Ballroom last night," she began, praying that she was doing the right thing, "he spent a good deal of time discussing some kind of business venture with Mrs. Byron the proprietress."

Tom Quick continued to gaze at her for a few minutes. He was convinced that she had told everything she knew. Undoubtedly Hattie Byron was Watson's connection in town, and she was hoping that this afternoon's playtime would give her immunity from the marshall's investigation. Tom thought about it and guessed that she was right. He wasn't about to put a woman with a body like that behind bars. He just hoped that Pathkiller could find that money for evidence. It was the only chance they had to nail him.

"Thank you kindly, Mrs. Watson," he told her at last. "I know this has just been a horrible ordeal for you."

"Can I see my husband now?"

"I think that would be fine."

Henry Lee Watson stood in the corner of a sparse, dreary cell in the basement of the Federal Courthouse. He was hatless, coatless, beltless, and shoeless. The pockets of his trousers had been emptied and slashed open. None of this bothered him. All his concern was focused on Hannah. He berated himself as fifty kinds of fool for getting her entangled. He vowed never to involve her again. He remembered the look on her face in the wagon when he finally told her the truth. She'd believed such wonderful things about him. It hurt so much to prove to her that she was completely wrong.

He heard a door opening down the hall and the sound of footsteps. Pulling his long frame away from the wall, he steadied himself for whatever was heading his way.

When Hannah came in sight, he couldn't stop his face from breaking into a smile of relief.

"Hannah!" He ran to the bars and reached through to take her hand. "Are you all right? They aren't going to hold you?"

"I'm fine," she insisted, smiling at him. She wanted to seem brave and courageous, that was what they both needed. She turned to the deputy beside her. "Could we have a moment to be alone?"

The deputy was one who had seen it all and was not in the least impressed by Hannah's wifely devotion. But he found it hard to believe that she would be thinking up an escape plan, so he tipped his hat to her and moved up the hall out of earshot.

"Marshall Quick had me in his office questioning me, but I think that he's satisfied with what I've told him. Anyway, he has decided to let me leave."

"Thank goodness. I don't know how much evidence they have against me, Hannah. So I don't know how long I'll be in here. Did you get any indication of how much they know?"

Hannah shrugged. "The marshall didn't seem to know very much." She related the conversation between herself and Quick, including the hedging that she had been forced to engage in.

"You singled out Mrs. Byron! That witch!" Henry Lee found himself laughing, something he would not have believed possible an hour ago. "Oh Hannah, you are a jewel."

"I'm just a wife. I promised 'for better or worse' and I'm sure I'll be held to it," she answered, beaming at his approval.

"From what you've said, it doesn't seem that they really have too much to hold me on. If they don't get some hard evidence, the judge will throw it out of court."

"What will that mean?"

"It means that, with luck, I'll be out of here by the end of the week."

Hannah was ecstatic and excitedly leaned through the bars, throwing her arms around his neck. He kissed her sweetly, longingly, and then quickly pulled away. He wanted her to have no loving memories of her husband behind bars.

"We have our whole lives ahead of us, Hannah. Our marriage hasn't really even started. I'm going to get out of here and we are going to go back to the place, live our lives, have our children and someday this will just seem like a bad dream," he promised.

"I know," she agreed smiling. "I feel exactly the same way. It's our future together that's important."

He planted a chaste kiss right on the end of her nose, causing them both to giggle.

"Do you think they will call on the Oscars?"

"Probably." He squeezed her hand, offering comfort. "When they find out about how I make my living, more than likely they won't be our friends anymore. I'm sorry about that, Hannah. I know you liked them, but the disapproval of a lot of folks is just part of the business."

In truth it bothered Henry Lee more than he cared to admit. He too had liked the Oscars and had cherished their approval. He figured that they would be singing a new tune when they found out about his moonshining. They would still be friendly, probably, like most folks were—slapping-on-the-back friendly. But they would not respect him. He knew Hiram would never see Henry Lee's ability to make good whiskey as his real gift.

Hannah offered him a smile of comfort. "I'm not a woman who needs a whole lot of people, Henry Lee. What I most need is to get my husband out of jail."

"I am a lucky man, Hannah, and I know it." He wished that he could say more. Wished he had the courage to say that he loved her, because he knew that he did.

"No, don't go getting too sappy on me. A wife stands with her husband and that's just the way of it. Besides, we're going to put all of this behind us," she told him cheerfully. "As soon as you get out of here, we'll begin again. Just start from scratch. A lot of men have a checkered past, but what's important is the future. Once you quit the whiskey business and start living right, people will give you a chance to redeem yourself."

Henry Lee pulled away from the bars and looked at her closely. He thought that she'd understood, but she didn't. Maybe she couldn't.

"I don't need to redeem myself, Hannah." His voice was very quiet. "I won't have to give it up. Of course, I intend to be a good deal more careful in the future. We are making plenty of money and there is no call for me to get greedy. As long as I am careful and stay close to the border, there shouldn't be any problem."

Hannah was incredulous. "But Henry Lee, of course you'll have to give it up. I know that you've been doing this a long time. The marshall said you've been making whiskey since you were a boy. But you must see that it is a criminal activity. It's landed you in jail and if you continue you'll end up in the penitentiary."

"There are risks in every business, Hannah. A farmer can get struck by lightning in his field. A merchant can be robbed by thieves. A cowboy can be trampled to death in a stampede. There are no guarantees in this world, but you do the job as well as you can and you try to avoid the risks."

"Henry Lee, the risk of being arrested is entirely different from the risk of being struck by lightning!"

"Maybe so, but a man takes the risks in his business and that's just the way of things."

"It might be the way of things to your mind, Henry Lee, but it doesn't have to be." Hannah felt herself grow-

ing frustrated and angry. She had grasped the bars to talk
to him, but he was now pacing back and forth in the cell.

"It does have to be the way of things!" Henry Lee
insisted. "At least it does for me."

"Why?"

"Look, Hannah, I like what I do. I like making whis-
key. I'm good at it. You know what they say about me?
They say I make the smoothest whiskey in the territory.
I'm proud of that; I don't deny it."

"How can you be proud of that!"

"Hannah, it's like you said about Cain and Abel," he
told her. "God establishes the work of our hands. He
gave me the ability to make fine whiskey, I'd be going
against my nature not to use that gift."

"God does not make thieves or outlaws, gunslingers
or moonshiners! A man makes himself that and has no
one to blame for his choice," she replied.

"I'm not talking blame, Hannah. I'm talking pride. I
taught myself to make this whiskey. I took a little bit of
corn and some half-baked instructions and I taught myself
to do it. And I do it better than anybody else! My father
couldn't do that. None of your upstanding farmboys
could hold a candle to me. That's how I can be proud!"

"But Henry Lee, don't you see what the whiskey
does? Don't you see how it ruins lives and causes trouble
in the territory?"

"Hannah, you don't know a thing about it."

She bristled at his arrogant disclaimer. "I know that
it destroys families! That men controlled by drink forget
about their responsibilities. That the wives and children
of those men never know when they can count on them.
I can't imagine what it must be like to live that way, not
knowing if the man who left the house sober in the morning was going to come home drunk during the afternoon.
I can't imagine what that is like. But I know that *you* can,
Henry Lee. Isn't that the kind of life you got from your
parents?"

Henry Lee flushed with anger at her direct hit. His
immediate thought was to retaliate. She hurt him, he

would hurt her back. But he didn't want to hurt her. He wanted her to understand.

"Hannah," he said, taking a deep breath to steady himself. "You are a good person, a Christian person, and I know you see the world as being good and bad, but things are not so clear-cut. I am careful with my whiskey. Like I said, I'm proud of the product I make. I make sure that it's clean and it's pure. People are going to buy whiskey. Even if I don't sell it, somebody else will and that whiskey might be fouled or corrupted. It could be poison if the distiller doesn't know what he's doing."

Hannah's jaw tightened with anger. "So you're trying to tell me that you make whiskey for the good of whiskey drinkers. You're doing it as a service to the community?"

Henry Lee kicked the wall in frustration. "I'm not trying to tell you anything!" He raised his voice for the first time. "I'm trying to make you see that making whiskey is something that I want to do, that I am proud of doing, and it is not something I'm going to give up just because you don't like the idea. The whiskey business can mean a lot to both of us if you'll just let yourself think about it."

"It means nothing to me."

"It means new pews for your father's church. It means no worries about too little rain, or too much. It's not like farming, Hannah. It's much more certain. People always buy whiskey. The demand is steady, no matter the price. It means a good future for our children. You'd like to see your child go to college or start up a business or buy his own place. The whiskey gives us money that can insure that."

"What's the use of having money for your children if you can't offer them a proper example and a father who won't make them feel ashamed? Do you think any child would want to have a moonshiner for a father?"

"Oh, I see, Hannah," he said, sarcasm creeping furiously into his voice. "The question is, do you think any child would want to have me for a father?"

"Henry Lee, I didn't mean . . ."

He was seething with anger. "I understand now how

it is with you, Hannah. You're all ready to stand by me, to be the perfect wife and helpmate, as long as I follow your rules. All I have to do is forget about the life I've made for myself. I just pick up your morals and your ideals and you'll be willing to do me the favor of staying by my side. You didn't get yourself a churchgoing farmer, so you just take what you did get and try to turn him into what you want. Well, Miss Hannah, no thank-you very much!"

"Henry Lee, I only want what is best for you," she implored. "What's best for us."

He turned his back.

"You are not giving up the whiskey business?" she asked finally, quietly.

"No, ma'am," he answered turning, at last, to face her with anger in every line of his face. "And if that don't suit you, well, I believe you know your way to the door."

They stood there separated by bars, but also by a thousand dreams and ideals.

Hannah turned without a word and walked away.

EIGHTEEN

Hannah sat on the arbor swing at her father's house watching the setting sun. She could hear Myrtie and Violet in the house cleaning up the supper dishes. She should be in there helping or there were at least a million other things that she might be doing. Harvest time was upon them, the busiest time of the year on the farm, but lately she seemed to find more time than she needed to lose herself in thought.

She had been back home for almost three weeks. Time enough for her anger to turn to dismay and her pride to stubbornness. Henry Lee was back at his place. The gossips had made sure she knew. He'd returned from Muskogee only two days after she had. Apparently, he'd been right: the marshall didn't have enough evidence. She was glad about that. Sighing she shook her head, she hated thinking about him in that cell.

He hadn't attempted to contact her. She'd left him a note on the kitchen table saying that she was moving back to her father's home. Somehow she expected him to at least acknowledge that. But she hadn't heard a word from him.

She had certainly heard a good deal about him. She was hardly back herself when word of his arrest in Muskogee was prime dinner conversation in every household in the congregation. The entire community seemed to have an opinion about their marriage, and most didn't hesitate to express it. Old Maude Ruskin seemed to sum up the feelings of most of the church people last Sunday

276

when she patted Hannah on the cheek and told her simply to "put that unfortunate marriage behind you."

Hannah discovered that, except for herself and most of the young girls Myrtie's age, virtually every person in the community had known all along about Henry Lee's whiskey business. She'd even asked her father point-blank why he hadn't told her.

He hesitated thoughtfully and then said, "At first I thought you must know. By the time I realized that you didn't, well, it wasn't my place. He's your husband," he said, as if that answered everything, "and it's really between the two of you."

That had continued to be her father's major theme on the subject. Somehow, to him, her marriage vows took precedence over all else. Her father made it clear that he thought Hannah should return to her husband. He believed it so strongly that, at first, he hadn't wanted Hannah to move back in.

"I've been helping married folks through rough times for a lot of years," he explained. "When a couple have trouble, they've got to stay and work it out. It does no one good if the wife can just pack up and go home to Daddy when things don't suit her."

"It's not a case of things not suiting!" Hannah had argued. "The man I married is choosing to break the law and has no intention of reforming. You can't expect me to stay there as if I approve of that."

"You'll never change a man by running out on him, Hannah."

"I didn't run out on him. He sent me away," she admitted in frustration. "He doesn't want to change. He says he likes making whiskey, that he's proud of what he does and that I should just accept that." She threw up her hands in disgust. "I'd certainly be a hypocrite if I did."

Her father was inflexible. "You wouldn't be a hypocrite, but you might be a better wife. Lots of women have found themselves married to men who don't live by the scriptures. As long as that man doesn't beat her, starve her, or threaten her, the good wife stays right with her man and shows him by her example how to live right. She doesn't just run off and say, 'It was all a big mistake, let's forget the whole thing.' "

"Some marriages are just big mistakes," she insisted, "and trying to keep something together that was never meant to be is just throwing water down a rat hole!"

"Are you saying you don't care for Henry Lee?" her father asked pointedly. "You forget, I've seen you two with your heads together. It'd be obvious to a blind man that you got feelings for each other, strong feelings."

"What I feel is relief that I've put that chapter of my life behind me!" Hannah lied vehemently.

Finally, when it became clear that the father and daughter who had once been so close were determined to remain completely opposed to the other's view, Violet intervened. Hannah was sure that her father hadn't heard a word she had said, but he listened to his wife.

"I know you are right," Violet assured her husband. "But I think these two just need a little time. Let their anger cool a bit and see what's left of their other sentiments."

Her stepmother convinced the preacher that Hannah should be allowed to have some time to think about what she wanted.

Time to think was what she got. She had trouble eating, trouble sleeping, but no trouble at all thinking. Her thoughts were constantly in action. She would recall a story that he had told her with his wide-eyed look of mischief and find herself smiling at the memory. She would imagine the sight of him working in the yard or chopping wood and a warm glow of desire would settle around her. In her mind she was talking with Henry Lee, working with Henry Lee, laughing with Henry Lee, dancing with Henry Lee and at night when her exhausted brain had finally given over to sleep, her dreams were writhing in passion with Henry Lee.

She rebelled at the injustice of it all. They had just begun to know each other. She thought that he could make her happy, she knew she wanted to make him happy. Why couldn't he be a farmer like everyone else? But Henry Lee could never be like anyone else.

Hannah heard a horse coming up the road, breaking into her thoughts, but she didn't even bother to turn. It was Saturday night, so she knew exactly who it was. The rider spoke as he trotted past on his way to the hitching post.

"Good evening, Miss Hannah."

"Good evening, Will."

She watched him dismount and wrap the reins around the hitching post before stepping on the porch. He straightened his jacket and ran a hand across his head, making sure that his hair was lying down before knocking briskly on the front door.

That was another surprise she'd discovered when she'd returned. Will Sample was courting Myrtie. The two were so in love they would sit and make calf eyes at each other all evening. It was strange to see them together. Will's shy, red-faced clumsiness disappeared completely when he was with Myrtie. He talked to her with confidence and never seemed to stammer or stutter around her. And Myrtie was a sight to behold! The mischievous little doll was now amazingly serious about such things as the making of pork sausage and the canning of pickles. The bright-eyed little girl who thought all material should be made up into dresses now carefully folded sheets and dishtowels and placed them in her hope chest.

Hannah remembered her own surprise and Myrtie's giggling blushes when she heard of her new beau.

"I've always thought he was just wonderful. He was always so sweet to me, treating me just like I was grown up. But I assumed he was coming around all the time to see you, even though you two never really seemed that interested in each other. It never occurred to me that I was the one he was here to see." The young girl's eyes were soft and starry.

"He said he just wanted to be close by while he waited for me to grow up. Claims to have loved me from the first minute he saw me, and he just wanted to be sure he was right in my path when I went looking for a husband."

Hannah had listened, startled. She fervently offered extravagant thanks to heaven that her well-planned trap had failed so miserably. How close she had come to making her sister—and the man she loved—miserable. How blind and foolish she had been to think that a man, any man, who cared for a woman would be unable to show that feeling. No man is so shy that he wouldn't go after what he loves.

At least the way things had worked out, the only person who was really unhappy was the person who deserved it: Hannah.

She would have liked to believe that Henry Lee was unhappy, too. He had seemed to be learning to care for her, and surely he had become used to her being around. Did he miss all those good meals and those finely laundered shirts? Apparently not. At the prayer meeting on Wednesday night, one of the women told her that he was seen dancing and laughing at a barn dance near Ingalls.

"He was flirting and carrying on, just as if everyone didn't know that he's a married man!"

Hannah could see him, dancing and flirting. But, in her mind, he was always dancing and flirting with her.

She shook her head with disgust. Never in her life had she been at such cross-purposes with herself. Leaving him had been the right decision. He wasn't about to change and she could not live with a lawbreaker, imagining the lives that he was ruining, even, maybe, her own life. She had lived with him less than a month and had actually imbibed spirits herself. Living with him for a lifetime might have changed her into a gin-soaked derelict!

She stopped herself before her mind got carried away. Her fall from grace was none of Henry Lee's doing. And for all that he was guilty of many things, he had never hurt Hannah or treated her in any way except like a good husband should treat a wife.

She couldn't seem to regret even one small moment that she had spent with him. They were all so precious to her now. Even when he was acting strange and staying out all night, he was still with her. Now she was alone.

She had carefully gone over all of their time together, realizing how foolish she was, making grits for pigs and cleaning out the fermentation barrels. But she also realized why he'd spent so much time away from her. He was obviously at his still and he hadn't wanted her to know.

She wished that he had made a woman of her and given her a child to be with her forever. She remembered with a wistful smile her discussion with Myrtie on the morning after her wedding. She pictured the child she dreamed of that morning and the hope that had sung through her veins with pleasure at the touch of her husband. Neither of these things would ever happen now. Because he was a whiskey man.

It was ridiculous for a woman to sit and sigh at the moon, wishing a man was something that he wasn't. It was especially ridiculous when the woman was much better off on her own, she reminded herself. She needed to get on with her own life. Decide what she was going to do. But the decisions were harder than ever.

Staying here with Violet and her father was even less possible now than before she'd taken such drastic action to get married. With Myrtie sure to marry next spring, there was truly no excuse for her to stay even if her father would allow it, and she was not too sure about that.

Another marriage was not an option. Even if she could get an annulment instead of a divorce, she would never be considered marriageable. Unmarried women really couldn't work outside the home or the family business unless they were teachers, or maybe nurses. Hannah had neither training nor skills in either of those areas. Perhaps she could find an elderly woman with no family who needed a caretaker. The thought didn't fill her with optimism.

She imagined herself ten years down the road, cloaked in faded, gray bombazine and spending her years in quiet, silent isolation as she watched aged dependents slowly slip from this world to the next. The face of her mother, weary and emaciated at the last, superimposed on the image of her future client and inexplicable tears stung her eyes.

Oh, how she dreaded tying her life to that of the sick and dying. She wanted life and laughter. She wanted a future with love, a future with her man beside her, his arms around her, his lips in her hair. Duty and respect seemed to pale by comparison.

A breathy giggle joined by a deeper laugh drew her attention to Myrtie and Will who were just coming out on the porch. Hannah gathered up her things to leave. She knew the young couple would want the privacy of the arbor swing to steal a few quick and desperate kisses. She gladly gave it over to them, with only a slight twinge of jealousy. She knew how it felt to be in love.

Henry Lee sat at a corner table in Zanola Little's barn listening to the strange mournful sounds the musicians had chosen to play. All around him dancers slowly undulated to the strange mix of African and Indian rhythms, bodies slick with sweat and eyes closed, feeling only the music. He wished he could lose himself in the dance also, but lately nothing seemed to be able to work for him.

The truth of that statement managed to bring a wry smile to his face. He had tried to banish Hannah from his mind with a pretty little dance hall girl in Stillwater. She was still fairly young and very skilled, but at the last moment he'd paid her and sent her on her way. He ached with desire, but could no longer find relief among the women of his past. The woman's painted face had offered no allure and the body that she eagerly pressed against him repulsed him and served only to remind him of what he really wanted. He wanted Hannah, only Hannah, and he knew now that he would never have her.

When he'd returned to his cabin, he'd been hopeful. Hannah had a good mind, realistic and practical like his own. He was sure that after the first rush of anger, she would see that they could have a good life selling whiskey. She needn't ever worry about herself or her children doing without the things that they needed.

When he'd found the note on the table, he'd wanted to lay his head down and cry. He'd sat staring at it for the better part of an hour. Thinking about her sitting at the table, writing out the conclusion of their life as one. He couldn't make out a word, except his name, but he knew she was telling him that it was finished.

Henry Lee had chosen Zanola's place on purpose. The blacks mostly kept to themselves and he was tired of his every word and deed being the grist for the gossip mill. Elsewhere he would have felt like he had to look pleased, like he was quite content with the direction his life had taken. Here, at least, he had the luxury of displaying all the misery that he felt.

Zanola hadn't asked for a word of explanation about his ill-fated marriage. "Your business is your own," she had told him. "You want to talk, I can listen, but sometimes you just got to think on it yourself."

"She's left me," he told her simply. "Guess there ain't much more a man can say about that."

"You can go after her, you know."

Henry Lee shook his head sadly. "There's no purpose in it. Nothing has changed between us. I'm still the whiskey man and she's still the preacher's daughter. It was foolish to think for a minute that those two could make a pair."

Zanola was not as sure as Henry Lee, but she was a woman who had seen a good deal of misery in her own life, recognized it, and knew that the whiskey man was best left alone to see his own way through his troubles. She passed the word and Henry Lee found himself undisturbed by well-meaning advisors or cheerful comrades.

He'd had plenty of advice already. The morning after Hannah left, the Oscar brothers had arrived at the jail. Putting their good reputation on the line, they insisted that charges against Henry Lee be dropped.

When the judge heard Hiram Oscar's glowing description of Henry Lee's character and then looked at what little evidence Tom Quick had managed to scare up, Henry Lee was released immediately.

The Oscars, with Henry Lee in tow, had made their

way to the McCulley Dining Hall where he was given a
very strong piece of their collective mind. "I try to judge
a man by what he is, not what he does," Hiram told him
solemnly. "But there is no way that I can countenance
the kind of evil that you are doing. Sure, lots of folks
drink, and most of the Indians, well, they think they
ought to have a right to drink just like whites."

The woodworker turned to Willard as if to enlist his
support. "Drinking makes a man crazy, he don't know
who he is or what he is anymore. He gets to caring nothing 'bout right or wrong, all he cares about is that drink
and where he can get another one."

Henry Lee continued to eat his dinner, listening, but
unwilling to reply.

"You didn't invent liquor, boy. It was here long
before you were and it'll be here after you've gone. But
that don't mean that you've got to invest your life in it."

"Hiram, I make good whiskey," he finally told him.
"It's like working with the wood, it's a gift I've got and
it'd be a shame for me not to use it."

"A gift to do evil ain't no kinda gift at all!"

The old man lowered his voice, and spoke to Henry
Lee more gently and with emotion.

"I don't know nothing about you, except what you
need to know 'bout a man. I done worked with you and
seen that you're mighty fit to run the river with. Who
your folks was, or how you was brought up, I don't know
none of that. But Henry Lee, I tell you like a son, like I
would have told my own, when you live your life outside
the rules, outside what folks believe is right, it ain't no
fit life. You get no respect, except from other 'uns as bad
as you. And you got no respect for yourself 'cause you
didn't play it straight. It's like cheating in a card game,
you know even if you win that the others are all better
than you."

Henry Lee flinched at that and the Oscar brothers
didn't miss it.

"Henry Lee, you've got a strong back, a good mind,
you're not afeared of work and you're plenty capable. You
got that sweet little wife, and 'fore you know it, you'll

have a house full of young 'uns. I'd say this boy's got some
pretty serious thinking to do, wouldn't you, Willard?"

The two brothers left shortly after that. Henry Lee
hadn't the heart, or the guts, to tell them that Hannah
had left him. He couldn't bear to speak of it. But everybody already seemed to know anyway.

Holding up his glass, Zanola mercifully came by and
filled it. Henry Lee stared at the clear liquid that was his
pride and his livelihood and thought only of his Hannah.

He'd tried staying out at his place, working, keeping
busy. He'd reaped his harvest as soon as it was barely
ready and worked like a madman sunup to sundown until
it was in. He mowed his hay field all alone, not wanting
the help that he usually hired. He needed the work, he
needed to sweat and ache and hurt. He needed to cry,
but a man didn't do that.

Everything seemed to remind him of Hannah. He
would sit at the table and imagine her sitting with him.
Her serious talk interspersed with his teasing chatter. He
would dress and remember it was this shirt that she'd
mended. He ate his food straight from the can, when he
bothered to eat at all. He tried sleeping in the bedroom,
but the pillows had the scent of that thick, honey-colored
hair and remembering it kept him awake all night.

Sometimes, just for a moment, he would forget that
she was gone. He'd seen a doe with her fawn taking a
drink at the creek and he was rushing back to the house
to have her come look, when he remembered she wasn't
there anymore. He was walking through the corn field
nearest the house and decided that it would be the best
place to put Hannah's garden next year. Then he remembered that there would be no garden, because Hannah
wouldn't be there to tend it.

He kept telling himself that it was really for the best.
He was not much of a family type man. And he couldn't
help but agree that a moonshiner might not be the best
example for a child.

They were both really better off. He had his freedom.
He could continue in the whiskey business without wor-

rying about getting someone else involved or about leaving a wife and child when he went to jail.

The whiskey business was a good one, and he was
the best in it. How could she expect him to give up a
business that he'd built himself? Something he'd worked
so hard to perfect.

He saw himself as he had been back then. Just a
dirty-faced boy. Hungry. He was so hungry that winter.
Skut had been too drunk to do anything and too drunk
to care. Drunks never get hungry, they just get thirsty.
There was no food in the house and no money to get
any. Henry Lee had eaten the fodder from the corn crib,
and scavenged the forest for berries and nuts, robbing
the stores of the squirrels and woodchucks, but it wasn't
enough.

An old Indian showed up to buy whiskey. There was
none to sell. Skut had drunk up everything they had
made and had wandered off to try to find more. The old
man had brought carrots and potatoes to trade. Henry
Lee's mouth had watered at the sight of them. He had
begged the old man. He had dropped down on proud,
young knees and begged for the food.

"Please mister," he heard his high childish voice
pleading. "I ain't et nothing but roast acorns for more
than a week. I'd do anything, anything, for one of them
taters."

The Indian had eyed him somewhat disdainfully, but
had generously given him one potato and one carrot.

Even today thinking back, he could still taste the bitterness of his humiliation with that sweet, half-burnt,
half-raw food that he had wolfed down. The food had
done more than fill his belly and recover his strength, it
had brought home to him that he was very much all alone
in a rough world and that if he wanted to eat regular, he
would have to depend upon himself.

He was too small to hire out, if anyone would have
had him anyway. And it was too late in the year to try
to get a crop into the ground. He could have taken off to
town and tried to flim-flam or outright steal, but he didn't

have the nature for it. So he did the only other thing that he knew could make money, he made whiskey.

He'd watched his father and others before. While his father had drunk and talked with the Ozark moonshiners, Henry Lee had watched and listened. He carefully tried to recall all that was said. He experimented and learned to trust his own judgment.

The whiskey he produced wasn't very good at first, but he was able to sell it and get enough to eat and money to buy more corn, to make more whiskey. As he continued to distill, he learned from his mistakes and once he had it down, once he could shake a jar of his own liquor and see that the proof was right by the size of the bubbles, he began not just to eat, but to make a living from whiskey.

He'd done it on his own. No one ever helped him. He was a child alone, who taught himself to be a man. And no one, not Hannah or anyone else, would tell him that what he did was wrong. Alcohol was bad. He knew that. He'd had a drunken lout for a father and a mother that wasn't a lot better. But people chose to drink, he didn't force them. Even if he never made another batch of whiskey, there would still be fathers who drank up all the cash and left their sons to go hungry. They were guilty, but he was not.

He would do what he had to do. What he wanted to do! He would sell whiskey whenever he could to whoever he could. And if the law didn't like it, let them try to catch him. And if Hannah didn't like it, well, she'd made her choice.

He took another slug of corn liquor.

That was another thing that didn't seem to work for him. All his life, he had been careful not to get too drunk. Now, he wanted to be so drunk he was senseless. To not be able to remember who he was or where he'd been. But as he gazed at the clear liquor in the glass, not his first of the evening by a long shot, he was cold sober.

NINETEEN

The noonday sun beat down on the green alfalfa, shimmering in the heat, as the women in the wagon arrived at the hay meadow. Without a word to the other two, Myrtie scampered off to find Will for a private moment alone, leaving Hannah and Violet to set up a camp lunch for the hay haulers.

The two struggled with tent poles, erecting a lean-to shade on the side of the wagon. "It's a good thing you're here, Hannah," Violet said. "With Myrtie's mind so full of Will Sample, I never would have been able to put this thing up by myself."

"One of the men would have come to help," Hannah replied, making light of her stepmother's gratitude. "But that Myrtie, she really does have her head in the clouds these days."

Violet laughed. "It's kind of silly to watch from the outside, but you know how it is. When you're in love, you just can't seem to help but make a fool of yourself."

Hannah let that comment pass. The last thing she wanted to discuss was how foolish a woman in love could be.

"What do you think about Myrtie and Will?" she asked Violet, diverting the subject.

"Well, to tell the truth," Violet answered, "I suspected it all along, not that Will ever let on in any way. It's just that a man who's kind of shy and backward, why, he'll fall for a bubbly, little magpie like Myrtie every time."

Her stepmother's perceptiveness surprised Hannah. She had become so accustomed to thinking of Violet as light-minded, it hadn't occurred to Hannah that she might have some very keen observations.

When the two managed to get the poles firmly into the ground, about ten feet from the wagon, Hannah climbed into the wagon bed and brought out a tarp and attached it to the wagon. They rolled it out on the ground and attempted to secure the other two corners on the tent poles. Neither woman was quite tall enough and after numerous failed attempts the two were laughing so hard the tears were coursing down Hannah's cheeks and Violet was doubled over gasping for breath. They finally managed with Hannah holding Violet up, so that she could get a good grasp on the tarp and secure it to the upright.

"It worked!" Hannah exclaimed when the shaded area was finally constructed. "That was a good idea, me holding you up. I never would have thought of it."

"I don't know why not?" Violet answered, still smiling. "You've been helping to hold me up through the whole first year of my marriage. Covering for me at every turn."

Hannah felt genuinely embarrassed that her assistance had been so obvious.

"I meant well, Violet. I know I seem to always have to have things done my way. I truly didn't mean to intrude on you like that."

"Lord, Hannah! I'm grateful that you did. I don't know how I would have made it without you." She put her arm around her stepdaughter and hugged her closely. "I never had any idea of the things that were expected of a preacher's wife. When I married your father, I truly thought of nothing but making him happy." She smiled as if having chanced upon a precious memory. "If it hadn't been for you, I would have had this whole congregation up in arms."

"The congregation loves you!" Hannah insisted.

"Yes, I think they love me all right, now. They've begun to accept me as I am. But when I first married your

father, you weren't the only one that had doubts about
it."

Hannah's mouth dropped open in surprise. How
could Violet have sensed her concern over her father's
choice?

"I always liked you," Hannah said. "I just couldn't
understand what you and Papa could possibly have in
common."

Violet smiled knowingly. "Your father and I have a
lot in common. We have our love of the church and our
attraction to this prairie. But, Hannah, it's not always
what you have in common that makes a good marriage.
Like I said with Will and Myrtie, sometimes it's the things
you don't have in common that are the most important."

"You mean opposites attract?"

"No, not really that." Violet pursed her lips as if trying to gather up the words. "It's more that when you
marry you do become one flesh, like the Good Book says.
And for that marriage to work, the one flesh needs to be
a whole person. So each one brings part of that flesh to
the whole."

The idea made a furrow in Hannah's brow.

"A marriage should represent all sides," Violet continued. "And it takes differences in people to do that.
Your father and I, together, make one whole person."

"And Myrtie and Will make one whole person," Hannah agreed. "Because he is shy and hardworking and she
is so vivacious and carefree."

"Yes," Violet said, "Will and Myrtie make one person. And of course, you and Henry Lee."

Hannah stopped dead still and turned to look at her.

"What are you talking about?"

"You and Henry Lee make one person, too," she
said.

Hannah quickly shook her head. "No, Violet, we
really just don't suit at all."

"You suit each other perfectly," the older woman
insisted, waving away Hannah's hasty denial. "I've seen
it! When you are together, it's plain as pancakes. You
become more like him and he becomes more like you."

"No, I just—"

"Just think about it, Hannah," Violet interrupted her. "Don't dismiss the truth before you've even given it a look." Her stepmother's words were kindly, but serious. "Think about how you feel when you are with him. How he makes you laugh. He makes you think and say things that you would never have done on your own. And you do the same for him, whether you realize it or not."

Hannah assured herself that her stepmother was seeing things that definitely were not there. But, rather than argue, with so much work to be done, Hannah pushed the disturbing thoughts into the background and began unloading the wagon.

Planks set between two sawhorses became a table beneath the shade covering. As Violet covered it with a cloth Hannah began toting the food.

Hay mowing was hot, hard work and a man could build up an appetite in a hurry. With that in mind, the table was laid with six frying chickens, perfectly golden brown, a huge kettle of butter beans, potatoes, sweet carrots, greens and salad. A mound of cornbread sat at each plate and a whole crock of buttermilk was cooling in the shade.

When Violet finally rang the dinner bell, the crew quickly hurried to the small oasis in the hot hay field. Water came first, each man serving himself a dipperful to drink out of the bucket, and a bit to scrub up with out of the washtub. Will and Myrtie were the last to arrive. Hannah watched in wonder as the storekeeper carefully explained to her younger sister how the market prices for commodities were calculated in Kansas City. Myrtie listened with the rapt attention she had formerly reserved only for gossip and gee-gaw peddlers.

The crew, made up mostly of young men about Myrtie's age, were sons of the farmers in the congregation. They wolfed down the food as if they had never eaten before. Although hot and tired, even a moment's respite encouraged their youthfulness, and they began laughing and teasing each other. Will and Myrtie came in for a lot of ribbing, but they didn't seem to mind very much.

The young men joked about how hot and tired they were. It was a rough job, a man's job, and they were proud to be doing it.

A freckled-face teener, one of Dillary's brood, spoke up. "Can you imagine that Watson, doing his hay meadow by himself without asking a hand from nobody?"

There was a sudden silence at the table, and then as the freckled-face remembered where he was, he blushed fiery red. To his credit he looked straight up at Hannah and murmured a sincere and stricken apology.

Hannah gave him as genuine a smile as she could manage. "It is perfectly all right to mention my husband," she told him with more confidence than she actually felt. Her heart had stopped suddenly when his name had been mentioned, and then to catch up had begun beating like a tom-tom. Her stomach had developed a mass of fluttering wings, which seemed to twist in anguish and pain.

"Mr. Watson and I both intend to live in this community for a good long time," she said bravely. "It's not possible that we would not see or hear about each other. Please don't distress yourself on my behalf."

The boys went back to eating and joking, but it was an echo of the lighthearted mood that had prevailed earlier.

Hannah began talking a blue streak to Will and Myrtie. She was determined that no one would think she was pining over her husband. In a desperate search for a subject to discuss, she found herself regaling them with an amusing story that Henry Lee had told her. She was trying to tell it as he had, with all his gestures and facial expressions. She was doing such a good job that she had captured the attention of the whole table.

"And then the old man said," Hannah mimicked a deep masculine voice, " 'That goat didn't die by itself!' "

Hannah expected a giggle from Myrtie and maybe a chuckle from Will, but when the whole table erupted in gales of laughter, she jumped with surprise. She hadn't realized that they were all listening.

"You sure tell a good story," one of the crew complimented.

Will smiled almost in disbelief. "I never realized you were such a cutup, Miss Hannah."

Hannah glanced down at the end of the table to see her father studying her. He had known her all her life, and one thing she certainly was not, was a cutup. His gaze was so searching, so full of concern that Hannah had to look away. Unfortunately, she turned her gaze to Violet, who was smiling with an "I told you so" expression.

Hannah began clearing the table as the men dispersed to head back to their labors. She watched Myrtie and Will say their chaste good-bye, and her father planted a quick kiss on Violet's lips. She missed Henry Lee.

Three days later, Farnam Bunch, all his hay in, saddled up his old roan mare and went off to make a few calls. Violet had sent a ham to Emmitt Travis, whose wife was ailing and who had three young children to tend as well. When Farnam arrived, Mrs. Travis was up and around, insisting that she was perfectly fine, even with a flush still in her cheeks. They were grateful for the ham and Reverend Bunch only lingered long enough to insist that Emmitt send for him if they needed anything.

He made his way to Tulley's place to see how they were recovering from their young son's funeral. They asked him to stay to dinner, but he insisted that he had to get on to other calls. He had a cold dinner packed in his saddlebags and he ate it as he made his way to the edge of the Territory.

With no real plan of what he wanted to say or do, Reverend Bunch rode up to Henry Lee's place. The yard was clean and well kept as usual. Henry Lee had obviously been doing a bit of laundry. Several rough grey shirts hung on the clothes line, flapping in the slight breeze.

Henry Lee came up from the direction of the creek. His expression was cautious.

"Morning, Reverend."

"Morning, Henry Lee."

The two men stood facing each other. Each waiting for the other to speak first.

Farnam wondered if any good could come of this meeting. Prying into his daughter's business was not the way a father ought to behave. But these two were more than his daughter and son-in-law, he was their pastor. If it had been any other young couple in his flock that was having marital trouble, he would have immediately gone to counsel them. His own needn't be any different, he assured himself. But he knew it wasn't true. He wanted happiness for his daughter and he couldn't remain impartial between them, but he was willing to try.

Henry Lee wondered if the preacher had come to give him his comeuppance. He was certainly ready. Nothing anybody could say to him now could make him feel any worse than he already did. He hadn't even the heart to make whiskey these days. He just worked in the fields as long and as hard as he could, then he came back to the house and spent the late afternoon and evening working on the church pews. They were his last contact with Hannah. They would be in that church for the rest of Hannah's life and every time she saw them or touched the wood, she would know that he had made them.

As the minutes dragged on, Henry Lee couldn't wait any longer. He broke his tough waiting stance and asked the question he wanted to know.

"How is Hannah?"

The reverend heard the loving concern disguised in the casual curiosity of the young man's tone.

"She's well."

Henry Lee nodded. The silence dragged on for another few minutes. Surely, if the man had something to say, he would say it. When he didn't Henry Lee finally took over. A businessman never finds long periods of silence comfortable.

"Looks like it might rain this evening," he commented. "Hope you've got your hay in."

"Yep," the preacher replied. "Just got the last of it in yesterday." Henry Lee nodded his approval.

The preacher gestured toward the washbench that

was sitting in the shade of the big red oak. "You think I could have a seat there? I'm getting kind of old for these long standing-up conversations."

Without any sign from Henry Lee, Reverend Bunch made his way to the bench and sat down. Henry Lee followed, but didn't sit. Leaning back against the tree with one knee raised and bracing himself with his foot behind him, Henry Lee stood with his arms crossed, solemnly waiting to hear what the preacher had to say.

Farnam didn't much like having to look up to his son-in-law, but decided not to insist that he sit. He had things he wanted Henry Lee to hear and if he pushed too hard, it was certain that he wouldn't listen.

"One of the men on my haying crew told me that you brought in your hay all by yourself."

Henry Lee shrugged.

"Did you think that no one would help you?" the preacher asked.

Henry Lee didn't answer at first. It had occurred to him that the church folks might not be feeling real friendly toward him, but he didn't really think that neighbors would refuse to help get in a crop. That wouldn't be smart, a man never knew when and where he might need help next time.

"I had plenty of time," Henry Lee finally said. "I knew I could do it myself. If I'd needed help, I would have asked for it."

"Good," the preacher replied. "I want you to know that your troubles with Hannah, well, that's really between the two of you. I'm sure every soul in both Territories knows exactly what you two should do, and most will be quite willing to tell you. But whether you and Hannah work out your problems or not, I still consider you a member of this community and my son-in-law."

This unexpected inclusion among the people of Plainview embarrassed Henry Lee. He had expected to be raked over the coals and cast out like refuse; instead, he was being offered kinship. The surprise compelled him to move away from the tree and walk a few paces in front of the preacher, staring out over his fields.

He wanted the respect of the preacher. The respect of other men had always been a hunger that he had sought to satisfy. Unfortunately, with his background, and in his kind of business, respect was hard to come by and even harder to maintain.

"You're being a bit too fair, aren't you, Bunch? You are a preacher and I'm a moonshiner. Shouldn't be too much common ground between the two of us."

Farnam had to stop himself from smiling. It was as if the young man wanted to push him away. He was leery of any offer of friendship. And certainly not his.

"I'd say there is some common ground between us," he replied, twisting a blade of grass into a fine sprig and slipping it into his mouth like a toothpick. "After all, we both love Hannah."

Henry Lee turned to stare at the preacher. His first thought was to deny it, but he knew that he wouldn't be believed. He loved Hannah, he had never said it out loud, but he knew that it was so. Slowly he nodded his head.

"Yes, well, there is that," he agreed. Henry Lee turned back to gaze out over the landscape in front of him; he wasn't seeing anything but it kept the feelings he couldn't strip from his face from being on display. When he'd gained a modicum of control he turned back, crossing his arms again, looking impassive.

"She's glad to be home, I suspect," he said finally.

Farnam smiled and offered a bit of a chuckle. "I wouldn't exactly say that. She spends most of her free time alone, these days. She stares into space, kinda dreamy like. She was never that way before. I think she misses you."

Henry Lee shook his head with a gesture of disbelief. "I'm sure she's just pining away!" he said sarcastically.

"No, Hannah's not like that," the preacher admitted. "She's doing her work, trying to stay busy and be pleasant to everyone."

Reverend Bunch straightened his legs and scratched his head in contemplation as he gave Henry Lee a long thoughtful look. "I still think she misses you."

The preacher let that soak in for a few minutes.

"She did the funniest thing the other day," he began, then waited. When the younger man gave a nod to indicate his interest, he continued. "She told a joke."

"Hannah told a joke," Henry Lee replied, not quite understanding what his father-in-law was getting at. "I don't remember her telling jokes too much."

"That's what was so strange," the preacher insisted. "I have known that girl all her life, and she has a fine sense of humor and is as willing to enjoy a funny story as anyone. But I have never heard her tell one, ever. And she did it so well. She had all the haying crew hanging on her every word." The two stared at each other momentarily, until Henry Lee shrugged.

"It was the one about the goat getting on top of the house."

Henry Lee smiled. "That is a pretty good joke," he admitted.

Farnam smiled back. "I knew it was your joke. I could see you in the telling of it."

Henry Lee was confused. The old man seemed to be giving him his genuine approval, and there was definitely no reason for that. The reverend should be furious that he'd dragged Hannah's name through the mud, not talking to him as if he were a friend.

"I know you think that you can just walk out of her life and everything will just go on like it has always been," the preacher told him. "But it's not so. She's changed. You've changed."

"I didn't walk away from her. She left me," he pointed out. "And she's better off, we both know that."

"I don't know that."

Henry Lee ignored the dispute. Whether she was better or worse was not a consideration. She'd made her choice and they would both have to live with that.

"I think she'd come back if you asked her, Henry Lee."

"Why do you think that?" Henry Lee's voice was hoarse with controlled anger. "I'm still the whiskey man," he replied bitterly. "I don't intend to give up my business, just 'cause some starchy, stiff preacher's daughter doesn't approve."

"Starchy stiff, is she?" The preacher laughed. "It's funny, when I've seen her look at you, it reminded me more of melting butter."

Henry Lee's mind was immediately drawn to the image of Hannah melting in his arms, hot and eager against him. He quickly put a hold on those thoughts. "You said yourself that what's between me and Hannah is our business. I think you would do best to remember your own advice."

"That's true, Henry Lee. I did say that, didn't I?" Farnam leaned down to scrape a bit of mud off the side of his boot. He was buying time, but time was important when discussing matters of the heart.

"So what else is new with you?" he asked. "I take it you're not to do any jail time over the Muskogee escapade?"

"Nope, they didn't have enough evidence to hold me."

"I've heard Tom Quick is a bad man to cross. You'd best be watching out for yourself."

Henry Lee shook his head in disbelief. "Hasn't anyone told you, Preacher? You're supposed to be praying that the moonshiner gets caught, not worrying that he might be."

"I'm not worrying about the moonshiner. I'm worrying about Henry Lee."

"I'm always careful," he answered. "At least I usually am, and I will try to take even more heed in the future."

Farnam Bunch nodded his acceptance. There was no way to change a man, unless he was willing to change. Hannah was right about that at least. Badgering or threatening, giving ultimatums, only made a person angry, more rigid. Henry Lee would have to decide on his own what he wanted to do with his life, and the rest of them would just have to wait until he decided.

The reverend decided it might be prudent to change the subject and asked Henry Lee about the lumber for the church pews. Henry Lee proudly led him to his workshop where, except for a second coat of varnish, he had one pew finished.

"It's beautiful." The preacher couldn't keep the reverence out of his voice as he lovingly ran his hand along the satin finish of the walnut top.

The five-foot bench had a straight seat and a curved back. The end pieces reflected the gentle curve in design and were attached by perfectly hand-cut, dovetail joints. The varnish Henry Lee used shined the wood while enhancing the natural beauty of the grain.

"Try it out," Henry Lee said.

"Henry Lee, I never imagined that they would look this good!" He seated himself, running his hand along the expertly finished surface. "This is as nice as any big city church pew I've ever seen."

Henry Lee was very pleased at the compliment, but eased it away with a joke. "With the way you get wound up and preach on for hours, a man's got to do something to protect his behind!"

Farnam smiled, but would not be dissuaded from his point. "This is fine quality workmanship, Henry Lee. I don't claim to know a thing about woodworking, but it's clear that you have a talent here, a talent you're not using like you should."

He waved that away with an impatient gesture. "I like working with the wood and I do a good job, but I haven't got that much time for it, or the proper tools to really do it right. You should have seen the Oscar brothers' factory in Sallisaw. It was really something. With good wood and the right kind of tools, why, a man could make things so pretty it'd hurt your eyes to look at them."

"Maybe you should take the time, and get yourself the proper tools. It's a long way to Sallisaw. Folks around here could use some furniture, too."

Henry Lee considered for a moment and then sat himself down on a sawhorse, facing the reverend.

"I know what you are trying to do, Preacher, and it won't work."

"What am I trying to do?"

"You're trying to get me to give up my business and try making a living building furniture."

"You could, you know," the preacher replied.

"Maybe," Henry Lee said. "I'm pretty sure I could make some nice things, things people might want to buy. But that isn't all there is to a business. The farmers around here, they might buy a table or a few chairs once in a while, but you can't live on that, Preacher. To be successful you've got to get yourself established on a big scale. Folks buy a table, it's supposed to last a lifetime. Even if they like your work, you can't expect them to buy another table next week."

His father-in-law nodded his understanding. "Not like the whiskey business, where you know they will always be coming back for more."

"That's right, Preacher." Henry Lee leaned forward, resting his elbows on his knees. "I know that you mean well. That you think my life would be better if I gave up moonshining, but I'm not going to do that. I've built a good business. I have everything I need and money in the bank. I know the whiskey trade, I make good liquor and I know how to sell it. There is no reason in the world why I should throw all that away to try to do something else, something I really don't know anything about."

"I think you're a little inaccurate about what it is that you know," the preacher answered. "You started up a business and made a success of it. I see that, Henry Lee, and I'm proud of you for it. But, you didn't make a success of it because you are inherently good at making whiskey. You had to learn to make whiskey. You worked hard at it, I'm sure, and you were determined to make the best; from what I hear, I understand that you do. You sell that whiskey all over the territory and people go out of their way to buy from you because they know you sell a good product and that you are fair and honest in your dealings."

The preacher leaned back and crossed his legs, looking into Henry Lee's eyes to make sure he had the man's attention.

"What you've learned, Henry Lee, is that if you make

a quality product that people want to buy, and you deal fairly and openly with them, they will buy it from you. That is what you've learned. That is the talent you have. It wouldn't matter if it's whiskey or furniture or brushes, you are a man who will be successful because you expect nothing less of yourself."

Henry Lee felt a swell of pride stirring in his breast, but he quickly beat it down. He was a whiskey man, that was who he was, who he had always been. The preacher might know about a lot of things, but it didn't mean he knew about him.

"That's all well and good, Preacher. And I appreciate your confidence in me, but it's a lot easier to be successful in the whiskey business."

"Yes, I guess so." The preacher smiled his agreement. "But then success in the whiskey business doesn't really mean as much, does it? Nothing worth having ever comes easy. When you don't play by the rules, being the winner doesn't seem much of an accomplishment."

Farnam stood up and stretched. "These are going to be mighty fine benches, Henry Lee. I'll be very proud to have them in the church."

"Thanks," Henry Lee replied quietly. He was still mulling over what the preacher had just said. He was trying to push it away, telling himself the preacher was wrong. But he was no longer sure.

"I'd best be getting on my way," Farnam told him, heading for the door. "It's bad enough when you've got one woman watching out the window and worrying about you. With Hannah at home, there's two hens to fuss after me. I'm thinking that's one too many."

As the two men walked across the yard, Henry Lee was lost in thought while Farnam rattled on about the crops and the weather.

When he got to his horse, he turned to Henry Lee as if just recalling an errand.

"By the way, thought I'd invite you to the house on Saturday night for dinner. I suspect you're getting pretty sick of your own cooking and I know that we'll be having a big spread 'cause Myrtie's beau is coming. I'd enjoy having you there, and I suspect it would ease Hannah's mind a bit to see that you are all right after your time in jail."

"Did Hannah say to invite me?"

"No, she had no idea that I would be coming by this way. I don't know that she'd even want me to ask you, but I do know that she'd like to see you."

"Saturday is my busiest night. I've got no time for socializing on a night when folks are serious about buying corn liquor."

The preacher nodded in understanding. "If you're too busy, you're too busy. But I'll leave the invitation open anyhow. If you can find your way clear to come, we would love to have you."

Henry Lee shook his head as he watched the preacher ride out of sight. The last thing he needed was to see Hannah again. Things were just fine as they were, she'd soon forget about him and he'd get on with his life. But even as he thought it, he wasn't sure he would be able to resist the opportunity to see her.

In the Federal Courthouse in Muskogee, Tom Quick, three of his deputies, Neemie Pathkiller, and two Indian cohorts sat around a table planning the end of Henry Lee Watson's whiskey business.

"We're not sure that we'd be able to find the still and if we start nosing around, he's bound to spot us," Quick explained to his men. "What we'll need to do is to get him to sell whiskey to you three. The money will be marked and the deputies and I will be able to testify that we saw the sale take place."

The marshall nearly licked his lips in anticipation.

"Once we've arrested him, we can take our time combing those hills until we find that still. This time we'll be able to put him away for twenty years."

The men asked few questions. Everybody knew the job they had to do. It would be easy. No moonshiner would expect the marshall's office to go to this much trouble to arrest him. The three deputies wondered, among themselves, why they were doing it.

It was what Marshall Quick wanted and they would all be getting paid for travel and a portion of the arrest payment, so why complain. There was very little chance of danger. This moonshiner was known to carry a gun only on very rare occasions. There would be no reason for him to be armed at his own back door. It would be like taking candy from a baby.

As the men filed out, Quick motioned Pathkiller to stay.

"I don't want any slip-ups. We want him dead to rights. I'm not about to be made a fool of a second time."

Pathkiller understood the marshall's anger, and he too intended to be extremely careful that everything went smoothly.

"Are you sure the Indians can be trusted?" Quick asked him.

"Don't know why not," he answered. "Neither of them are drinkers and they both need the money."

"I've seen the scar-faced one around town before, do you think Watson will recognize him?"

"No, he's never seen Watson, I asked him first thing. He'll just be another drunk Indian to the Whiskey Man."

"What about the young one? Where does he fit in?"

"He's up from around Locust Grove. He's a college boy out at Bacone, clever and desperate for cash, just the kind we need."

Tom Quick digested that information and finally nodded his head.

"We are going to get him this time. I'm putting that no-account out of business forever."

TWENTY

L ate Saturday afternoon, Hannah sat at the kitchen table slicing tomatoes for supper. She watched Violet struggling with the canning of the last of the green beans.

Will was coming for supper, and although Myrtie saw him several times a week, she continued to go into a tizzy each time, worrying about her dress and her hair. It was clear to all that Will already knew that she was the prettiest girl in the territory. Apparently Myrtie wanted to insure that he didn't change his mind.

Hannah's mind wandered back, as it had dozens of times this week, to what Violet had said about Will and Myrtie as two parts of a whole. And about her and Henry Lee being the same way.

At first she had tried simply to dismiss the idea. But things that made sense were difficult to just ignore. She realized how she had changed in the few weeks she had lived with Henry Lee. And she had enough honesty to admit that those changes were for the better. Had he changed too? Had she had some influence on his life? She didn't know. She would probably never know.

As she began to set the table, Myrtie rushed in and stood in the doorway looking at Hannah. Her body blocking the view to the outside, she held herself stiff and her face revealed anxious agitation, as if some terrible calamity had occurred. She kept darting her eyes back over her shoulder as if someone were coming up behind her.

"What is it?" Hannah asked her, but when she only

answered her sister with a pleading look of dismay, Violet took up the questioning.

"Wasn't that Will I heard ride up?" Violet questioned. "What are you doing still in the house?"

Myrtie darted glances back and forth between the women and then with a somewhat indecisive whine, said, "No, it wasn't Will."

The older women waited in silence for a moment, expecting Myrtie to continue. When she didn't, Violet and Hannah exchanged confused looks.

"Well, who was it?" Hannah asked.

Myrtie took a deep breath and then looked sympathetically at Hannah.

"You'd best set another place," she said finally, lines of concern marring her pretty face. "Papa has invited Henry Lee for dinner."

Hannah set down the plate she was holding as if it were a hot skillet. Glancing through the door behind Myrtie, she saw nothing but wasn't reassured.

"He's out there?" she asked nervously, her voice barely above a whisper.

Myrtie nodded furiously, her face contorted with misery. "I'll help you, Hannah," she offered. "If we hurry, we can still have you fixed up nice before you see him."

"See him?" Hannah asked stupidly, and then as if suddenly getting a grip on her senses she quickly reached behind her and pulled the ties on the apron and handed it to Violet.

"I have no intention of seeing him," she told them. "I'm going to my room. You'll just have to tell him that I am indisposed. I can't see him."

"Hannah!" Violet sounded dismayed and almost angry. "He's made the first move, you can't just ignore it."

"I have to. I can't see him. I just can't."

As Hannah turned to go to her room, Violet grabbed her arm. Her worry and concern for her stepdaughter altered her normally placid visage into a reflection of anguish.

"This is your future you're throwing away. Please don't do this."

Hannah pulled away without answering and hurried to the sanctuary of the bedroom. She couldn't face her husband. Her feelings were so raw, and so near the surface, she feared she would shame herself.

The supper table that night was a curious affair with everybody talking cheerfully and all feeling distinctly uncomfortable. Even Will and Myrtie, normally so wrapped in their own world, seemed to be caught up in the problems of Henry Lee and Hannah.

Henry Lee had nearly turned the buggy around four times before he finally made it to the reverend's place. And then, to find that his wife wasn't even willing to sit at the same table with him was humiliating. He had been ready to leave right then. He had tried to make his excuses, but Violet would hear none of it. He had come to supper and he would stay and eat, Violet insisted. Despite her usual cheery temperament, she brooked no argument.

So he did eat what he could. It had been so long since he'd had good food that he should have been diving into his plate. But he was having a difficult time forcing anything down at all. Being told that almost everything on the table was cooked by the woman he had come to see didn't help a bit. He wanted to cherish this meal, probably the last she would ever cook for him. But every time he looked around the table and was reminded that she wasn't there, his throat tightened with grief.

As Henry Lee sat in the kitchen, Hannah paced in her room. She told herself that she would take a much-needed nap and that when she awoke, the man in the kitchen would be gone forever. Although she'd stripped down to her chemise and drawers, the idea of sleep was totally ridiculous. The blood seemed to be pounding through her veins and she couldn't, for the life of her, even sit still. Lying down would have been impossible.

Her mind played over and over the memories of Henry Lee. It was as if there were no other memories in her life, no life at all before he became part of hers. This room that she'd shared with her sister for five years now only represented the one night the two of them had been here together. That one night when she was so embarrassed and frightened, and he was so kind. And that wonderful morning when she had first discovered what it felt like to be held close by a man.

Before the dreamy smile could take over her face, she pushed the memory away. All the kisses they had shared, all the incredible heat that she had learned from his body, couldn't change the facts. Her husband was a moonshiner and he intended to live his life on the wrong side of the law. She could not approve of that, not ever.

He was a gentle man, and he was good to her, she couldn't deny that. He was not frivolous and shallow as she had thought at first. Nor was he shiftless and lazy. She remembered her surprised pride when she heard about him bringing in his hay alone.

She also remembered the depths of pain in his eyes when they had shared their childhood grief at the loss of their mothers.

He was strong and worthy and admirable. He could make her heart soar and her pulse race with desire. But he was a moonshiner. A purveyor of that evil elixir that could turn a man into an animal. Despite that, she knew she loved him.

She saw him again, in her memory, on that day under the catalpa tree. Armed with a singletree, he had come running to protect her. He had shown tenderness and offered comfort. Teasingly, he'd agreed to slay all her dragons, to keep her safe from lizards and spiders. And he had made her body sing with passion. It was a husband's bargain he had offered. And she had accepted it so casually, never dreaming of the leap of faith he was taking.

She, the pious preacher's daughter, had been willing to accept him as a husband, graciously forgiving him for his good humor and frivolity, when he had proved himself to be a hardworking farmer.

But he had accepted her, believing her to be a sinful

and wicked Jezebel willing to draw an innocent man into scandal to guard herself. Even being saddled with another man's child had not deterred him from trying to be a good husband to the woman who had deliberately tricked him into marriage.

Henry Lee was just that way. He accepted the cruel and difficult life that heaven had handed him and he made the best of it.

Looking beyond her obvious misdeed, he sought the strengths in Hannah, to see what was really true about her, what was really inside. It was not a condescending forgiveness that he offered, it was acceptance of the human frailties of all and an opportunity to move on without penance or remorse.

"It's too bad, Miss Hannah May Bunch," she reviled herself, "that you aren't a good enough person to be able to do that. You know already that, inside, he is a man of tenderness and depth, inestimable value and honor. But you are willing to discard all of that because, outside, he doesn't live up to your measure."

Hannah stopped her pacing. Leaning her head against the wall, she covered her eyes with her hands. Violet was right. She was throwing away her future, her only chance for happiness and, for the life of her, she didn't know why.

The long, uncomfortable meal in the kitchen was drawing to a welcomed conclusion. Violet was just getting ready to ask if everyone was ready for dessert when she heard the door to Hannah's bedroom opening. As if frozen in place, everybody waited as footsteps came determinedly down the hall.

As Hannah stepped into the doorway, Henry Lee immediately rose to his feet. His good manners prompted Will and the preacher to quickly do the same.

The couple stood at opposite ends of the table, drinking in the sight of each other. It felt so good just to see, just to know, just to remember.

Hannah was wearing the silver-leafed blue calico that Henry Lee had given her, the one she had worn on her glorious Cinderella night in Muskogee. Her hair was loosed from its stiff confining braid and worked into a gentle topknot that softened her features. Her cheeks flushed with excitement and her eyes softened with love, she had never looked more beautiful.

"What a delicious dress!" Myrtie exclaimed. "I've never seen you wear that before."

"It's my favorite," Hannah answered her sister, as her eyes remained on her husband. "I saved it for a special occasion."

The silence lengthened, until Violet broke it abruptly. "Sit, Hannah, I'll get you a plate. Henry Lee, you want more of those potatoes?"

The food was passed around another time and everybody at the table took another portion as if the meal that had gone on before had never existed.

She had changed her mind! The reality screamed through Henry Lee's brain as he ate now with a vengeance, not tasting a thing and not taking his eyes off her for a moment. He was almost as ill at ease now as he had been when she was in her room. What did this mean? Was he to be accepted, forgiven, or simply offered another chance? The anxiety almost overwhelmed him. But it felt so good just to look at her. He had forgotten how desirable she really was.

"Are you feeling better?" he asked, giving her a polite alibi.

"I have never felt better in my life," she answered, wanting him to have no doubt that she had stayed away because of him, and now she was here because of him.

"You do look very well," Henry Lee said, thinking that she was even prettier in reality than his memory had been able to render.

"Thank you. You look well yourself," she responded both truthfully and with concern. He was as handsome and vital as ever, but she found herself thinking that he looked tired. He'd lost weight and there were new lines of worry in his face.

Farnam Bunch was nearly choking on the couple's

strained politeness and the undercurrents that seemed to be shifting across the room.

"Henry Lee brought me the blackberries that you put up," her father said, hoping to shore up a sinking conversation. "He said that he'd never cared for them, but he was sure if you made them, they were bound to be good and he wanted someone to be able to enjoy them."

"That's nice," Hannah said, but never allowed her glance to stray from her husband.

"I remembered that you said they were your father's favorite," Henry Lee told her.

"I'm surprised that you remembered that."

Henry Lee's eyes were dark and fathomless, and his voice was breathy with emotion.

"I remember everything."

Hannah felt the words shiver through her in pleasure. She also remembered and although she didn't speak a word, her hot look conveyed that fact to Henry Lee.

When Violet decided that surely they had lingered at the table long enough, she rose. "You don't need to bother with the dishes, Hannah. I'll take care of them."

In truth, Violet would have been hard pressed to get Hannah to help. For once in her life, she seemed unconcerned about the necessary household chores. She was totally wrapped up in Henry Lee.

As her father seated himself in a rocking chair on the front porch, it was only natural that the young people "walk out," the traditional way for courting couples to be alone while still under the watchful eye of a chaperone.

Hannah walked calmly next to Henry Lee. They were not touching in any way, but they were close enough to touch and Hannah didn't seem either shy or ill at ease about that. It surprised him a little, but pleased him a great deal. They followed Will and Myrtie as they sauntered around the yard whispering and laughing in front of them.

Henry Lee found that the amusing small talk that always came so easily to him in his business failed him as he walked with the woman he loved. Not one diverting tale came to his mind, and had it not been for Hannah, filling him in on the doings at the church, there would have been no conversation at all.

Will and Myrtie made an abrupt detour in their route and Henry Lee would have followed, except for Hannah's hand on his arm.

"I'm sure they are headed for the arbor swing," Hannah told him. "That's their private place on Saturday nights."

Henry Lee nodded and, gently placing his hand on the back of her waist, diverged from the direction of the swing. The night was not yet cool, but a breeze made it comfortable and the hefty slice of moon in the sky lighted their path and gave silvery highlights to their faces.

"We didn't have a private, Saturday night place," he commented, matter-of-factly. "This is the first time we have ever walked out."

Hannah nodded. "It does seem strange, doesn't it?" After a moment she added, "It might have helped if we had."

Henry Lee thought about that.

"Yes, I guess it would have. You would have known about my business before we married and you could have been saved from tying yourself to me."

"Maybe," she answered. "But the point is, we never walked out because you never even knew that I was alive before you woke up in the wellhouse that morning."

Henry Lee found it difficult to argue with that. He had hardly given the plain, hymn-singing daughter of the preacher a second thought. But looking at his wife now, he couldn't imagine that she and that other Hannah Bunch were the same woman.

"I didn't know you, and I thought you were surely too good for me anyway."

Hannah shook her head ruefully and offered an ironic little laugh. "One thing I am not, Henry Lee, is good. You of all people should know that. What I've done to you, forcing myself into your life. That's a terrible sin."

"Don't talk like it was a mistake, Hannah. I guess you'd say I'm not much of a believer, but things happen

for a reason. I believe that. This whole thing was meant
to be, I'm as sure of that as anything."

He slid his arm around her waist, pulling her close
beside him, and planted a sweet, chaste kiss in her hair.

"Hannah, there are things about me that you don't
know. Things besides my whiskey making that maybe
you've got a right to hear."

He took a deep breath and glanced up at the moon,
gathering strength to share words he had kept to himself
for a lifetime.

"Skut Watson was not my father, Hannah," he told
her, carefully avoiding her face, unsure of her reaction.
"My father was an army major named Walter Henry Lee,
who was once the post commander at Fort Gibson. When
my mother knew him, he was at least twice her age, married, and with grown children. She knew all that, of
course. It didn't matter. She was young and pretty and
wild, and he bought her presents and paid her for her
services. She was his mistress and when she began blossoming with me in her belly, he sold her to Skut Watson
for cash."

They had stopped still in the yard and, taking a
cleansing breath, Henry Lee turned to look at her.

"That's who I am, Hannah. Three parents and all of
them put together not fit to wipe the boots of my wife."

Hannah wrapped her arms around her husband's
waist and looked determinedly up into his eyes.

"That is not who you are, Henry Lee!" she contra-
dicted. "Do you remember what Harjo told us about his
birth, how the midwife said he would never walk? He
walks, Henry Lee. He even dances. Maybe those three
weren't the best start for a child in this world, but you've
overcome that handicap. You're walking as straight and
tall as any man in these territories and you've even
learned to dance."

Henry Lee felt a strange surge of joy. He nodded,
too full of feelings to speak words. He turned her again
to the path and gently urged her beside him. They walked
in silence for several minutes. There was something comforting in just being together. Simply sharing the close

proximity of the other created a kind of haven. He realized that no matter the terrors and hatred of the outside world, with Hannah beside him like this, believing in him, sharing his sorrows, he could survive the worst. Having Hannah as his woman could ease a world of hurt.

The solemn stillness of their introspective moments was finally broken by Hannah as she questioned him about the church pews. With enthusiasm he related the work he had done and his pride in his finished product.

They talked of the harvest and weather, the pigs and the pecan trees. Not once did either mention their marriage or the trouble between them.

Taking her hand in his he set a course to the left and a couple of moments later they stood in front of the door to the wellhouse. Neither could hide from the funny, terrible, embarrassing memories associated with the small building.

"I guess we do have a private, Saturday night place, after all," he said, giving her a bantering smile.

He opened the door to the cool interior and they seated themselves in the doorway with their feet on the steps.

The moon, the night, the memories, the quiet between them seemed to stretch too long and both became somewhat ill at ease. Hannah, seeking something to do with her hands, reached down next to the steps to pull the long grass that grew unmolested there. She jerked her hand back with a startled cry.

"What is it?" Henry Lee asked urgently reaching for her injured hand.

"It's just a sandbur," Hannah answered him, somewhat embarrassed at her reaction. "I'm not hurt, just startled, I guess."

"Let me see."

She gave him her hand and he held it gently in his own as if it were a treasure. Tenderly his rough finger sought the place of her injury.

"Does it still hurt?"

"No, it's fine, really."

Henry Lee brought his lips to the upturned palm he

held in his hand and gifted it with a healing kiss. The sweet tenderness of his lips coupled with his hot breath on her skin sent a current of fire up her arm. Henry Lee felt her reaction, which was no less startling than his own, and he reveled in it.

"Kiss me, Hannah," he whispered to her. "Oh, how I have ached in my bed at night dreaming that you would kiss me."

Hannah raised the hand he had so lovingly pleasured to his cheek. She felt that slight roughness, evidence of the lateness of the day, and she slowly moved her face toward his. Tilting her head slightly to meet his mouth, she drew closer and closer to the wonderful lips that she sought. An instant before the kiss was met, Henry Lee raised his hand and, with his index finger, gently urged her lips apart.

"Open for me, Hannah."

She did, both her mouth and her heart.

With the earnest yearning of their fragile love, they kissed softly, delicately, with such reverence for the emotion between them.

They drew back to look at each other, to see if the sorcery that held them was mirrored in the eyes of the other. Finding the truth there, they offered another gentle kiss, and then another. Again their eyes met, seeking, exploring, testing. Tiny little kisses, gentle little bites, were not dangerous. Just a diminutive peck. A whisper on the lips. A brief spark of jeopardy. A chancy taste of the forbidden. Then with a sigh of gracious surrender, Hannah grasped his muscled forearms and kissed him dangerously.

The blood surged through Henry Lee's veins as he recognized Hannah's building passion. He returned her kiss with full measure, trying valiantly to bank the fire that threatened to flash out of control. His arms encircled her, eagerly drawing her close, possession and protection warring in their clasp.

Hannah had learned from him the pleasure that lips could give and she sought to teach the teacher as she allowed her desire full rein to enjoy him. The pressure of his mouth pulled her to him as if he would consume her, and she wanted nothing less.

He deepened his embrace, seeking to pull her closer, so much closer, as if to make her a part of him at last.

Even through the layers of clothing that separated their bodies, Henry Lee could feel the tense, hardened nipples that crowned her bountiful bosom. Though her lips were sweet, he wanted badly to taste her nipples, to tease them with his tongue and suck them into his mouth. He consoled himself with the tender flesh of her throat and ear.

Hannah did not remain idle. Her hands eagerly explored the powerful muscles of his back, caressing and investigating the strength of the man she loved. Touching him was such pleasure, but not nearly enough. Her body ached with desire. She wanted to feel him against her. She remembered the heat of his rigid eagerness pressed against the juncture of her thighs and she wanted to feel him again. She wanted to lie here on the wellhouse floor and have him cover her body with his own, to press against her. Her hand strayed from his smooth, sleek ribs to his thigh, where her quest continued. When her inquisitive fingers discovered his hard, heated manhood, they instinctively curled around it.

"Hannah!" Her name was a gasp on his lips. Henry Lee clenched his teeth and held himself perfectly still as he struggled for control. He knew he should take her hand and move it away from him, but he could not. No skilled harlot or experienced widow had ever given him the pleasure he felt as her hand simply held the object of her desire. In another minute he would go off like a green kid. He had meant only to kiss her, not to lose control. With abject regret, he eased her out of his grasp and took her hand in his own, bringing it to his lips.

"Oh, Hannah, if you knew how much I want to have you right here, right now, you'd be running in terror back to the house."

Hannah's eyes, still glazed with desire, assessed him lovingly and her lips pressed a small tender kiss on the side of his mouth.

"I'm not running, Henry Lee. I'm not running from you ever again."

A surge of joy poured through Henry Lee at her words. She was not running. She was his for the taking. Had he proved to himself that he was worthy of such a gift? Would pulling her skirts up and having her now prove just the opposite?

Assembling all his wit and control, Henry Lee concentrated on steadily breathing in and out. After a moment he felt stronger and he laid his forehead playfully against hers.

Looking down into her eyes he teased, "Your father may have forgiven me for one indiscretion in his well-house. I'm not sure he would be so forgiving a second time."

She laughed delightedly. Henry Lee loved that deep throaty laugh. If he could have his heart's desire, he would want to hear that laugh every day for the rest of his life.

Putting his arm around her, he drew her close beside him, touching her only lightly. They were not yet willing to part, but they needed to cool the fire that was burning so brightly between them.

Wanting to store the sound of her laughter for the silent days to come, he quietly told her all the amusing anecdotes that came into his mind. Surprisingly, she had a few of her own to offer. They talked together until quite late, but never once mentioned the trouble between them, or the walls that continued to keep them apart.

It was after midnight when Henry Lee finally walked her back to her front porch. Will had ridden out long ago and the household was already in bed.

Standing beside her in the moonlight, Henry Lee didn't know exactly what to say. They had not resolved the problems in their marriage, but he knew now that they could. He hoped she would say something, ask him back tomorrow, anything. But she seemed to be waiting for him to speak. What could he say, his offer was the same it had always been.

Hannah waited. She waited for him to tell her to

come home. She waited for him to say he wanted her to be his wife. As the silence dragged on, she became afraid. The perfection of the night could be marred by words misspoken or conclusions drawn too quickly.

Rising on the tips of her toes, she quickly planted a kiss on his warm, firm lips.

"Good night, Henry Lee. I hope you know that I love you."

She hurried into the house, shutting the door behind her. Henry Lee stared after her, replaying in his mind the words she had just spoken. She had said she loved him. Hannah, his Hannah, the woman that gave his life sunshine and purpose, actually loved him. He suddenly felt as if he were a giant, ruler of the universe, master of his own fate. Hannah Bunch Watson was in love with him, and she had said so right to his face.

He knew she stood on the other side of the closed door. With a smile of triumph, he leaned up against the door and spoke just loudly enough to make himself heard.

"Good night, Mrs. Watson. I love you, too."

With his face brimming with smiles, he leaped off the porch like a young colt and headed to his rig. He wanted to laugh and dance and shout his excitement to the world. But he managed to contain his dignity until he had made his way down the road out of earshot of the house. Then he sent a whopping "wahoo" to the heavens.

He laughed at his own foolishness. Then as he calmed, he became more serious. Being given Hannah's love was not just a prize to be accepted with delight, it was a responsibility that he needed to live up to. A gift to be treasured and secured for safekeeping, he could not just accept it and be done. Hannah, his Hannah, deserved a better man than him. But it was him that she loved and she wasn't a woman to give her love easily.

Throughout the trip home, he brooded and planned. His future with Hannah was the only thing that mattered. Summer would turn to fall and winter, some would be born, some would die. Henry Lee would put food on their table and keep the wind from the chinks in the cabin.

Life, his life, was with Hannah. Without her, it was only existence.

As he stepped up to his back porch he saw a piece of paper hanging against the door. He carefully took it down and carried it inside the cabin with him.

Lighting the lamp in the kitchen, he unfolded the paper and laid it out on the table. He stared at the ink marks on the paper for a few moments; then, as if it were a map, he turned it ninety degrees. When it still failed to make sense, he turned it again. Finally recognizing some of the letters, he knew it was the right direction.

He cursed his lack of schooling. He knew some of the letters on the page, but they meant nothing to him. He would just have to wait until he saw someone to read it to him. He pulled his suspenders down from his shoulders and started to walk away. He was tired and wanted to lie in his bed and think about the future. One last look at the paper honed in on an unusual letter. There at the bottom of the page, the first letter of the word was "z."

A strange feeling of dread washed over him. There was only one word that he could think of that started with "z" and that was Zanola. If she had bothered to come all the way up to his place at night, something must be terribly wrong.

He shrugged tiredly; surely whatever it was could wait for morning, he thought to himself and started to continue with his undressing. Then he went to stand and stare at the paper again, worried and wishing that he could make sense of it. With a sigh of self-disgust, he readjusted his clothes, shoved the rumpled note into his pocket, slammed his hat on his head, and went out to hitch a fresh horse to the buggy.

The night train pulled into the station at Ingalls. Seven men got off. Three were Indians; dressed in beat-up hats and stained clothes, they appeared to be dirty and unkempt, but their movements were sober and sure as they made their way across the platform. With them were three lawmen, heavily armed and wary-eyed. The seventh man followed behind them. His face was totally void of emotion. No anxiety or fear or excitement was going to cause him to make a mistake. He was experienced and experience had taught him to be careful. Train robbers, murderers, hired guns, and bloodthirsty lunatics, he had seen them all. If a lawman wanted to live long enough to die in his own bed, he needed to expect the unexpected. He was prepared for anything, except failure. Tom Quick had arrived at the border to take care of Henry Lee Watson, once and for all.

TWENTY-ONE

Hannah pulled her father's rig to a stop underneath the big red oak outside Henry Lee's cabin. She was surprised that he didn't seem to be around. She couldn't imagine where anyone might be on Sunday morning, unless it was church, and she would have passed him on the road if he had headed that way.

Admittedly, she didn't know a good deal about what non-churchgoers did on Sunday morning. But today she was going to find out for herself. When she told her father that she intended to move back to Henry Lee's house this morning, she had half expected him to tell her to wait until after the service. He hadn't and she was glad, because she didn't think she could have.

She had tossed and turned most of the night, before she finally got up and went out to sit on the porch. Her decision had not been easy, but there was no other choice. She loved Henry Lee, despite what she knew about him, maybe even because of what she knew about him. She loved him. And last night, through the door, he had said he loved her, too. Two people who loved each other and were married to each other should be together. There was just no other way to figure it.

Hannah unloaded her things near the back door and then led the horse to the barn to unhitch her. It felt good to be home, she thought. This place was hers now, as well as Henry Lee's.

Working with the horse, she thought about the family that she had left behind. Her father had been proud of her decision, though he hadn't said a word. She had finally realized that he was right, but at least he'd had the good grace not to say "I told you so."

Violet's warm hug and encouraging smile gave her comfort. It was amazing what a rock of strength Violet had turned out to be. More evidence, Hannah thought ruefully, that Hannah Bunch Watson did not know as much as she thought she did.

Myrtie had been bubbly and excited for her as she helped her pack. "So you talked it all out, and got your troubles squared away last night?"

"No," Hannah answered her with a light laugh. "Our troubles are still as big as Texas and nothing was solved last night. But I love him and I can't just stop loving him because I think that I should. He's still a moonshiner and I can't approve of that, but he's my man and I'm going to be right next to him, disapproving, for as long as we both shall live."

Hannah thought of those words as she headed back up toward the house. She'd heard a story once about Bill Dalton. How he'd courted his wife and won her before she realized he was an outlaw. Hannah had always wondered why she hadn't left him when she'd found out. Now she knew.

A woman can't change a man. She can't make him what he's not. But if she can see the good in him, she can nurture that. It's like working in the garden. The weeds grow right along next to the carrots. People do their best to encourage the carrots; if not, the weeds will just take over.

The cabin was clean, as she knew it would be. Henry Lee wasn't a man to let things go. She was anxious, however, to scrub it herself. After a trip to the creek for two buckets of water, she began to make it her house again. The work was not drudgery, but pleasant. Making a home for Henry Lee and herself was a pleasure. A tune came to her lips and she began to sing as she worked.

Tom Quick and his men arrived only shortly after Hannah. But, unlike her, they did not approach the house

at first. Staking out their horses about a half mile down
the creek, Quick sent Pathkiller to check out the house
while he went over the plan one more time. He wanted
no slip-ups, no mistakes.

Pathkiller returned shortly. "Watson's not there."

Tom Quick muttered an obscene expletive.

"Only the woman is there, she's cleaning the house
and singing up a storm."

"The woman is there?" Quick had heard the woman
had left Watson. That had pleased him. A criminal didn't
deserve such a fine female. When he'd learned she had
walked out on Watson, he'd considered her just the
proper woman. But maybe she was not. Pathkiller had
said she was drinking whiskey at the Ambrosia Ballroom,
and the story told about their wedding indicated that she
was no better than she should be.

Quick leaned back on his heels, studying the situation. If she was there in the house, then Watson would
obviously be returning pretty soon.

"Is she cooking anything?" he asked Pathkiller.

"Yep," the Indian replied, "smells like turnips."

Quick smiled.

"Then she expects him back for dinner. If we wait
any longer, it will be hard to believe that these three have
been out drinking all night and just run out of liquor."

The men nodded in agreement.

"We'll proceed with the plan," Quick announced.

He turned his attention to Pathkiller and the other
Indians. "If she doesn't sell you the whiskey, just plant
yourself in the yard, take a nap or whatever and wait for
her man to come home. I'll be watching and I'll have you
covered."

His gaze moved to the deputies. "You can spend the
time combing these woods looking for that still. It has to
be fairly close to the house. I want every inch of ground
within a half mile covered."

The deputies set out on foot and Tom Quick followed
the creek to get himself into position. He found a bluff,
not far from the cabin, with a couple of toe holds up high
enough to have a clear view of everything that went on.

The ledge he was sitting on was not much, but it gave him a good perspective. He looked above him and saw an outcropping with a larger ledge, but he knew that was too high. He'd be too easily spotted. So he settled down right where he was, content, not realizing that Watson's still was in a cave hidden not ten feet above him, behind the ledge he thought was too high.

The Indians mounted up and taking a circuitous route approached the cabin from the west, riding fast and hollering.

Hannah heard the racket and was momentarily startled. She hurried to the door to see the three Indians riding up hell for leather and yelling in an obvious state of intoxication. Slightly fearful, she was dismayed at her haven being invaded by whiskey-wild Indians. But, she remembered Harjo as a friend of both Henry Lee and herself and she stiffened her spine and walked to the back door.

Pathkiller saw her at the back door and recognized her apprehension. He immediately dismounted and spoke sharply to the others in Cherokee, warning them not to overplay their hand. He walked toward the back door but stopped before he got too near. Doffing his hat, he gave her a low bow that he hoped was a parody of politeness.

"You are Mrs. Watson, I presume," he said to Hannah, his voice was cultured, but his words were slightly slurred.

Hannah nodded. "We've come to do some business with your husband," he said. "Is he at home?"

Hannah shook her head. "He had an errand to run this morning, he should be back anytime," she answered, hoping that it was true.

The Indian accepted this, but then after turning to his cohorts for a consultation, came back.

"Perhaps you can help us, Mrs. Watson. My friends and I have been having a little celebration, and it seems that we've run out of one of the necessary ingredients." He dug into his pocket and pulled out a fifty dollar gold piece. "Could you sell us a couple of jugs of Mr. Watson's fine corn liquor?"

Hannah knew that this was why they had come to the place, but it still angered her that they would think her a party to this evil whiskey business.

"No, sir, I could not," she answered sharply. "You should take yourself and your business elsewhere." She turned and went back into the house, slamming the door primly.

Pathkiller hesitated a moment, a little surprised by her reaction. Then he shrugged. There was really no understanding women. That was one certainty.

Calling through the door he told her, "We'll just wait out here in the yard until your husband returns, ma'am, don't mind us. We're not going to be a minute's trouble to you."

The Indians tied their horses to the hitching post and sat down in the shade of the red oak and waited for Henry Lee Watson.

Tom Quick, in the woods within earshot, lay his rifle across his knees and settled himself also for the long wait. Waiting was one thing a lawman had to learn to do a lot, and Tom Quick was a master at it. Watson would return and sell the Indians the liquor. By that time, the deputies would have found his still and Quick would see that he stayed locked up for twenty years. Tom Quick smiled to himself, justice would be done.

As the morning stretched longer, Hannah continued her work in the house. She no longer sang, and a good deal of the joy had gone out of her return home. She didn't want to go outside, because the Indians were still waiting there under the tree. And their presence was a constant reminder of the distance still unbridged between herself and Henry Lee.

She tried to concentrate on the decisions she had made last night and this morning. How she would learn to tolerate the whiskey business, while continuing to disapprove of it. She would not be a part of it. Somehow, having those men waiting around to buy liquor from her husband made her feel that she was a part of it. That she did condone it. It made her ashamed. She shouldn't be simply ignoring the existence of those men, she should be encouraging them to give up their sinful devotion to strong drink.

Realizing her duty, Hannah filled the coffee pot and put it on the stove.

Pathkiller and his men sat together, occasionally talking, but mostly just trying to outlive the boredom of the moment. Watson could return anytime and they needed to be ready, but he might not return for hours, so they remained relaxed yet alert. Nothing could have surprised them more than Mrs. Watson suddenly appearing at the back step.

"I'm sure you gentlemen are getting tired and hungry," she said sweetly. "I've got a batch of butter cookies just coming out of the oven and some fresh brewed coffee. Why don't you come in and have some?"

The men were stunned. After her earlier behavior, they didn't figure she would have a word to say to them. Now she was inviting them into the house. The two cohorts looked to Pathkiller for guidance.

He quickly considered his options. To refuse would look strange. No man would turn down coffee and food if he was just sitting around, especially if that food was prepared by a woman. And cookies were something that a man couldn't make over a camp fire. They were not a thing to be sneered at.

Pathkiller rose and the other two with him.

"That's very nice of you, Mrs. Watson. We'd be delighted."

The three tromped into the house and Hannah had them sit at the kitchen table. She poured a cup of coffee for each of them and placed a bowl of sugar and a pitcher of milk in the middle of the table and urged them to help themselves. The kitchen smelled wonderfully and the men found themselves forgetting the seriousness of their mission as she handed each of them a plate with at least a dozen cookies for each man.

Hannah wanted their mouths full, because she intended to be doing most of the talking. When she saw that they had what they needed and were all busily consuming their unexpected treat, she picked up her Bible

from the counter where she had laid it and began reading
from the passages that she had marked.

> *"And they shall say unto the elders of his city, this
> our son is stubborn and rebellious, he will not obey
> our voice; he is a glutton and a drunkard, and all men
> of the city shall stone him with stones."*

Pathkiller stopped chewing abruptly and nearly
choked on the tasty morsel he was consuming. He looked
at the other two, who were just as astonished as himself.
He thought that he had seen everything, but he had never
heard of having the Bible read to you when you visited
the whiskey peddler.

> *"But they also have erred through wine, and through
> strong drink are out of the way."* Hannah continued her
reading without pause. These men might not be led away
from their chosen path, but she was sure that hearing the
words of the Good Book could do them nothing but good.

> *"They are swallowed up of wine, they are out of the way
> through strong drink; they err in vision, they stumble in judg-
> ment . . ."*

Tom Quick sat patiently in the woods. He had been
as surprised as the others at her invitation and worried
that it might be a trick. Now after better than half an hour
waiting for them to come back out of the house, he was
getting a little concerned.

He heard Wilson coming up behind him and turned
his attention to the deputy.

"Have you found that still?" he asked.

"Marshall, I'm not sure there is one."

"Of course there is one. Do you think he makes this
liquor from thin air?"

"Well," the deputy told him firmly, "it must be in
the house or one of the outbuildings. We've searched
every inch of ground within a mile. There is no shack, no
cave, no dugout, nothing."

Tom Quick's face was a mask of displeasure. He had
counted on finding that still before they nailed Watson.
It would insure that he had no bargaining chips. He

looked off over the horizon toward the road. He didn't see any sign of Watson. Perhaps there was time to find it yet.

"The Indians are all in the house. I don't know what they are doing, but they're bound to keep that woman occupied. You and your men scout around those outbuildings."

The deputy nodded as the old man continued.

"Get some long sticks and check for hidden cellars under those buildings. I want everything including the outhouse looked over completely."

"Yes, sir," the deputy replied.

"And get somebody up to have a look in that cabin, they've been in there too long. I want to know what's going on."

"I'll do it myself," he replied and headed off to give the men their orders.

Quick continued to keep watch. Within a few minutes he could see the deputies making their way stealthily to the outbuildings. He saw Wilson slowly moving from obstacle to obstacle trying to get closer to the house. Finally he was on the ground near the back door. He remained seated there for several minutes as the marshall watched. Then he made his slow careful retreat in the same manner in which he had come.

The marshall waited patiently as the minutes dragged on, knowing that Wilson could not afford to hurry and be seen. Finally he heard him coming back through the woods.

"What's happening in there?"

"They're having a damn prayer meeting!"

"What?"

"She's reading the Bible and they're singing hymns. You wouldn't believe it. Hell, I'd never a guessed that Pathkiller could sing like that."

Tom Quick stared at his deputy, totally dumbfounded. Out of the corner of his eye, he saw movement on the horizon. He turned his attention that way and Wilson quickly followed his glance. The whiskey man was returning home.

*   *   *

Henry Lee held the horse at a leisurely pace as he scanned the horizon. He was nervous, but then he had a right to be. There were men out there watching him. Men who wanted to put him in jail. He had better plans for his future than that.

Following his instinct may have saved him, that and a few friends. If he hadn't had such a terrible feeling about the note, he might well have ignored it. That would have been a disaster.

When he'd arrived at Zanola's, her place was just closing up. She was surprised to see him.

"I sent a boy out to your house," she told him. "He says he left you a note."

"He did." Henry Lee pulled the note out of his pocket and showed it to her. "I can't read, so I came to find out what it says."

"You best be getting someone to teach you, this is too dangerous a world to go about it like a blind man."

She invited him into the tack room of the barn, which doubled as the office for her business.

"A man come riding in this afternoon from Okmulgee," she told him. "Seems he works for a friend of yours name of Harjo." Henry Lee felt a wave of anxiety wash over him.

"This Harjo fellow's got a boy at Bacone College, and that boy done heard another boy bragging that he was working for the U.S. marshalls. The marshalls got a big plan, and the boy's to be a part of it. He's going to pretend he's a bad drunk Indian. Going to catch him a whiskey man name of Watson."

Henry Lee listened to the plan, both surprised and not a little concerned. It was not good to have a man like Tom Quick on your bad side. Quick was like a toothless bulldog; he might never draw blood, but once he clamped those jaws on you, he could be a long-term nuisance.

He'd sat up most of the night, thinking, worrying, making plans on his own. He had purposely stayed away from his place this morning, knowing that they would spend the long day in the hot sun, waiting for him to come home.

That was both good and bad. The long wait would make them tired and careless, he hoped. But it could also give them time. The time they needed to locate the still. If they found the still, Henry Lee would go to jail. It was as simple as that.

If he had been his father, he would have ridden over to Guthrie or maybe even further west and waited for things to cool down. But he wasn't Skut Watson. He wanted to have this confrontation, get it over with, for good or bad, and get on with his life. He would as soon spend time in jail as spend time hiding out from the law.

Of course, he would rather do neither. If he could have what he wanted, he'd spend all his days with Hannah. But that was up to Hannah, she had to make her own choice. Right now, Henry Lee just hoped that he wouldn't be locked up in the penitentiary when she decided.

As Henry Lee rode up into the yard, his face broke out in a cold sweat. He expected Quick and his men to be hiding in the woods, but there were three horses tied at his hitching post. That could mean that they had found the still and no longer saw any reason to try to catch him in the act of selling whiskey.

In that moment of uncertainty, when he was trying to hastily reevaluate the situation, a sound from the house captured his ear.

> *"I have found a friend in Jesus,*
> *He's everything to me,*
> *He's the fairest of ten thousand to my soul;*
> *He's the Lily of the Valley,*
> *In Him alone I see,*
> *All I need to cleanse and make me fully whole.*
> *In sorrow He's my comfort,*
> *In trouble He's my stay,*
> *He tells me ev'ry care on Him to roll . . ."*

Henry Lee sat on the wagon seat listening in disbelief

for several minutes. Then in the midst of the deep male baritone and the poorly tuned tenors, he heard the throaty beer-garden soprano that he loved. Hannah was home.

Henry Lee pulled on the hand brake and jumped down from the buggy. With a lightness of his heart that was inexplicable in the current dangerous situation, he made his way to the house.

From the doorway he surveyed the scene in wonder. Hannah stood at the head of the table, her Bible clasped in one hand, the other moving rhythmically up and down marking time of the music for the singing. At the table sat three disreputable-looking Indians. Studying them, he easily picked out the young college boy and silently thanked him for his braggart ways and his big mouth. The quartet was mismatched and discordant, but it sounded heavenly to Henry Lee.

> "He's the Lily of the Valley,
> The bright and morning star,
> He's the fairest of ten thousand to my soul."

"Amen!" Henry Lee called loudly from the doorway as the song ended.

All four jumped slightly, but all Henry Lee saw was Hannah's face. Delight at seeing him warred with trepidation for her interference. Henry Lee wanted to set her straight immediately. Ignoring the men at the table, Henry Lee walked directly to his wife and pulled her tenderly into his arms brushing her lips with his own.

"Good morning, Mrs. Watson," he whispered huskily. "Nothing could make me happier than hearing you sing again in this kitchen."

At his words, the little bubble of apprehension that had been plaguing Hannah for the past few hours burst into warm sparks of happiness. She couldn't seem to take her eyes off him, and she couldn't stop smiling.

Hearing one of the Indians moving uncomfortably in his chair, Henry Lee remembered what he was about and decided that it was time he took charge of the situation.

Releasing Hannah, he turned to the man he assumed to be the leader, a nondescript Cherokee of indeterminate age. He offered his hand.

"Welcome to my home. I'm Henry Lee Watson, you've already met my wife, Hannah."

"Pathkiller," the man answered to the implied question, but didn't volunteer the names of the other men. He didn't like the way things were going here. He'd had a bad feeling about the operation as soon as the woman had invited them into the house. And now, after an hour of Bible reading and hymn singing, he was even more sure that things were going terribly wrong.

"We know who you are, Whiskey Man. Friends have told us that you make the finest corn liquor in the territory, and we've come to buy some." His smile didn't quite make it to his eyes, but Henry Lee knew that he would never have noticed it had he not been warned.

"I'm afraid your friends have led you wrong," he answered, keeping his voice friendly and purposely not looking at Hannah. He hoped that she wouldn't say anything to contradict him, or give him away with a facial expression. There was no time to warn her, he would simply have to trust her to trust him.

"You won't sell us your whiskey?"

"I don't sell whiskey," Henry Lee answered him calmly. "And I don't own a still."

Pathkiller stood up. Pulling a bag from inside his coat, he poured out coins of silver and gold onto the table.

"We have money," he said angrily, fruitlessly, already knowing that the trap had not worked.

"I'm sure your money's good," Henry Lee agreed. "But I have nothing to sell, unless you'd be willing to buy some of my wife's blackberry preserves?"

Pathkiller picked up his money and prepared to leave. He knew when the game was over. When a man couldn't win he made a dignified retreat.

Tom Quick, who with his deputies had come quietly up to the house, listened with anger at the interchange between the two men. Watson had already got the best of him once and he would be damned if he'd let him do it again without a fight. With all the pent-up anger of a man who's been sitting patiently in the hot sun all day, Quick burst into the kitchen.

Hannah gave a little startled scream before she recognized the angry marshall. Henry Lee drew her to him protectively. He had hoped they would accept defeat and just go away, but he could see that Quick was too enraged to do that.

"You don't get off that easily, Watson," the marshall barked angrily.

"Marshall," Henry Lee said, refusing to act surprised that he was there. Henry Lee just hoped that he hadn't found the still. If there was no still, there was no way he could take him to jail. The marshall's next words caused Henry Lee to give an inaudible sigh of relief.

"It's got to be here in the house," he said to his deputies. "You men search every inch of this place, I want that still found!"

The men began turning over the furniture, pulling things out of the cabinets and generally creating havoc in Hannah's well-ordered house. When one of the deputies carelessly knocked over the dainty little milk pitcher that belonged to her mother, she moved to stop them. Henry Lee's strong arms came around her and held her fast.

"Let the men do their job, Hannah," he told her, planting a consoling kiss on the top of her head. As his arms held her, she relaxed. Having a group of lawmen tear up your house is not a pleasant experience, but being cuddled in Henry Lee's arms made it bearable.

The mattress off the bed was lying in the middle of the sitting room, her clothes from the wardrobe were scattered everywhere. The deputies had a field day figuring out the Dufold: Hannah hoped it was not permanently ruined.

The men were stomping around on the floors when one said, "Marshall Quick, there's a cellar beneath this kitchen."

"Where's the door?"

"Don't see one, sir."

"Wilson," he called out. "Go get an axe and bust open this floor."

"No!" Hannah screamed furiously. Pulling away from Henry Lee she spoke sharply to the man called Wilson. "For heaven's sake, there is no need to tear up the floor! The door to the cellar is right over here. Follow me and I'll light a candle."

As Hannah opened the well-hidden door, she led the deputy down into the cellar. Picking up a candle and matches from the stock kept back behind the ladder, she lighted his way. The deputy looked around for several minutes, noting the well-stocked shelves of vegetables and examining the rows of potatoes and barrels of cured meats. He finally nodded and they returned upstairs.

"Well?" Quick boomed the question at him.

"Looks about like my mother's cellar," the young deputy answered.

Quick was mad as well as disgusted.

"We must have missed it," he told the men roughly. "Get back out there and search this place again, and I don't want to hear from you until you've found it."

Deputy Wilson shot Pathkiller a look and a bond of understanding emerged between the two of them.

"Marshall," Wilson told his superior. "There is no still here. He knew we were coming. I don't know how he knew but he knew. Do you think that he would still be here if there was evidence to be found? He'd be sitting in Amarillo resting his can if there was anything to find."

Quick realized that his deputy had the right of it. And cursed himself that he hadn't realized the truth himself without having to be told by a whippersnapper still wet behind the ears.

The marshall turned to Henry Lee. He didn't look much like his father, the old man thought. None of the snake-eyed evilness showed in this one. And he was a hell of a lot smarter, that was for sure. He could almost have liked him, if he hadn't been a lawbreaker.

"Watson, I guess luck was with you again this time. But it won't always be. I don't like wasting the taxpayers' money trying to catch no-accounts at their thieving business. If I so much as catch you spitting on the sidewalk, I'll throw you in jail and toss away the key."

"I'll keep that in mind, Marshall."

As the men filed out and headed on their way, Henry Lee turned to Hannah.

"Wasn't much of a welcome home, darlin'." His voice was a loving, velvet caress. "But I'm glad you're here."

Hannah was still slightly overwhelmed by the events of the last hour. But she, too, was glad to be home. No matter how unlawful, or frightening, or dangerous, she wanted to be with Henry Lee. Without a word she stepped eagerly into his embrace.

TWENTY-TWO

The sunlight was fading as Hannah hung the last of the soiled curtains on the clothesline and used the hot soapy water in the huge black kettle to douse the fire in the outdoor hearth.

After Tom Quick and his men had made their angry exit, she and Henry Lee had spent the better part of the day trying to put the house back in order.

Henry Lee told her the whole story, from the indecipherable note to the decision not to run away, but to risk imprisonment by standing his ground.

Once Henry Lee got her to see the funny side of it, they laughed together until Hannah couldn't stop. The shock the lawmen must have suffered at going to the whiskey peddler's to attend Sunday prayer service was enough to make her clutch her side in painful hilarity. When she could no longer stand she collapsed on the Dufold.

When Henry Lee lay down beside her and pulled her to his chest, the laughter gently subsided.

"I love you, Hannah," he stated firmly. "Last night I hadn't the courage to say it to your face, but I do have it now. I love you and I'm so glad you've come back to me."

Hannah smiled at the memory of the love that had shone in his eyes. He had been quick to loose her. The sparks that flew between them were too volatile to ignite unintentionally. They had laughed together and worked in harmony, taking care of the place they both now called home. They exchanged bashful blushes and confident looks as they both dutifully took care of responsibilities and secretly indulged in fantasies of the night to come. Hannah glanced toward the western horizon. She had never known the sun to take so long to go down!

Henry Lee brought down the last load from the cave to the small clearing in the woods. The cave would remain a secret. He would never tell a soul about it. Well, he reconsidered, perhaps he would tell Hannah. The wedding whiskey was still there. Carefully stored in barrels, he planned to let it age a good long time. Maybe for their twenty-fifth wedding anniversary, he'd take her there and they'd break into a barrel. He imagined the two of them, hiding out from a flock of grandchildren and making love in the afternoon when everyone thought them busy at work. The idea made him smile. Any idea of making love to Hannah could put him in a good mood.

They had talked at the wellhouse about their lack of a proper courtship. Well, perhaps it was too late for a proper one, but Henry Lee could easily imagine a very improper courtship between the woman he loved and himself.

With that in mind, as he started toward the cabin, he began looking around for wildflowers in the grass. It was hopeless. Too late in the year, too hot and too dry for wildflowers. He did, however, see a big ugly brown-faced sunflower staring at him from the corner of the pigsty.

Taking his pocket knife out and carefully cutting it with about a foot of stem, he decided to carry it home to his pretty wife. It wasn't a bouquet of roses, but theirs was not an ordinary love.

As he walked to the house, he spotted her. Standing near the back door, she was gazing off into the sunset; her work dress was dusty and several of those precious honey-colored curls had escaped the confines of her neatly twisted plait. She was beautiful, Henry Lee thought. A strong, beautiful woman, so full of heart and love. He truly did not deserve her. He was very glad that men don't always get what they deserve.

Hannah looked up to see Henry Lee coming toward

her and a buzz of excitement fluttered through her. In his hand he carried a sunflower and she knew that he had picked it for her.

He handed it to her and she held it in her hands as if it were precious and fragile.

"Oh Henry Lee, this is beautiful. Thank you so much. You are so sweet to me."

"I wish it were something better, Hannah. You deserve something better than a sunflower and a mixed-breed whiskey peddler."

She brushed the bright yellow petals tenderly against her lips. "No, Henry Lee," she protested. "I've been a very good girl for so very long. I deserve to have exactly what I want."

Laying her hands on his shoulders she raised herself on tiptoes and angling her head slightly kissed him with all the expertise she had learned from her whiskey man.

"Oh Hannah," he whispered moments later. "That's what I want, too."

Henry Lee slipped his arm beneath her knees and lifted her into his arms, whirling around in a circle. Her skirt flew in the breeze, giving her a strange surge of wanton freedom and him a tantalizing glimpse of black cotton stockings.

"Henry Lee, it's still daylight!" she objected half-heartedly as he leaped up the back steps with her laughing and squealing in his arms.

In answer he tossed her lightly in the air and then clasped her to him tightly.

"Don't expect me to wait until tonight, Mrs. Watson. Your husband has waited all that he's going to!"

He whisked her on into the bedroom, whirling her around twice more for good measure, and then leaped onto the bed. He landed on his back with Hannah astraddle him, both laughing like wayward children playing hookey from school.

As he gently rolled to the side, they faced each other; their bodies close, touching and trembling, they became more serious. Spending a moment just looking at each other, they realized that they were both anxious, both excited, both a little scared.

"Sometimes it hurts the first time, Hannah," he told her solemnly. "I'll try not to hurt you, but I can't promise."

"I'm not afraid, Henry Lee. I belong to you, it was meant to be this way."

He smiled lovingly at her. He'd never felt about a woman like this, and he wanted to make it so good for her.

"Take down your hair for me."

Hannah sat up in the bed and quickly undid the braided coil. She handed him the pins and he merely tossed them on the floor, not willing to look away long enough to set them on the table. Hannah giggled at that and then loosened her braid until her hair was a mass of wild curls around her head.

Henry Lee pulled her toward him and ran his hand lovingly through that mass of hair. Rubbing it against his cheek and offering it a kiss, he wrapped it around his fist like a rope and pulled her to him. Their lips met, gently at first and then with more passion as they both reacted to the fire that blazed between them.

Henry Lee had to remind himself to go slow as his hands explored her, cherished her. Tenderly he stroked her from her throat to her knees, then back again. He eased open the buttons of her bodice, untied the neckline of her chemise and bared her bosom to his eyes. Whispering words of praise and devotion he lowered his mouth to her firm, white breast. He sucked gently, then with more pressure as his tongue teasingly flicked the turgid nipple. He gave equal attention to the second breast, until both were full, hot, and wet.

Hannah, gasping for breath, couldn't seem to hold herself still and her reaction delighted Henry Lee. He ran a loving caress down her hip and leg to where her skirts bunched up at her knees. Running his hand underneath her dress he slowly explored the inside of her thigh, bringing the skirts up with him. When he reached the apex of her thighs he covered her womanhood and she immediately raised her hips from the bed, pressing against his hand. He returned the pressure, reveling in the heat and dampness he found there.

He brought his lips back to hers with fiery little kisses and cooing words, promising release and bliss. He struggled momentarily with the tie ribbon on her drawers, but it gave way and he pulled them down off her legs and threw them from her.

He sat back on his knees, surveying the abundance before him. Her bodice was spread open and her chemise down as if to frame the work of art that was her generous bosom. Her skirts were rucked up around her waist like a curtain at the theater and the show they displayed, the gentle curve of her belly, the riot of honey-colored curls covering her secrets, the long sturdy thighs, naked until just above the knees where plain white garters held her stockings in place, delighted him.

Her thighs trembled under his regard. His glance went to her face to see she was looking at him, awaiting his decision.

"You are beautiful, Hannah. More so than I ever realized." He laid his hand gently upon her belly. "I want to touch you, I love to touch you."

Hannah sat up in bed taking him in her arms. "I want to touch you, too!" With that she eased the suspenders off his shoulders. With a smile of tender delight, he helped her. He pulled the shirt out of his pants, and without bothering to unbutton it, pulled it off over his head and cast it away.

Hannah pulled him to her and cried out in rapture as she felt his naked flesh against her own. Henry Lee grasped her naked bottom in his hands and they rolled on the bed, teasing and kissing, stroking and learning the feel of the other. Henry Lee's trousers became not only uncomfortable but an impediment and he quickly loosed himself from them.

Hannah didn't yet have the courage to look, but she felt him hot and hard and massive against her. Their kisses became hotter and Henry Lee's hands seemed to be everywhere at once. Coaxing, teasing, finding the places that could pop Hannah's eyes open and quicken her breathing.

He lovingly stroked her hillock of curls and gently parted her, easing his finger a little inside. She jerked responsively at the contact and he knew she was ready.

To hold himself off, he thought only of her. Her laughing, her dancing, her grinding corn at the mill, singing hymns in his kitchen. He brought himself into position and kissed her repeatedly on the lips, the throat, the eyes. He whispered lovingly in her ear.

"I love you, Hannah. I'll try not to hurt you, but you're very tight. Trust me, Hannah."

He entered her then slowly, she was hot and eager, but her maidenhead was strong. When he tried to breach it, she cried out.

"Easy, Hannah, easy." He gentled her with sweet kisses, trying desperately to maintain control when her hot, tight cavern offered such relief.

"It doesn't fit!" she cried pitifully.

Henry Lee couldn't keep the smile from his face and the humor helped rein in his desire.

"Don't worry, Hannah, we're going to make it fit."

And he did, slowly stroking, coaxing, kissing, easing his way past her barrier until the pain was swallowed in a maelstrom of desire.

Hannah lay beneath him crying and pleading for what she didn't yet know. She opened her eyes and saw him above her, the power, the intensity, the glaze of passion in his eyes. Then she could hardly see at all as a red haze clouded her vision and she fell into an abyss of sensual pleasure, screaming his name.

They lay in each other's arms, still touching, still stroking, not willing to stop even as they waited for their breathing to return to normal.

"I'm sorry I hurt you." His voice was husky and his breathing labored.

"Oh, Henry Lee, it was worth it."

He smiled and planted a kiss on the end of her nose.

"Is it always like this?" she asked him.

"Hannah, it has never been like this for me. Nothing

I have ever done, no woman I have ever known, has even come close to the feelings I've had with you today."

She smiled a pleased but weary smile and they held each other close.

The sun was well up in the sky the next morning as the weary but sated couple woke to the distinct sounds of a wagon coming up the road.

"Somebody's coming," Hannah screeched, leaping out of bed, grabbing her dress and looking for her drawers.

Henry Lee only rolled over on his back and looked up at her. They had spent the entire evening and most of the night discovering each other and the meaning of conjugal bliss. Lack of sleep shadowed his eyes and every muscle in his body ached, but he had never felt better in his life.

"Get out of there and get dressed, Henry Lee! What will folks think if they come here in the middle of the day to find us still in bed."

"They'll think we are newly wed," he teased, "and they will be exactly right." But with her anxious prodding he slowly rolled himself off of their comfortable nest and began the search for his own discarded clothing.

"Hurry, they are almost here!" she told him, trying unsuccessfully to tie her drawers and braid her hair at the same time.

"Don't panic, darlin'. You can take your time getting dressed and I'll go out and keep them busy for a few minutes. It's just Zanola and Jones and they won't be speculating on anything or spreading any, absolutely true, gossip about us."

"How do you know it's them?"

"Because I told them to come over this morning, that I'd have the still ready and they could pick it up."

"The still?"

"Yep, Zanola's always admired the whiskey from my still, so I decided to sell it to her. I've promised to give her a few whiskey-making lessons and then she's on her own."

"You've sold your still?"

"That's right, Hannah." His smile was self-effacing, but he continued in mock solemnity. "It was a business decision. Not everybody drinks whiskey, but everybody sits at a table. For better or worse, the whiskey man is now in the furniture business."

"Oh Henry Lee, did you do this for me?"

"No. I did it for our marriage, and our children, and for myself. I want to know if I'm good enough to win even when I play by the rules."

Hannah went into his arms and laid her head lovingly against his chest.

"This business is not a sure thing, like whiskey," he whispered gently over the top of her head. "Morelli and I are in a partnership with some land, just south of Tulsa. There's some good wood there we can use. It'll save us from having to buy from somebody else. I've got enough money put by to give us a good start, but I can't promise that you'll be dressing in silks."

"I'd be looking mighty foolish hoeing my garden in silks!" she said humorously.

"It won't be nearly as exciting either. I doubt seriously if we'll have even one visit from the Federal marshalls."

"Well, we will just have to find our houseguests elsewhere!"

They laughed together for a minute, then Henry Lee held her at arm's length to look her directly in the eye. There was no humor in his look. He wanted her to understand the gamble they would be taking and that, success or failure, she would be a part of it.

"There is always a risk in any business, I want you to realize that. But if we work hard and pull together in this, we have a good chance of making a go of it."

"I know you can do it, Henry Lee. I said I'd be beside you for better or worse, and I think the worst is already behind us!" She embraced him lovingly, then he raised her chin with a teasing smile.

"There is one thing I need to do, before we start off on this new business venture."

"What's that?"

"I need to build myself a wellhouse. If my wife takes it into her head to venture out at night, I want to make sure she never finds anybody but me."

ABOUT THE AUTHOR

PAMELA MORSI is a native of Oklahoma who now resides in Texas with her family. Winner of numerous awards, including two RITA Awards, she is the author of *Heaven Sent, Courting Miss Hattie, Garters, Wild Oats, Runabout, Marrying Stone, Something Shady, Simple Jess, The Love Charm, No Ordinary Princess,* and *Sealed with a Kiss.* A former medical librarian, Pamela Morsi has been praised as "the Garrison Keillor of romance" (*Publishers Weekly*) for the down-to-earth flavor of her delightfully romantic novels.

CPSIA information can be obtained at www.ICGtesting.com
Printed in the USA
LVOW06s2127120813

347558LV00001B/61/A